The Book
of
Bob

As revealed to Paul Chasman

Helluva deal!

[A Novel]

THE BOOK OF BOB
As Revealed to Paul Chasman

REVIEWS AND LETTERS

"Your book is laughing magic."
—**J.H., Clearwater, Nebraska**

"This is an excellent satire that had me laughing out loud."
—**Patti Siberz, Oregon Coast Today**

"We're mighty lucky Paul Chasman got his inspiration for **The Book of Bob** *because it's going to help all of us laugh and think and change and laugh some more . . . so much wit and wisdom . . . I couldn't wait to sit down with the book, reread pieces and after laughing myself silly, I felt really healthy. I've converted my old holiday gift list, and scratched out a lot of other things, and written in:* **The Book of Bob.**"
—**Marlena Smith--KBOO-FM, Portland, Oregon**

"What shines out is the brilliance of a prismatic clarity of mind. I love the complexity and compassion. I love 'helluva deal' and CONTRA-DICTIONS. You have given us a humorful mythic masterpiece, which is also a frightening, searing commentary. MAY IT INSPIRE."
—**S.S., Yachats, Oregon**

"What an engrossing and enjoyable serio-comic novel! **The Book Of Bob** *addresses just about every social and cultural issue in today's world . . . You have created a little masterpiece of commentary on the contemporary scene with all its frightening possibilities, but also with its redemptive and hopeful potential that stem from caring for our fellows with love and kindness.*

*"***The Book of Bob** *is a drama of options and choices about how life can play out, examining as it goes, the good and the evil. You have peopled it with characters strong and weak, with agendas altruistic and self-serving, and brought them together as fully developed individuals with all their strengths and idiosyncrasies. I commend you for portraying them all so skillfully within a plot that has many venues and many moral issues for both the best and the worst of humankind. You are a skilled and insightful writer."*
—**Nadine Cobb, Baker & Taylor**

"Flipper me fingers, this might be the best babbling book I have ever read. As with the previous book, those who can't handle a little teasing about religion or a few humorously rewritten Bible verses might be offended, but I think Paul Chasman, who channeled this book after the second election of the second George Bush, may have received a bit of divine inspiration . . . Laughs, tears, and lessons abound."
—**www.suelick.com**

"I want to be the first to tell the world about this wonderful book . . . It's one of those books that you can't wait to find out what happens, and when it does, you are sad that it's over. I laugh out loud, wake the dog, cats, husband, and go back for more. Helluva deal!"
—**K. Morris, Amazon Book Review**

*"***The Book of Bob** *should be subtitled* Candide Meets the Political and Religious Equivalents of the Marx Brothers' Evil Twins. *It features a naïf who just wants to do the right thing. And . . .*
-- a picaresque confederacy of saints & crazies on one helluva road trip
-- an elected leader who is hilariously linguistically challenged. The Right Reverend Spooner has more than met his match. (And so has anybody with even an advanced case of Satyriasis)
-- the loopiest, unlikeliest, loveliest love story since, say, Burns & Allen, or Auntie Mame and Beau, or, what the hell, Gargantua and Pantagruel
-- a chilling story of a decent man gone crazed assassin
-- a happy ending!! (And just as an aside, the story involves the coolest dog since Rin Tin Tin. Asta. Lassie. Scooby Doo)
Never has Christmas shopping been so easy. My wife and I bought 20 copies. We don't have that many friends, but we might meet someone— and whoever it might be, they'll need this book. So do you."
—**Robert Clapp, Amazon Book Review**

*"***The Book of Bob** *is one of those rare books that made me laugh out loud in public. Just describing the premise—that God (aka "Dad") has chosen to write a new blockbuster through a new prophet (Bob)—is enough to provoke giggles. It also suggests there may be irreverent satire ahead. Knowing Paul Chasman and his work as 'Carl Estrada,' I was prepared. However, if you're looking for angry political rants against conservatives, go find a blog. All forms of 21st-century wackiness are fair game for Dad's mockery. This book is so funny, I forgot it had an agenda!"*
—**Jeff Allen, Executive Director, Oregon Environmental Council, Amazon Book Review**

"One helluva romp!! Move over Hunter S. and Bill Burroughs! Make room for Paul Chasman. Great fun! Heavy intellectual input. A real classy piece of writing."
—L. H., Port Angeles, Washington

"Got in touch with E.S. and M.B. to tell them **The Book of Bob** *is waiting for them. I warned them they were not going to get through it quickly—what with all the laugh breaks."*
—E.O., Joyce, Washington

"It is the first time I've cried out loud over the death of a character since Garp. I will have to order another copy, for sharing. I will not hand out my copy, I'm afraid I won't get it back!"
—K.M., Meriden, Connecticut

And this, straight from the pen of Dad:
"I just finished reading **The Book of Bob** *for the fourth time, and for the fourth time I'm stunned by the relevance of (the) work . . . For the fourth time I'm struck by the perfect pitch of the satire. The sparks of brilliance, the pages of sheer poetry, the outrageous humor, the wild array of characters, and the passion of* **The Book of Bob** *make it a 'must read' for everyone who is frightened by the speed at which George W. Bush and his gang are bulldozing our country. This book may well have been inspired by Dad. It's a helluva deal!"*
—DLC
(Note: The fact that I'm one of the editors of **The Book of Bob** *and that I happen to be the author's father in no way affected the objectivity of this review.)*

The Book of Bob

of

Bob

As revealed to Paul Chasman

[A Novel]

DANCING MOON PRESS
NEWPORT. OREGON

CONTENTS

THE CAST OF CHARACTERS
(IN ORDER OF APPEARANCE)

Bob — *a blank slate who first converses with his dog, then with God.*
Helen — *Bob's wife who leaves him on his fiftieth birthday.*
Bud — *Bob's ragged old dog.*
Eldon & Larry — *forever indebted to Bob for breaking up their fight.*
Lakshmi Jackson — *young woman who feels like a "kite without a string."*
Ivan Bunt — *wheelchair-bound veteran with a colorful language all his own.*
Dad — *what does "doG" spell backwards?*
Sophia Wise — *her life's goal is to cover her entire body with tattoos.*
Roland Brand — *a chameleon on the fast track to power.*
Natalie and Phil — *Sophia Wise's parents.*
Delbert Thorne — *Chosen Leader of the Free Nation.*
Orvil Swain — *collector of fossils and wives.*
Aruna Jackson — *Lakshmi's mother whose life's goal is to stay clean.*
Ben Jackson — *Lakshmi's father; Aruna's jealous husband.*
Professor Tyrone T. Matters — *the scientist.*
Normal Bea Freee — *the seer.*
Thaddeus Well — *the shrink.*
Donald LaFarge — *discoverer of the Sacred Text for his eyes only.*
Venecia Bosco — *counselor at the Veteran's Resource Center.*

Also starring:

Reverend Rufus — *the faith healer.*
Rod Barkley, Gennisaw Tubbs, Conrad Shanks — *failed Secretaries of Religion.*
The Evil Abdul Kashmir — *dictator of Yurkistan, arch enemy of Delbert Thorne.*
Aides #3, #2, and #1 — *Chosen Leader Thorne's trusted sounding boards.*
Virtuous Liar — *caretaker of the Forest of Truth and Lies.*
Allan Famous — *Number One talk show host.*
Logan Berry — *star reporter for the Free Nation Network (FNN)*

And a thousand extras!

I. IN THE BEGINNING

IN THE BEGINNING, BOB DIDN'T PLAN TO START A RELIGION; IT just happened. That's how Bob viewed most of his life up to that point. It just happened.

It just happened that he was born fifty years ago in the Northwest Region of the Free Nation. When he was twenty, it happened that a strong, stout woman named Helen would pick him out and decide to marry him. It happened they would inherit a house from her parents where they would live for thirty years until it happened she would leave him on his fiftieth birthday.

When Helen married Bob, her father put him to work framing houses. Thirty years later, he was still at it and his back was sore. It happened that Bob would never be able to give Helen a child. Maybe it was for the best. Parenting is tough. Like most people, they probably wouldn't have done a very good job.

The day after Helen left him, Bob discovered he was ragged, middle-aged, childless, wifeless, going-on-old. He found himself living in a ragged old house on a ragged old street, talking to his ragged old dog named Bud. That was before Bud started talking back to him. Pretty soon God would talk to Bob, too. God would call him "Son."

Bob had no clue why Helen left. One day everything was normal, the next day, it was his birthday and she was gone. The night before his birthday, he shuffled home tracking sawdust into the house. He pulled a cherry soda from the fridge, plopped down on the sofa, aimed the remote, flipped the channels, nothing on, flipped the power off, drank cherry soda, patted the top of Bud's head, and stared at the blank screen. Pretty much the same as every night.

"Bob . . . BOB! Bob, do you hear me? We need to talk."

That was Helen. Nothing new. She'd been saying that for years. Bob continued to stare at the empty TV. Bud, the ragged old dog, nudged Bob, turning the power on in Bob's hand and making it pat his head some more.

Helen began to cry. Nothing new there, either. "Bob, I'm living alone! This house is more empty when you come home than when you're gone!"

Same old . . . .

"Bob, if you won't be my husband, I'm leaving you. I mean it this time!"

She meant it every time. But tonight something different happened. On this night, the night before Bob's fiftieth birthday, something happened that would set in motion a chain of events that would change his life and change the course of history.

He kissed her. It wasn't much of a kiss. But he kissed her just the same. On the lips. Then he said, "Good night, Helen. I'm tired. I'm going to bed."

Nothing new except the kiss.

You could say it didn't have the intended effect, but as far as Bob was concerned, there probably was no intended effect. Just a kiss out of the blue. For Helen it was the final betrayal, the kiss of death. Being the first time in years Bob had done such a thing, it took her by surprise. She stumbled aside, eyes wide watching his dusty back as he lumbered toward the bedroom. She felt the aftershock of his sticky lips on hers, the sweet cold of cherry soda, an absent peck and nothing . . . .

Helen finally knew. Bob was an empty frame on a vacant lot. The wind blew chilly through the beams. She had to go.

Dry eyed, Helen wrote him a note and set it on the kitchen table. She didn't pack. She put on her warm coat and the little beanie she always wore. She stuffed some pills and a toothbrush into her purse. She didn't bother saying goodbye to ragged Bud. He was sleeping with Bob anyway. She took the car keys off the hook and left the house as if she were going shopping. Bob didn't hear the engine start. He didn't hear its trail disappear into the night. He slept on.

* * * * * *

In the morning, Bob arose with the light. He peed and farted and reached under his blue striped pajamas to scratch. Catching a glimpse in the mirror, he saw a prickly gray face with thin white hair sticking out the top in an abstract design. He guessed it must be him.

Bob stumbled into the kitchen, figuring Helen would find him there; figuring on the empty bowl at his place at the table, set next to three sizes of spoons and a serrated knife lined up neatly on the right; figuring on the four boxes of cereal standing at attention like soldiers guarding the rear flank, a quart carton of milk leading the brigade; figuring on the grapefruit stationed to the left, sliced and quartered.

Figuring on that which came to him the day before and the day before that, coming to him again. Instead, what came to him was an eight-by-ten photo where he usually found his morning feeding. It was a picture of the exact layout of his breakfast. On it was a yellow sticky that said:

> *Here's how to make your breakfast. It's time*
> *you learned to do it yourself.*

Beside the eight-by-ten sat Helen's note, which he didn't pick up. He only craned his neck a little as he stood and read:

Dear Bob,

When I married you, I vowed, "Till death do us part." You haven't kissed me for years so how was I to know? Well, you kissed me tonight and now I know. You're dead. Guess I'll go.

Bye,
Helen

"Well, that's that," Bob said aloud.

Bud heard him where he was sleeping and pulled himself up in sections. Fourteen years ago, Bud would have sprung to his feet, wet tongue flopping eagerly from his smiling face. But now the dog was ragged and old and he labored to stand, one quarter at a time.

"Well, Bud old boy," said Bob, "I guess it's just you and me now."

Bud panted, smiled, and wagged.

"Yeah Bud," he continued, "I must have worn her out."

More panting, smiling, and wagging.

"What d'ya say we take the day off, Bud?"

Fine with Bud. They took the day off. And then some.

Bob never went back to work. When the phone rang, Bob would say, "Let it ring, Bud. I hate the damn phone anyway."

When Bob saw the mail fall through the front door slot, he'd order Bud, "Leave it be. It's just people who want my money."

Bob didn't do much of anything but sit in his dark house with the curtains closed, talking to Bud. Sometimes he'd watch TV, but usually there wasn't anything on. There was one show Bob did like. It was the preacher who was on every day at four o'clock. Reverend Rufus wore a white suit and a hairpiece that looked like road kill without the tail. People would roll up to Reverend Rufus in wheelchairs or stagger up to him on crutches or cry because they were dying of cancer. Some people had smaller complaints like a kink in their neck or ringing in their ears. It was all the same to Reverend Rufus who would close his eyes and shiver and lay his hands on their heads. A handsome young man was there to catch them as they fell or rolled backwards, and the next thing you knew, they were walking out of their wheelchairs or throwing their crutches away or turning their necks in every imaginable direction. They were healed!

"Praise the Lord!" everyone would cry.

Bob would cry, "Praise the Lord!" along with them.

Then he'd clap his hands, snap his fingers, and shake a fist above his head and shout, "*Helluva* deal!"

Reverend Rufus had an 800 number you could call to send money. Sometimes Bob would send him some.

Bob became a typical bachelor. He never thought to wash his clothes. When he ran out, he dug through the dirty pile and started over again. He ate ok for awhile, but the cupboards got pretty empty. The cookies were the first to go. Then the Cheeze Puffs. There were a few Hot & Hardy Soups that got him by for a few days. The vegetable bin never got opened, so pretty soon, the bin began to take on a life of its own. Bud ate what Bob ate.

Bob never left the house. You can imagine the smell. Bob didn't notice, but Bud sensed something weird. Bob did remember to let Bud out back to do his business—except when he forgot—at which time, Bud would whimper and do his business in the corner of the living room. Bob didn't wash, brush, or flush. His skin turned pasty and he had raccoon rings around his eyes. You could say Bob let himself go.

One day, Bob was talking to Bud as he always did:

"Just you and me, Bud." And:

"Ha, ha, Bud. Doesn't it just go to show?" And:

"What a life, eh Bud? Never a dull moment."

But on this day, Bud talked back. "Bob, how long are we going to go on like this?"

"What's that you say, Buddy boy?"

"I said, we can't do this forever Bob. Something's gotta give. For one thing, I'm hungry. Aren't you hungry?"

"Well, I guess I hadn't given it much thought."

"Man can't live on love alone. Also, a little fresh air would do us both a world of good."

"Fresh air . . . Hmm . . . Right again! It *is* getting a little stuffy in here. See, Bud? That's what I keep you around for—you save me from myself!"

"I'm happy to. That's my job, Bob."

"And it's *my* job to see that you're fed and exercised and groomed! I have an idea," Bob said, his voice cracking with emotion. "Let's make a pilgrimage to the In 'n' Out grocery and get some chow!"

"Chow?"

"You know—grub . . . vittles . . . food!"

"I like that idea, Bob. Will you get me some milk bones?"

"I think that can be arranged," said Bob. "Well then Bud, what are we waiting for?" He clapped his hands, snapped his fingers, and shook a fist above his head.

"*Helluva* deal!" he declared.

* * * * * *

Off they went on their In 'n' Out pilgrimage. For the first time in ages, there was a spring in Bob's step. As he and Bud walked briskly, their talk was lively and animated.

"Bud, I've got to hand it to you," Bob exclaimed. "Sometimes you're inspired!"

"Well, Bob," said Bud, "it takes a wise man to know when he hears the truth."

Passers-by gave them a fairly wide berth.

Bob and Bud merrily made their way past ragged houses, over ragged railroad tracks, and onto a boulevard of ragged shops. Gun shop, liquor shop, porn shop. Beauty shop, shoe shop, tattoo shop. Everything you could possibly want.

Fast food. Espresso. They passed a church. They passed a bar . . . .

"Bob?" asked Bud. "About those milk bones . . . ."

A loud crash disrupted their conversation. Bob turned to see a large, young black man pitching backwards out the bar door and collapsing on the ground, holding his head which trickled blood. A wiry white man followed fast, raging toward him with evil intent. He aimed a kick at the downed man's ribs, but the black man caught his leg, blunting the force of the blow. The white man tripped and down he went. The two rolled around in a scuffling heap, disengaged, then scrambled to their feet, banged up and panting, facing off for the next round.

That's when Bob said, "There's a fight! *I* have to stop it!"

Bob waded in, a man on a mission. He strode between the foes, parting them like the seas. There they were—two strong young men facing off, the poisonous juices of hate and destruction pulsing through their bodies. And there stood Bob between them—white-haired, a head shorter, paunchy, pasty, and past his prime. Bob talked earnestly, reasonably, and fast, waving his arms while he swiveled from one man to the other.

"Oh my! What in heaven's name have we here? I know at this moment both you guys want to kill each other and hate fills your hearts but please please stop and think what you're doing. When you woke up this morning did you think you were going to get yourself in such a fix today that you would have to kill or be killed? Think back to when your mother brought you into this world! Think back! I know she wasn't the mother you wanted her to be, but when she begat you she loved you more than anything and wanted you to be happy, warm, safe, loved and protected from all the hard knocks of life.

"Think back! Think back to your mother's love! You have the same choice now that you have every moment of your life— you can hate or you can love. If you choose to hate this man before you, you will hurt him and you'll feel better for oh maybe ten minutes and then the pain you caused will seep into your soul and eat you from the inside out. But if you love him, if you forgive him, you will love and forgive yourself and you will be healed! Look at this man! Look! Look! He's your brother! All your brother wants is what you want: To be loved and healed! Love thy brother! Heal him! Heal thyself!"

The two men fidgeted. They looked down and around and everywhere except at each other. They sneaked peaks at Bob out of the corners of their moist, sheepish eyes.

"Come, come . . . There, there . . . Isn't this better? No one hurts. We're all in this together. We're all the same flesh. Prick us and we all bleed. You are him. He is you. Come now. Heal yourselves. Brother . . ." Bob addressed the black man on his left. "What is your name?"

"Smith . . . Larry Smith," the man muttered toward the ground.

"And you, sir," said Bob to the wiry white man on his right. "How may I address you?"

"Um . . . I'm Eldon. Last name's Smith."

"You see?" exclaimed Bob. "Eldon and Larry Smith! You *are* brothers! Now please . . . please . . . no more fighting among brothers. Shake hands and walk away. That's the spirit . . . Come closer . . . Shake on it . . . ."

Eldon and Larry Smith reached out tentatively. They grasped hands gingerly, then more firmly. Bob extended both his hands to clasp the backs of their heads, and as he did so, they fell into an embrace. Their bodies wracked with sobs as they wailed tears of a millennia.

Bob stood outside the hug, hands resting on the men's heads, absorbing the two men's pain as his eyes gazed heavenward. Once cleansed, the two brothers stepped back, but their hands lingered to grip.

Bob released Eldon and Larry, and when he did, they let go too. Looking sheepish again, they mumbled a few words, then walked away, arms around each other . . . .

Bob returned to Bud who had been watching the event from a distance. "I'll be happy to buy you those milk bones, Bud," he said, as if he'd put a bookmark in the discussion and opened right to the page they had left off. "Which kind did you say you liked?"

* * * * * *

Bob and Bud resumed their merry conversation and their lively step.

"Look, Bud. There's the In 'n' Out now."

"What a bargain!" Bud exclaimed. "Soup is only $1.99!"

"That's *soap*, Bud. S-O-A-P. Can't you read?"

"I'm just a dog, Bob. I don't read very well, but it's a miracle I read at all!"

Bob and Bud continued talking in this vein as they entered the store. Behind the counter, Lakshmi Jackson looked up from the science text she had been studying. She was perplexed because she could only hear Bob's half of the conversation. To her, it sounded like:

"So Bud, what kind of milk bones do you want . . . ? Well, that's a surprise to me, Bud. I always thought you liked . . . Bud! You're interrupting me again! Haven't I taught you . . . I know, I know, Bud. But you're just going to have to wait till we get home."

Lakshmi Jackson stepped out from behind the counter. She wore a Levi jacket over her traditional *sari*. The label on her tennis shoes said, "Free Nation." Her eyes were blurred behind the thick lenses of the black-rimmed glasses that covered most of her round, brown face. Although she was nineteen, Lakshmi still wore the small black *kajal* dot her mother put on her forehead every day of her life to mar her beauty. This protected Lakshmi from evil.

"May I help you, sir?" asked Lakshmi Jackson, eager to please.

"Thank you. That's very kind of you. Bud here would like milk bones."

"We have several kinds, sir. Which kind would you prefer?"

"I'll let Bud field that question," said Bob. "Bud?"

Lakshmi Jackson looked at Bob, then at Bud, and back to Bob. She wished this ragged man would take his ragged dog and go away so she could get back to her science book, but she was polite. "Sir, I don't quite understand . . . ."

Bob gave a little chuckle. "That's Bud. I keep telling him he has to speak more clearly, but it's hard to teach an old dog new tricks. He says he prefers the flavored ones that come in several colors. Would you happen to have . . . ?"

Bob noticed that the store appeared to wave. It seemed to him like a fun house with the curly mirrors that make everything look strange and distorted. Just so you don't think he was going crazy, that's the way it looked to Bud and Lakshmi Jackson, too. The three of them felt like they were on a small boat in the high seas.

The wavy sea began to shake. Cans rattled and fell from the tipping shelves. Lakshmi Jackson's black-rimmed glasses bounced all the way to the end of her nose. She heard Bob shout: "Get under cover, Bud! We're having an earthquake! I know, I know . . . Yes, yes, you already told me . . . ! But you'll have to wait till we get home . . . No, Bud, stop arguing with me!"

Then she couldn't hear him at all above the clatter and the crash. The earthquake meant business. In fact, Lakshmi Jackson had to get out of the way quick because things were flying every which way and—*look out!* A high, heavy shelf teetered right over her head, ready to fall and it would certainly crush her . . . But Bob leapt in front of Lakshmi Jackson, knocking her out of harm's way and catching the falling shelf in his outstretched hands, ducking to absorb the blows of jars and cans that rained upon his head. The earth rattled and rolled while Bob heroically held his position, a human wedge against a rogue shelf, knee deep in peanut butter, fruit cups, and canned stew.

When at last the ground stopped shaking and the earth's tectonic plates settled, Bob pushed the empty shelf upright and backed away. Bud and Lakshmi Jackson looked on as he casually picked through the rubble, gathering shopping items.

"Do you have a bag?" he asked Lakshmi Jackson. "I don't have enough arms to hold all this stuff," he chuckled.

Lakshmi Jackson didn't know how to act. The floor had just given way under her, a strange man who conversed with his dog had appeared from nowhere to save her life, and now he was rummaging through the fallout and asking her for a shopping bag? She scurried behind the counter, dug out a bag, and hurried toward Bob. Holding it at arms length, she presented it to him.

"That'll do just fine," said Bob. "Are these the kind of milk bones you wanted, Bud?"

Lakshmi Jackson watched as Bob filled his bag to the brim, talking to Bud all the while. When he could hold no more, Bob stumbled toward the counter and set his treasure down. "Well," he announced grandly. "Let's square up."

Lakshmi Jackson was flustered. "Oh no, sir. You saved my life. Besides, you can see we've lost power—the computer won't work. The cash register's crushed. Please take it."

"I would no sooner take groceries without paying for them than would I slay my first-born son!" Bob declared emphatically. "I insist. This should cover it," he said as he reached into his pocket and pulled out a crumpled wad. He stuffed it into her palm and closed her hand over it.

"Bud, the hour is late. No time to waste. Young lady, it's been a pleasure doing business with you. Bob's my name. And yours?"

"Lakshmi Jackson, sir."

"Goodbye, Lakshmi Jackson. Till we meet again . . . ."

Bob and Bud exited the In 'n' Out while Lakshmi watched, dazed and perplexed through her thick, cracked glasses, the wad of bills still clutched in her outstretched hand.

* * * * * *

Bob and Bud headed home, wading through a maze of mashed cars, cracked pavement, and downed power lines. People emerged like squirrels on the first day of spring, peaking out with looks of shock and wonder. Gingerly, they tested the ground, checking their limbs to make sure their arms and legs, fingers and toes were still there. Others, not so lucky, lay littered every which way, crying and struggling to escape the rubble that buried them. Bob moved quickly, a man on a mission, setting his shopping bag down to lift this beam and roll that slab with superhuman strength, releasing one grateful victim after another.

"It's ok, ma'am," he reassured an elderly lady. "I think I can pull you out if you'll please give me both hands."

She reached out and Bob gave a mighty pull, dragging her squirming and straining like a child being born out of a concrete womb. Bob was pulling with every measure of strength and tenderness in his being, when he heard off to his left:

"Help! Hurry! Blast your teeth, man! Hurry up and help me!"

The first time Bob laid eyes on Ivan Bunt, he was upside down. Propped against his toppled wheel chair, his wild red hair spread on the ground in all directions, a bushy red beard springing up from his chin covering half his green flannel shirt. Desperate blue eyes stared trapped and angry behind brows as red and bushy as his hair. Two knee stumps pointed like pillars toward the sky.

"Fry you for breakfast, man! Help me up!

"Just one moment, sir. I'm helping this dear lady. As soon as I've got her out of . . . ."

"Measles!" exclaimed Ivan Bunt. "I'm standin' on my fiddlin' head in my wheel chair and all my blood has left my torso! Break your nose! Help me up I say!"

Bob focused on the task at hand, while Ivan Bunt's litany of curses played loudly on.

"Mold your mayonnaise! A pox on your pajamas! May your tongue grow hair!"

"Patience, my brother. I'm on my way." Gallant Bob helped the lady dust off and made her promise she was fine. Reaching into his grocery bag, he produced a can of pears.

"For you, ma'am." He presented her the gift. "And now, the squeaky wheel . . . ."

Dazed, perplexed, and clutching a can of pears, the rescued woman watched her savior as he carried his grocery bag toward the upside-down and sputtering Ivan Bunt. "Good day to you, brother. I suppose you'd like me to help you get upright."

"It's about tinkerin' time!" barked Bunt. "Stop standing there scratchin' yer fleas and set me straight!"

"I'll fix you up right away," said Bob, and with that he lifted Ivan Bunt, wheelchair and all, turned him over and placed him right side up.

"There now," Bob said with a satisfied smile. He wiped his hands. "Good as new."

"Good as noodlin' new," Ivan Bunt mimicked. He was breathing loudly and sweating profusely. "If'n I was good as noodlin' new, I could waddlin' walk, now couldn't I? If'n I was good as noodlin' new, I wouldn't have to ride around in this wart-ridden wheelchair. Needles!" he muttered.

Bob felt Ivan's pain. A magenta warmth enveloped Bob's body and he tingled from head to foot. Energy poured through him, hot and strong. He was overcome with love of life. He was overwhelmed by the heartbreak of the world. His entire body vibrated with surging magenta force. He laughed a mournful laugh. He cried a joyous cry. He stood pigeon-toed before Ivan Bunt, gazing blissfully toward the heavens, rocking side to side, hugging himself like Ray Charles.

"Uh . . . What's goin' on, pilgrim?" asked Ivan Bunt. "You'd better get a grip on the reins, hoss. Yer startin' to scare the drool outta my doodle."

But Bob hardly heard him. "I'll save you, brother! I'll save you!" he cried joyously. "You will walk again, brother! You will walk!" he chanted. "Feel the current that burns like a torch through my fingers! Stand up and walk!" Bob cried.

"What the wallowin' . . . ?" Ivan's shaggy blue eyes were open wide. If he *could have* walked, he *would* have walked as far from Bob as he *could have.*

Bob slowly and steadily approached Ivan Bunt, eyes rolled up, arms outstretched. "Walk, my brother!" Bob laid both hands on Ivan's head. "Stand up and walk!" he commanded. Bob was in a zone.

"Ow! Howdy doodlin' Doody! Get your hammerin' hands off'n me! Ow! That's hot! Duelin' dingbats! That hurts!"

But Bob would not yield. He stood tall, smiling, as electricity seethed through him, fusing his hands with poor Ivan Bunt's head, the two men fixed for an eternal moment in a vibrating magenta rapture.

It was over.

Bob jerked back and released as if repelled. Wild-haired, wild-eyed Ivan stared at him, no words escaped his wide-open mouth. Red prints blazed on his forehead where Bob's fingers had burned.

"It's over, my brother," Bob smiled. "You may stand up and walk now."

Ivan snapped to. "Walk?! Are you blind, man? Blast your bunions! Look at me, you loon! Have you lost your lugnuts? I ain't got no livin' legs! Flies, man! What kind of crazy crock are you, anyway—ya come over here an' burn the bats out of a guy's noggin and then ya tell 'im to walk when he ain't got no limpin' legs? Mangle your maggots!"

Bob looked puzzled. "You mean you can't walk?"

"Binge 'n' purge, man! Of course I can't walk! Didn't you hear me? How can a poor wayfarin' ranger walk when he AIN'T GOT NO LUMBERIN' LEGS!?"

Bob unbuckled Ivan Bunt. With love and patience, he lifted him out of his chair and set him on the ground.

He couldn't walk.

"Thanks for nothin,' Ahab," said Bunt. "Now put me back in my chuggin' chair!"

Bob put him back. "Some day you will walk, my friend. As for now . . . ."

He reached into his shopping bag, withdrew Bud's box of milk bones, and handed the remainder of his treasure to Ivan Bunt. "Take this, brother. It will give you sustenance."

Bunt rummaged through the bag, muttering as he dug. "Rr-rr . . . chili. Rr-rr . . . artichoke hearts. Hmm, I *like* chili . . . I *like* artichoke hearts . . . Rr-rr . . . Oh, looky here . . . Got some of them wieners in a jar . . . Sleepin' slumlords! I do like them wieners in a jar!"

Bob looked on, pleased that he had brought such happiness to his new friend. "May I ask, sir, since our paths have crossed, by what name should I address you?"

The bushy red face was buried deep in the bag as he

continued his exploration. "Bunt," he said into the bag. Then he emerged and looked Bob square in the eye. "Ivan Bunt. That's mighty kind of you to give me all them vittles. Mighty cuddlin' kind."

Bob could see Ivan's eyes were glazed and moist. He took Bunt's hands in his. "I'm proud to meet you, Ivan Bunt. I am Bob. Whenever you need a friend, you will find me."

"Mighty kind. Mighty kickin' kind," Ivan nodded, his eyes overflowing. Then: "Rattle yer rats, man! Blacken yer blood! Now you've gone and plundered my peepers!" Ivan Bunt sniffled as he turned and wheeled himself over the rubble, towards home.

"Well, Bud," Bob announced. "I think it's high time we went home ourselves."

"I'm glad you didn't give him my milk bones, Bob," said Bud.

* * * * * *

Bob and Bud arrived home shortly before dark. Lamps and dishes were toppled from the earthquake, but to tell the truth, after a couple weeks of Bob's bachelorhood, things hadn't changed all that much.

"Home sweet home," said Bob. He sank satisfied into his stuffed chair.

"Uh, Bob?" said Bud.

"Yeah Bud, what is it?"

"Would you mind if I had some of those milk bones now?"

"Why, of course, Bud. Silly me."

Bud took his milk bones and was happy. "These are the kind I like," he said.

"Nothing but the best for you, Bud." Then: "Well, I guess you could say it's been quite a day."

"Yeah, Bob. Quite a day," said Bud as he chewed.

Then Bob clapped his hands, snapped his fingers, shook a fist above his head and exclaimed, "*Helluva* deal!"

"Helluva deal, Bob."

II. Conversation With Dad

That night Bob had a dream.

He dreamed *he was an eagle soaring high above the earth, overseeing the Free Nation below. Flying over the coast, he saw green surf crashing like white foam fireworks into lava flows that had hardened into tall, black, craggy mounds . . . .*

. . . Drifting north, he patrolled a river, starting at the outlet and winding through ancient forest. He skimmed green tops of maple and hemlock, alder, spruce and fir. Beneath the canopy, autumn vine maple blazed red . . . .

. . . Far north, the land turned rugged, barren and wild. He saw herds of caribou crossing vast white plains, making their way south for winter. Catching a wind current, he glided far beyond the Free Nation and looked down upon white glacier peaks rising toward him from the top of the world . . . .

. . . Then, he was Bob again, picking his way through hordes of men, women, and children squatting dirty and hungry outside stinking hovels in a haggard city. Humanity's failure on display . . .

. . . On to the outskirts and into a forest where rusty machines clanked and cut, screeched and roared. Bob had to dodge giant trees that toppled on all sides of him, rattling the ground as they fell. Creatures of every species sprinted past— horses and deer, leopards and chimps, polars and pandas, birds, bats, and rats—flushed out in desperate flight. When Bob reached the clearing, he faced a firing squad of hunters in camouflage, automatic rifles methodically mowing down the prey as they escaped the falling woods. . . .

. . . The hunters transformed into soldiers. The panicked animals became an outgunned enemy . . . missiles searing the sky, bombs obliterating the woods . . . tanks crushing the terrain beneath them and blasting terrible fire . . . tanks morphing into horses with riders fighting hand-to-hand, sword to blood-soaked sword swirling in hellish chaos of violence, death, shrieks and roars of men who now were hairy and ape-like, pummeling each other with enormous clubs. . . .

. . . Bob stumbled away to a clearing, the sounds of battle becoming miniature beyond a distant hill. He came upon more ape-like men, circled around a bonfire . . . the fire dwindled . . . dwindled . . . an ember . . . He joined the crowd of naked men— no, apes . . . walking backwards, migrating to the ocean. He followed as they waded in . . . let himself down down into white foam surf, a frog slipping deep along the floor . . . didn't think about breathing. Wasn't troubled by the cold . . . a fish gliding in the ocean . . . squeeze through a dark tunnel of pink coral and emerge a jelly . . . tentacles dangle soft transparent lace . . . shrinking shrinking . . . amoeba . . . and gone.

It was a helluva dream. Freud would have had a field day.

* * * * * *

When Bob awoke, the world was dark. He lay half asleep, staring groggily into the black void. His dream lingered in hazy photos, but as he tried to remember, the gray pictures escaped and slipped away like smoke . . . .

"Bob . . . ."

He thought he heard a deep voice.

"Oh, Bob . . . ."

Louder this time. It seemed to come from the ceiling.

"Bob, wake up."

The voice spread out and wrapped around the room.

"Who's there?"

"You're not going to believe this, Bob. No one ever does."
The voice sounded like Johnny Cash—only lower.

Bob leapt out of bed and turned on the light. His eyes raced
around the room. Nothing. He shivered once, then bolted to the
closet where he fished out his baseball bat. He took a batting
stance near the bed, his eyes darting here and there, a disheveled
ballplayer who doesn't know where the pitcher is.

"You ready, Bob? Here comes the pitch . . . ."

"Who are you? Where are you? What do you want?" Bob
trembled in his pajamas as he held his stance.

"I'll answer all three questions in due time," said the voice.
"Let's start with the first one. Here's a Zen question: If a train
leaves the station going fifty miles per hour and your foot is
caught in the railroad tracks and the train is one hundred yards
away and coming toward you at an increased rate of speed, who
do you call? Answer my riddle and you'll have the answer to
Question Number One."

"What the . . . ?"

Bob dashed to the bedroom door and opened it. He looked
around the living room. Nothing. The house was still as stone.
The only sound was Bud snoring. Bob crept cautiously through
the open doorway.

"Try this one." The voice enveloped the house. "Fill in the
blanks: "(Blank) dammit, I swear to (blank), I pray to (blank),
(blank) will get you for this, in (blank) we trust, so help me
(blank), it was (blank's) will, he has a (blank) complex, one
nation under (blank), never take (blank's) name in vain, (blank)
bless you, (blank) bless our daily bread . . . ."

"Stop!" Bob interrupted, holding his ears. "What are you doing?!"

"What does "doG" spell backwards?"

Silence. Only Bud's tranquil snoring. Bob gazed around the living room speechless, holding his bat one-handed and slack on his shoulder.

"I know," said God. "The next thing you're going to want is proof. You're all so predictable. Ok . . . Let's see . . . Here's one: LET THERE BE LIGHT!" He commanded.

Presto! On went the lights in the living room, kitchen, and in every room of the house. Helen's candles lit up on the mantle, and a roaring fire ignited in the hearth.

"Hey, that was pretty good," said God. "Here . . . Let's try this one."

Bingo! An apple appeared on the dining table. "Don't eat it," laughed God. "One more. Ready?"

Shazam! The bat Bob brandished became a snake. Bob let out a yell as he threw it and leapt back. The snake hissed and slithered on the floor toward Bob, backing him into a corner.

"Watch this," said God. "Pick up the snake."

"Pick up the . . . ? You must be crazy!" cried Bob. "I'm not picking up that snake!"

"BOB . . . THIS IS GOD SPEAKING! I ORDER THEE TO PICKETH UP THE DAMN SNAKE!"

"B-b-but . . . ."

"C'MON, BOB. I HAVEN'T GOT ALL NIGHT!"

Whimpering, Bob reached with trembling fingers toward the snake. Its forked tongue darted and Bob yanked his hands back as if they'd been burned.

"Be careful," said God. "Grab it by the tail . . . CAREFUL! Not the head! The tail! The tail! There . . . you got him . . . Don't hold him too close to you, now! Keep him away from your body!"

"Now what?" screamed Bob. "Do something! I can't hold him here forever!"

"Ok, ok," said God. "Just a second . . . Let me think . . . Ok, here we go . . . ."

VOILA! The snake became a baseball bat in Bob's hand. Bob held the bat as far from his body as possible, watching it for a moment with pop-eyes. Then he threw it on the ground, eyes following as it rolled away.

"We're getting closer," God declared. "But you're confused and scared. You want to believe me, but you're not totally on board yet—you don't know what to think. Maybe this will help: You have a scar on your right knee from when you were nine years old and went careening down that hill and crashed your bike—it got you out of the military. You have a large mole on the lower left side of your back—you should probably have it looked at. You're not circumcised."

"What do you want?" exclaimed Bob.

"I want you to accept me into your heart. I want you to call me God. 'My Lord' will do."

"But I don't . . . ."

"Marsha Ginsburg, August 22, 1969, Gabriel Park, Day Three of the Total Eclipse Rock Festival—in her teepee . . . ."

"Wait a minute . . . How do you . . . ?"

"I AM THE ALMIGHTY GOD! WALK WITH ME AND BE THOU PERFECT! BOW DOWN BEFORE ME AND CALL ME YOUR LORD OR I WILL GIVE YOU SUCH A SMITE! BOW DOWN! BOW YE DOWN, I SAY!"

"Ok, ok," Bob shriveled and bowed before God.

Outside, lightning crashed and thunder roared and hail pummeled the roof. "CALL ME THY ONE AND ONLY GOD AND BEG MY MERCY, O LOWLY SINNER!" God ordered.

"Um . . . You are my one and only God. Please have mercy, Sir."

"*DAD!* 'PLEASE HAVE MERCY, *DAD!*' YOU ARE MY SON. CALL ME *DAD.*"

"Please have mercy, Dad," Bob begged.

Dad chuckled and whispered to himself. "Works every time."

"What did you say, Dad?" asked Bob.

"Nothing, nothing." The room was still. The hail and thunder had stopped. Dad: Master of the Pregnant Pause.

Finally, Bob could take it no longer. "What do you want from me, Dad?" he asked meekly.

"I thought you'd never ask, Son," said Dad. "I'm thinking about writing a new book. A couple centuries ago, I had a productive period in which I cranked out one book after another. But it's been fourteen hundred years since my last big hit. I've got lots of new ideas."

"A new book, Dad?"

"Yes, Son. And I want you to help me write it. I'll tell you what to say and you can transcribe it for me. Then when we're finished, you can go forth into the world and spread the word. You can be my P.R. guy."

"What's the book about?" Bob asked.

"It's a sequel, really. A variation on a theme. But with new perspectives and insights, and a new maturity that comes with experience."

"You've matured?"

"Well, I like to think so. But I'm stagnating. I need a creative stretch. An artist has to grow. Look at the difference between the Beatles' first single, "Love Me Do," and their "Abbey Road" album ten years later. They're such an inspiration! If they can change, why can't I?"

"Abbey Road?"

"My favorite album. Anyway, I want to clarify some of my positions. I think people took me too literally."

"I'm afraid to ask."

"I'll accept part of the blame. I was young and irresponsible. You know how kids are—they think all their opinions are written in stone. My answer to every problem was to smite somebody. I've lost count of how many of my creations I've smitten. And the tantrums I used to throw! I have to say, with twenty-twenty hindsight, I'm a bit embarrassed. Remember when I spake to Moses and made him tell the Pharaoh to let the Israelites go? And Pharaoh wouldn't, so I threw a tantrum and had Moses smite the river so all the fish would die, and it turned to blood and stank?

"Then remember when I spake to Moses and ordered him to tell Pharaoh again, but Pharaoh still wouldn't cooperate so I smote all the borders with frogs, and sent them stampeding all over Egypt? But Pharaoh was still stubborn so I smote the dust of the land and infested the whole place with lice. After lice, I tried flies. When flies didn't work, I smote all of Egypt's cattle. I still feel bad about that one—it wasn't those poor oxen's fault. After that, I smote every herb and tree with hail. Talk about biting your nose to smite your face! Then it was locusts. After locusts, I sent Moses out to spread darkness over the land. The final straw was when Pharaoh wouldn't even sacrifice an ox for me. I got so mad, I did another thing I'm ashamed of. I smote all the Egyptians' first-born sons."

Bob heard Dad sniff. Then the house shook. It sounded as if He was blowing His nose.

"All those innocent babies," Dad cried. "It wasn't *their* fault Pharaoh was such a jerk. Anyway, I admit, I could've handled the whole situation a lot better. I should have talked to Pharaoh personally. As you've seen, I have lots of powers of persuasion. I guess I was pretty stubborn too."

Bob sat down. "Is there anything . . . ?"

"SILENCE! I'M TALKING!" snapped Dad. "Since then, I've done a lot of work on myself," He continued. "I've learned a lot about anger management, and I have a better understanding of my issues. I'm not so quick to fly off the handle. I think I have better coping strategies now. I feel bad for all the innocent beings who have suffered because of my unskillful behavior, but the important thing is, I've grown. I feel better about myself than I ever have."

Dad went on. "The other thing I'm sorry about is this: I set a bad example. People are so cruel and destructive. But what can I expect? You've been copying me all these years. You start wars at the drop of a hat—so did I. You scorch the earth as if you own the place—so did I. I'm afraid I was a dysfunctional father and I raised a bunch of dysfunctional kids. Oh well, *c'est la vie*," said Dad. "That's French. Did you know I'm multi-lingual? I'm fluent in any language."

Bob didn't dare respond.

"Try me. *Parlez-vous Francais? Donde esta el bano? Ooday ooyay eakspay igpay atinlay?*" Dad laughed at his own joke. "*Oy vey!*" He roared.

Bob sat very, very still.

"Just trying to lighten things up a little."

Bob thought he'd better try to laugh.

"I do impressions too," said Dad. "Check this out: *Tonight we have a r-r-really really big shew!* Guess who?"

"Umm . . . Ed Sullivan?"

"Ok, how 'bout this:

What'choo want, baby I got it . . . ."

"Aretha Franklin?"

"It's like she's right here in your living room, isn't it? Ok, one more: *Thou shalt not lie with mankind, as with womankind; it is abomination.*"

"Wasn't that you?" asked Bob.

"Leviticus 18:22. I've got to change that one. Don't get me wrong—*I'D* never lie with mankind as with womankind. But if it's between two consenting adults, I say: To each his own. *Que sera sera.* Besides there's too many damn people! If thou liest with mankind, and if womankind liest with womankind, maybe we can get a handle on this population problem. You guys are always throwing my words around: '*Go forth and multiply. Go forth and multiply.*' I said that ages ago! It's so *retro*! Did you think I wanted you to go forth and multiply *forever*? Do the math! Haven't you noticed how crowded the world is getting? But I digress," Dad continued. "Where was I?"

"Um . . . you were talking in different languages and then you were doing impressions," Bob reminded Him.

"Right!" exclaimed Dad. "Hey—you're a good listener! Ok, heads up—I want you to start jotting some of this down. Got a pen? Good. You're going to need lots of paper. Maybe when we take a break you can go to the store and stock up. I know you just got back from the In 'n' Out, but sometimes you need to come home from shopping to find out what you forgot to buy at the store. Hey—that's good! Write that down!"

Bob scribbled fast.

"Sometimes you need to go shopping to find out what to buy at the store."

"Now—take this down:

> *I speaketh the language you speak;*
> *I only show what you can see.*
> *If I'd spoken to Moses in Chinese or Greek,*
> *Tell me, then, o where would we be?*
> *If I address a Russian in French,*
> *Will he findeth the answers he seeks?*
> *I thinketh not.*
>
> *Some harken my voice in the wind;*
> *Some folks find me in the earth;*
> *Some people will say there's a heaven and hell,*
> *Some travel from birth to rebirth.*
> *You all think you're right and they're wrong;*
> *And guess what I think that is worth?*
> *I thinketh not*
> *A helluva lot.*
>
> *I speaketh the language you know;*
> *I'll be what you want me to be;*
> *A round-bellied Buddha with aura aglow;*
> *A schmuck you once saw on TV.*
> *Allah or Yahweh or Joe;*
> *You pick: a, b, c, d, or e.*
> *The answer I love,*

It fits like a glove:
All of the above.

"Do you think I should say, *'All of the above'* or *'None of the above'* at the end?"

"Wait, wait," Bob panted. "I can't write that fast. I'm still on 'A duck you once saw on TV.' What comes after that?"

"Not *duck!*" said Dad, exasperated. *"Schmuck!"*

"A schmuck you once saw on TV," mumbled Bob as he wrote. "Ok, then what did you say?"

* * * * * *

Dad and Bob worked through the night. And the next and the next. They worked for six days and six nights with no time off except for bathroom breaks and to feed Bud who lay in a corner with his eyes on Bob, his ragged head resting flat on crossed paws. Often, Dad would get to talking too fast and Bob would have to race to keep up. He developed a shorthand filled with symbols and abbreviations so he could catch most of what Dad said.

For example, Bob would have written the last sentence in the above paragraph like this:

H dvlp-ed sh fld w/smbls & abrev so h cd cach mst o w D" ".

On the third day, Bob ran out of paper while Dad was on a roll. Dad didn't want to block His creative flow, so rather than take a break for Bob to buy more paper, He ordered him to remove all the books from his shelves and tear pages out of them. Then Dad rendered the torn pages white, clean, and new. In this manner, they were able to keep working.

On the fifth day, Bob ran out of pages to tear. By this time, Dad had worked up such a head of steam He didn't even notice Bob's dilemma. So Bob frantically began to jot Dad's words on his arm. When he ran out of room on both arms, he took his shirt off and made notes on his chest. By the sixth day, Bob was stripped naked, and his legs were covered with Dad's words too.

On the seventh day, Dad said, "Hey—that's pretty good!" Then He and Bob rested.

* * * * * *

Lying exhausted on the living room floor, Dad's graffiti spread over his naked body, Bob had a nagging question.

"Dad?" he began.

"Yes, Son," Dad replied.

"Why me?"

"Well, Son," said Dad. "You know the old saying: You can pick your friends, but you can't pick your family."

III. Sophia Wise

Dad's Instructions for Life

According to *The Book of Bob*; as written on Day V on Bob's chest, directly below the left shoulder:

1. *Be Kind to Every Man, Woman, Beast and Sprout.*
2. *Think! That's Why I Gave You a Brain.*
3. *Use Your Imagination.*
4. *Turn Off the Damn TV.*
5. *Buy Organic.*
6. *Recycle.*
7. *Walk More; Drive Less.*
8. *Clean Up Your Mess.*
9. *Thursday is Garbage Day.*
10. *Don't Forget to Floss.*

* * * * * *

Sophia Wise needed a new tattoo. Last week, the genius Roland Brand had drawn two beautiful fish on her right shoulder, symbolizing her Double-Pisces Sun and Rising sign. Now she felt out of balance. She would need an Archer on her left shoulder to help her get more in touch with the Sagittarius energy she derived from her Moon sign. Ever since the genius Roland Brand gave her the Double-Pisces tattoo, Sophia Wise had been propelled by a rush of creative energy. She wrote two new songs. She worked overtime at The Shelter where she served up soup and sympathy, sang songs and played her mandolin. Her friends at The Shelter loved the new songs.

On the downside of her Double-Pisces nature, she hadn't been totally straight with Roland. He wanted her and she had toyed with him. While he created the rainbow-colored masterpiece on her shoulder, she realized he had a deep hunger that couldn't be satisfied. After the tattoo, she gave in to his desire like a yawning, indifferent cat (was she picking up on his Leo energy?), but she knew one time wouldn't quench his hunger for long. She had also neglected to inform him she was only trying women for a while. Her friends Dorothy, Lisa, and Lakshmi had talked her into that one. It was fun.

Too much Pisces energy. She needed a Sagittarius Archer tattoo to balance her out. But how to pay for it? She had already used up all her money on the fish, even though Roland had only charged her half. She would have to go back to the Moonshadow Café and play her mandolin for tips. If she did it every night for a week or two, maybe she could swing it. She wondered if Roland would give her an advance. She knew he would—*if* she violated her "girls only" policy. Sophia figured Dorothy, Lisa, and Lakshmi wouldn't have to know.

Sophia's goal was to someday have every inch of her body covered with tattoos. She believed she was God's living, breathing art installation. Her job was to decorate the temple God had created for her. She smiled a squinty smile. She was still young—just nineteen—so she still had plenty of time to complete her task. But like most nineteen-year-olds, she was in a hurry. Her biggest fear was that she would die before she finished decorating.

Sophia Wise got her first tattoo at fifteen. It was just a small stock image of a rose. In her inexperience, she found somebody cheap who turned out to be a "scratcher"—the rose looked like a little lollipop and he placed it too close to her ankle bone. This caused more pain than necessary, and it would be almost a year before Sophia would try again.

On her sixteenth birthday, Sophia got a vine, which started at the rose on her ankle and climbed up her leg to just behind the knee. This began her "Dense Vegetation" period, during which time her lower limbs became a fertile tangle of shoots, stems, blossoms and leaves.

She soon graduated to what she would later think of as her "Across the Universe" period. She graced one butt cheek with a smiling sun, the other with a moon. On the right side of her belly, she experimented briefly with planets and stars against a night sky, but she got bored and left it unfinished.

She became interested in religious icons for a while. She created a ring around her right bicep, linking a Cross, a Star of David, and an Islamic Crescent, symbolizing the unity of all religions. Later, she created another ring around her left bicep, linking the faces of Einstein, Newton, Galileo, and Copernicus. One day, Lakshmi applied tattoos of the word *Mythos* under Sophia's scientists' ring, and *Logos* under her religion ring. At the time, Sophia and Lakshmi thought this represented the balance and ambiguity of myth and logic.

Until Sophia met Roland Brand, she was unsophisticated. Most of her tattoos were either stock designs or pictures copied from a book. It hadn't yet occurred to her that designing a tattoo could be an opportunity to collaborate in the creation of High Art. In her naiveté, she would simply thumb through a catalog and say, "I want *that* one."

She'd have to go back to Angela—she knew that. Angela was her therapist. Sophia had made a deal with Natalie and Phil, and she was on her honor. The deal was this: They would let her move out and they would pay her living expenses if she stayed in school. The other part of the deal was if she got a tattoo, she had to go see Angela and talk about it.

Natalie and Phil were her parents. That's what Sophia called them—Natalie and Phil. Why not? Those were their names. When she was young, she started therapy with Angela, studied French and mathematics, and learned to call her parents Natalie and Phil.

Sophia wondered if she should borrow from her therapy money to get the Sagittarius tattoo and pay Angela later? No, that wouldn't be honest. She'd just have to play more nights at the Moonshadow. And she was pretty sure she could get an advance from Roland.

She wondered what color to dye her hair before she went to see Angela. Last time it was bright orange. Maybe purple this time. It had been a couple months since she'd gone with purple, and there was a new shade she wanted to try. She liked to distract Angela with different colors. Angela would always comment on it, and they would spend most of the session talking about her hair. It was fun.

Maybe she'd spike it.

Maybe she'd talk to Angela about piercing again. Sophia wasn't really into piercing. She limited her rings to bunches in her ears, a couple in her nose, and one in her eyebrow. Once she put a ring in her tongue, but she took it out because it got infected. Unlike some of her friends, she never pierced herself in all the weird places. What would be the point?

If she played her cards right, she could talk about her hair and her piercings for most of the hour. She could bring up the tattoo at the very end, and just when she was getting started, Angela would tell her their time was up. That way, she'd keep her promise to Natalie and Phil that she would talk to Angela about her tattoo.

Sophia also kept up her end of the bargain by staying in school. She was taking a drawing class.

On the other hand, this time she might really *want* to talk about tattoos with Angela. She would tell Angela she needed a Sagittarius Archer on her left shoulder to balance out the Double-Pisces on her right. It might take a couple weeks to come up with the money—maybe she and Angela could brainstorm.

* * * * * *

Most men weren't taller than Sophia, but Roland Brand was. He was mysteriously handsome, wrapped in a cloak of feminine-macho vagueness. He had a strong jaw that always sprouted a three-day stubble. It's an interesting phenomenon how some men can keep a perpetual three-day stubble. You would think they could only have it once every three days, but some men seem to be able to keep the stubble all the time. It's probably a generational thing—men in Sophia and Roland's generation can have a three-day stubble every day. Men in Bob's generation cannot. Evolution of the species.

Sophia understood that Roland was handsome, but she didn't notice his good looks any more than she noticed cardboard boxes. She didn't smoke, but it didn't bother her that he did. Maybe this was what Angela meant when she talked about disassociation. Whatever.

She did find it strange that Roland Brand didn't have a single tattoo on his body. She found that out the first time she let him make love to her after he created the exquisite Double-Pisces Fish on her right shoulder. She thought he looked more like a GQ pretty boy than a tattoo genius. When she asked him why he didn't have any tattoos, all he would say was, "I'm saving myself for the perfect one." Cool.

The important thing was that Roland *was* a genius and he introduced her to the world of custom tattoos the first time she entered Roland Brand's House of Body Design. Roland emerged from behind a partition—three-day stubble, cigarette dangling from feminine lips, dark hair disheveled just so. Skinny, busy, and distracted, he welcomed her, then disappeared to finish working on his current human canvas. While Sophia waited and tried to hear the conversation behind the screen, she thumbed through a catalog to pick a tattoo. She chose an owl.

Roland emerged with a giggling couple in tow. Good spirits

all around—relief at the end of an ordeal and a job well done. As they joked and laughed, saying their goodbyes, Roland sneaked peaks from Sophia to the catalog in her lap, then back to Sophia again.

After he let them out the door, he turned to Sophia. "You don't want that."

"What?" she asked, caught off guard.

"That owl—it's too generic for your regal bearing."

"How did you know?" she began.

"Call me psychic. Or observant. I see the page you're perusing. You've been fixed on the singular image of the owl since I first laid eyes upon your splendid countenance."

"I like this owl," she admitted.

"You must be heedful of owls," Roland warned. "What is your general knowledge of them?"

"I know I like them." Sophia was stubborn. "I know I want one tattooed on my belly next to my unfinished universe."

"The Apaches believed if an owl appeared in your dreams, it was an omen of death. Have you had any dreams about owls?"

She hadn't.

"Have you had any dreams about Apaches?"

No.

"We mustn't give you a Screech Owl," he continued. "The Cherokees believed it would inflict infirmity upon you."

Sophia had not thought all this through.

"You might enjoy a Little Owl," suggested Roland. "They're quite exquisite. Athene, the Greek Goddess of Wisdom believed they had an inner light that gave them night vision. She fancied them a symbol of wisdom and the protector of her armies. Yes, yes . . . the more I consider this matter, the more I'm convinced the Little Owl is the image I will create for you . . . Are you aware that the Greeks honored Little Owl on two different coins?" Roland asked.

He pondered a moment, then declared, "It's settled! I'll give you a Little Owl. *Athene Noctua*—perfect! Would you like him standing or in flight? Head or full body? A profile would be regal—no, no, a full facial image is more majestic—let's perch him on top of a snag . . . ."

Sophia didn't much mind the pain from tattoo needles anymore. Actually, she kind of welcomed it—a small price to pay for glorifying God. The familiar buzz of the machine cued her to drift into a blissful trance. As the needle vibrated and snarled on her skin, beautiful images came alive in her mind. For Sophia, electric heat was the burning of creation. Everything was right.

The Little Owl Roland Brand painted on Sophia's belly that first day was a masterpiece. Each tiny, brown, speckled feather emerged in such sharp detail, you wanted to touch it. You wanted to feel the soft, warm owl coat and skin, feel the little heart beat. Roland's creation glared into your eyes with his own. No compromise in the intense black pupils surrounded by musty yellow. No compromise in the grim wisdom of Little Owl.

After Roland finished, he inspected his work and said, "Yes, yes . . . That's marvelous." Sophia looked down on her belly, smiled her squinty smile and agreed. After that, Sophia always went to Roland Brand for her tattoos. She had attained a higher level.

* * * * * *

It would be a relief to get back in balance. Sophia had felt off center ever since she'd gotten the Double-Pisces Fish tattoo. She looked forward to having a majestic Centaur—half man, half horse, drawing back his bow string, preparing to let an arrow fly—applied to her skin. As soon as she could get Roland to tattoo a Sagittarius Archer on her left shoulder everything would be right again.

Tonight, after she finished working at The Shelter, she would go to the Moonshadow alone. She wouldn't bring Dorothy, Lisa, and Lakshmi with her this time. Their band, *Dis Funkshun & The Famlee Die-namics* was fun, but she didn't want to split the take four ways. Besides, Dorothy always wanted to quit early and Lisa always messed up the harmonies. Lakshmi was ok, but Sophia could make more money by herself. She was on a mission.

The northwest autumn night was biting cold. The Shelter line was long. Sophia knew it would get longer when winter set in. She knew some of these patched and tattered people wouldn't make it through. She also knew there would be more babbling nut cases in February than in November.

She wondered if Mr. Thurston came to the shelter because he was a babbling nut case, or if he had become a babbling nut case from living a desperate life on the street. Maybe Mr. Thurston was operating on a higher plane than she could understand. She imagined sitting at his feet and learning from him.

Then again, if she could be a fly on the wall inside the brains of everyday dentists and teachers and shoppers, she wondered which of them would turn out to be babbling nut cases.

Sophia loved her friends at The Shelter. How could she not? Their needs were so simple. A little warmth, a little food, love and compassion and care. Help them through a moment; help them through a night.

Feed them, clean them, listen to their stories. Touch them. Most people didn't want to touch them because they were dirty. They smelled bad. Most people didn't want to deal with piss and hawked up spit. For Sophia, it was ok. She held hands. She hugged. She laughed and cried with them. Most people worried about germs, but Sophia never got sick.

Ladle, pour it, hand it out . . . Here, take this bowl of soup. It's warm. Smile a squinty smile. Scruffy Mr. Davenport, eyes on his bowl, wordlessly drifting away . . . Ladle, pour it, hand it out . . . Mumbles of thank you . . . You're welcome . . . Thank you . . . You're welcome . . . Old glowing Mrs. Stearn, smiling through bloodshot eyes . . . Sophia glowed too.

She loved them all.

* * * * * *

At the same time Sophia Wise was ladling soup at The Shelter, Roland Brand was closing up shop. He'd had a good day. He'd started by giving another serpent to Big Roy. Big Roy had been a regular for a decade. That's how it usually went—once they got a tattoo from Roland Brand, they never went anywhere else. Big Roy would have to find someone else to go to after Roland was gone. That was fine—there wasn't much room left on his body anyway.

Next, he had a couple that requested matching rings tattooed on their wedding fingers. Cute. A first-timer got a heart with her boy friend's name inside it. Roland entertained her with war stories while she hung in there. Oh well—pretty soon he'd be outta here and wouldn't have to waste his time with that crap anymore.

His favorite of the day was the "mural" he was creating on Zigbee's back. Zigbee was the lead singer in a grunge band by the same name. Zigbee understood art. The mural was a depiction of Genesis. Today, Roland had recreated the Great Flood. Two more sessions and he would be done.

Roland thought he'd walk over to the Moonshadow Café. Chances were good Sophia Wise would be there, and he wanted to see her. He suspected soon she'd ask him to paint a Sagittarian Archer on her shoulder. Ever since he'd told her the Double-Pisces Fish was "creating a hazardous imbalance," he knew she'd come back for more.

The Moonshadow was just a short six blocks away. Roland didn't wear a coat or hat. Cold never bothered him, especially not tonight—he had Sophia dead in his sights and was focused like a bullet. He remembered Sophia's question about why he didn't have any tattoos.

"Just saving myself for the perfect one," he had said. He was glad she didn't ask any more questions.

As Roland approached the Moonshadow, Sophia was finishing her shift at The Shelter. She wasn't in a hurry to leave—she liked to hang with her friends and play tunes. She sat on a foldout table, surrounded by adoring companions who talked to her while she tuned her mandolin.

* * * * * *

Ivan Bunt sat in his apartment, feeling lucky. This month, Veteran's Resources helped him find a new room with wheelchair access. Not only that, he was the only tenant in the building with his own bathroom. The rest of those pathetic slobs had to use the toilet down the hall. He had his own TV too—with cable.

Now that Veteran's Resources had agreed to start up his disability again, he was in fat city. They'd messed him up good when, out of the blue, they sent a letter announcing they were cutting him off because he had been dishonorably discharged. Dishonorably discharged, his nose! He hadn't been dishonorably diddlin' discharged! He left the service with full freakin' honors and no flippin' flanks, thanks to the grimy grenade that had walloped him in the East World while he was busy defendin' the friggin' Free Nation!

It had taken eight months to sort out the snafu. If the folks at The Shelter hadn't let him in, he'd have been out on the street. But they did, and they even hooked him up with a Veteran's Service Officer named Betsy who went to battle for him. No harm, no foul. Everything was aces now. Maybe next month he'd ask the landlord to change the peeling wallpaper and fix the rusty pipes. And maybe put in a jigglin' jacuzzi and a big stone fireplace an' while yer at it, why don'tcha bring me up a chompin' champagne breakfast! And wouldja mind turnin' up the honkin' heat a little bit?! Festerin' filberts!

Never mind. Water under the bridge. Now it was time for Reverend Rufus. He dug his thumb and finger into a jar of little wieners and turned on the TV. He sure liked them little wieners in a jar. As he watched Reverend Rufus knocking people down and saving their souls, his mind drifted to the man he met last week. The man who gave him that bag of groceries. Mighty kind. Mighty kindly kind. Somethin' about that guy . . . He couldn't make me walk, but at least he tried. Nobody's tried before . . . But it wasn't what he did so much as how he looked. Somethin' in his eyes . . . .

Knock, knock!

"Who's there?"

"Bob."

"Bob who?"

"Brother Bob, The Lord's Loyal Servant and Dutiful Son. I am Dad's Carrier Pigeon, Flying Home with His Message."

"You the same Bob that gave me them wieners?"

"No, my brother, I am not. The Bob who gave you the wieners had not yet heard the Lord's voice. I have since spoken with Dad, and I am reborn. Will you please let me in? These books are getting heavy."

Bunt wheeled to the door and released the chain. He undid the dead bolt then he fished for his keys. When at last he found the key he wanted, he released the final lock and opened the door to see Bob's head, legs, and feet. The rest of him was hidden behind a tall stack of *Books of Bob* clamped at the top with his chin.

Bud wagged his tail at Bob's side.

"May I come in?" Bob asked. Bud was already through the door and sniffing the wieners in Ivan's hand.

Ivan Bunt wheeled backwards, making way for Bob who staggered in with his burden of books. Bob carefully set them on the floor, letting go ever so slowly, mindful that the stack stood in perfect balance before he cautiously backed away. There . . . .

"How did you know where to find me?" asked Bunt.

"Dad told me," replied Bob, removing his battered hat. "He tells me everything. He tells me what to say and what to do. I am His instrument. I play whatever tune He requests."

Bob was radiant in the second-hand gray suit Dad had instructed him to buy. The coat was a little tight in the shoulders and fit best when left unbuttoned. The sleeves were a bit short, but no matter. Bob especially liked his Hawaiian tie. It had palm trees swaying in a tropical breeze.

"Why me?" Ivan wanted to know.

Bob laughed hard and loud.

"Do you believe in synchronicity? 'Why me?' you asked. That's exactly the same question I asked Dad. 'Why me?' Do you know what He said? He said, *'You can pick your friends, but you can't pick your family.'* Ivan Bunt, my friend," Bob continued, "I pick *you!*"

"But why?"

"Because you are a perfect instrument to play in the Lord's band. You have suffered. You've been poor. You feel compassion, my brother, because you have walked in the shoes of the afflicted. Remember I told you I could make you walk? I can! I can! Go wherest I go and you will no longer walketh in the shoes of the poor, you will walketh in the shoes of Dad! And if you can't walk, no matter! You will fly! Join me and we will be Dad's Carrier Pigeons! Together we will Fly Home with His Message!"

"And the meddlin' message would be . . . ?" asked Bunt.

"It's all right here," answered Bob. He picked up a book at the top of the stack and handed it to Ivan.

"*The Book of Bob,*" Ivan Bunt read from the cover. "*The True Word of Dad as Transcribed by His Son.* Did *you* write this?"

"No, brother. Those are Dad's words. I just took dictation."

"Let's see . . ." said Bunt, thumbing through. "Says here on page 217:

> *Look ye at the Bigger Picture:*
> *When polar icecaps melt,*
> *Curseth not the red wine you spill that staineth*
> *your white carpet.*
> *When hurricanes doth smite your cities,*
> *Curseth not the mud that splatters your car;*
> *Washeth your damn car!*

Get thee over it!
When morons and despots rule the earth,
Curseth not thy neighbor's bumper sticker;
Educate thy idiot neighbor!

"From the *Book of Outlooks: 4:13*," Bob reminisced.

"Scottish kimonos," said Ivan in awe. "Listen to this:

Knoweth Me and thou knowest thyself;
Knoweth thyself and thou knowest Me.
I am not only Bob's Dad,
I am your Dad, too;
For verily, I say unto you,
Thou art the Fruit of My Loins.'

Geneology 2:16

"Filibusterin' frogs," Ivan Bunt whispered.

"Ivan, I am Dad's Carrier Pigeon. He has sent me out to lead His flock. I want you to be my First Carrier Pigeon. Come fly with me and together we will spread Dad's message. We will tell every man, woman, beast and sprout that we are all brothers and sisters! We are all the Fruit of Dad's Loins!"

"The fruit of His lanky loins," Ivan Bunt echoed.

"Are you with me, Ivan Bunt? Will you be my First Carrier Pigeon?"

"I will! I wallowin' will!"

"Then repeat after me . . . ."

And so it was that Ivan Bunt became the first to take the following oath from the *Book of Loyalty: Verse 1*:

"I, Ivan Bunt, do embark on this terrible journey with no heed for comfort, safety, or well-being, to be Dad's Carrier Pigeon and spread His word to every man, woman, beast and sprout. Though it's into the jaws of death I may go, I do so with good cheer, for when I emerge, I'll fly away with Dad."

"Ivan Bunt," Bob declared, placing his hands on Bunt's head, "through the awesome power vested in me by the Lord,

Our Dad, I hereby pronounce you Brother Bob's First Carrier Pigeon!"

Tears all around.

Then, "Bang my bananas, man! What're we dawdlin' in this doodlin' dive for? Are we gonna bring the falootin' flock on home to Dad, or we just gonna sit around here playin' checkers?"

"Right again!" exclaimed Bob. "I knew Dad was on to something when He told me to find you. Where to first?"

"The Shelter," said First Carrier Bunt, without hesitation.

So it was off to The Shelter. Bob's stack of books was shorter by one now that Ivan Bunt carried his own treasured copy of *The Book of Bob* in his lap. As Ivan locked the door behind them, Reverend Rufus was still knocking people down and saving their souls on the crackling TV.

* * * * * *

Back at The Shelter, Sophia Wise played a fiddle tune to warm up. By now, Roland Brand was already waiting at the Moonshadow. Brothers Bob, Ivan and Bud were only a couple blocks away.

Sophia closed her eyes, swaying with her mandolin to the music. She didn't play the fiddle tune fast like some people did. She wanted to hear every note. She liked the tune's relentless drone. She liked its certainty and inevitability. You knew where the tune was going; you knew what came next. She found security in the directness of the music, the predictability and precision. Play it right, follow the rules, and the music will be beautiful. Don't get fancy. It was fun to play fiddle tunes and pretend life was a straight line.

The fiddle tune Sophia played that night was called "Chickens in the Outhouse."

Next she sang the two songs she had written that week. Her favorite was the second one, "Please Put Your Brain Away." It went:

Verse:
Pardon me,
Don't mean to complain,
Is that your mind I see,
Or is that your brain?
I just think you should,
Keep your thoughts to yourself,
Especially when,
Your mind's an empty shelf.

Chorus:
Oh, put your brain away,
Back where it belongs,
Don't say you know it all,
When you're all wrong.
Stop saying the time of day,
With each new dong,
Please put your brain away,
Where it belongs.

Verse:
So sorry,
Don't mean to offend,
But I say "Beginning,"
You say "The End."
You've got all the answers,
But I can tell,
You're brain is showing,
It doesn't work too well.

Chorus:
Oh, put your brain away,
Please let me choose,
Stop telling me the facts,
When you're confused,
Save your ideas half-baked,

For another day,
Please give us all a break,
And put your brain away.

* * * * * *

Dad's Carrier Pigeons Bob, Bud, and Ivan arrived at The Shelter just as Sophia Wise started singing the first verse of "Please Put Your Brain Away." They, along with everyone else, listened with rapt attention.

Roland Brand bided his time at the Moonshadow.

IV. DAD'S CARRIER PIGEONS

EXCERPT FROM *THE BOOK OF BOB*:

> *The only thing that never changes is:*
> *Everything changes.*
> *Change is chaotic.*
> *Change hurts.*
> *Change is death, birth, death, rebirth . . . .*
> *Question: What came first, the chicken or the egg?*
> *Answer: To get to the other side.*

When you scratch an itch on your back, you change the lives of thousands of skin cells. You brutally kill them. One day they were minding their own business, being good citizens and contributing to the skin cell community. Then they bothered you because they were so busy. So you scratched, and in so doing, you ripped those poor innocent cells to shreds and smote them.

When you took your morning shower, you sent millions of screaming bacteria down the drain, to a soapy, watery grave. Which brings up another point:

Use biodegradable products.

Hurricanes, tornadoes, volcanoes; fires, famines and

floods; pestilence and drought. You call them disasters. I call them nature scratching Her back. I call them nature washing Herself. She has to scratch and wash just like you do. But:

Dad's Law of Physics #1: *The more you make nature itch, the more She wants to scratch.*

Dad's Law of Physics #2: *If you mess up the house, get out of the way—there's going to be some cleaning to do.*

Fly over the top of Mount St. Jude, the great volcano of the Northwest. What do you see? A base of cracked gray lava, hardened and cooled. And—what have we here? Green shrubs and sprouts springing out of ash and rock, the beginnings of junipers poking through. In the spring will be wild flowers and frogs.

Go to the red rock canyons of the Southwest. Look up. What do you see? YOU see rust colored pillars that almost touch the sky. YOU see majestic mountains springing forth from a dusty dry desert sprinkled with lupin and sage. Do you want to know what I see in the red rock canyons? I see the ocean floor. Look— there's a fish fossil. I remember when whales migrated right over there . . . This whole place used to be under water.

The tide comes in, the tide goes out . . . .

I've been watching your human tides. You people started out as a few trickling streams. Your human streams flowed into human rivers and tributaries, which flowed into great human oceans, and now you human oceans are rivals to the great saltwater oceans of the world. You're flooding the damn place! Pretty soon it will be time for the great water oceans to push back.

I've been watching your tides of history. For thousands of years, your violent ocean of war has thundered in and swamped the beach, then rolled back, revealing a new human landscape. Just when you breathed a sigh of relief and said, "Whew! Finally I can get some peace and quiet around here," another war roller came in and knocked you on your butts again.

You piled sandbags. War rolled in and blew them up. You put up some riprap. It worked fine till the next high tide. You kept tinkering and fixing. "If we can just get rid of this race or that ruler or this religion, we'll turn this cruel ocean into a placid lake," you said.

I once made a folksinger who asked the musical question, "When will they ever learn?" What's wrong with you people? Don't you get it? You have about as much chance of learning to stop war and suffering as the ocean has of learning not to go in and out?

Progressions 5:12

* * * * * *

Bud was worried about Bob. In the fourteen years Bud had been with Bob, he couldn't remember him ever smelling this way before. Once when Bud was young, Bob lay in bed for many, many days with his leg sticking straight out, and a strange wrapping all around him. He had a sick smell then. Bud remembered bad flesh smell and bone marrow smell. He remembered how happy he was when he smelled Bob's flesh and bones healing.

Bud could always smell when Bob was happy or mad or sad or scared. Early on, Bob used to come home smelling strong, like rotten fruit. The smell would last for days. But Bob hadn't had a rotten fruit smell for a long time now. Come to think of it, Bud couldn't remember the last time Bob smelled happy, mad, sad, or scared, either. For many, many days, Bob had smelled tired and musty and old.

But lately, Bob smelled different from anything Bud had ever experienced. He couldn't figure it out. The closest he could come was once when he was riding in the car with Bob and they were going too fast on a windy mountain road and Bud was getting thrown from one side to the other and Bob's eyes were closed tight and he was laughing and shouting and the car was tipping and screeching and then they were tumbling through the air . . . and the next thing Bud knew, he was waking up on a nice sunny spot on the grass. It was the same sunny spot where he had lain down to take a nap before he found himself flying through the air in a car with Bob, and now he was back on the grass where he started. Bob's new smell reminded him of that time in the car.

Bud was fourteen years old, which would make him ninety-eight in dog years. If Bob's sense of smell was the size of a postage stamp, Bud's was the size of a football field. Don't you wish you could pick his brain?

Bud didn't know he could smell so much better than Bob. He thought Bob knew *everything*. Bob knew how to open doors and boxes and cans so Bud could eat. Bob rewarded Bud when he was good and scolded him when he was bad. He gave him shelter from the rain and let him in and out when he wanted to. He gave him soft places to sleep. He told Bud what to do and he was always right. Sometimes Bob patted his head, sometimes he didn't. Bob gaveth and Bob tooketh away.

You can imagine how scary it was for Bud to worship Bob like he did, and then have Bob smell so weird. Bud thought maybe Bob had started smelling weird about the same time he started talking more. Lately, Bob had been talking a lot. He'd talk loudly, then he'd seem to be listening, then he'd talk some more. He talked like that to Bud and also to the ceiling. Sometimes he scared Bud when he yelled loud. Sometimes he scared him when he shook his fist in the air. But most of the time, Bud liked when Bob talked to him or to the ceiling. He liked the sound of Bob's voice.

They had also been going to lots of new and different places lately. Bud didn't care where Bob went, just so he got to come with him. It seemed that Bob had lots of new friends. He liked Bob's friend in the rolling chair. That man had many interesting smells. The man smelled like he had metal inside him. He also smelled salty, like tears.

But Bud was puzzled by Bob's new smell. *Oh well,* thought Bud. *Bob knows best. He'll take care of me.*

* * * * * *

Sophia Wise finished her second song at the Shelter. Happy applause all around. In back, Ivan Bunt stuck his two forefingers in his mouth and whistled. Sophia looked in the direction of the sound. When she saw Ivan, her squinty eyes opened wide and she smiled.

"Well, fry me for breakfast!" she cried. "It's Ivan bubblin' Bunt!" Her smile grew wider as she made her way through the crowd. When she reached him, she bent down and gave him a hug.

"That song was prettier'n toe nails," said Ivan, hugging her back.

"Where have you been?" asked Sophia. "I haven't seen you around for awhile."

"Mighty busy. Mighty bloomin' busy," answered Ivan. "Doin' great 'n' important things, an' bein' such a honkin' hero, I don't think you can stand the heat o' me."

"Oh, Ivan," Sophia said. "Is this your friend?"

"Allow me to introduce myself," said Bob. "My name is Bob, Son of Dad. God speaks to me, and it is His words I speaketh to you. He calls me Son; I call Him Dad. Dad wants us to be His Carrier Pigeons and spread His word. I don't make decisions anymore—Dad decides. Dad told me to find Ivan Bunt and make him my First Carrier Pigeon. Dad told me to come here tonight and spread the news. Dad tells me what to eat and when to sleep. When I go to the bathroom, it's because Dad tells me to. At this very moment, you think I'm speaking to you, but I'm not. Dad is. Watch this:

"I SAY UNTO YOU, THIS IS THY LORD, DAD, TALKING! HEED MY WORD, WHICH I SPEAKETH TO YOU THROUGH MY BLOOD SON, BOB!

"You see? I'm nothing but an empty vessel. Dad fills me up."

"Cool," said Sophia.

When Dad spoke through Bob, a hush swept through The

Shelter. All eyes turned toward him and the crowd gathered around.

"Brother Ivan is my First Carrier Pigeon. He has taken the Sacred Oath from the *Book of Loyalty: Verse 1*. Brother Ivan, please pass the books."

Ivan wheeled around the room, and passed out copies of *The Book of Bob* to the congregation. As he did so, he carried on a stream of thought:

"*Book of Bob, Book of Bob*, right off the poppin' presses! Get it while it's hot! Here are the words you've been waitin' to hear—straight from the hollerin' horse's mouth! These are the instructions, folks—from The Big Guy to you! Who-o-oa—onions an' ketchup! I feel good tonight! The spirit of Dad is overtaking me-ya! No strings attached-a! Just follow the recipe and you'll have your pie! Who-o-oa—chatterin' chipmunks! One helluva pie-ya! Getcher book! Getcher gropin' book-a! Right this way-ya! Climb on board and don't be late-a! O-O-OH—I flippin' feel it! I flippin' floppin feel it now-a! O-O-OH Dad-a! The spirit's overtakin' me-ya! Here you go, ma'am. Dad loves you! Here you go, sir. Read *The Book of Bob-a*! *Praise* Dad! *Praise* Dad-da!"

When people opened their *Books of Bob*, they were astonished at the truth of what they read. They knew they were in the presence of the Lord. They began to wail and fall on their knees and wave their arms and shriek and exhort the heavens and pass out. If you had just walked in and didn't know what was going on, you'd think they were all crazy.

Sophia Wise stood next to Bob, smiling as she read. Watching her friends roll on the floor, crying, moaning, banging their heads and kicking their feet in the air, she was reminded of a wonderful night long ago, when she sat in Phil's lap and they watched TV together. She remembered Phil's lap, safe and warm; the sweet smell of his pipe—she remembered how they laughed and laughed. She laughed so hard she peed. Everything about the memory made Sophia feel loved and nurtured and whole. In that moment, she even secretly called Phil, "Daddy."

The show Sophia and her daddy watched together that night was called *The Three Stooges Go to Mars*.

"That's so cool," she said to Bob.

"Yes, Sophia, it's very cool," replied Bob. "And Dad has an important job for you. He told me He wants you to join me and be His Carrier Pigeon. He's asking you to fly away with me and spread His word to every man, woman, beast, and sprout."

"That's nice of Dad to ask," said Sophia. "But I've got a lot on my plate right now. I'm taking a drawing class and I'm working here at The Shelter—and I've got to make enough money so I can get a Sagittarius Archer tattoo. Ever since I got my Double-Pisces Fish tattoo, I've been so out of balance—the only way I'll ever get straightened out is to get my Sagittarius Archer tattoo. I don't know how my life got so busy, but here I am—way over-committed and I can't take on any new projects. So, could you tell Dad thanks a lot for asking, but I just don't have the time?"

"Sophia, I'm nothing but a blank page waiting for Dad to scribble what He pleases. There is nothing I can say that will sway you. But please—open your *Book of Bob* to page 117 and read, *Dad's Plea: Verse 1*."

Sophia found the passage:

> *O lowly sinner,*
> *Thou art not worthy to touch*
> *the slime between my toes.*
> *Thou art not worthy of the raw sewage*
> *you dump into thine rivers.*
> *Thou art a worthless little turd,*
> *Who will suffer a hideous eternity of:*
> *Shackles and chains,*
> *Fire and flaying,*
> *Torment and torture—*
> *Unless—*
> *Unless you walk with Me.*

Unless you love Me.
I love you so much,
Ple-e-ease love Me too.
Ple-e-ease be My Carrier Pigeon,
And things will go much better for you.

And it became so that upon reading these words, Sophia Wise fell upon her knees and cried, "Yes! I will be Dad's Carrier Pigeon! I will fly away with you, Bob, to spread Dad's word to every man, woman, beast, and sprout!"

"Dad's got such a way with words," Bob said. "Sophia Wise, I hereby proclaim you Dad's Carrier Pigeon. And I appoint you to be my Minister of Wisdom."

And it became so that Bob and First Carrier Bunt and Minister of Wisdom Sophia conferred and decided on their next course of action. Sophia thought they should lead their flock from The Shelter to the Moonshadow Café, where they would spread the word, and while they were at it, she could sing a few tunes and make some money to pay for the Sagittarius Archer tattoo she needed to balance out her Double-Pisces Fish.

And it became so that Bob gathered his new flock at The Shelter and invited them to take the very same Sacred Oath from *The Book of Loyalty: Verse 1* that he had given to Ivan Bunt. And after they took the oath, Bob told them they were all Dad's Carrier Pigeons and he would lead them to spread Dad's word to every man, woman, beast, and sprout.

At which point, Bob clapped his hands, snapped his fingers, shook a fist above his head and exclaimed, "*Helluva* deal!"

And First Carrier Bunt and Minister of Wisdom Sophia and all the flock from The Shelter clapped their hands, snapped their fingers, shook their fists above their heads and exclaimed, "*Helluva* deal!"

* * * * * *

The Moonshadow Café, where Roland Brand waited, and where

Bob and his friends would soon arrive, was the latest link in the evolutionary chain of hip hangouts. In the Free Nation during the "Beat Era," the Moonshadow's forerunners emerged as beat coffee houses. The beatniks drank cappuccino and read free-form poetry that told stories of nihilism and what an existential bummer they were on. They sipped red wine and smoked cigarettes and pot. They dug jazz. They developed their own language that borrowed and stole from their hip jazz heroes.

Beat coffee houses evolved into folk clubs in the "Hippy Era." There were two breeds of folk clubs: One species specialized in "authentic" folk music. These clubs brought in musicians from the rural south who had never seen a big northern city. Imagine their surprise! The clientele consisted mostly of stoned young hippies wanting to get back to basics— so they tripped out on old black sharecroppers and real live white crackers who played music from a simpler, far away world.

The other species was a hybrid of the "authentic" folk club and the beat coffee house. These clubs showcased performers who borrowed and stole ideas from their black sharecropper and white cracker heroes, then mated them with ideas borrowed and stolen from their beatnik heroes. The crossbreeding begat lots of existential songs about freight trains.

Coffee houses became an endangered species. They proved unfit to survive the onslaught of disco, metal, and rap cultures. Like innocent field mice caught in the middle of a nuclear crossfire, the quiet little coffee houses didn't stand a chance.

But just when people thought coffee houses were extinct, the unexpected happened. The Free Nation was overrun by an invasive species: Coffee! Suddenly, every corner, every airport, hospital, and cornfield had a coffee shop. Wherever you looked, you saw people wandering aimlessly, carrying steaming paper cups of Double Soy Latte, Triple Caffe Au Lait, Cappafrappuccino, and Mocha Java Kahlua Kreme.

Out of the ashes and coffee grounds sprang a new type of habitat. Enter the Moonshadow Café. The lifeblood surging through the veins of the Moonshadow carried the DNA of its ancestors: Rage against The Man in the Gray Flannel Suit, rage against The Pigs who brainwashed and brutalized us. And now the latest: Rage against the Corporation.

Most beatniks and hippies could no more recognize their descendants at the Moonshadow as one of their own than a wolf would recognize a chihuahua. What's with the belly buttons? What's with the rings in weird places? What's with the baggy pants? The green hair? The shaved heads? What's Goth?

Kids these days . . . Don't you know your beatnik and hippy ancestors sacrificed so you could say what you think, be who you want, dress how you want, and be sexually free?

It worked! We won!

* * * * * *

While Roland Brand was sipping cappuccino at the Moonshadow, two more familiar faces showed up: Eldon and Larry Smith. They sat down at the table directly behind him. And no—they were not the Smith Brothers.

It turns out Bob was mistaken about Eldon and Larry when he broke up their fight. They weren't brothers at all. They were married. The day he stepped between them, Bob thought he was breaking up two thugs in a barroom brawl, when in reality he was meddling in a marital spat.

You could make up lots of rationalizations why the Smiths were fighting: Larry spent too much money, Eldon had recently had an affair, which made Larry jealous and sent him on another spending spree—but the truth is they had a lot of issues and neither of them handled his anger very well, especially when drinking. They went through these rifts several times a year. It always ended up the same way, with both of them crying and apologizing and promising it would never happen again.

But tonight, nothing could ruin their good mood. They were celebrating two big events. Today, Eldon had been awarded a commission to paint an enormous mural on the side of the FreeCorps bank building. The mural would depict the evolution of money, starting with the exchange of beads, and bringing the observer right up to present day credit cards. *Most people aren't aware of the exquisite beauty to be found in monetary designs,* Eldon thought. He looked forward to educating the public.

Larry was happy because that day, the doctor had told him he was still AIDS-free. Twenty years ago, he was diagnosed HIV positive, and here he was today—still alive and kicking. He was precise and disciplined in caring for his body, mind, and spirit. He took the exact combination of meds at exactly the same time every day, and he never missed. He worked out religiously and was buffed like a marine. His only transgression was drinking. He knew he shouldn't do that. Also smoking. He knew he shouldn't smoke either, but he was cutting down.

Eldon didn't worry about that stuff. His main complaint about Larry was that he spent too much money. Eldon secretly knew that Larry had made a down payment on a sports car that very day. Larry did it because he was relieved to still be AIDS-free. But he didn't tell Eldon that night because he didn't want to ruin their celebration.

Pretty soon a whole crowd of Larry's friends from the AIDS Prevention Center would join them. Larry was their well-loved director. Eldon thought, *Larry's friends can love him all they want—it's not* their *problem if he buys a new sports car every time he gets good or bad news.*

* * * * * *

Bob, Sophia, Ivan, and Bud triumphantly led the procession of Carrier Pigeons on their trek toward the Moonshadow Café. Bob walked in front of the flock, head held high, eyes blazing toward some distant light. Staring unswervingly ahead, he trumpeted a steady stream of testimony for all to hear. He testified about Dad's great love for every man, woman, beast, and sprout. He invited one and all to join him in loving Dad, becoming His Carrier Pigeon, and spreading the good news. Many brothers and sisters on the street heard Bob's message and were overjoyed. They waded into the tide, and their numbers swelled.

As Bob and his happy parade approached the Moonshadow Café, Roland Brand sat inside, wondering if Sophia would show up. He was patient. But he couldn't afford to wait long. He looked around, knowing he wasn't wise to be there.

He'd been thinking about the Southwest lately. That's where he would go. He liked the stark dry of the desert. Sometimes the Northwest Region's abundance gave him claustrophobia. Too much life—you couldn't get away from it. He felt oppressed by the forest—trees bore down on him, so tall he couldn't see their tops; nurse logs down for decades, sprouting whole forests from their bark; life growing out of life; life growing out of death. He thought he'd be strangled by blackberry vines. Escape the woods and look up: More oppression. Swollen gray clouds; damp heavy air that weighs on you like a full backpack. And always the rain.

"Looks like it's gonna rain today."

"That sure was a storm we had yesterday."

"I hear we're gonna have rain tomorrow."

"What's it supposed to do this weekend?"

"They say it's gonna rain."

The Southwest desert was where he should be. You could get lost in the vastness of it. The big blue sky kept its distance. A guy could live whatever kind of life he chose down there and not have the whole world crowding in to judge him.

Roland Brand looked toward the back. A cop sat near the door. Definitely time to move on. He'd have to leave some of his tattoo equipment at the studio. Oh well. He was bored with the little tattoo business anyway. He was made for bigger things . . . .

He should leave now. The only reason he was still in town was Sophia. He wanted her to come with him. He had plans in the Southwest and she figured in. He could convince her—of that he was sure. But there wasn't much time.

The sign over the men's room said, "Y Chromosomes." The sign over the women's said, "X Chromosomes." A girl in a tie-dyed shirt brought Roland another cappuccino.

Eldon and Larry's party arrived. They clicked wine glasses

at the table behind Roland and drank a toast. A singer banged his guitar and sang a song about what an existential bummer it was that the corporations owned all the freight trains.

Still leading the parade, Bob realized he had given away his stack of books. He'd need to stop by the house and pick up some more.

Roland Brand lit another cigarette and wondered if he should go now or wait for Sophia.

V. SERMON AT THE MOONSHADOW

There was a smart dog named Horatio,
Who devised a mathematical ratio:
The sum total space
From his groin to his face,
Was equal to solo fellatio.

Limericks 5:9

* * * * * *

ASIDE FROM BEING THE CHOSEN LEADER OF THE FREE NATION, Delbert Thorne had two other claims to fame. The first was, standing in his stocking feet, he barely cleared five-feet-two inches, making him the shortest Chosen Leader in the history of the Free Nation. The other claim to fame was that he had an enormous, permanent erection.

It came up many years ago when he was first campaigning to be Chosen Leader. At the time, his good friend Conrad Shanks was CEO of a little-known drug company that became a colossus when they marketed a sure-fire pill to remedy erectile dysfunction. Delbert Thorne, who was then governor of the Southern Region, thought he'd like to give the little pill a try. Not that he *needed* it. He just thought, with all the stress of campaigning, he'd enjoy a boost. So he gave his CEO buddy a call and asked for some samples.

The first night he took it, his wife Martha was horrified. She told him to stay away from her with that thing. When he awoke in the morning, he was surprised to find the erection had grown even more, and he had left Martha nowhere to sleep but at the farthest edge of the bed. He was forced to curtail his campaigning. He made no public appearances that week. While the public thought Governor Thorne was home with the flu, doctors and aides streamed in and out of his mansion, trying to figure out what to do. The damn thing wouldn't go down.

Finally, Delbert Thorne did what he had done his entire career: He took a handicap and called it a strength. He made the bold decision to walk out in public, erection preceding him, and go on about his business. He made the correct calculation that there would be a buzz of gossip in the press, but nobody would dare say a word to his face, and when it all came out in the wash, he could parlay his erection into a net gain. People would think it projected power. His short stature had dogged him his entire life—now he would finally have something to balance it out.

Pants were a problem. He had to have every pair refitted to accommodate his new physiology. Seating arrangements at dinners and public events needed to be carefully thought through. Now, when he spoke at the podium, along with the risers he had always demanded, he also required a long goose neck attached to the microphone so he could stand further back. Thorne had never been one for hugging, but when forced to hug, he learned to stand sideways. He and Martha slept in separate beds.

As he had predicted, his erection was all the rage among the pundits and gossip columnists, but no one ever forced him to address the issue. Although his opponent in that first election was vastly more intelligent, knowledgeable, and experienced, Thorne proved there's more than one way to be smart. His way was to convince people that his enormous erection was just what was needed to make the Free Nation safe and prosperous.

At this moment, Chosen Leader Thorne's biggest dilemma was whom to appoint as his next Secretary of Religion. He was still fuming about how the last guy worked out. Reverend Rod Barkley had been Thorne's handpicked choice!

Barkley had been pious and he'd been loyal. When Thorne started his first war, Reverend Barkley had turned out his flock in full support. When Thorne mistakenly bombed the little country of Borak because he got it confused with Boran, it was Barkley who bailed him out by coining the slogan, "Crusaders leave no stones unturned."

Secretary of Religion Barkley had been a staunch supporter of Chosen Leader Thorne's drive to drain the Free Nation's economy. The two men wanted to keep only enough money to pay for the expensive weapon systems needed to protect the country, and leave a little left over to lock up criminals, critics, and violators of the Sex Code. Only then would the Free Nation live up to its name and truly be free.

Thorne also had a powerful ally in Barkley when he launched his Air and Water Initiative, in which he declared it was the "fundamental right of every Free Nationer to breathe air and drink water." Barkley had helped him sell that one.

Delbert Thorne and Rod Barkley shared the belief that the sooner they crashed the car, the better. It was only after the earth was scorched and everybody eradicated that the Lord would come down and handpick the Chosen Leader, the Secretary of Religion, and a few others to sit happily at His feet for eternity. They couldn't wait to thumb their noses at the poor bastards down below who didn't make the cut.

But Barkley was gone, done in by a flurry of scandal. If he had only been caught embezzling millions to support his voracious life style, he might have been able to finesse it. The public seemed ready to forgive and forget after he said, "If *you* had sixteen wives, *you'd* need to skim a little off the top, too."

Damn! We could've ridden it out, thought Thorne. But, at a conference of religious leaders, Reverend Barkley made a fatal error. Mistakenly thinking his microphone was off, Barkley was overheard by the media, the public, God, and Delbert Thorne, making the following statement: "Delbert is dumber than a donut hole."

It took a whole week of aides fanning out over the Free Nation, repeating their talking points to every newspaper, TV and radio show, before Free Nationers were convinced Delbert Thorne was, in fact, smarter than a donut hole.

Whom to replace Rod Barkley with? Barkley was the third Secretary of Religion to melt down. This time, Chosen Leader Thorne would probably have to recruit from the outside. Thorne hated outsiders. Outsiders came in full of new ideas and questions. Thorne hated new ideas. He hated questions.

It would be so much easier if I didn't have to have all these secretaries and I could do everything myself, thought Chosen Leader Delbert Thorne, adjusting his prodigious protrusion. Maybe someday. But for now, his aides had better get cracking. He needed a new Secretary of Religion, and he needed one now.

* * * * * *

As the Carrier Pigeons approached the Moonshadow, Bob stopped in his tracks and listened. Dad was speaking to him. Dad was telling him to go home this very minute and get more books.

After explaining his latest directives to the flock, Bob instructed Sophia and Ivan to take charge in his absence. They were to soldier on and lead the flock to the Moonshadow where they would wait for Bob.

When Bob arrived at his house, he had to push with all his strength to open the door. The entire living room was bursting from floor to ceiling with boxes of books. Last week, when he had taken Dad's manuscript to the printer, Bob had asked Dad if maybe they should order a smaller batch for their first run, but Dad had admonished Bob to think big. Bob made a joke about needing to think big about buying a new house to hold all those books, but Dad didn't laugh. Bob was learning that Dad only had a sense of humor when *He* was the one telling the jokes.

Dad ordered Bob to remove all the books from their boxes and stack them in the front yard. Bob was also learning not to ask questions. He went straight to work, doing Dad's will. While Bob stumbled in and out of the house, stacking boxes and straining his sore back, Dad entertained him with a story:

"You know, Son, this reminds me of another son of mine. Have you ever heard of Hercules? You'll meet him some day. Be careful with him—he's a bit unpredictable, and he's awfully strong. That can be a dangerous combination."

Bob was about to tell Dad that *He* was strong and unpredictable too, but he decided to keep his mouth shut.

Dad grew expansive as he warmed to His subject. "This brings back fond memories of when Hercules had to clean out the stables where thousands of cattle had been housed. It was a big job, much bigger than stacking a few books. So, stop feeling sorry for yourself. Also, my boy Hercules had to divert *two entire rivers* to flow through the stables and flush them out. This little errand you're doing is nothing.

"The reason he had to clean the stables is a long story. But let's just say he suffered an abusive childhood. His evil stepmother threw a poisonous serpent into his cradle. Fortunately, little Hercules was really strong for his age, and he killed the thing. But I don't think he ever got over it. After that, he seemed to have a need to act out his trauma over and over by killing lions with his bare hands, and eventually killing his wife and three children.

"You can imagine how guilty my poor Hercules felt after that. To help him atone for his sins, King Eurystheus gave him twelve tasks, the fifth one being to clean out the stables. Other such assignments were to fight a nine-headed snake, a wild boar, a lion, a bull, a three-headed dog—all with his bare hands!

"Finally, Hercules was free. He married Deianira who was a

very suspicious woman. One day, she falsely accused him of having an affair, and in a fit of jealous rage, she tried to poison him. But before he could die, he ascended Olympus and came up here to live with me. It's so nice to have your children close by—families are so scattered these days. I can't wait for you to meet him. I think you'll like him a lot. Just one piece of advice: Don't ever wake him from a deep sleep. Aren't you done yet?"

Bob propped himself on a pile of books. Panting and perspiring from his labors, he looked heavenward and said, "I'm done, Dad."

"Not quite done yet," replied Dad. He told Bob to cut a piece of cardboard from one of the boxes. Next, He ordered Him to make a sign saying:

THE BOOK OF BOB
THE TRUE WORD OF DAD. TAKE ONE.

When that task was completed, Dad told Bob to tape the sign to the book pile, facing the street.

"Good!' said Dad. "Now call a cab."

* * * * * *

Roland Brand listened distractedly as a red-faced rapper, who looked as though his jugulars would burst, barked out a song called, "The Corporate Crap Trap." At thirty-two, Roland was getting too old for this stuff. Back when he was a kid, songs had a melody you could sing. These days, nobody sang at all, they just screamed. You couldn't understand the words, and even when you did catch a few, they went by so fast, you couldn't keep up.

Not that he much cared. He mainly wondered what he was doing here. Maybe he should leave right now. The hell with Sophia Wise—he could make it work without her. He'd find somebody else. Maybe he'd call her when he got safely to the

Southwest and she could catch up with him there . . . .

He heard a commotion outside. The noise grew as it approached the entrance. At first, it sounded like a tsunami, but he was able to pick human voices out of the wave, then an entire chorus, and then he realized they were chanting something. The door opened and the tsunami choir rushed in. And there, leading the chant was Sophia. She was joined by a wild looking red-haired guy in a wheel chair, pounding his fists in time to the chant. As they made their way through the door, a ragged horde swarmed in behind them. Now Roland was able to make out what they were saying:

> *Dad is great!*
> *Dad is good!*
> *Come and love Him*
> *Like you should!*
> *The Book of Bob*
> *Is understood!*
> *Re-e-eal . . .*
> *Re-e-eal . . .*
> *HELLUVA-deal!*

The throng continued its mystic chant until it became infectious. It spread among the patrons, swelling the entire room with the Spirit. Pure energy expanded the little coffee house, and some swore the Moonshadow levitated that night. Ecstatic people, packed in so tightly they threatened to blow the roof off its beams. It was lucky for them the fire marshal had the day off.

The only person not caught up in the pandemonium was Roland Brand. He remained in his seat, sipping cappuccino and calculating. *Raw energy can be dangerous or harnessed*, he thought. Should he stay to see how this force can be channeled? He looked beyond the human sea that buffered Sophia, and he scrutinized her. She was clearly tapped into something. What was it and how could it be used? Danger was near, but Roland was intrigued.

Sophia stood on the small wooden platform that sufficed as a stage, grinning her squinty grin, and leading the chant like an orchestra conductor. She spotted Roland and waved to him. Still smiling, she pointed to her left shoulder, where she wanted the Sagittarius Archer to be. Roland nodded slightly and showing a trace of a smile, he rested his chin on intertwined fingers. His thoughts began to crystallize.

Two Carrier Pigeons rolled Ivan Bunt onto the platform, and together he and Sophia rallied the crowd.

"Who is great?" she cried.

"Dad!" they answered.

"Dumpin' donkeys!" cheered Bunt. "Let's hear it for Dad!"

"Who is good?" asked Sophia.

"Dad!" they replied.

"Drunken dwarfs!" Bunt exclaimed. "It's Dad!"

"Come and love Him! Love Dad!" Sophia exhorted the flock to new heights.

"Give it up for the Big Dipper!" cried Ivan.

"Dad! Dad! Dad!" the crowd uttered as one.

And as one, a hush fell over them. For at the door, arms spread wide to greet the gathering, a resplendent look of bliss upon his face, surrounded by an aura of radiant gold, stood Bob. Following behind, looking as if he had stumbled into a stranger's bedroom, was the taxi driver carrying a tall stack of books.

Bud came in, too. He was happy and smiling and wagging his tail. He knew there would be lots of nice people to pet him and give him scraps.

Bob asked the taxi driver if he would kindly pass out the books. The sea of humanity parted as Bob, in his luminescence, glided as if off the ground, toward the stage. Once there, he ascended and was greeted by Sophia and Ivan. They each kissed Bob's hand and departed, leaving Bob to stand before his expectant flock. Bob raised his arms until his light spread over every man, woman, beast, and sprout in the room.

And then he spake:

"My friends," he began. "You who are poor, you who are humble, you who try to live by higher principles, you who are merciful, peaceful and pure, you who are persecuted; I say unto you, I have good news tonight! And that good news is: This world sucks! There's no place for you here. But hang in there. It'll get better."

A joyous uproar exploded when the people heard Bob's good news.

"Look at the big picture. Your problem is you're living in the material world. But there's another world—a world you can't see, and it's even more real. Dad calls it the Spirit Zone. But those are only words. Call it the Collective Consciousness, call it Energy, the Infinite, Heaven, Nirvana—call it what you want. Words don't matter—that's just you getting caught up in your material world again. Call it 'Hamburger World.' Don't you get it? I DON'T CARE! The point is, if you send out good, pure, loving energy, it will spread light throughout the Spirit Zone. If, on the other hand, you put out bad energy, all you're going to do is bum everybody out.

"Do you get it?"

"We get it, Bob!" they all cried.

"And," he continued, "it's not enough just to be good in the world. You have to be good in the Spirit Zone, too. Here's an example: Say you're mad at your brother and you want to blow his head off. It's not good enough that you decide not to kill him. If you were thinking, 'That no good sonofabitch deserves to die,' that's unacceptable because you're putting out bad energy.

"Ok, let's try another one: Say the reason you want to kill your brother is because he has a really hot wife and you think with him out of the way, maybe you'll have a chance with her. Do not, I repeat—*do not* lie with that woman as you would your wife. Or any other way, for that matter.

"Also, don't even lust after her. Don't picture her undressing slowly before you, revealing herself one soft luscious inch at a time until she's completely naked and slipping under the sheets with you and rubbing her warm body up against yours until . . .

" . . . Hmm . . . Where was I? Oh yeah—do you remember that guy who was running to be the Chosen Leader of the Free Nation, and he told a men's magazine that he never committed adultery but he 'lusted in his heart?' If you're ever running for office, don't say that."

"We won't Bob!"

"And always remember Dad made all of us. He didn't just make you and your friends. He also made that no good shyster who scammed you out of your life savings. Dad made the dumb lady who cut in front of you in line at the grocery store then held you up for fifteen minutes because she couldn't find her coupons. Dad made that idiot who rear-ended you and gave you a whiplash while you were sitting at a red light. They're Dad's children! They're your brothers and sisters! Love them all!"

And Bob's Carrier Pigeons shouted as one, "*Helluva* deal!" Buoyed by their enthusiasm and the Spirit of Dad, Bob continued: "If you do a good deed, don't go around advertising it. Keep it a secret! Don't let your right hand know what your left hand did, especially if it's doing that thing you're not supposed to do. Or if you do it with your right hand, don't let your left hand know.

"Ok, now I'm going to teach you how to pray. Repeat after me:

Our Dad who is the Source of all,
Your name is sacred.
Be with me in the material world,
As you are in the Spirit Zone.
Feed me and forgive my debts,
Especially those Visa and MasterCard bills I ran up last
*   year.*
Don't dangle rich desserts

Or loose women in front of me,
And if you do, make sure I don't mess up.
Because you're the Big Guy,
And I really don't want to piss you off.
Amen."

But still there was more.

"Don't invest in the material world. It's a risky market. Invest in the spirit. The rate of return is much better.

"Don't bother trying to enlighten your dog—he won't get it; don't hand out pearls of wisdom to your pig—you're wasting your time. As a matter of fact, what am I talking to *you* for? I could be addressing a convention of holy men or a theology seminar. If it hadn't been for a few bad breaks, I could have really gone places. Do you know I almost got on the Reverend Rufus show? But no—instead here I am, talking to a bunch of street people at the Moonshadow Café . . . ."

"*Helluva* deal, Bob! *Helluva* deal!" they urged him on.

Bob took a deep breath and drew sustenance from the exuberance of his flock. "If you want something, all you gotta do is ask Dad. Just ask nicely.

"Treat others the way you would like them to treat you.

"Don't go through the wide gate. It's really crowded. Go through the straight and narrow gate. The line is a lot shorter, but you might have to lose some weight to get through.

"Beware of the preacher who wears a hair piece. Or one who wears a Rolex. If a preacher invites you to his private quarters to see his etchings, get out of there fast.

"If you build your house on a foundation of sand, Dad will huff and puff and blow your house down. But if you build it on a foundation of rock, you'll get to sit with Dad in the Spirit Zone and He might give you a break."

Then he clapped his hands, snapped his fingers, shook a fist above his head and exclaimed, "*Helluva* deal!"

This brought down the house. The audience stood as one, shaking the walls with thunderous applause. Never had the Moonshadow seen such a standing ovation. Bob took his bows, but they couldn't get enough. They kept calling him back for more, crowding around him, wanting to be closer, wanting to touch him, wanting him to autograph their *Book of Bob*. And he stayed, signing each book with a personal inscription, and not leaving until he had satisfied every person in the room.

Throughout Bob's sermon, all eyes were riveted on him—all eyes except Roland's. His were fixed on Sophia. He studied every rapturous movement, each exuberant reaction. He noticed when she led the flock in wild chants and when she held back. He came to know when her eyes would water and when her face would contort in wild abandon. He came to anticipate every movement and twitch. He thought her thoughts and felt what she felt. He came to know her as a lion knows his prey.

Behind him, Eldon and Larry found something new to celebrate. This man with a golden glow who called himself Bob, was the very same man who, last week, had broken up their fight and saved their marriage. Now, here he was again, passing out books and giving them the good news from Dad. They found themselves caught up in the passion of the crowd. When Bob shouted, "*Helluva* deal," they snapped their fingers, shook their fists above their heads, and shouted "*Helluva* deal!" as loud as anybody in the room. After the sermon, hand in hand and teary-eyed, they made their way through the snarl of people to thank the man who had saved them. They were drunk on wine and Dad.

First Carrier Pigeon Bunt and Minister of Wisdom Sophia had their hands full. Circling fast around the crush of people who wanted a piece of Bob, Ivan herded them like a sheep dog, barking orders, rounding up stragglers and keeping them in line. Meanwhile, Sophia stood at Bob's side, greeting the awe-stricken worshippers with a smile as they made their way to the front. With loving arms, she led them to Bob, supported them in his presence, then helped them disengage. She serenely revived those who fainted. Most of the congregation wanted her to sign their *Book of Bob* too, and she was happy to oblige. One man shyly asked her if she thought Ivan Bunt would be willing to sign his Book.

"Hey, Ivan!" she called over the noise. "Would you like to autograph this gentleman's book?"

"Would I?" he cried. "Maids a-milkin'! I never had anybody ask me to scribble my autograph before!" He wheeled over to sign, and to his great pleasure, many others asked for his signature, too.

"May I be so bold as to request that you grace the pages of my *Book of Bob* with your inscription?" Sophia heard a familiar voice.

"Hey, Roland!" she exclaimed happily. "What brings you here?" She gave him a warm hug.

"Fate," Roland answered. "This fortuitous coincidence is further evidence of Dad's plan."

"It just goes to show," she said. "Have you met Bob yet?"

"I don't believe I have had the honor."

"Hey, Bob!"

Bob looked up from a plump, middle-aged woman who was gnawing on his leg. "Hey to you, Sophia. I think our friend needs a hand."

Sophia made her way over to Bob and gently pried the woman's fingers loose, cooing lovingly. "There you are, Ma'am . . . So sweet of you to come . . . Don't forget your book, now . . . Bob loves you . . . So does Dad . . ." Sophia waved bye-bye as she watched the shell-shocked woman drift away.

"Bob, I have a friend I want you to meet. Roland, Bob . . . Bob, this is my friend, Roland Brand."

"This is a distinct honor," said Roland.

Bob took Roland's right hand in both of his. "Bless you, my son. Dad loves you." He released Roland's hand and removed a pair of pink panties from his shoulder.

"Roland is a tattoo genius," Sophia told him. "He gave me a Little Owl and a Double-Pisces Fish. Pretty soon he's going to give me a Sagittarius Archer to balance me out."

"You are blessed to have such a friend," said Bob. "Tell me, Roland, are you right with Dad?"

"Am I right with Him?"

"Yes. If you were to walk out of here and be hit by a bus, would Dad take you with Him to the Spirit Zone?"

"I cannot reply to your inquiry with total certainty. I was quite taken with your sermon this evening. Your *Book of Bob* appears to be a profound work with far-reaching implications. However, whether I'd be deemed worthy to walk with Dad . . . I believe it would be presumptuous for me to say."

"Dad says, *'He who knoweth Me knows he knoweth Me not. He who claimeth to know all the answers with his tiny pea brain is an idiot,'*" quoted Sophia.

"Contradictions, 6:13," added Bob.

Roland nodded. "Yes, that was quite a passage, wasn't it? It brings to mind a similar sentiment from *The Book of Contradictions—8:14*, I believe it was, in which Dad stated, *'Fool Me once, shame on you; fool Me twice and you'd better hide.'*"

"Yes," answered Bob. "And one of my favorites is, *'I only speak in metaphor; on that you can take me literally.'* Contradictions 4:24."

"Ah," exclaimed Roland. "And lest we forget, *'There are absolutely no absolutes; and that's the absolute truth.'* Contradictions 12:11."

"How do you know your *Book of Bob* so well?" Sophia was incredulous.

"I'm a quick study," Roland answered.

"That you are," said Bob. "Hold on a second . . . Yes, Dad? Oh, ok, but . . . Remember when you told me . . ? I know, Dad, but . . . Sorry, sorry, I know You hate it when I interrupt. You really think so? Well, if You say . . . Right, right . . . Right again,

Dad . . . Ok. Give my regards to Brother Hercules."

Bob turned to Roland. "Dad wants you to work for me. He wants you to be His Carrier Pigeon and spread His word to every man, woman, beast, and sprout. If you agree to shoulder this terrible burden, I will appoint you my First Deputy Messenger."

"This is a great honor you bestow upon me. However, I am afraid I have previous commitments. I am due to leave in the morning for the Southwest Region, where I plan to take up residence."

"The Southwest Region?" exclaimed Sophia. "But what about my Sagittarius Archer tattoo?"

"Of course," Roland continued, "there are many men, women, beasts, and sprouts in the Southwest as well. It is conceivable I could be your representative in that area, and in so being, spread Dad's word to a virgin community."

"But . . ." The beam in Sophia's smile grew dim.

"Dad's speaking to me again," said Bob. "He likes the idea. Ivan—come on over here. There's somebody I want you to meet."

Sophia frowned.

"First Carrier Pigeon Ivan Bunt, meet my new First Deputy, Roland Brand. Roland is going to travel to the Southwest Region to spread Dad's word."

Ivan tentatively held out his hand. "Buttered to meet ya," he grumbled under his breath.

"The butter is mine, Mr. Bunt," said Roland, shaking his hand. "I have been watching you ride herd. You seem well suited for your vocation. And such a colorful way with words—the likes of which I have rarely heard."

"Jello!" exclaimed Bunt. "Who is this jiggler?"

"He's a friend of mine," Sophia told him. "He's given me some beautiful tattoos, and he was going to give me a Sagittarius Archer, but now . . . ."

"Now I'm going on a mission from Dad, to spread His word to the Southwest Region. Maybe you'd like to accompany me on this sacred quest, Sophia?"

"Me? Go with you to the Southwest?"

"Bob, what do you think? It appears that you and Bunt here are quite equipped to carry the message in this locality. Sophia, on the other hand, can provide invaluable assistance to my ministry."

"Sufferin' squash! Stutterin' stallions! I don't like . . . ."

"And another consideration is that if you come with me, Sophia, the tattoo you so desire will be yours, and you will finally achieve the equilibrium you so long for."

"Brambles in my buns! Bob, I don't think . . . ."

"Dad seems to like the idea," said Bob.

Sophia was deep in thought.

"It's settled then," declared Roland. 'We'll leave first thing in the morning. Ivan . . . ," he curled his lips into a smile, "may I have a word with you?"

Roland wheeled Ivan Bunt briskly to a far corner. He walked around to face Ivan. Gripping the arms of the chair, he leaned forward and, still smiling, talked for what seemed like a very long time. Ivan nodded his head slightly as sank into his seat.

Eldon and Larry were thrilled to finally get their audience with Bob. They jabbered excitedly as Bob closed his eyes and held the backs of their heads, just as he had the day he broke up their fight. They poured out their gratitude and their love for Dad, pledging total loyalty and devotion. Then, while Bob posed with his arms around them, they said, "One, two, three, cheese!" and their friend snapped a picture.

Roland continued his deep conversation with Ivan Bunt while Sophia pondered the situation. She had a lot on her mind.

VI. Sophia's Tattoo

You can lead a horse to water;
But you can't make him drink.
You can lead a woman to drink;
But it's probably your own fault,
For treating her thataway.

Parables 8:13

* * * * * *

"HE'S WRITTEN ME FROM RED ROCK EVERY DAY THIS WEEK," Sophia Wise told Lakshmi Jackson. They lay facing each other at the head and foot of Sophia's bed, like two sisters at a slumber party. There were two choices in Sophia's cozy one-room apartment: The bed or the floor. "He totally wants me to come to the Southwest with him. Bob thinks it's a good idea, too. Dad told him I should go. Want to see my tattoo again?"

Lakshmi nodded. Her eyes were heavy and sleepy. Of course, she had seen Sophia's new Sagittarius Archer tattoo lots of times now, but it made Sophia happy to show it to her, so she would admire it again. Also, as many times as Lakshmi had seen the new tattoo, that was how many times she had heard Sophia's story of how she got it. She knew she was about to hear the story again. She would listen.

"It was so cool," said Sophia, turning her back and lifting her shirt to display the magnificent Archer on her left shoulder. "We were all high from Bob's Sermon at the Moonshadow. But then, when Roland said he was moving to the Southwest, I got totally depressed. I know it was selfish of me. It's important to the world that Roland go there to spread Dad's word, but all I could think was, I'll never get my Sagittarius Archer tattoo and I'm doomed to a life out of balance."

"What a predicament," Lakshmi agreed.

"Most of the crowd had gone home, and I was hanging out with Bob, Roland, and Ivan, plus a few people who worked there. Also, there were a couple of cool guys named Eldon and Larry who loved Bob so much, they wanted to follow him everywhere."

Lakshmi's mind drifted to that day at the In 'n' Out.

"Isn't it the most incredible tattoo you've ever seen?" Sophia exclaimed. "Nobody does colors like Roland. And look at the detail. Can you see how the muscles ripple as he pulls back the bow? And check out the eyes . . . He's got his prey right in his sights. Roland says the Centaur represents our duality. I love how he fused the man with the horse's body. Isn't he perfect?"

"Mm-hm. He's perfect."

"So Roland comes up to me and he's like—you know how he talks—he's like, 'On this sacred night, so that we may honor the blessing of Dad's re-emergence among the Earth's populace, I shall grace your left shoulder with a Sagittarius Archer tattoo.' Then he takes me by the hand and starts to pull me away and then, I forget—did I tell you what Ivan said to me on the way out?"

"I think you did," answered Lakshmi.

"It was so weird. He rolls up alongside me and he whispers one word and then keeps right on going. The word he said as he rolled by me was, '*Cuidado.*' Do you know what that means?"

"It's Span . . . ."

"It's Spanish for 'be careful.' I love how Ivan talks. He says the funniest things."

"I wonder if Ivan . . . ."

"So Roland takes me to his studio and the whole way over, he's telling me about the town of Red Rock in the Southwest Region and how awesome it is and how I've got to come with him. Do you think my Fish and my Archer look like they need support?"

"Well, I know that's what Roland told . . . ."

"That's what Roland said. All night long while he was drawing my Archer, he kept talking about how perfectly in balance I was going to be, but then when he finished, he was like, '*Oh dear. I believe we have a problem.*'" Sophia mimicked his voice again. "'*It appears your Double-Pisces Fish and your Sagittarius Archer are free falling through the universe. This is all wrong. Until they have support, you will find it impossible to be grounded.*'"

"So now he wants you to come to Red Rock so he can draw Bob on your back, balancing the Fish and the Archer in his hands."

"Exactly!" exclaimed Sophia. "Ever since that night, I've been feeling totally uprooted. I'm afraid unless I have Roland give me a Bob tattoo to support my Double-Pisces Fish and my Sagittarius Archer, I'll be doomed to a life of drifting like a kite without a string."

"I know the feeling," sympathized Lakshmi Jackson. For most of her life, she had felt like a kite without a string.

"Bob wants me to go. He says there are lots of men, women, beasts, and sprouts in the Southwest who need to hear Dad's word. Bob is so awesome. I wish you could hear him."

"He saved my life . . ." Lakshmi started to say.

"He saved mine, too!" Sophia declared. "Ever since Bob brought Dad into my life, I've had direction and meaning and a purpose for living."

"Sophia, who is Bob—really? I mean, that day I told you about when he saved me at the In 'n' Out . . ."

"Bob is the Son of God. God told Bob to call Him 'Dad.' Dad came to him one night and asked him to transcribe His new book, which He calls *The Book of Bob*, in honor of His son. Bob and Dad talk all the time—they have a really good Father-Son relationship. You should see Bob sometimes—he'll be talking and then he's like real quiet and you know he's listening to Dad, and then he'll talk some more. It's totally awesome to be with someone when they're talking to Dad."

"I was with him when he talked to his dog," Lakshmi volunteered.

"Then you kind of know what I'm talking about," said Sophia. "Bob has a sixth sense. He's in tune with something you and I can hardly imagine."

"My mother says . . . ."

"Bob totally wants me to go to the Southwest and help Roland. Roland writes me every day. Want to hear the letter he sent me today?"

"Sure," said Lakshmi.

Sophia rummaged through her backpack. "Ok, here it is:

My Dear Little Owl.

"That's what he calls me," Sophia said, "Little Owl."

Ever since that (dare I say?) cosmic night in which we first heard Bob's momentous Sermon at the Moonshadow, followed by our tryst in my studio during which time I created for you the most magnificent Sagittarius Archer capped by our romantic episode which was so memorable I am quite certain it still lingers in your mind—where was I? Oh yes—but of course—Little Owl, it is imperative that you come join me in Red Rock. There is important work to be done here, spreading Dad's word to every man, woman,

beast, and sprout, and I fear I am incapable of completing
that task alone. Your Yin is needed to compliment my Yang.
Dad needs you in Red Rock. Would you forsake Him in His
hour of need? Further, I fear for your safety. Now that your
Fish and Archer are floating in space, you will have no
ground beneath your feet until I am able to draw Bob on
your back to bear the burden of your astrological signs. I
implore you, for your own well-being—come to Red Rock
soon.

Praise Dad,
Roland Brand

"He's hard to say no to," said Sophia.

"Believe me, I know," Lakshmi replied.

"I've never been to the Southwest Region. Have you?"

"No."

"There's so much I don't want to leave behind—my friends
at The Shelter and the Moonshadow; Natalie and Phil; you and
Lisa and Dorothy . . . I especially don't want to leave Bob, now
that I've found him. I've never felt so close to Dad before."

"There's something about Roland I think you . . ."

"But it would be an adventure. I like seeing places I've
never been, and everybody seems to think Dad needs me there.
Also, I'm feeling so ungrounded lately . . . ."

" . . . should know . . . ."

"I don't want to go by myself. Lakshmi? Do you want to go
to Red Rock with me?"

"Me? Oh no, I couldn't. My mother would never . . . ."

"Of course you can! Let's take a trip to Red Rock together.
It'll be fun!"

"But my mother . . . ."

"Lakshmi, how old are you, nineteen? Have you ever done
anything your mother told you not to do?"

Lakshmi thought. "I'm sure I can think of something if you
give me a while," she said.

"Well, it's about time you learned," replied Sophia. "And what could be a better cause than to spread Dad's word?"

"I don't even know what Dad's word is," Lakshmi protested.

"Read the *Book of Bob* I gave you and you'll find out. Bob is speaking at the Moonshadow tomorrow night. Come with me to hear him. Ivan Bunt will be there, and so will Eldon and Larry. Once you hear Bob speak, your life will be changed forever."

"I'm not sure I want my life to be changed forever," Lakshmi sighed.

"Promise you'll come with me?"

"Ok, I promise."

"That's a good girl," Sophia stretched and yawned. "I'm tired. Let's go to sleep."

So Lakshmi Jackson cuddled up next to Sophia in her best friend's bed, and like two sisters at a slumber party, they fell fast asleep.

* * * * * *

Orvil Swain liked to say, "If the Red Rock Fossil Shop don't have it, we ain't got it." Then he'd laugh.

Perched in the shade of an enormous, rust colored, egg-shaped boulder, Orvil's shop was the best place to be in the whole town of Red Rock because it was the one place a guy could chill out in the summer. Orvil had been chilling out there for over forty years now, and he didn't seem likely to be chilling out anywhere else soon.

Of course, the bones he had piled up in his dusty old shop had been around for a lot longer than that. He had, if he could find it, a caudal vertebra from the Jurassic period, probably off an Allosaurus. It was around somewhere. He had a Diplodocus cervical bone buried under one of them piles over there—he just seen 'er the other day. There was a Sauropod femur and a

Dryosaurus knuckle joint. If'n you wanted one, you could come back in a hour and he'd dig 'er up for ya.

And it weren't just dinosaur bones. There was lots o' petrified wood. He had genu-wine stuff like a petrified conifer that was fossilized in calcite, from the Triassic period. He did! An' that weren't all. He had crystals 'n' quartz 'n' agates 'n' such. All you had to do was look. They was all around somewhere.

Orvil remembered the old days. It was simpler then. You had yer Tyrannosaurus Rex, which was the baddest dude on the planet. You had yer Brontosaurus who was eighty foot long and weighed thirty-five tons, an' ate nothin' but leaves 'n' shrubs, an' had a brain no bigger'n a pea. You had yer Stegosaurus with them bony plates on his back an' that spiky tail. Then you had yer Triceratops with them three horns stickin' outta his face. Orvil liked to say the Triceratops was one horny sonofabitch. Then he'd laugh. That about covered it in the old days, 'cept for maybe yer Pterodactyl, which weren't really a dinosaur anyhow—they was more of a flyin' reptile.

That was about it. But nowadys they got so many fancy names for dinosaurs, a guy can't keep track. Abrosaurus, Bactrosaurus, Campylodoniscus, Diplotomodon—goddamn scientists. Always tryin' to show off how much they know by makin' up a bunch o' fancy names an' confusin' regular folks. Same with planets. Remember when there used to be nine planets? Well, now there's as many planets as there is dinosaurs. But don't get Orvil started 'bout scientists. Or the gov'ment. Don't get 'im started on the gov'ment, neither.

Orvil liked to say he'd lost more old stuff than most people ever seen. Then he'd laugh. An' not only fossils 'n' such. That Allosauros vertebra he was looking for was hiding under a Donnie and Marie lunch pail. If'n ya moved that Howdy Doody clock outta the way, you'd find that Dryosaurus knuckle joint. He had all kinds of stuff. Old comic books. Some busted up furniture. All it had to be was old and Orvil Swain had it.

He also had three wives. Two of 'em was old, one weren't. Goddamn gov'ment. If'n there weren't a law fer every time a guy wanted to piss, he'd have him four by now. All the kids was up 'n gone now, but his new wife Maggie had two fine ones from her last marriage, an' as far as Orvil could figure, the fourteen-year-old looked ripe enough to marry anyhow. Screw the gov'ment. If'n he wanted to marry the fourteen-year-old, he'd damn well marry 'er. An' if Maggie had anything to say about it, he'd whup 'er good and then she wouldn't have nothin' to say about it no more. Then in a year or two, the twelve-year-old wouldn't be twelve an' he'd marry her too.

But on this day, Orvil was in a mood that was going from bad to worse. He had a toothache. Goddamn dentists. The only dentist in town was that little feller with the hairy arms, Dr. Dark, and he'd let all his teeth rot and fall out before he'd let that sonofabitch pull one. Fact o' the matter was, a lot of his teeth was rotting, but that sure weren't no concern fer Dr. Dark. He'd make his first wife, Ruth, pull 'er. She was good fer that sort o' thing.

If'n he could find her. Last night, he come home and the house was empty. *What's this world comin' to*, Orvil thought, *when a guy can't even keep track o' his women?* He was hungry an' in a mood that was goin' from bad to worse. He musta paced around the house for fifteen minutes before they showed up. All five of 'em—Ruth, Barb, an' Maggie an' the two step-daughters, too. They was a bit flushed in the face an' looked a little worried. Ruth says real sweet, "Orvil! So good to see you! We didn't expect you home till 6:30."

"Well, I come home early. And where does it say in the Scripture that a guy can't come home early if'n a guy wants to?"

It turns out, the gals was at that new preacher's trailer, over at the south end of town, doin' God-knows-what. They says he's got this new brand o' religion that's the closest thing to the Holy Spirit they's ever seen. All Orvil knew was he wanted his women home where he could see them, and he was hungry. He whupped 'em good that night—all three of 'em, and he got in a few licks on the two step-daughters, too.

Them gals was quite taken with that new preacher that come to town, Orvil thought. Young skinny guy. Orvil seen 'im a few times. He even come into the shop. Bought 'im a few thises an' thats. Guy introduced hisself—he come right out and says, "Brother, are you right with the Lord?"

Orvil replied, "I believe I'm 'bout as right with the Lord as I'm gonna be an' 'scuse me, but I believe I got three brothers an' you ain't one of 'em."

Roland Brand laughed. "Brother is just a figure of speech. May I call you friend?"

"Why, I don't rightly know if'n yer friend or foe," Orvil fiddled with his suspenders.

"The Lord, Our Dad, says," and Roland quoted:

> *He who lifteth you to righteousness,*
> *Call him brother;*
> *He who passeth you by,*
> *Call him brother;*
> *He who smiteth you with his sword,*
> *Call him brother;*
> *She who looketh at you with a lustful eye,*
> *Call her wife.*
>
> Proclamations 7:4

"Hey, that there's pretty good," Orvil exclaimed. "Where'dja get that?"

"It's all in *The Book of Bob.* I regret that all my copies were destroyed in a great fire. However, every word is branded up here." Roland pointed to his brain.

Orvil reached under his stained undershirt and scratched his large belly. "My wives don't much look at me with no lustful eye, but I don't pay *that* no never mind. I call them 'wives' anyhow." Then he laughed.

"And how much for this dinosaur bone?"

"That'd be thirty-four, ninety-nine. Cash. That way I don't have to pay the goddamn gov'ment no goddamn tax every time I piss. You ain't with the goddamn gov'ment, are you?"

"No."

"Ever notice how a guy can't take a piss without the goddamn gov'ment tellin' you which side o' the bowl to piss in?"

"*The Book of Bob* has a lot to say about that issue."

"It does, does it? Does it talk about marryin' laws? Does it say how a guy can't marry his own fourteen-year-old stepdaughter if'n he cares to, but the goddamn gov'ment says it's perfectly ok for a white guy to go an' marry a gal of any color he wants? Does yer *Book o' Bob* have anything to say 'bout the fact that if'n all the white guys starts marryin' brown gals an' yeller gals an' any other color gal they wanna have, pretty soon the whole white race'll get watered down with half 'n' halfs and there ain't gonna be no white race no more?" Orvil had hit on one of his favorite touchy spots.

"Actually, my friend, *The Book of Bob* is quite clear on those points," Roland answered. He quoted again:

> *Whoa to him who corrupts his errant seed. He doth distort Mine own image. Verily, if thine wife beareth a daughter from thy neighbor's seed, that daughter be yours as well.*
>
> Proclamations 8:13

"Well, that pretty much sums it up, don't it," Orvil rubbed his bald head.

"Rather nicely," Roland replied. "Is there a price tag on this crystal?"

"Eleven, ninety-nine. Cash. Does yer *Book o' Bob* really say them things?"

"Every word I have quoted you is in *The Book of Bob*."

"An' what does yer *Book o' Bob* have to say about the Unnaturals?"

"Excuse me? Unnaturals?"

Orvil went on to explain about the "Unnaturals." He'd seen 'em before when they come a-visitin' from outta town. They was boys that liked boys, but not just to go fishin' with. He'd heard about the things they done. It was like what he done with his wives and what he'd do with his step-daughters too, when they come around a little bit, only it was unnatural. He'd heard there was gals that liked gals that way, too. What would they wanna do that for? But Orvil knew one thing—if a guy ever tried to do somethin' like that with him, he'd shoot 'em an' ask questions later. He'd shoot 'em twice, once in the pecker an' once in the head. *Crazy goddamn world*, Orvil thought.

Of course, Roland Brand had just the right quotation to address Orvil Swain's concern. He recited:

> *If thou desirest electricity, insert thine plug into thine wall socket. Do not strive to insert thine plug into a another plug; electricity wilt not be yours. Verily, do not strive to insert thine socket into another socket; electricity wilt not be yours.*
>
> Home Improvements 2:9

"Couldn't be clearer 'n that," declared Orvil.

Reverend Brand pulled a wad of bills out of his wallet and paid Orvil for his treasure in cash. As he was leaving, he informed Orvil of the Great Renewal Meeting coming up Sunday at the vacant lot on the south end of town, and he invited him to come learn more about how Dad spoke to us all in *The Book of Bob*.

Then he said, "Dad loves you, brother," and with that, Reverend Brand strolled out of the Red Rock Fossil Shop with a bag of bones and crystals, and quite a bit of new information to digest. It had been a fruitful conversation.

Orvil Swain spent a lot of time thinking about it, too. Every time his tooth throbbed, his thoughts went back to Reverend Brand. His mood was going from bad to worse. Maybe he'd walk down to the south end an' have a talk with this Brand fella. Leastwise, he knew his wives would be home when he got there. They wouldn't be showin' their faces anywhere today.

* * * * * *

Chosen Leader Delbert Thorne was starting to think there was a jinx on the job of Secretary of Religion. He'd lost three so far, one to scandal, one to mental meltdown, and one to death. The problem of finding a Secretary of Religion he could hold on to was closing in on him and making him tense. When things started closing in on him, Delbert Thorne had a secret way of releasing his tension that nobody knew about, not even Martha. Things were closing in on him now, and it was time to let off some steam.

In the attic, stashed behind suitcases and boxes of memorabilia, was a long, black vault, securely sealed with a padlock. With the help of a flashlight, Delbert crawled through the cubbyhole and sifted through the obstacles in the tight dark attic, finding his way to the vault. These were the times, he thought as he squeezed through the attic, that he most regretted his enormous erection.

Finally, he arrived at the vault. Grunting and straining, he pulled it backwards out of the attic and into the bedroom. He made his way into the open light, and heaving a sigh of relief, sat down on the vault to catch his breath. But he didn't have the time or patience to sit for long. Reaching into his pocket, Delbert pulled out the familiar key that would open the padlock and transport him to another world where he didn't have to worry about things like finding a new Secretary of Religion.

First, he scanned the area one last time to make sure he was alone. Then he dragged the vault a few more feet until it was sitting directly in front of the full-length mirror. He opened the lock.

The secret game Delbert Thorne liked to play to relieve his tension was called, "Dress-up." In the box were elaborate outfits he would put on. Then he'd parade in front of the mirror and pretend. Which ensemble to wear? He considered putting on the Spanish soldier's uniform dating back to the Inquisition. Or maybe the tattered gray uniform that had been worn by a Confederate during the Old United States' First Civil War. The suit of armor had been out of the question ever since he'd gotten his permanent erection. Another outfit he liked to wear was the bearskin from the Viking days, complete with the broadsword and bull-horned cap. After a moment of deliberation though, Delbert decided to go with his favorite standby, the outfit he prized most: The Nazi Storm Trooper's uniform he'd bought from some old fart at a fossil shop when he was campaigning in the Southwest Region.

Now that Delbert had his humongous erection, he was no longer able to fit it into his pants when he played "Dress-up." *That's ok*, he thought, pulling up his jackboots. *Give it some air. It adds to the effect.* He slipped on his S.S. cap and, riding crop in hand, he paraded in front of the mirror.

As he watched himself marching back and forth, Delbert felt an uneasy gnaw in his gut and realized his mind was wandering. Being Chosen Leader of the Free Nation wasn't as much fun as it used to be. There was a time when everybody followed orders, and that was that. But then he created the new post of Secretary of Religion and all hell broke loose.

He tried a goose step to bring his mind back to center. He never should have let his aides talk him into picking Gennisaw Tubbs as his first Secretary of Religion. Anybody could see Gennisaw Tubbs was a crackpot. And sure enough, Gennisaw melted down right on cue. His very first day on the job, he demanded an emergency audience with The Chosen Leader and breathlessly told him the Lord had informed him that all

Congressmen from the Progressive Party were agents of the devil and should be arrested immediately. Fair enough. There weren't too many Progressives left anyway, but Delbert figured better safe than sorry, so he took Gennisaw's advice and had 'em rounded up.

Then Gennisaw started performing exorcisms on the poor incarcerated congressmen. While subjecting them to extreme duress, he ordered that they renounce the devil or be burned at the stake. But he didn't stop there. He began accusing members of Chosen Leader Thorne's own Regressive Party of devil worship. It got to the point where every innocent, God fearing Free Nationer, Regressive or not, was worried that he would be the next to be accused by the red-faced, raw-boned, book thumping, devil-chasing, holy-hollerin' Secretary of Religion Gennisaw Tubbs.

Staff members took to tiptoeing quickly and quietly passed his closed office door, from which they heard all kinds of ungodly growls and snarls on the other side. Some swore they had seen the door expand, contract, shake and rattle, as if a wild hyena was pounding on the other side, trying to knock it off its hinges. There were reports from people who had entered Tubbs' office that they were barraged by multi-colored strobe lights. One intern swore she had opened the door to find him leering bug-eyed behind his desk, while his head spun around like a top.

Still, Chosen Leader Delbert Thorne felt compelled to stand behind his man. To fire Gennisaw Tubbs would be to publicly admit he had made a mistake, and Delbert Thorne wasn't made of that kind of stuff. Events started spiraling out of control when Tubbs accused the entire High Court of practicing devil worship, and ordered them hauled away. Thorne knew the circle was closing in and it was only a matter of time before he too, would stand accused.

Chosen Leader Delbert Thorne huddled with his aides and they hatched a plan. On a late Friday afternoon when most staffers had gone home, three Secret Service agents dressed as medics pulled up to the front of the Falwell Memorial Building in an ambulance and discreetly climbed the stairs to the twenty-second floor, where Gennisaw Tubbs' office was located. With trained efficiency, they entered his lair, marched without hesitation behind the desk where he sat, and while two of the agents held Tubbs down, the third silently answered his desperate protests with a needle in the neck, rendering him unconscious. They strapped him to a stretcher, whisked him into the ambulance and drove him to the hospital.

That night, the citizens heard on the Free Nation Network (FNN) that Secretary of Religion Gennisaw Tubbs had had his appendix removed. This was true. However, the surgeons only removed his appendix as a cover. The part the Free Nationers didn't hear was that while Gennisaw lay unconscious, the medical team, under the supervision of the Secret Service, also inserted a tiny computer chip into his brain. The chip would cause Gennisaw Tubbs, when he awoke, to hear a continuous, twenty-four-hour-a-day loop of Frankie Valli singing, "Big Girls Don't Cry."

This was an "extreme duress" interrogation technique that Chosen Leader Thorne had been wanting to experiment with for quite some time. He couldn't have been happier with the results. Within days after Tubbs was released from the hospital, he was seen running naked down Capital City Boulevard, holding his ears, shaking his head, and singing in a high, falsetto shriek:

BI-IG GIRLS,
DO-ONT CRY-YI-YI!!!

All that was left to do was haul Gennisaw Tubbs away in a straightjacket and tell the public that due to a rare medication reaction, Gennisaw Tubbs would no longer be able to fulfill his duties as Secretary of Religion.

Chosen Leader Thorne frowned in the mirror. He couldn't get it off his mind. He tried a little *Sieg Heil!* and marched around some more. He considered getting out Martha's eyeliner and painting a little brush of a mustache on his upper lip, but he thought better of it. Last time, it took a week to wash off.

Delbert's mind drifted to his second Secretary of Religion. Conrad Shanks didn't even last two days. Right after Shanks was sworn in, the former CEO of the drug company that became a colossus based on the success of its erectile dysfunction remedy, gave a major speech addressing the pharmaceutical industry. He told of the sweeping reforms he planned to introduce to the Free Nation's religious policy. Central to his strategy would be the mandatory use of "God Realization" drugs for anyone who was diagnosed as "God Deficient." It was an ambitious plan with far-reaching implications. His speech was enthusiastically received by the pharmaceutical giants, all of whom agreed this would be a major breakthrough for mankind and the industry.

But Secretary of Religion Shanks made a big mistake. He was going along fine, sticking to the text: *"The generous prescription of God Realization drugs will benefit every citizen of the Free Nation! We will finally see a day in our lifetime when all people will follow The One True Religion! Then and only then will we be free to live our lives without the burden of another man's bogus beliefs!"*

But rather than leave well enough alone, in a fit of rhetorical inspiration, Shanks spontaneously improvised these closing lines: *"And to those cynics who claim that, as former CEO of the company that will distribute these drugs, I will make stupendous profits, I say unto you: I will not make one dime! And if this is a lie, may God strike me dead here and now!"*

To Conrad Shanks' surprise, God took him up on his offer.

The autopsy showed Shanks had been high on just about every medication known to man, and the combination had been enough to knock out an entire city. This probably explained Shanks' puzzling closing remarks which required Thorne's aides to go on a week-long education campaign before the entire incident fuzzed over in the public's mind.

Gennisaw Tubbs, Conrad Shanks, Rod Barkley—three Secretaries of Religion down. Maybe there was a jinx. Chosen Leader Thorne sighed. Even "Dress-up" wasn't much fun anymore.

So much to worry about, Chosen Leader Delbert Thorne thought as he removed his Nazi Storm Trooper's uniform, folded it neatly, and placed it back in the vault. He sadly clamped the padlock shut and began sliding the vault through the cubbyhole to the back of the attic. He cursed in pain as he banged his erection into a suitcase. Finally, the vault was back in place and he slid backwards out of the darkness.

Being Chosen Leader isn't as fun as it used to be, thought Delbert Thorne as he latched the door.

VII. PURIFICATION

Wade in the water,
And cleanse thyself of thy sins.
But first check the mercury levels,
And make certain thou art not
Downstream from a chemical plant.

Purifications 12:8

* * * * * *

THE MAIN REASON ROLAND BRAND LEFT THE NORTHWEST Region was Lakshmi Jackson's father wanted to kill him. There were others who wanted to kill him too, but Ben Jackson was the one Roland worried about the most. Ben didn't take it well when he found out what had happened between Roland and his wife. He didn't even know the whole story. If he had, he wouldn't have wasted so much time and let Roland get away.

Let's back up:

Lakshmi's mother, Aruna Jackson had two priorities in life. Her top priority was warding off evil. Her second priority was to keep her body clean, which she hoped would help her achieve her first goal. She believed each event in life presented an opportunity to wash, and she took advantage of every chance she could get. She took a minimum of three baths a day, one upon rising, one to clean up in the afternoon, and one before sleep. On the evenings she and Ben made love, she took a bath before and after. Sometimes she would wake up in the dead of night when the world was dark and still. She would feel evil creeping in, and she'd run the tub.

Hand washing was practiced as regularly as inhaling and exhaling; as predictable as the tides. Aruna was on a constant lookout for the perfect scrubber that would eliminate every particle of bacteria once and for all. Each day, after she had washed her hands from her morning chores, she would peruse her piles of catalogs for new cleansing devices. Then she would wash her hands. Usually she found a soap or scrubber she'd like to try, so she would wash her hands, call the 800 number and order it, after which she would wash her hands again.

Aruna kept canisters of anti-bacterial hand wipe tissues in every room in the house. She also kept her car well supplied. She had a bumper sticker that read:

If the Lord called you today, would you be clean?

Aruna didn't want to be obsessive about it—she just thought with so much evil in the world, keeping it at bay was a constant job. If you had been her friend, she would have told you washing wasn't *all* she did. She had lots of other methods for fending off evil too, such as hanging cloves of garlic over each doorway, giving her home a daily incense smudge, protecting each room with ankhs and crosses and mandalas, and placing a welcome mat on her front porch that read:

Devil Be Gone!

It bothered Aruna Jackson that her daughter Lakshmi didn't value cleanliness the way she did. Aruna couldn't remember the last time she had seen Lakshmi take more than two baths in one day. Sometimes she still had to remind Lakshmi to wash her hands before she used the bathroom. It was so hard to instill proper values in children. Maybe when Lakshmi grew up and calmed down, she'd understand the importance of staying clean and warding off evil.

One day, Aruna was reading the classifieds, hoping to find a device that could get under her fingernails better, when an ad caught her eye. It said:

CLEANSE THYSELF OF EVIL.

Nothing more but a phone number. She didn't call, but she kept the ad. Every day for a week, she glanced at the simple statement and wondered. Once she even picked up the phone and started to dial, but stopped before she had punched the final digit. When the daily paper came, she would go straight to the classifieds to see if the ad was still there. One day, a week later, the ad was gone. Worried that she'd hesitated too long, she washed her hands, went straight to the phone, and dialed the number.

"I thought you'd never call," Roland Brand said on the other side.

"Who are you?" Aruna asked.

"I am but a simple practitioner of body art who, through years of ritual and deep meditation, has learned the mystic secrets of purification. But that is of little importance. The question is: Who are *you*?"

"Well . . . I don't . . . ."

"Wait," Roland interjected. "I'll tell you. There are two kinds of people in this world: Seekers and finders. You, my love, are a seeker. You have a gaping hole in your heart. That chasm exists because you have not yet found the answers you are looking for. You want to know God. You are so close, you can almost touch Him. You have looked and looked. You've reached out to Him but He has slipped through your fingers like mist. You have done all the right things. And yet . . . and yet . . ."

To Aruna's surprise, she found herself on the verge of tears. "How do you know all this?"

"Because, my love, I am a finder. I have been to the depths of hell and the pinnacle of heaven, and this much I know: If you wish to stop being a seeker and become a finder, you must purge yourself of all evil! You must cleanse yourself in the spirit of the Lord! Purge your body! Cleanse your spirit! Then, my love, the hole in your heart will heal without a scar."

"Yes! Yes!" she exclaimed. Never had she felt so seen. Finally, her long, tormented search seemed about to come to an end.

Aruna never harbored secrets from her husband, but on this occasion, for reasons she could not explain, she kept her conversation with Roland and her plans to meet him to herself. On the appointed day, she waited anxiously for her husband Ben Jackson to don his police uniform, strap on his gun and eat his eggs. Then she peeked out the window as Ben backed the cop car down the driveway and disappeared around the corner. Quickly, she scurried into the bathroom to fill up the tub for a second time. Climbing in, she said a prayer asking that on this day of days, she be made pure and cleansed of all evil. Then she scrubbed her body until it was red.

After her bath, she locked the house, got into the car, and drove the three miles to Roland Brand's House of Body Design. Upon arriving, she pulled out one last anti-bacterial wipe and nervously gave her hands a good going over before walking on shaky legs toward the shop door. But before she could knock, Roland threw the door open and announced, "Quickly, my love. We haven't a moment to lose."

He grabbed her hand, rather roughly she thought, and led her in. Wordlessly, he whisked her through the waiting room where she caught a glimpse of wild tattooed bodies framed above her on the walls, then he thrust back the partition revealing a dentist's office? No—a real tattoo parlor with some sort of electric instrument looming over—what? A massage table? And next to it, canisters of colored ink neatly lined up in a row and needles, but Aruna Jackson had no time to think because Roland led her past all that and through the next door and into a room with soothing pink lights, candles flickering around the perimeter, luscious green philodendrons hanging low from the ceiling, and in the center, a bubbling, steaming cedar hot tub.

"I will wait in the next room while you undress," Roland almost whispered. "Please make yourself comfortable in the tub and call me when you're ready." With that, he left.

Aruna stood where he left her. If her heart would just stop pounding so hard in her head, maybe she could think. His voice—it was so low and smooth and soothing . . . Like warm chocolate . . . calming her down . . . penetrating her pores . . . It was so hard to think with her heart pounding like this. Something about how he looked at her—like he knew. He knew. She felt watched and seen and naked . . . Even though she stood there in her *sari*, she felt naked and didn't mind. She didn't mind being seen by him. Maybe she liked it. It was hot in here. Her clothes were starting to stick. So hot . . . so hard to think. Oh, what she would do for a bath right now—she was sticky and sweaty and needed to be clean. If she could just get out of this *sari* and get into a nice, cleansing bath, everything would be all right. She wanted to be clean. Free herself of all those evil thoughts that swirled in her mind . . . the germs . . . evil was everywhere . . . so much evil . . . She needed a bath, needed to be purified . . . .

"Are you ready?" Roland called from behind the door.

"I'm in," she said.

* * * * * *

"Great grindin' gorillas! Buggerin' buffaloes!" exclaimed Ivan Bunt. "Bust my noggin, I feel better 'n a bag o' roosters today!"

"Wasn't Bob incredible?" Larry said, tears running down

his puffy face. Eldon had a black eye and Larry's face was swollen from the fight they'd had after Eldon learned that Larry had bought a new sports car. But that was water under the bridge. Since then they had made up, and now they were reveling in the stunning success of Bob's second Sermon at the Moonshadow.

Eldon wanted to relive every magic moment. "Remember when Bob said, *'When you leaveth the water running and you floodeth the kitchen, sue not the plumber; when you forget to turn off the oven and you burn down the house, sue not the fireman. Buy some gingko biloba and get thee over it.'"*

"*Helluva* deal!" cried Ivan.

Eldon went on. "Yes, oh yes! Remember when he said, *'Beware the clever man with an answer for every question; he will twisteth your little brain like a pretzel and show you for the moron that you are. Follow the fool who knows nothing; you're more on his level.'"*

"*Helluva* drunkin' deal! Praise Dad!" Ivan chimed in, raising a fist triumphantly.

Sophia added, "My favorite line was when he said, *'Let us live a life of love, free of hate. I HATE hate!'"*

"Bash my bananas! Pound my pies! I feel it now! *Helluva* doodlin' deal!"

"You were right," Lakshmi Jackson told Sophia. "You have to see Bob in person to understand how awesome he is. How does he come up with all that stuff?"

"Dad writes the script," Larry explained. Just thinking about it made him burst into joyful tears again. He continued, his voice wavering with emotion. "Bob told me ninety percent of everything he says is Dad's material. Bob just fills in a few blanks every once in a while. Praise Dad! *Helluva* deal!"

"Yes, oh yes," wept Eldon. "And sometimes Dad gets mad if Bob improvises too much."

"Stick to the squawkin' script!" cried Ivan.

"Praise Dad! *Helluva* deal!" they all declared.

Bob stood in the farthest corner of the Moonshadow, surrounded by worshipful followers, microphones, and television cameras. There was no way anyone could have anticipated the stunning success of his second Sermon at the Moonshadow, which would later come to be known simply as "THE SEQUEL."

Earlier that afternoon, a large crowd had gathered, anxiously awaiting the arrival of Bob and his Carrier Pigeons. It overflowed into the street and halfway down the block. At first, Bob tried to lead his Pigeons to the building, but it was no use. The crush was too thick. Then somebody shouted, "There he is!" and the crowd turned into a mob. Like dry kindling that catches all at once, the crowd exploded into a hysterical, thousand-armed beast, reaching for a piece of Bob.

Those who couldn't get to Bob settled for Sophia, Lakshmi, Ivan, Eldon, and Larry. Even poor old Bud was mobbed. The worshippers tore away patches of clothes, pulled out hair samples, and somebody made off with Bud's expired dog tags. But Bob stood serenely in the midst of the melee, and just when it looked as though disorder would devolve into disaster, Bob lifted his hands high and shouted, "DAD SAYS ENOUGH!"

The fire was doused. An eerie hush fell over the crowd, which now spread over several blocks. Spontaneously, the multitudes fell to their knees and bowed their heads, while Bob continued to stand motionless with arms stretched toward the heavens.

Bob held his pose for a pregnant pause, then dramatically whispered, "You may rise." Then, while thousands of worshippers cast their anxious eyes upon him, he launched into THE SEQUEL.

* * * * * *

Over the next two months, Aruna Jackson seemed to be getting purer. The sessions with Roland Brand had become increasingly intense, and the excitement was almost too much to bear. At their last meeting, Roland told her she was on the verge of a breakthrough.

Because the purification sessions had increased, not only in intensity but in frequency, Aruna was having a harder time keeping her secret from her husband, Ben. If she could only hold out a little longer, she would finally be pure, and then she could tell him the whole story. But for now, she would have to sneak around.

That wasn't hard to do because Ben worked so much. The biggest problem was acting normal. There was a week in which she found herself at, unpredictable moments, clucking like a chicken. This was after Roland had handed her a flapping, squawking chicken and invited her to bite off its head. When Aruna uncontrollably clucked in front of Ben, she would pretend to have a coughing fit and quickly leave the room. She was having so many coughing fits these days, Ben asked if maybe she should go see the doctor.

Roland had cautioned Aruna that the purification sessions might intensify her home hygienic program. Sometimes she spent the entire day in the tub, scrubbing and scrubbing. She just couldn't get clean enough. Roland encouraged her to go with it.

Then there was the sex. The purifying sex she had with Roland was like nothing she had ever experienced before. He violently purged her of every trace of wickedness, and then transported her to a world of cleanliness, purity and bliss. Roland instructed her, at all costs, not to make love with her husband during this critical period, or it would not only undo all the progress they had made, but could actually create a dangerous split in which she would descend headlong into irreversible evil. It required a good deal of creativity on Aruna's part to continually invent new stories to keep Ben's ardent advances at bay. She noticed that as she came closer to becoming purified, her stories became more elaborate and convincing.

And now, the main event.

Roland had been preparing Aruna for the day when she would be ready for Advanced Purification, and that day was finally here. She performed her familiar morning ritual of seeing Ben out the door, watching through the window until she was sure his shiny black and white car was out of sight, slipping into her second bath and scrubbing herself raw, quickly throwing on her *sari*, saying a prayer asking that today on this day of days she be purified once and for all, and hustling out of the house to start the engine and drive the three miles to Roland Brand's House of Body Design.

She no longer knocked. She knew Roland would leave the door ajar. She let herself in, tip-toed anxiously through the waiting room with the pictures of tattooed bodies staring down at her from the high walls, through the partition into the tattoo studio that still looked to her like a dentist's office, and took one last, deep breath before opening the door to the purification chamber.

There stood Roland directly before her, stark naked and eyes a-blaze. Behind him, in the hot tub and out, was a tangle of naked men and women writhing and moaning in every conceivable configuration. Off to Roland's left was a white goat, tethered to a pole. The goat looked up at her with a childlike face and said, "Baa-aa." She noticed the knife in Roland's hand.

"Come in, my love," he said.

* * * * * *

"Bob, I'd like you to meet Lakshmi Jackson," said Sophia.

Bob had finally managed to disengage from his admirers, the microphones, and the questioning media and return to his Carrier Pigeons. Lakshmi felt bashful, not only to be in Bob's presence, but because she wasn't used to having television cameras on her. Everywhere Bob went, the cameras followed.

"Of course! We're old friends. We had quite an adventure at the In 'n' Out market, didn't we? Dad be with you, Lakshmi,"

Bob greeted her.

"Dad be with you, too," she replied. Then realizing what she had just said, she thought she'd better qualify. "Oh, I'm sorry . . . I didn't mean it that way. I mean . . . I'm sorry . . . I know Dad is with you . . . Of course, that's so obvious. You're the one who told us all about Dad, and I know he speaks to you all the time, and I'm so stupid to say that . . . of course Dad is *already* with you, but I just meant . . . ."

Bob placed his hands on Lakshmi's head and she calmed right down. "You're a beautiful girl, Lakshmi Jackson. There, there, don't cry. We're all flustered when we're in the presence of Dad. Carrier Pigeons, come heal Lakshmi Jackson."

All the Carrier Pigeons gathered and formed a circle of love around Lakshmi, and she was healed.

"Lakshmi," Bob continued, "I have a very important mission for you. I am sending Sophia to the Southwest Region to help Roland Brand spread Dad's word to every man, woman, beast, and sprout. Will you join Brother Roland and Sister Sophia in their ministry?"

"I'd like to," Lakshmi Jackson began, "but there are some things . . . ."

"Lakshmi's so shy," Sophia told Bob. "She always thinks she's not good enough or smart enough or pretty enough. Lakshmi, if you only knew how wonderful you are, you'd know you'll be a perfect Carrier Pigeon."

"Yes, oh yes," Eldon agreed.

"Undoubtedly true," said Larry.

"Whistlin' weasels! That's a natural fact!" added Ivan.

"You're all so kind," Lakshmi said. "I don't deserve your love. I wish I could go to the Southwest with Sophia. But, Roland . . ."

"You should see Roland now," interjected Sophia. "Ever since he heard Bob's good news about Dad, he's been so full of The Spirit!"

"Yes, oh yes," said Eldon. "Roland's got The Spirit."

"The Spirit of Dad," added Larry.

"Hi ho and it's ho hum! Great gobs of goats!" declared Ivan. "Roland's got the chicken cluckin' Spirit!"

Then Bob spoke. "Lakshmi Jackson, I sense your hesitation. That's all right, my child. You needn't go to the Southwest and spread Dad's word if that is not your wish. You may stay right here and live your little life in the Northwest Region, studying your books, working at the In 'n' Out market, living in your parents' home where you will be safe and bored. You have the free choice to not do what Dad asks you to do in His time of need. Chances are Dad probably won't be offended and smite you, anyway. He has a lot on His mind and a lot of people to keep track of without worrying about one puny little ungrateful pigeon who disregards His request without even considering the consequences of His wrath. Chances are nothing will happen to you. It's a free country. You decide."

"Yes, oh yes! Decide!" chorused Eldon.

"It's a free country," Larry agreed.

"Decisions, decisions! Festerin' incisions!" contributed Ivan.

"Lakshmi," Sophia said, "will you please come with me to the Southwest?"

"I will," Lakshmi relented. "I will."

"She will!" cried Eldon. "Yes, oh yes!"

"Yes she will!" echoed Larry.

"Will she?" Ivan asked the rhetorical question. "Believe your boots she will!"

Sophia kissed her, and Bob wrapped her up in his arms with a loving hug. Then all the Carrier Pigeons clapped their hands, snapped their fingers, shook their fists above their heads and exclaimed, "*Helluva* deal!"

* * * * * *

Ben Jackson might not have found out if it hadn't been for the

Purification Tattoo. And he might not have discovered the tattoo if Roland Brand hadn't been so damned arrogant. But power begets arrogance, and arrogance born from power begets the heady belief that you are exempt from the laws that ordinary people live by. Roland Brand claimed that exemption when he drew a green-blue teardrop directly over Aruna Jackson's butt.

He gave it to her as the finale of their marathon Advanced Purification session with his naked friends and the goat. As the participants gathered around, Aruna lay face down on the table and accepted her tattoo. The one original member to not witness the tattooing was the goat. The only trace left of him was his blood smeared on the sated bodies.

Roland told Aruna that the single drop of water he would draw over her butt symbolized the purification she so longed for; the purification that was finally within her grasp. The tear depicted Aruna's newfound compassion. Further, Roland explained that a tear comes from the eye, representing Aruna's vision and awareness. Her new friends laid their hands on her and chanted mysterious, otherworldly sounds as she lay in an altered state, joyously receiving her tattoo. She welcomed the pain that felt like a cat scratching the last cells of evil out of her body. She was purged and purified and never felt so clean.

Once she got home, the purification sessions, orgies, animal sacrifices, and tattoo had mixed results. On one hand, she was ecstatic to hear Roland say she was finally cleansed of all evil, although she would need some supplemental sessions to assure they kept wickedness away. Furthermore, Roland would ask her from time to time to help purify a novice, which he assured Aruna would help *her* in her own cleansing process.

On the other hand, she found it difficult to get out of bed. She was surprised to find her newly purified world looking so gray. Where had all the colors gone? She felt heavy and tired and sad, and she cried at odd times for no reason. Roland explained, now that she was pure, she was feeling a deep compassion for humanity. What she was experiencing, he pointed out, was the pain all saints endure when they bear the burdens of the world. He assured her she'd learn to integrate it.

Aruna suffered another setback when she learned she wasn't allowed to take a bath for three weeks while her tattoo healed. She made do in the shower where she tried to keep her tattoo dry while she scrubbed her body till it bled. Though she was purified, she never felt clean.

Then there was the problem of her voice. Sometimes it was quite normal. At other times, however, she would open her mouth to speak and the utterance that emerged sounded like Darth Vader. She still had occasional clucking problems. At various times, both her husband Ben and her daughter Lakshmi walked by the locked bedroom door and heard what sounded like a "BAA-AA!" coming from the other side.

Ben sensed something was different with his wife, but they had been shorthanded down at the station and he'd been doing a lot of overtime, so he may have missed some of the subtleties. But being a detective, his job required him to have an intuition about problems, and something was up. He probably would have connected the dots eventually anyway, but when he saw Aruna's tattoo, he found the clue that broke the case. The smoking gun.

"I don't get mad," Ben Jackson repeated his lifelong motto through clenched teeth, as Aruna tearfully blurted out the story. "I get even." A festering knot formed in his stomach, and over several days it grew to a simmering rage.

Before work each morning, Ben drove his police car directly to Roland Brand's House of Body Design and parked across the street. He paid several visits to the same spot each day, and parked there one last time each night before going home. He studied Roland's habits. He knew Roland never arrived before noon, and rarely left before dark. Sometimes there was a steady stream of customers; sometimes Roland was in there by himself for a long time. Roland often walked a block to the deli around four o'clock and came back with a veggie sandwich and tea.

The night of Bob's first Sermon at the Moonshadow, Ben Jackson told Aruna he had to work late and he parked by the House of Body Design to stalk Roland. At 9:15, Roland emerged by himself, locked the door and began walking. Ben lurked a block behind with his car lights off and trailed him to the café. Ben watched his mark disappear behind the door, followed him in, and found a seat in the back. For two hours, he drank coffee and set his sights on the back of Roland's head.

Then all hell broke loose. First a motley band, led by some girl with a purple mohawk and tattoos all over her came marching in, chanting something about "Dad" and yelling, "*Helluva* deal!" That couldn't be Lakshmi's friend Sophia, could it? Then there was this crazy red-headed guy in a wheelchair, who kept yelling things like, "Chatterin' chipmunks!" and "Bust my bananas!" And then, this pasty dude in a bad suit walked in with his dog, and everybody chanted, "Bob! Bob!" and he got up in front and started talking about Dad and some book he wrote and god-knows-what but people were going crazy and rolling on the ground and yelling, "*Helluva* deal!" and pretty soon, Ben found himself caught up in it, and the next thing he knew he was jumping on the table and yelling, "Yes, Bob! Yes! *Helluva* deal!"

Ben's plan that night had been to follow Roland to his home and kill him. But in all the excitement, Roland slipped out and disappeared and the trail went cold. Ben wasn't worried—he was a patient man. There would be other days. Besides, after Bob's inspiring Sermon at the Moonshadow, he wasn't much in the mood for killing, anyway.

It turned out there wouldn't be other days after all. The next morning, Roland Brand was gone, and Ben had squandered his chance. All he had left was his daughter who informed him only a week after Roland disappeared, that she was leaving for the Southwest Region; and his shell-shocked wife who claimed she was cleansed by her tattoo, who bathed constantly, and who clucked like a chicken and baa-aad like a goat.

"*Helluva* deal," Ben Jackson grumbled to himself.

* * * * * *

Poor Lakshmi Jackson. She loved Sophia and couldn't say no to her. She couldn't turn down Bob, either. When he talked about Dad, she knew she was in the presence of something bigger than herself. She dreamed of Bob and Dad taking her away to a place where everything was safe and clean and good. Truth was, it was hard for her to say no to anybody. She wanted so much to make people happy.

But how could she make Bob and Sophia happy and make her parents happy too? Her father needed her more than ever, now that her mother spent most of her time in the bathtub, clucking and baa-aaing. These days, her father spent his evenings cleaning his gun and muttering, "I should've got him while I could."

Lakshmi knew his story about being suspended from the force because he let a serial killer get away wasn't true. She knew he had asked for a leave of absence because his wife was cracking up and he was afraid to leave her alone. She also knew what Roland Brand had done, and that her father was taking it hard. He blamed himself for letting it happen and for letting Roland get away. Lakshmi was afraid he might crack up too. How could she leave her parents like this?

Then there was Roland. She didn't trust him, but who knows? Maybe he was different now. People change. She saw Bob's power to transform people. He transformed Sophia. He transformed Lakshmi a little, too. Maybe he transformed Roland.

You should always give people the benefit of the doubt, Lakshmi thought. *Sophia thinks he's a genius, and Bob made him his First Messenger. They know best.* Still, when she allowed her mind to drift to the things he did to her mother . . . .

No, she'd better not dwell on it. How could she give Roland the benefit of the doubt if she thought about *that*? She remembered the first day she met him, when he strolled into the In 'n' Out market—he was quite handsome, in a vague, feminine-macho sort of way . . . He was so sure of himself, and she remembered how flustered she got . . . The two things he bought would always stick in her mind: A box of Mr. Binky's Bath & Body Bubbles and a butcher knife . . . .

No, she wouldn't think about it anymore. She would go with Sophia to the Southwest and help spread Dad's word to every man, woman, beast, and sprout. She would write to her mother and father every day and call when she could. This would be the most important thing she had ever done in her life. She'd not only help Bob and Sophia, but she'd serve Dad and make the world a better place. She couldn't wait to go to the Southwest with Sophia. It would be fun.

* * * * * *

Orvil Swain's tooth was workin' up to quite an ache. Guess he'd make Ruth pull 'er tonight. She didn't have nothin' better ta do. Before he come home though, he thought he'd oughtta take a walk down to the south end and have a talk with this new Reverend Brand fella. He had a few questions he wanted to clear up. But when he got to Reverend Brand's trailer, Brand was nowhere to be found. He thought he'd let hisself in anyhow, but the goddamn door was locked. Even though he stood on tippy-toes to get a view inside, them windows was too goddamn high. All he could see inside was them same posters that he seen plastered all over Red Rock. They read:

RENEWAL MEETING SUNDAY AT DUSK!
COME HEAR THE TRUE WORD OF DAD
AS WRITTEN IN "*THE BOOK OF BOB!*"
CLEANSE THYSELF OF EVIL & PURIFY THY SOUL!
First Messenger Roland Brand
presiding at the vacant lot on the south end of town.

Orvil thought he just might come down to this Renewal Meetin' on Sunday and see what this First Messenger Brand had to say. He was in a mood that was going from bad to worse.

VIII. THE SCIENTIST, THE SEER, AND THE SHRINK

Row, row,
Row your boat,
Gently down the stream;
Merrily, merrily,
Merrily, merrily,
Life is but a dream.

Dad's Book of Children's Verses 1:1

* * * * * *

THE MORNING SUN SHONE BRIGHTLY ON SOPHIA WISE AND Lakshmi Jackson as they stepped out onto the highway and pointed their thumbs toward the Southwest, chirping happily about Dad and the awesome things Bob had taught them. With light hearts and backpacks heavy with *Books of Bob*, they were exhilarated to finally be out on the road, poised for their grand adventure.

It rarely takes long for two young women to hitch a ride, and this day was no exception. No sooner had their thumbs poked the air, than a long wide relic from the Chrome Tanks With Fins Era careened past them, swerved to the right, and with a screech of brakes, lurched abruptly to a stop on the side of the road, less than twenty feet away.

"We're in luck," cried Sophia. "Dad is with us today!"

They scampered to the car, tossed their packs in the trunk, and climbed into the back seat. Sitting in front were two short, skinny middle-aged men on either side of a rather plump woman. The men wore black suits; the woman wore every color in the rainbow.

"And where, pray tell, are you going?" asked the driver whose black top hat crushed against the ceiling of the car.

"Hush, hush! Let me tell *you*," said the woman, holding her temples. "You're go-o-ing . . . *that* way!" she declared, pointing straight ahead.

"I think the more relevant question is," stated the man with the beard in the passenger seat, "where are you going in a philosophical sense?"

"We're going to the Southwest Region," answered Sophia.

"I knew it, I *knew* it!" declared the woman. "That's just what I was about to say."

"Ah, the Southwest Region," said the driver, as he maneuvered onto the highway. "Land of sedimentary sandstone canyons, metaphoric mountains, and exclusive volcanic (also known as 'igneous') rocks; a geologist's gem; an archaeologist's archive; a paleontologist's paradise."

"Let's examine why you feel a need to go to the Southwest Region," probed the passenger on the right.

"We're going to spread Dad's word to every man, woman, beast, and sprout," said Sophia. "It's all right here in *The Book of Bob*." She handed the woman the book.

"*The Book of Bob*," read the large woman. "I think I've seen this before."

"I hypothesize, if we were to trace this book's historic data it would reveal itself to be firmly rooted in the Pathological Period," the driver speculated.

"And what," asked the man riding shotgun, "is the motive for conceptualizing God as 'Dad' rather than 'Mom'?"

"I sens-s-se an imbalance somewhere," observed the woman.

"That's amazing!" Sophia exclaimed. "How did you know?"

"I was right, wasn't I? I feel that someone here is not grounded."

"Grounding occurs at the angle of repose," remarked the driver. "This is a theory based on the concept that when gravitational forces cause an imbalance in mountainous materials, the earth and rocks will slide until they once again achieve a balance. The angle at which they settle," he explained, making his point with his index finger, "is known as the 'angle of repose.'"

"Have you had any dreams lately that might give us a clue to your ungrounded feelings?" asked the man on the right, clasping his hands around his knee.

"What is your astrological sign, dear?" asked the woman.

"Funny you should ask," said Sophia. "I'm a double Pisces with my moon in Sagittarius."

"You, young lady," the woman turned to Lakshmi. "Do you by any chance have any tattoos?"

"Um . . . no I don't, ma'am. But . . . ."

"That's strange," continued the woman. "I'm sure I sense tattoos."

"If you study anthropology, you will learn that tattooing is an ancient ritual that has long been practiced for purposes ranging from depicting prowess and rank, to sexual proclivities, to coming of age," the driver contributed.

"Can you share with us your earliest childhood memory of tattoos?" inquired the bearded passenger.

"There are tattoos in this car. I can feel it," said the woman with her eyes closed and fingers to her temples.

Sophia pointed to her bare arms and said, "You can see these right here. I have more under my clothes."

"I knew it, I *knew* it!" The woman was triumphant. "Could

they possibly have anything to do with your Pisces Sun and Rising signs and your Moon in Sagittarius?"

Sophia and Lakshmi exchanged amazed glances.

"I think it's high time we all got acquainted," announced the man in the passenger's seat. "Please allow me. My name is Thaddeus Well." He reached back and shook the girls' hands. "I will join you in your journey toward self-awareness, however, you will have to *want* to change."

"I knew he would say that," the woman chimed in. "During this lifetime, I go by the name of Normal Bea Freee. I am a very old soul who sees past and future. Pleased to meet you." She smiled a red lipstick smile; her face was framed by a shock of bushy hair.

"Pleased to meet you, Miss Freee," said Sophia.

"Oh, heavens sakes! Call me Normal Bea."

"Pleased to meet you, Normal Bea," said Sophia and Lakshmi in unison.

"And that would leave me. I am Professor Tyrone T. Matters, Ph.D. You may call me Professor or Professor Matters, whichever you prefer. I am professor of the sciences, specializing in anthrobiological physiostronomy with an auxiliary expertise in anatocellular neutrophysics."

"Names are a good place to start. Would you like to share yours with us?" invited Thaddeus Well.

"My name is Sophia Wise, and this is my friend, Lakshmi Jackson."

"I find it interesting," Well observed, stroking his beard, "that Ms. Jackson does not speak for herself."

"Oh, that's ok . . ." Lakshmi started to say, but Normal Bea had a vision. "Lakshmi had much pain in her last lifetime. She was a mute, so this time around, the poor girl is just beginning to learn to speak."

"It's fascinating you should bring that up," said Professor Matters. "I just finished writing a paper about the different causes of *speechus impedimentia*, which you lay folk refer to as 'mute' or 'dumb'."

"My question is: What's in it for you to remain mute?" Well probed.

"It's not that I don't want to speak," answered Lakshmi. "It's just that other people always have so much to say."

"The reason we're on this trip," said Sophia, picking up where Lakshmi left off, "is to meet up with Bob's First Messenger Roland Brand in the Southwest Region, where we will help him do Dad's work and spread His word to every man, woman, beast, and sprout. It's all right here in *The Book of Bob*." She passed around the book again.

"Ah yes, *The Book of Bob*," said Normal Bea. "I believe I've seen this somewhere before."

"This is quite the coincidence," declared the Professor. "It seems we all have books to sell. You see, we are on our way to the Annual National Book Convention in the Southwest Region, wherein each one of us will be plugging his or her book."

"This is mine," Normal Bea jumped in, handing Sophia a thick volume titled, *I Knew it, I KNEW it!: A Chronicle of My Lives as a Psychic, by Normal Bea Freee*.

"I have a modest little book, myself," stated Thaddeus Well. "If you would like to see it, we can make arrangements."

"Of course, we'd like to see it," said Sophia.

"Well then, here it is. It's called, *I'm Not Sleeping; I'm Listening, by Thaddeus Well*."

"This looks like an interesting book, Mr. Well," Lakshmi volunteered.

"That would leave me," Professor Matters announced weightily. "My latest opus has won numerous awards, most notably the Hubris Prize, the Alvin B. Addled Award for Audacious Research, and First Prize in the International Practical Obfuscations Competition. Normal Bea, please show them my book."

Normal Bea Freee reached under the seat and pulled out a rather slim little volume, which she held up for Sophia and

Lakshmi to see. The title was simply, *The Complete Compilation of All Things Known, by Professor Tyrone T. Matters, Ph.D.*

"I have read your treatise, Tyrone," said Thaddeus. "I wonder if there is a bit of grandiose thinking on your part to claim that you list *all* things known?"

"Of course it would seem so to the lay person, unversed in the practice of empirical study," the professor responded. "My book deals only in proven fact, not unconfirmed speculation."

"Are you implying that my profession does not conform to a rigorous discipline of evidentiary hierarchy?" interrogated Thaddeus.

"There are degrees of truth in every belief system, but I daresay, Thaddeus, your stew has not yet reached a full boil."

"My stew has not . . . This is an outrage!"

"I knew it, I *knew* it," lamented Normal Bea Freee. "I had a strange feeling that you two would get into an argument again."

"Take, for example," continued the professor, "your profession's bizarre obsession with the ego, the super-ego, and the id . . . ."

"Bizarre?! Obsession?! Why, the concept of the ego is the cornerstone of modern psychological thought! That and the theory of Oedipal fixation, in which the son secretly lusts after his mother, making it necessary for him to jealously destroy his father in order to actualize his perverted wish. It is clear to me, Professor Matters, that you are suffering such a torment yourself. In your unresolved desire for your mother, you are transferring your jealousy toward your father onto me, and in an act of rage, you are symbolically trying to destroy me. Let's explore your feelings toward your mother."

"My mother?!" What's she got to do with this?!" Professor Matters cried. "Just because she wanted me to become a famous violinist, but all I wanted to do was play with my chemistry set, and my father beat me because I blew up the garage . . . ."

Normal Bea handed the professor a tissue. He blew.

"This is going to take years," said Thaddeus.

"*The Book of Bob* tells us about all things known, too," said Sophia. "God came to Bob one night and told him to write the whole thing down. When Bob ran out of paper, he wrote it on his arms and legs and the rest of his body. God told Bob he was His son and to call him 'Dad,'" she added.

"I knew it, Professor Matters!" exclaimed Normal Bea. "I *knew* there was a reason I told you to pick them up!"

"There have been 2311 confirmed reports of extra-terrestrial sightings since man began keeping records of such contacts," interjected the Professor. "I hated the violin," he added.

"How long has Bob been hearing voices?" Thaddeus wanted to know.

"Only since Dad started talking to him," Sophia answered.

"Before that, I heard him talk to Bud," added Lakshmi.

"And, who is Bud?" Thaddeus probed.

"Hush, hush! Let me tell *you*," said Normal Bea. "Bud is—I feel something soft and cuddly. Is Bud soft and cuddly?"

"I guess you could say . . ." Lakshmi began.

"I knew it, I *knew* it! I feel Bud's energy! He's soft and cuddly, but right now Bud is worried."

"Let's find out what in Bud's past would give him cause to worry," suggested Thaddeus.

"I don't know, but something smells very weird," said Normal Bea, sniffing the air. "Does Bud smell weird?" she queried.

"The olfactory sense is the most primal of our five basic means of discerning our surroundings," Professor Matters informed them. "Why, just last week I wrote an important paper on the subject."

"I wonder if Bud has issues with early potty training?" Thaddeus speculated.

"Whatever smells weird seems to have traveled from our Northwest Region to somewhere in the Southwest," Normal Bea said with her eyes closed, rocking forward and back. "An-n-nd . . . hush, hush! Don't say anything! Bud is trying to get through!"

She was in a trance. "Bud is trying to tell me something! He's worried! He's worried about somebody in this car!"

Sophia and Lakshmi exchanged questioning looks.

"Bud says he's worried about Lakshmi!" Normal Bea announced. "Yes! There's no mistaking it! Lakshmi, do you know Bud?"

"I know him a little bit," Lakshmi replied. "He was with Bob when he saved my life at the In 'n' Out market. Bob was talking to him, which I thought was strange, but then . . . ."

"But then," Normal Bea continued, "Bud sensed danger and he saved your life! I knew it, I *knew* it!"

"Well, that wasn't . . . ."

"Lakshmi," Normal Bea turned to look her directly in the eyes, "I want you to level with me. Will you do that?"

"It has been necessary for you to build up strong defenses," Thaddeus Well stated. "But until we are able to speak with utter candor, progress will be minimal."

"You must understand that your declarations will be subject to the scrutiny of rigorous, unbiased, scientific testing before they can be validated as fact," added the professor.

"I will level with you the best I can, Miss Normal," Lakshmi said.

"Now," Normal Bea continued, "this Bud person . . . Under no circumstances should you trust him. He doesn't have your best interests at heart. I know he saved your life and he's soft and cuddly and . . . ."

"But . . ." When Lakshmi tried to protest, Normal Bea held up her hand and silenced her.

"You're so young, dear. There are things you don't understand yet. Sometimes it's the people who seem the most trustworthy, the most lovable, even the ones who you think are saving your life—*those* are the ones you have to watch out for. I sense peril when I'm around Bud. He smells weird. He has caused great harm to some people you love. And now, I think he may be trying to destroy you."

"But, Bud is . . ."

"Bud is dangerous, dear," Normal Bea's voice trembled. "Tread lightly. I see a fork in the road, Lakshmi Jackson. On one path, I see a fragrant garden blooming with the most exquisite flowers and vines. You are the good steward of your dominion, and you serenely go about nurturing all that grows and, like a midwife, you assist its beauty to spring forth. You are very happy and wise on this path. But on the other . . . ," her voice darkened again. "On the other path, Bud awaits you with his terrible black force. On this path, I see nothing but death and destruction and doom."

"That's amazing!" exclaimed Sophia. "It reminds me of a passage in *The Book of Bob*, where Dad is talking about the two roads and He says:

> *Stay off the worn road;*
> *Beware the less-trekked road, too.*
> *Too many RV's.*
>
> Haikus 5:7:5"

"That's beautiful," said Normal Bea Freee. "I think I've heard that before."

"What do the two roads represent to you?" wondered Thaddeus Well.

"The road I'm on is Dad's road," said Sophia.

"It is a peculiar fact in the Free Nation," expounded Professor Matters, "that a special permit is required to drive a motorcycle, however, any imbecile with a driver's license can drive off the lot in an RV with no prior experience."

"Dad says," continued Sophia:

> *My road is The Way;*
> *Take my road but don't forget:*
> *Pay at the toll booth.*
>
> Haikus 57:5

"Dad must be very wise," nodded Normal Bea.

"You are so right," Sophia declared. "Dad is the wisest of the wise."

"Faith can serve an important function in the healing process," Thaddeus concurred.

"You are right too, Thaddeus. My faith in Dad has healed me to the core."

"There are mysteries even science can't explain," admitted the professor.

"But Professor Matters," answered Sophia, "Dad can explain all mysteries. And He does so in *The Book of Bob*."

"I have an idea!" exclaimed Normal Bea. "Why don't you two come to the Book Convention with us? You can share our booth and sell lots of *Books of Bob*."

"I think a successful convention would be a positive building block toward greater self-esteem," agreed Thaddeus.

"Furthermore," added the professor, "you can assist me in an important study I am currently conducting comparing the chemical effects of faith on people from the different regions of the Free Nation."

"We don't sell *The Book of Bob*," said Sophia. "But the convention would be an excellent place to give them away. And we can get lots of new people to join our flock. Won't Roland be surprised when he sees all our new Carrier Pigeons? What do you think, Lakshmi?"

"I think we should . . . ."

"Then it's settled!" cried Normal Bea. "Oh, we're all going to have such fun together at the Book Convention!"

"Yes," said Thaddeus. "This should provide us all a real opportunity for growth."

"Not to omit the important data we will acquire," mentioned the professor.

"I knew it, I *knew* it!" Normal Bea Freee exclaimed.

And so it was that the jovial band set off for the National Book Convention in the Southwest Region. Sophia played her mandolin while the others entertained each other with stories and songs, and of course, Sophia and Lakshmi had lots to tell their new friends about Dad and *The Book of Bob*. They read many passages from their sacred book, but the verse that all agreed was the most powerful and moving was the one Sophia recited with hauntingly hushed tones:

> *Don't live in a cave;*
> *Use the stuff that makes folks rave;*
> *Buy it: Burma Shave!*

Haikus 5:75

IX. FOREST OF TRUTH AND LIES

You believe Heaven is sky full of bliss,
And Hell is a fiery tomb;
I say unto you
Believe all you want,
But all is not what you assume.

For Heaven and Hell are your own state of mind,
They spring from the same fertile womb;
I say unto you
The seeds that you plant,
Will surely take root and will bloom.

The chambers of Heaven and Hell in your brain,
You furnish with sunshine or doom,
I say unto you
You have work to be done;
I sayeth: Go clean up your room!

Proclamations 21:7

* * * * * *

THAT NIGHT, IN A PEELING ROADSIDE MOTEL, CURLED UP NEXT
to Sophia on a springy bed, Lakshmi had a dream . . . .

She dreamed *she was back in the Northwest Region,
standing on the brink of some great and mighty river, watching
the gray-green torrent rush downstream, watching the white
foam bubble up and draw pictures. How did the patterns stay put
when the whole thing kept moving? Watching fat waves
undulating in place, smelling the clear-water ocean. A large,
sawed-off log bobbed toward her and by; so much more power
and speed underneath than she could see on the surface. She
could tell the strength by its sounds: An infinite chorus chanting
a mantra of raindrops and snowdrops, rolling headlong,
grinding, crushing, eroding boulders, dragging sediment,
reconfiguring. The punctuating bass voice on the far shore, the
tinkling soprano of the arterial creek, the tenor singing against a
rock, and the masses—the masses in the middle drowning them
all out unless you listened carefully. Lakshmi's heart leaped
when, high above, the clarinet song of a bald eagle rang so
clearly that, for a moment, it silenced the river. The eagle was
more at home on this river than Lakshmi would ever be any
place in the world. She wished she could be so at home . . . .
Guess she shouldn't jump in. But, oh how she longed to.
The water would be frigid—that she knew. Her limbs would
cramp and her heart would burst and her twisted body would be
thrown mercilessly, indifferently against hard blunt rocks. She
would be blinded and bruised in the chaotic swirl; she would die.
And yet . . . she needed to be part of this river. Standing on its
shore, she was HERE and it was THERE . . . No good.
The size, scope, strength—the sheer LIFE of it—too much
for her little brain to absorb; she couldn't take it in. The only
way was to let the river take her. The low-lying fog lifted, and a
pastel sun peaked through, reflecting off the top, illuminating the
bed. How clean the water is! Look how pure. Lakshmi wanted
more than anything to be this river. So she let it take her . . . .*

. . . *found herself swimming hard upwater with salmon; salmon so thick you could walk across 'em, just like the old-timers say it used to be. It was true—they really were that thick; but you could no more walk across them than you could walk across the river. No time to think about that now—she was losing ground, thrashing face forward while the river dragged her back. The salmon were huge—bigger than she—the size of dolphins or that log she had watched drift by. But these giant salmon sure weren't drifting. While she fought the river that pulled her backwards, the giant fish pressed forward, passing her up. She caught glimpses of glistening silver backs sparkling with gold, green, and red as they lunged and bucked with strength and purpose, mouths open like some marathon runner on the last mile, fatigued and disciplined. Focused fish eyes—what did they see?—pushing heroically toward some great and distant goal, where they intended to spawn and die. She had never seen anybody work so hard in her life. She couldn't keep up. The giants smashed her out of the way as if she weren't there. They banged her sides and trampled her back and swatted her face with their tails. They knew where they were going—where their ancestors had gone for thousands of years. And where was SHE going? What was she doing besides trying to hang on? Maybe if she could grab hold of one, she could ride it home. If she could just—grab this one around her slippery sides, mount her like a bucking mare, hang on for the wild ride, hold on hold on—but the giant fish said "No!" She lay tight against the salmon's back, head against head, arms wrapped desperately around the slimy body, clinging to the cold life and power of the fish, who once again said, "No! I can't take you. You'll drag me down and we both shall die. Go back to your own world." And with one mighty flip, the salmon tossed Lakshmi off her back, clear of the river, and onto the bank . . . .*

. . . *she stood with her back to the water, on the lip of an ancient forest . . . didn't notice that her clothes were dry and her glasses were intact. Being in a dream, she saw a different set of details. She saw ferns abundant as leaves, sprouting from thick maple trunks with green beards of shaggy moss, a mystic orange-brown cedar emerging from a shroud of vine maple, rising rising straight up straight up—she lay on her back so she could see the top. On the ground around her, little emerald mosses and spongy lichens and oxalis looking like clover and maiden hair, and earth so rich and chocolate she wanted to eat it. Most of what Lakshmi knew about forests was from childhood fairy books. This was different. In her books the woods were orderly and clean, all trees were straight and in rows. No roots to trip over, no mangled logs blocking the way. No mud, tangles of vines, contorted limbs. No trees propping up trees—slanted and felled by the wind. In her books, there were trails. No coyote scat. In her books, death was an exception, not the rule . . . .*

. . . out in the woods, punching steadily through a tangle of salmonberry, a figure emerged. Small, old man, not more than four foot high. Down the left side of his face hung a white-gray beard reaching his waist. The right half of his face was bare. His head was also bare on the right, but long straight white hair dangled to his wide, leather belt on the left. A cap sat on top with the inscription: "EARTH: LOVE IT OR LEAVE IT." Peculiarly, his waist, to which his left-sided hair and beard reached, was less than a foot above the ground. Long torso, short legs. The legs themselves were covered by decomposing brown boots in which his feet turned sideways at a ninety degree angle as he waddled toward Lakshmi. He carried two gnarly wooden walking sticks, one in each hand, like a cross-country skier. Smiling and not too scary, he planted himself in front of Lakshmi and said, "Hello, Lakshmi Jackson. Welcome to the Forest of Truth and Lies. I am the caretaker—name of Virtuous Liar. Ask me a question and I'll tell you the truth and I'll tell you a lie."

"Pleased to meet you, Virtuous Liar," she said. "But, I don't know what question to ask."

Virtuous Liar chewed on this. "Let me tell you something, Lakshmi Jackson—but I warn you, half the time I speak the truth, half the time I lie. It's up to you to decipher which is which. Now tell me, what did I just tell you—truth or lie?"

"Um . . . the truth?"

"Exactly, Lakshmi Jackson! Of course it was the truth! Except for the part I made up." He laughed a hearty laugh.

"What do you mean?"

"I mean what I say; I don't say what I mean."

"Do you mean it?"

"No, I do," Virtuous Liar answered.

"I'm confused," confessed Lakshmi.

"YOU'RE confused?! How do you think I feel?"

"I can't imagine . . . ."

"Neither can I. It's hard to imagine ANYTHING when truth and lies get confused. When there's so much fantasy, the first thing to go is the imagination. You're so busy sorting out what's real and what's not, you don't have the luxury to IMAGINE something."

"I think I see what you mean."

"What you just said—truth or lie?"

"Why, it was the truth . . . I think . . . ."

"Let's ask Maple With A Thousand Arms." Virtuous Liar turned to a fat, craggy maple tree with mossy branches grabbing in every direction. "Maple With A Thousand Arms, does Lakshmi Jackson tell us the truth or does Lakshmi Jackson lie?"

"Everything Lakshmi Jackson says is the truth, and that's a lie," said the maple through the large hole in her trunk. "Everything Lakshmi Jackson says is a lie, and that's a lie, too," she added.

"There you have it," said Virtuous Liar.

"What do I have?" asked Lakshmi.

"The lies about truth. The truth about lies!" roared Virtuous Liar, and he fell on his back, laughing.

"I don't understand."

"Neither do I, Lakshmi Jackson!" He was crying from laughing so hard. He stood up, still chuckling and dusted himself

with his cap while Lakshmi tried not to stare impolitely at his half bald, half hairy head.

"Let's ask Spruce In The Sky. Maybe he can explain this dilemma to you. Spruce In The Sky, can you shed some light on the subject for poor Lakshmi Jackson?"

From the highest branch of the highest tree in the forest, she heard a deep voice call down to her, "Lakshmi Jackson, I tell you the truth: Don't believe anyone who tells you the truth."

"That means I shouldn't believe you," said Lakshmi.

"I said it, not you," replied Spruce In The Sky.

"Let me explain," said Virtuous Liar. "It's simple math: Multiply a positive times a negative and you get a negative. Multiply a negative times a negative and you get a positive. What we have here is a positively negative situation in which every negative gets negated positively by . . . ."

"But wait," interrupted Lakshmi. "You forgot to mention that if you multiply a positive times a positive, you get a positive."

"Truth or lie?" bellowed Virtuous Liar, pointing his stick. "Thirsty Fern, what do you have to say on this subject?"

Lakshmi looked down at the lush green fern that spread a graceful circle of fronds from the ground near Virtuous Liar's foot. "A positive times a positive," pondered Thirsty Fern in a soft, feminine voice. Her leaves waved gently as she spoke. "I've always not thought that was not true."

"There you have it," said Virtuous Liar. "Lakshmi Jackson, we here in the forest are truth tellers, and the truth is: We're lying. You see how honest we are? Do you think a liar would be so honest as to admit to his lie? Beware the man who claims to be honest; he might be a liar. Trust the man who admits he's a liar; he might be telling you the truth. Now a woman—that's a different story."

"Truth is a lie, Lakshmi Jackson," said Maple With A Thousand Arms. "For example: You think I'm a tree. Not true. I'm just something you're making up right now in your dream."

"Lies are the truth, Lakshmi Jackson," said Spruce In The Sky. "Your dream is more true at this moment than death and taxes."

"Beware of the Serial Liar, Lakshmi Jackson," said Thirsty Fern. "The Serial Liar will tell you lies so big, bold, and often, you will think they must be true, because no one could possibly make up anything so incredible and say it with a straight face. Beware of the person who sticks to his story."

"Your life depends on it, Lakshmi Jackson," said Maple With A Thousand Arms. "There are two kinds of people in this world: Those who lie when they must, and those who lie when they can. Only lie when you must, Lakshmi Jackson. And beware of those who lie when they can."

"I'll try . . . ."

"AND!" shouted Spruce In The Sky. "Never EVER lie to yourself, even if you can, even if you must. You can and you must tell yourself the truth at all times!"

"And, you are right, Lakshmi Jackson," said Thirsty Fern, sweetly. "A positive times a positive DOES equal a positive."

"AND! . . ." Virtuous Liar pointed both his sticks and gave her a steely stare. "Listen to the river, Lakshmi Jackson. The river tells no lies."

And with that, Virtuous Liar disappeared. Thirsty Fern and Spruce In The Sky and Maple With A Thousand Arms disappeared. The forest and the salmon and the river fell into a black hole. For a while, Lakshmi could still hear the rushing of the river. Then it, too, faded away . . . .

With the morning still new, Lakshmi awoke, recalling nothing of her night's journey but a vague memory of a river. However, in some strange way, a fog had lifted. As she rolled out of bed and padded to the window to let in the light, she felt more steady on her feet than she-couldn't-remember-when.

* * * * * *

It was becoming clear that Bob had outgrown the Moonshadow. The place burst at the beams with humanity every time he spoke. It got to the point where he had to set up a stage in front of the building and deliver his sermons outside. Carrier Pigeons camped out day and night, inside and down the block, shivering in blankets and clutching *The Book of Bob* to their breasts, waiting for Bob to show up and give them more good news. It was becoming a burden on the management. The only person in the whole neighborhood who was happy was Ralph Blodgett, owner of Blodgett's Outdoor Store. Sales on tents and camping gear were way up.

Bob's orations were becoming progressively more electric. He wasn't trying to work the crowd—far from it. He would stroll in, frumpy hat, tropical tie, hands in pockets of his wrinkled slacks—and people would go crazy. He never knew what he was going to say. Dad had taught him to clear his mind and wait for Him.

It was phenomenal. As Bob and his entourage made their way through the crowd, people would go berserk trying to get a piece of them. Ivan Bunt had gotten so exasperated, he took to beating people away with a large stick, yelling, "Blast your billiards! Clean your clocks! Get off'n me hammerin' hide!" When the crowds got out of control, Eldon and Larry ducked under a large tarp and staggered through, heads down. Bud stayed as close to Bob's legs as possible. But Bob floated serenely in the eye of the hurricane, the half-smile on his face giving no hint of the hysteria surrounding him.

Bob's casual expression never wavered as he stepped on stage. However, a transformation came over the crowd. It was as if, in ascending the platform, Bob flipped a switch that turned off the delirium, chaos, and noise. Now all was silent, and people looked on reverently as Bob stood before them, waiting patiently for Dad to show up.

Nobody, including Bob, had a clue to what Dad would tell him to say. Once He made Bob preach for four hours on the virtues of rotating the tires and checking the pressure. Once He had Bob harangue his flock for not going solar. Then, there was the famous Mother's Day Sermon. Once Dad turned Bob into a stand-up comic and had the audience in stitches—He killed 'em! Bob gave what was arguably his most powerful sermon on the day he stood before the hushed crowd, hands in pockets for a full forty-five minutes, waiting for Dad to reveal himself. Finally, Bob's half-smile became full. He gazed over his beloved flock so each person thought Bob looked him directly in the eye. With silence so thick you could hear time breathe, Dad said through Bob:

"Be kind to your neighbors and friends."

Bedlam! When Bob descended smiling from the stage, it took the town's entire police force to keep his frenzied flock from trampling him. This became forever remembered as the "Less is More" sermon.

Then there was the healing. Bob had progressed—he was better than Reverend Rufus now. No condition was too big—cancer, heart disease, renal failure—you name it. Bob cured them all. He'd lay his hands on their foreheads, and an electric current would zap through his arms, through his hands, and explode through their bodies—you could see it. People would go flying backwards as far as the fourth row, the congregation would catch them as if they were falling into a mosh pit, and they were healed. They'd walk away. You could hear people shouting, *"Helluva* deal!" for a mile, and then the next crying and ailing victim would ascend the stage to be cured. No infliction was too small—heartburn, hangnails, hangovers—Bob cured them all.

Dad kept nudging Bob to find a bigger venue. He'd say, "You gotta get out of this dive," or "Raise the stakes," or "You're a big fish in a small pond." Bob was willing to do whatever Dad told him to do—he just wasn't sure what the next move should be. He'd been getting lots of offers from Sunny Sunnyland, The Entertainment Capital of the World. A record producer wanted to cut a double CD of him reading *The Book of Bob*. There were movie offers and feelers for a TV series. Someone wanted to film a documentary on his life. Bob was asked to host a radio talk show. Agents were swarming like insects. The sky was the limit!

Although Bob wasn't sure, Ivan Bunt had no doubts. "Sunny Sunnyland?" he'd say. "Beat my bongos! Punch my doggies! Send me to Sunny Sunnyland! Land of movie maestros, mental midgets, and bulging bikinis! Slap on the lotion and give me a blisterin' tan! Buy me some shades 'n' a cell phone and pull down the top! I wanna recline in a traffic jam!"

Eldon and Larry wanted to go, too. They had always dreamed of seeing Sunny Sunnyland, and now was as good a time as ever. Lately, they had been fighting a lot—maybe it was the pressure of finding Bob. Everything was happening so fast, it was hard to keep up. The stress was causing a lot of strain on their relationship and they both thought if they could just get away where the air was warm and people weren't so uptight, maybe they would get along better.

Bud didn't care. Bob still smelled weird, but on the other hand, it seemed there were always nice people to pet him and give him treats now. Life was pretty good.

Bob wasn't sure how to proceed. So far, Dad had been vague, so Bob was waiting for the final word. Dad seemed to be hinting when He said things like, "What're you waiting for?" or "You're missing your date with destiny," or "Vision, Bob, vision! That's your problem—no vision." Bob just wanted to make sure he was doing Dad's will and not misunderstanding his message in any way. So he kept asking. But Dad continued to answer in cryptic messages such as, "Bob, sometimes you're as dense as a Rottweiler's skull."

Bob was patient. He knew when Dad was ready, He would give him a definitive answer.

* * * * * *

By dusk, the entire town of Red Rock had gathered in the vacant lot on the south end, waiting with delicious suspense for the arrival of First Messenger Roland Brand. Everyone knew by now, that First Messenger Roland had some powerful medicine. At the beginning of each week, the talk of Red Rock was all about Roland's last sermon. By the end of the week, the town buzzed with speculation about how he would outdo himself on the coming Sunday.

To get a good seat, you had to come early. Families brought picnic baskets full of fried chicken and potato salad, and made a wholesome day of it under lawn umbrellas. Many women hid their faces behind the traditional shawl, their exposed foreheads displaying the "T" for "Temptress" tattoo they had received at First Messenger Roland's trailer.

On this Sunday, the crowd packed in thicker than ever. As dusk darkened to night, the laser light show began. Multi-colored rays pointed in all directions, crisscrossing and swirling with herky-jerky strobe lights to create a phantasm somewhere between Heaven and Armageddon. Then all beams aimed toward the sky and drew every eye toward the helicopter hovering above where a white-clad figure stood poised to jump.

"LADIES AND GENTLEMEN: THE TIME HAS COME! TIME TO HEAR THE MAN WHO BRINGS YOU THE TRUE WORD OF DAD! LET'S HEAR IT FOR BOB'S FIRST MESSENGER . . REVEREND RO-O-OLAND BR-R-RA-A-A-ND OF RE-E-ED ROCK!!!"

Roland of Red Rock leaped from the helicopter and a gasp ricocheted through the crowd as his parachute opened. The light rays followed him as he glided over the multitudes, making a perfect landing on the stage, accompanied by music that sounded like the theme to "Dragnet." He ripped the parachute off his back and with a dramatic flourish, tossed it away like Houdini throwing off his shackles, arms outstretched to receive the adoration of his worshippers. Roland was stunning in his white jumpsuit with sparkling gold sequins; the collar turned up, top buttons open, revealing a large "D" for "Dad," hanging from a gold chain dangling over his bare chest. The belt was a red sash that swayed seductively over his groin; the pants, fringed and flaring at the feet, clung tight in all the right places; the boots were pointed and white. Roland's hair was so black and shiny from grease, it looked blue. He had fenders combed straight back on the sides, and a pompadour hanging impossibly over his forehead like a tree growing out of the side of a cliff—you wondered what kept it there.

Roland ripped the microphone from its stand and assumed the stance: left hand holding the mike below his mouth, pinky extended; right arm stretched behind him toward the sky; left leg forward, bent at the knee with the foot pointing toward the audience; right leg pushing off in back. He curled his upper lip, sneered, and held the pose. The crowd went crazy.

"ROLAND! ROLAND! ROLAND!" they chanted. They lit candles and held them high.

"Aha-hm," Roland answered.

Pandemonium. Roland had Red Rock in the palm of his hand.

Still holding his pose, Roland brought his right hand forward and silenced the crowd.

"I've got news from Dad tonight, ladies 'n' genlmun," he half-sung. "And do you know what that news is?"

"What's the news?" they cried. "Tell us! Tell us, First Messenger Roland!"

"The news is: Most of you assholes aren't gonna make it."

More uproar. "Tell us, Roland! Tell us why!"

"Why?" he asked. "Haven't you read your *Book of Bob* lately? Maybe you're just too dull to read. Well here—I just happen to have a copy on me. Let me read it *for* you."

Roland flipped to a book-marked page and read:

I'll be down in two years' time,
And when I come, your ass is mine.

"Aha-hm." Roland preened up one side of the stage and down the other. "So here's the deal, ladies 'n' genlmun," he continued in a hypnotic, singsong chant:

Dad come down and He talked to Bob,
Dad said, 'Get you a pencil and pad,'
Dad said, 'Bob, you are my son,'
He said, 'Son, you call me Dad.

Dad said, 'Bob, there is no doubt,
You gotta spread my word to every woman and man,
Spread my word to every beast and sprout,
And Bob said, 'Dad, I'll do the best I can.'

Bob said, 'Roland, Dad's got to be heard,
Go down to Red Rock and spread Dad's word.'
So Roland come down and what did he find?

"The sorriest bunch of lame-ass yahoos to ever dump a hay wagon!" Roland sat down on the lip of the stage. "Ok, we're gonna change the pace a little," he whispered. He spoke in intimate, conversational tones.

"Dad wants you to think of Him every waking moment and dream about Him when you sleep. Throw away your books, your magazines, and your newspapers! Only read *The Book of Bob*! That's the one place you're going to get The Truth.

"And if you had been reading your *Book of Bob*, you'd know that Dad has been stockpiling dynamite. He's been burying it under a canyon right here in Red Rock. He figures in two years, he'll have enough dynamite to blow up the whole damn planet, which is exactly what he intends to do. He's tired of you people. You were a fun experiment for a while, but you've gotten boring.

"Dad's got a new creation now: Planet Nebulon, about 400 million light years away. When Dad created Nebulon, He learned from His mistakes here on Earth—the people of Nebulon are a new, improved model. They're much smarter than you. They never have any wars because they all worship the one true Dad, so there's nothing to fight about. If anybody gets caught worshipping Dad insufficiently, he immediately gets put to death, which helps keep the Nebulonic race pure.

"Anyway," Roland continued his conversation, "Dad's been busy as a pack rat, stuffing dynamite under a canyon, and in two years, he's going to blow you all up. All except a chosen few. On the Day of Reckoning, Dad will choose one thousand, one hundred and eleven of His most loyal worshippers, put us in a space ship, and send us off to live happily ever after on Planet Nebulon. Then He'll push the detonator. All you other worthless worms will get blown to smithereens, and what happens from there isn't pretty. Your exploded particles will be blown to Planet Ug, home of Dad's hated evil twin, Uncle Ominus. There your particles will be reassembled and you'll be doomed to an eternity of suffering. Uncle Ominus is a master of torture, and he's very creative in its application."

The crowd gasped.

"That's where I come in," Roland announced. He bounced to his feet and began to strut the stage again. "I've got my seat reserved on the Rocket Ship Nebulon. I'll be sitting right next to Bob, waving you goodbye. Wanna go? Fat chance—now there's only one thousand, one hundred and nine seats left. You'd better be good.

"What's it gonna take?" Roland returned to his rhythmic, gyrating chant. "Gonna teach you how to pray. You'll have to say this prayer four times an hour, twenty-four hours a day, if you're going to even stand a chance," continued Roland. "There's a lot of competition. If you even miss one time, you're doomed."

A dreadful fear convulsed the crowd. "You ready?" Roland asked. "Repeat after me:

> *Dear Dad,*
> *I'm wicked and unworthy,*
> *Don't even have a clue;*
> *I know I don't have any right,*
> *To sit with the likes of You.*
> *So I'll follow Roland Brand,*
> *Who will tell me what to do;*
> *I'll follow First Messenger Roland,*
> *Who will maketh me brand new."*

Roland whipped out a handkerchief, wiped the profuse sweat from his brow, and tossed it into the mob. There was a mad scramble like a school of barracudas after bait. Roland posed, legs spread, knees a-wobblin', hips a-shakin', whipping his flock into a fever.

"Remember," Roland ordered. "Read your *Book of Bob.* Pray four times an hour, send your women to me for purification, and kill anybody who disobeys Dad. Then, maybe you'll have a chance. Aha-hm."

And with that, the laser lights swirled again, First Messenger Roland Brand of Red Rock wrapped himself in a red velvet cape, the stage went black, and when the lights came back on, Roland was gone.

"LADIE-EE--EES AND GENTLEME-E-EN, ROLAND OF RED ROCK HAS LEFT THE BUILDING!"

The town of Red Rock was never the same.

* * * * * *

Among the throng that witnessed Roland's historic sermon that Sunday was Orvil Swain. Even though he'd already had private counseling with First Messenger Roland and knew basically what he had to say, Orvil still got as caught up in the frenzy as everybody else. Fact was, Orvil was pretty happy with how things was goin' with the new minister. Roland even said he had a plan for 'im in the big scheme. Told Orvil he'd talk to Dad special and get 'im a place on that rocket ship to Nebulon. Now there was only one thousand, one hundred and *eight* seats left.

All in all, thought Orvil, sittin' in his fossil shop, *it was a pretty fair trade*. He swapped 'im his three wives—two of who was gettin' a little long in the tooth anyhow. In exchange, Roland married 'im to the fourteen-year-old. Also, Roland told 'im in another year, the twelve-year-old would come along some, an' maybe Roland would let 'im marry *her* in a swap for the fourteen-year-old. A year after that, Dad would be dynamitin' the damn planet, an' all them women would be payin' a visit to Uncle Ominus anyhow, whilst he 'n' Roland 'n' Bob would be settin' pretty in Nebulon.

Sometimes things just have a way of workin' themselves out, thought Orvil Swain. He was glad First Messenger Roland Brand had come to town.

X. At The Book Convention

You put your right foot in,
You put your right foot out,
You put your right foot in,
Then you shake it all about;
You do the Hokey Pokey,
And you turn yourself around;
That's what it's all about.

Dad's Book of Children's Verses 8:10

* * * * * *

THE REVIEWS WERE IN, AND IT WAS UNANIMOUS: *THE BOOK OF Bob* was a smash hit. Here is just a small sampling of the rave reviews. The *Daily Surface* said:

"It was a long time coming, but well worth the wait. Dad has once again proven Himself the unsurpassed master of prophetic prose and Poet Laureate of the Cosmos. Let's hope it doesn't take Him another two thousand years to write his next tour de force."

And this from the *Dubious Journal*:

"Once in a lifetime, a book comes along that has it all: A great story, impeccable craftsmanship, pathos, irony, sex, violence, drugs, and rock 'n' roll. The Book of Bob *has all of the above in spades!"*

And this from the *Faithful Messenger*:

Just when we, Dad's Pilgrims, found ourselves stranded in the desert, adrift at sea, lost in the woods, up a creek without a paddle, along came Bob, our Unassuming Savior and Messiah, armed with naught but The Book of Bob *to heal us and lead us to daylight.*

And this from the eminent literary critic Ignatius Simms in the *Urbane Book Review*:

In order to capture the essence of the multi-faceted discourse that springs forth with abundant prevalence from The Book of Bob, *one must digress to the foundations of the Abstract Maximalistic movement from which this opus surely derives its roots while maintaining a robust freshness which, unlike the multitudes of pale imitators who aspire to its Olympian heights and fall woefully short, consistently offers a potpourri of surprising homilies which, in their cumulative effect, lead the reader toward a complete and integrated conceptualization of God, while simultaneously serving to inspire and instruct with the muscular verbiage of Dad Himself, buoyed most competently by the assistance of Bob, His eminently loyal Messiah and faithful scribe.*

And this from Brad Cahoon, editor and publisher of *Rock On!* magazine:

Dude! The Book of Bob *rocks! I was over at my girl friend's the other day and she like had a copy and I like read it and I was like, Dude! Dad is so awesome! So is Bob! I especially liked the part where Bob writes all over his arms and when he runs out of room he strips till he's like totally buff, and then he keeps on writing all over his naked body! Dude! Whatever meds he was on, I want some! Also not to be missed: The part where Dad smites Uncle Ominus and sends him to planet Ug. Whoa! Dude is harsh! I'd recommend this book to anybody who knows how to read, and if you don't, hang on bro'—the movie'll be epic! Helluva deal!*

* * * * * *

A sense of jubilation filled the air at the National Book Convention. Although it was referred to as the "annual" convention, in truth, it had been three years since the last one. That was the event at which Chosen Leader Delbert Thorne declared a moratorium on new books. Thorne's point was, there were too many of the damn things already. Nobody had even come close to reading them all, so why not give people a chance to catch up? It wasn't that he was against free speech, he argued, but he'd never heard a book actually *speak*. All they did was sit quietly until someone came along and opened them, and even then, you could listen till the sun revolved around the moon and you'd never hear a book say anything. So he didn't see where not allowing books to be written for a while would violate anybody's free speech. Delbert Thorne was a strict interpretationist.

When Sophia and Lakshmi arrived with their new friends, Professor Matters, Thaddeus Well, and Normal Bea Freee, the convention was already in high gear. The giant warehouse took up an entire city block, and every aisle was lined with booths in which authors, publishers, and agents schmoozed and sold their goods. Everybody who was anybody was there: The eminent scholar, Lawrence T. Hutchins could be seen holding court on his latest work, *The Rise and Fall of the Mammalian Empire*, a two-thousand-page volume in which he brilliantly dissected the evolution of warm-blooded animals and made the case for their imminent demise. This was a sequel to his previous bestseller, written before the ban on new books. It was entitled *The Immortal Cockroach*.

The glamorous Leah Lafayette wore a slinky, low-cut dress designed by Raol Pannini himself. She smoked from a long cigarette holder. Surrounded by adoring fans and flashing cameras, she coyly shared anecdotes from her daring memoir, *A Discreet Life of Sex: Part 6*. She planned to write an installment for every year she had been sexually active. She was forty-two.

Of course, Guy Speller was there. He surely would have set the all-time record for most consecutive years with a number one best seller if it hadn't been for the moratorium. But no matter—he was at it again, starting a new run. His suspense thriller, which could be found in every airport in the world, was called *No Second Thoughts*.

The self-help gurus all showed up, each offering his or her common-sense recipes for life's everyday problems. Dr. Norman's new guide to realistic expectations was titled, *Staying Afloat in the Shallow End of the Pool*. Dr. Fred was plugging his newest recommendations for assertiveness in *Why Doesn't Anybody Do What I Tell Them to Do?* Dr. Hal had advice for couples in *When You Leave Your Underwear Lying in the Middle of the Floor, I Feel . . .* And no book conference would be complete without Dr. Linda's latest morality lesson: *You Deserve to be Abused, You Worthless Slut!*

But the surprise hit of the conference was *The Book of Bob*. No one besides Normal Bea Freee could have imagined the impact it would have, least of all Professor Matters and Thaddeus Well. The trio had generously offered to share their booth with Sophia and Lakshmi, but they were dismayed when throngs of people clambered over them to get their hands on *The*

Book of Bob, while ignoring their own wares on display.

By noon, Sophia had to call Bob and ask him to rush a new shipment. By evening, every booth at the conference was abandoned—every booth but one. Sophia and Lakshmi resembled the beleaguered yet cheerful Davy Crockett and Jim Bowie, valiantly holding off hordes of soldiers swarming the Alamo.

Most of the neglected authors were good sports. In fact, many of them were the first to abandon their posts and rush to what quickly became known as: The Booth of Bob. Volleys of questions flew fast and furious, and the two young women fielded them as best they could.

"Where does Dad cite his sources?" Lawrence T. Hutchins queried.

"Who is Bob's distributor?" Guy Speller wanted to know.

Leah Lafayette asked for Bob's phone number. Dr. Norman volunteered that *The Book of Bob* was really "neat." Dr. Linda harangued Sophia for ruining herself with tattoos and lectured Lakshmi for falling in with such a bunch of bad apples. "Your mother must be ashamed of you," she said.

"My mother loves me," replied Lakshmi. "So does Dad."

"But the question is, if Dad called you right now, would you be ready to go to Nebulon?" The questioner was none other than Donald LaFarge, author of the fabulously successful *Are You Ready?* series. With titles such as *Death by Dynamite*, *Uncle Ominus' Revenge*, and *The Good Ship Nebulon*, he had sold over a hundred million books and was the undisputed king of the Final Battle proponents.

Donald LaFarge claimed to have unearthed an ancient text predicting the impending doom of Planet Earth. He dug it up right in his own backyard. One moonlit night, as his wife lay sleeping, Dad told him to find a shovel, go out to the apple tree, and get to work. He dug all night, and at dawn his wife came out to find him standing in a hole as deep as a well.

"Donald! What on earth are you doing?" she asked.

"Keep digging," Dad implored him. "You're getting warm." LaFarge stayed at it all day, foregoing food and sleep. But when dusk arrived, he had turned up nothing but earth and rock.

"Donald, how long are you going to be?" his wife asked. "Your dinner's getting cold."

"If I had told you how far it was," Dad whispered in his ear, "you never would have started in the first place. Keep digging. You're almost there."

It wasn't until midnight that Donald LaFarge found his treasure buried in the eighteen-foot hole. With bloody fingers, he extracted a book the size of a small television. Shaking with emotion and exhaustion, he clutched the volume reverently to his chest and climbed up the wobbly ladder out of the hole.

He tiptoed back in the house, past his sleeping wife, brushed the dirt off his prize, held it under a lamp, and read the cover:

FOR THE EYES OF DONALD LaFARGE ONLY!

Donald LaFarge opened to the first page, which repeated the cover statement, followed by this warning:

Woe unto you, Donald LaFarge, if this Sacred Text falls under the gaze of another human eye. You will surely suffer a most painful death at the hands of Uncle Ominus.

The story that was meant for only Donald LaFarge to see was Dad's dire prophesy of the demise of Planet Earth and all but one thousand, one hundred and eleven of its inhabitants. For insurance, it was written in Nebulonic language, which only LaFarge could understand. While Dad didn't want anyone else to physically see his text, He sent Donald LaFarge on a mission to go out and give everybody the heads-up.

Which is exactly what he did, again and again. In the twelve years since Donald LaFarge found his treasure, he had published twenty best-selling books, telling the tale of Dad, Nebulon, and

Uncle Ominus. His books were translated into every language on Earth, omitting Nebulonic, of course. LaFarge had a knack for storytelling in a way that was accessible to everyone. His *Are You Ready?* books were written in big, bold print; sentences were short, and words rarely exceeded two syllables. Along with contributing mightily to modern theological thought, on a personal note, they enabled Donald LaFarge to afford several mansions, a yacht, and hefty alimony payments.

In truth, the end-of-the-world picture that Roland Brand had been describing in Red Rock was a sketch taken directly from the mural that LaFarge had been painting in primary colors for years. Curiously, *The Book of Bob* was the sole text First Minister Roland ever cited as his source of information, even though it contained only vague references to the impending disaster, and only indirect mention of Nebulon and Uncle Ominus.

Donald LaFarge was not one to waste time on useless speculation. All he knew was that he was not going to miss his ride to Nebulon. He carried a small, white suitcase, packed and ready to go. In his third book, *All Aboard*, Donald LaFarge discussed in detail the regulations for items passengers were allowed to carry on the rocket ship. The "immigrants," as they were called, were permitted one suitcase weighing no more than eighteen pounds and not to exceed seventeen inches in length, twelve inches in width, and eight inches in depth. Metric conversions were included. White was the preferred color for all items. Red was strictly prohibited—it made Nebuloners go blind. Toiletries were acceptable, although for their first five years on the planet, immigrants were not allowed to possess sharp objects. It was recommended that passengers bring bottled water—it was a long trip.

Donald LaFarge carried his regulation suitcase wherever he went. He kept a canteen attached to his belt. Beneath bushy gray eyebrows, his eyes constantly flitted from one place to another, forever on the lookout for the rocket ship that would soon land on earth and whisk him away to a better world. In conversation, he had a way of looking at people with a mixture of scorn and pity, as if they were inmates on Death Row. This was, in truth, how he viewed them—there were so few seats available and the standards were so high. Very few people would make the cut.

LaFarge eyed Sophia and Lakshmi with the above described expression as he stood in his white linen suit, stroking his Amish beard and asking them if they were prepared to follow Dad's summons to Nebulon.

"Actually," answered Sophia, "Bob told us to go to Red Rock and help Roland Brand spread Dad's word."

"That's where we're going right after the book convention," added Lakshmi.

"Blasphemy!" declared LaFarge. "I warn you girls," he said, his voice shaking, "you'd better get right with Dad or you will find yourselves in a fine mess with Uncle Ominus on Planet Ug."

"We're just Bob's humble Carrier Pigeons," said Sophia. "If he tells us to go to Planet Ug, that's where we'll go."

"We could bring *The Book of Bob* to Uncle Ominus," said Lakshmi. "Maybe he'd like to read it."

"You know not what you say!" cried Donald LaFarge. "Uncle Ominus will torture you in ways you can't imagine!"

"That's just like—everybody told me it would really hurt to get a tattoo," Sophia replied. "But it's not that bad, really. You just have to put your mind on something else. You want to see my owl?" She lifted her shirt. "Anyway, I couldn't possibly go to Nebulon or Planet Ug right now, because I have to go to Red Rock so Roland Brand can tattoo Bob on my back, holding up my Double-Pisces Fish and my Sagittarius Archer, which right now are floating on my shoulders without any support."

"She's been really ungrounded lately," added Lakshmi.

"I warn you girls," LaFarge continued. "You'd better get on your knees and pray to Dad to take you with Him. Look! It's 3:45. Time to face north!"

LaFarge meticulously spread a white blanket on the floor. He opened his suitcase, removed some pads which he strapped to his knees, then knelt facing north and with tears gushing from his eyes, he sobbed and prayed:

Dear Dad,
Ple-e-ease let Sacred Dancer win in the fourth race;
I have a lot of money riding on that one.
And ple-e-ease don't let it rain tomorrow;
I have to mow the lawn.
And ple-e-ease tell the chef not to overcook my steak tonight;
You know how I like it medium rare.
Praise Dad. Thank you, Dad.

LaFarge pulled a large handkerchief out of his coat, snuffled, and blew. "You'll be sorry you didn't pray," he said, wiping his eyes. "It's probably already too late for you."

"Bob says it's the spirit in our hearts and what we give of ourselves that's the important thing," said Sophia.

"Tell that to Uncle Ominus," said LaFarge, wagging his finger. "Young ladies, I have a multiple choice question for you. Consider your answers carefully. It may mean the difference between Nebulon and Ug. Are you ready?"

"We're ready," said Sophia and Lakshmi.

"Only one of these three people is going to Nebulon. The other two have a date with Uncle Ominus. Who is the lucky one:

a) The artist who devotes his life to glorifying Dad, however never prays, never apologizes for being wicked, and doesn't give Dad one dime of his earnings.

b) The woman who lives off the grid in the forest, recycles, grows an organic garden, heals people with herbs, never hurts a fly, and creates a paradise where all living things are happy to live and grow—BUT—she ignores Dad and worships something she vaguely calls "Spirit."

c) The murderer, rapist, and child molester, who, as he's walking to the electric chair, has an epiphany, tells Dad he's sorry, gets down on his knees and prays with all his heart for Dad to forgive him."

"Um . . . I'll go with the artist," said Sophia.

"Blasphemy!" declared LaFarge. "You will surely wind up along with that wicked artist on Planet Ug."

"The woman in the forest?" tried Lakshmi.

"Blasphemy!" cried LaFarge again. "Dad wouldn't put up with such a wicked pagan. It's clear that Uncle Ominus has his hooks in you. The answer to my puzzle, young ladies is: c) the murderer, rapist, and child molester. He is the only one who has the decency to apologize for being evil. And his timing is perfect! He lets Dad into his heart right before he dies, so he won't have time to screw up again.

"We have a lot of work to do," LaFarge continued. "I bet you don't even know how to Roll With the Punch. If you want to have any chance at all of going to Nebulon, you have to learn how to Roll With the Punch."

Sophia and Lakshmi looked puzzled.

"Let me show you," he said. Before they knew what was happening, Donald LaFarge had socked himself as hard as he could in the jaw. Then he hurled himself on the ground and began rolling every which way and crying, "I'm SO-O-ORRY, Dad! I'm so SO-O-ORRY! Look, Dad! Look! I'm Rolling With the Punch just for you!"

He stood up and dusted himself off. "There. I'm forgiven," he declared, rubbing his knuckles. His jaw was beginning to swell. "You must Roll With the Punch every Friday from noon till dusk, to cleanse yourself of wrong-doing and to apologize to Dad for being so wicked. Whoops—four o'clock. Time to pray again." He strapped on his pads, knelt on his blanket, and facing east, said another sobbing prayer:

Dear Dad,

I'm SO-O-ORRY—for I have committed the Sin of Greed:
You know that fifty-thousand-dollar royalty check I received
for my last book? I set up an off-shore account so I could cut you
out of your ten per cent.

Also, I'm SO-O-ORRY—for I have committed the Sin of
Pride:
While I was saying my 3:45 prayers, I imagined myself on
the Good Ship Nebulon, thumbing my nose at my heathen friends
who you're going to dynamite and send to Uncle Ominus.

Also, I'm SO-O-ORRY—for I have committed the Sin of
Lust:
When young Sophia Wise lifted her shirt and showed me her
tattoo, I had lustful thoughts that involved her, a feather,
handcuffs, and a can of Chunky Chicken Soup. Chunky Beef
would work too, but not as well. Also, I bet young Lakshmi
Jackson's not so bad under that sari, either.

Praise Dad! If the Good Ship Nebulon doesn't get here in
the next twelve minutes, I'll check back with You."

When Donald LaFarge had finished, he stood up and said,
"This Roland Brand you mentioned, he wouldn't be *the* Roland
Brand, would he? The famous Roland of Red Rock?"

"That's him," said Sophia. "Roland's a genius. Just look at
these tattoos. Nobody can draw tattoos like these."

"I've been hearing a lot about Roland of Red Rock these
days. They tell me he has become a leading proponent of my *Are*
You Ready? series. I hear he even has a seat reserved on the
Good Ship Nebulon."

"Roland usually gets what he wants," Lakshmi replied.

"May I see your owl again?" LaFarge asked.

"I hope he doesn't go to Nebulon before he gives me a Bob
tattoo," Sophia thought out loud.

"Roland Brand will not be going to Nebulon," announced
Normal Bea Freee, returning with bags of sandwiches.

"And who is this?" asked LaFarge.

"This is my friend, Normal Bea Freee," said Sophia. "Normal Bea, this is my friend . . . ."

"Hush, hush! Let *me* tell *you*," said Normal Bea. With fingers to her temples, she said, "You ar-r-re . . . a famous author. You have written bestsellers about the end of the world. Your name starts with an L . . . Large . . . no . . . LaFear . . . Lafore . . . no . . . Lafferty . . . no . . . ."

"LaFarge, madam. Donald LaFarge. At your service."

"Donald LaFarge! I knew it! I *knew* it! That's just what I was about to say!"

Thaddeus and the professor emerged through the crowd, balancing plastic cups of soft drinks. Lakshmi introduced them to LaFarge.

"Ah-h-h, Donald LaFarge," said Professor Matters. "The famous exponent of the Nebulonic Theory. Did you know that the earth's current atmosphere is known as an oxidizing atmosphere, consisting of seventy-nine percent nitrogen, twenty percent oxygen, and one percent other gases? Tell me, Mr. LaFarge, what is the make-up of Nebulon's atmosphere? Is it oxidizing or reducing? Is it realistic to expect that the Nebulonic troposphere would be compatible with earth's life systems?"

"An honor to meet you, Mr. LaFarge," said Thaddeus Well, passing out the drinks. "I think the more relevant question is how do you *feel* about going to Nebulon?"

"Normal Bea, I would like to know," said Donald LaFarge, "why you say Roland of Red Rock will not be going to Nebulon."

"I don't exactly know, Mr. LaFarge. I'm drawing a blank on Nebulon and Ug. I can't see them anywhere. But something is telling me loud and clear that Roland is not going to Nebulon and neither are you."

"Not going to Nebulon?" he exclaimed. "Blasphemy! Of course I'm going to Nebulon! I pray every quarter-hour! I apologize to Dad for all my sins! I Roll With the Punch every

Friday! Give me one good reason why I won't go to Nebulon!"

"I see," said Normal Bea, grasping her temples, "you were kind to somebody once, many years ago. You're saying something friendly—I think it was before you wrote your first book."

"Kind? Friendly? I'm kind and friendly to Dad every minute of every day. I praise Him constantly and tell Him what a great Dad he is. When was the last time *you* gave Dad some strokes? You'd better straighten up, Normal Bea Freee, or you'll be spending an eternity being kind and friendly to Uncle Ominus."

"I see . . ." she continued, "you're petting a dog. You're watering a flower. You're much younger—you have all your hair, and it's brown."

"I gave up petting dogs and watering flowers a long time ago. No time for that now. I'm busy doing Dad's work. You have no idea how much time it takes to tell Dad you love Him and apologize for your wickedness. By the time you're done doing all that—there goes your day."

"Bob says all men, women, beasts, and sprouts are Dad's creations," said Lakshmi. "He says if we love and care for all Dad's children, that's the best way to show Dad we love Him."

"Blasphemy!" cried LaFarge. "The only way you'll get to Nebulon is to beg Dad's forgiveness! Which reminds me," he said looking at his watch, "it's time to pray."

"I *knew* he was going to pray," said Normal Bea as she watched him get on his knees and face south.

Dear Dad (he began weeping),

Ple-e-ease help these wretched evildoers see the error of their ways. Show them that being kind and friendly isn't going to get them anywhere, and the only road to Nebulon is through you. Teach them the right path before it's too late and you dynamite the earth and send them to Planet Ug. Also, if there's not enough room on the rocket ship and it's a choice between them or me, ple-e-ease disregard everything I said.

"I have an idea," said Sophia. "After the convention, we're going to Red Rock to help Roland Brand. Would you like to come?"

"You and Roland would probably have a lot to talk about," offered Lakshmi.

"I predict Donald will come," said Normal Bea.

"I wonder what the atmospheric conditions of Planet Ug are?" wondered Professor Matters.

"Let's explore your preference for Chunky Chicken Soup," invited Thaddeus.

"All right, it's settled," declared LaFarge. "I'll come. I'd like to meet this Roland of Red Rock. I can mentor him on the finer points of the Final Battle prophecies."

"I knew it! I *knew* it!" exclaimed Normal Bea. "And now he's going to pray."

And sure enough, on cue, Donald LaFarge spread out his blanket, strapped on the knee pads, and knelt facing west, and with his body wracked with sobs, prayed:

Dear Dad,

I have a favor to ask you—when you come down with the rocket ship, could you make sure you come right after I'm done praying so I'll be sure to be forgiven when you get here? I'd sure hate to get caught in the middle—like say, twenty-two after the hour, and I've just pictured Lakshmi in a Cat Woman costume, and I've got eight minutes till my next prayer, and then you arrive and I haven't apologized yet and you won't let me on board.

Thank you, Dad!
You're Number One!

And with that, Donald LaFarge delivered himself a haymaker, right in the eye, and began Rolling With the Punch.

Sophia and Lakshmi watched in amazement, looked at each other, and together they said:

"*Helluva* deal!"

* * * * * *

The Annual National Book Convention was a bigger success than Sophia and Lakshmi could possibly have imagined. *The Book of Bob* was declared Book of the Convention by unanimous vote. In fact, for the first time in history, no other awards were given that year. Everyone agreed that *The Book of Bob* was so great, it should stand alone.

The new shipment arrived in time for each conventioneer to go home with a copy. However, many chose not to return. Hundreds of converts realized that everything they had thought was important in their little lives, now seemed trivial. They vowed to start over and dedicate their lives to Bob and Dad. The new Carrier Pigeons joined Normal Bea, Thaddeus, Professor Matters, and Donald LaFarge as they gathered around Sophia and Lakshmi at the Booth of Bob, awaiting their marching orders.

They were on their way to Red Rock.

XI. SUNNY SUNNYLAND

Some things have to be believed to be seen.

Abstractions 3:17

* * * * * *

CHOSEN LEADER DELBERT THORNE NEEDED A NEW SECRETARY of Religion, and he needed one now. It was time to start a new war, and it was so much easier to mobilize the populace when you had a strong Secretary of Religion to give you the moral high ground. Say what you want about his failed secretaries—each one had been a compelling spokesman for Delbert's wars, and they had been able to clarify for the public the concepts that Delbert found so difficult to articulate.

Delbert knew in his gut what he wanted to say—sometimes it was just difficult to find the right words. Just last week, he had attempted to make his case for the next war, and even he might have privately admitted his speech had fallen a little flat. It should have been a homerun—he was speaking to the League of Steadfast Devotionists (LSD), and his address was by invitation only. Usually, this would have been a job for the Secretary of Religion, but Delbert didn't *have* a Secretary of Religion, so he

thought he'd give it a shot. LSD had always been one of
Thorne's most loyal organizations, especially when it came to
war. All he had to do was make the case that the One True
Religion was being threatened by somebody somewhere, and
LSD was ready to go.

His speech started out well enough. He reviewed the
familiar facts: Yurkistan was a threat to the planet. The country
was run by the madman, Abdul Kashmir. The guy was a psycho.
He thought he was the Seventh Incarnation of God. Kashmir
forced all Yurkistanians to worship him fanatically, on pain of
death. Seven years ago, Kashmir had tried to spread Kashmirism
to the neighboring country of Borak. That was at a time when
Chosen Leader Thorne was stirring up the winds of war with
Yurkistan's other neighbor, Boran. Kashmir slyly thought he
could sneak into Borak while Delbert Thorne was distracted in
Boran. Big mistake. What Kashmir didn't count on was that
Delbert would get confused and bomb the wrong country, which
is exactly what happened. Abdul Kashmir got caught in the
crossfire and had to scramble out of Borak with his tail between
his legs.

Since then, the Free Nation had occupied Borak *and* Boran,
and Yurkistan was caught in the squeeze. Delbert reviewed this
history for the League, and everything was going along fine
until, to his horror, the teleprompter malfunctioned. Chosen
Leader Delbert Thorne had his strengths, but speaking
extemporaneously was not one of them. The screen went blank
and so did Delbert. For a heart stopping moment, he looked like
a deer caught in the headlights.

Fortunately, one of Delbert Thorne's strengths was a supreme
confidence that no matter how badly he screwed up, his aides
would fix it for him. So after an agonizing minute when time
stood still, all the members of LSD breathed a sigh of relief when
Chosen Leader Thorne collected himself and pushed ahead:

"It is impunitive," he continued, "that we dick the Evil
Stoptator near and how!"

The audience gasped, but it was too late to turn back.

"Seven years ago, Abdul Klezmer tried to invade the free nation of Boran—I mean Borak. It would have worked except I had bad intelligence."

Another strength of Delbert Thorne was he could keep a straight face under heavy fire.

"My bad intelligence told me to attack Boran—I mean Borak, when I meant to attack Borak . . ." Delbert blinked and recovered.

"I mean Boran."

Backstage, his aides were working furiously to develop their public education strategy for the next week. Delbert soldiered on.

"If it weren't for a quirk of state, the Free Nation today might be staining under the yoke of Klezmerism."

The LSD members applauded tentatively.

"Gentiles and ladymen, we're risking in livable times! Now, the Evil Tatedicker is trying to amass . . ." he paused dramatically, " . . . *weapons*! We have aerial phonograms which prove beyond the shallow of a drought that the country of Yurkistan has stickpiles of stocks and stones, which in the hands of the Evil Abdulla Kilmer could threaten our lay of wife! This is no time for the taint of fart!

"We must act now if we are to stop Abdullo Cashmar! We must tate the Evil Dickbeater before we are laid to mush under a restroom cloud!"

The League of Steadfast Devotionists leaped to their feet to applaud their Chosen Leader. They were like the mother at her son's piano recital—chewing her nails off with every clunker and so relieved when he made it through.

Chosen Leader Delbert Thorne stood squarely before the crowd, smirking and nodding his head slightly, as the adulation washed over him. Then he did his patented strut off the stage, his enormous erection preceding him. Backstage, his aides were ecstatic.

"Excellent speech, Mr. Chosen Leader!" said Aide #3.

"You outdid yourself this time, sir!" declared Aide #2.

"You are a true statesman!" gushed Aide #1.

Then they all fanned out and spent the next week hitting the airwaves and educating the Free Nationers about what a great speech their Chosen Leader had made. In private huddles, however, they emphatically agreed they had to find a new Secretary of Religion and find one fast.

* * * * * *

The power of Bob's message had lots of residual effects, not the least of which was to bring families closer together in the spirit of love.

Eldon and Larry, for example, had gone more than two weeks without a fight, and their commitment to Dad had infused their marriage with a new sense of purpose. They sold Larry's sports car, and in its place, they purchased a deluxe, double-decker, state-of-the-art motor home.

The RV had everything! Gold-plated faucets and toilet seats, a fully stocked wet bar, a wall-sized TV with built in video *and* DVD. The plush furniture and elegant wallpaper were coordinated in a tastefully understated motif of burgundy paisley, punctuated by lavender floral patterns. Eldon mounted a few Romanesque nude sculptures, adding to the atmosphere of sophistication and class.

Eldon and Larry took their jobs as Bob's chauffeurs seriously. They wanted to provide Bob, Bud, and First Carrier Pigeon Ivan Bunt all the comforts of home as they made their southern pilgrimage to Sunny Sunnyland. From the four varieties of body oils lined up neatly by the Jacuzzi, to the daily bouquets of fresh roses and lilies, to the little chocolate surprises laid on each pillow at night, no detail was too small to be overlooked.

The sign on the side of the bus said:

THE BUS OF BOB!
DAD: STRAIGHT AHEAD!

As the happy band approached Sunny Sunnyland, the crowds on the side of the road increased from a trickle to a crush. The Bus of Bob hopped from one gas station to the next. The smart worshippers figured out the best place to wait was at the nearest pump, where the odds were good that Bob and his Carrier Pigeons would have to stop and fill up. There, they mobbed their savior who characteristically stayed until every *Book of Bob* was signed. This slowed the entourage down considerably, but no one seemed to mind.

What was the hurry? Their business was to spread Dad's word to every man, woman, beast and sprout, and that's exactly what they were doing. By the time they reached the outskirts, the hordes of waving fans lined both sides of the highway, and traffic was backed up for miles.

The billboard at the city limit said:

WELCOME TO SUNNY SUNNYLAND!
THE FREE NATION'S
FIRST PAVED NATIONAL MONUMENT!

This was no false claim.

Twelve years ago, Delbert Thorne's first act as Chosen Leader was to declare Sunny Sunnyland a Paved National Monument. He did so in response to intense criticism he had received during the campaign in which his opponent had accused him of being unfriendly to the natural world. The new Chosen Leader Thorne wanted to extend an olive branch to Nature Lovers, and he thought giving Sunny Sunnyland Paved National Monument status would be just the ticket.

He also thought this act would be good payback to the Union of Flat Earth Believers, who had contributed mightily to his election.

Whenever the argument came up over whether the earth was flat or round, the Union of Flat Earth Believers used Sunny Sunnyland as the most powerful piece of evidence to support their position. Fly over Sunny Sunnyland in an airplane, and any fool could see the earth was flat. "Get out your binoculars!" they would say. "Get out your telescope! Look in any direction as far as your eyes will take you, and what do you see?"

Most days what you would see was a brown cloud that blanketed the entire city, obscuring the evidence in the Flat Earth versus Round Earth debate. The locals called this brown cloud "haze." But on a clear day, you'd have to admit the Flat Earth Believers had a point—the earth was flat as an enormous pancake.

From an airplane on a clear day, you'd see that the pancake was overrun by billions of busy bumper-to-bumper ants streaming down a vast and complex maze of arteries, as far as the eye could see. You'd look down on rows and rows of tiny rooftops scrunched into straight lines like a farm crop of miniature homes; or maybe the regimented rows were some immense rag-tag army, leaning shoulder-to-shoulder at undisciplined attention.

Touch down to earth and you'd see that driving each and every one of those scrambling little ants was a warm-blooded human being with fingers, toes, muscles, kidneys, and lungs. A full-sized mammal with hopes and dreams, love and hate, pain, joy, and drama as big as your own. Each and every one was the center of his or her universe. You'd see that each and every flat roof that you'd viewed from above covered a flat house, standing in a flat row on a flat street stretching over a flat landscape. A vessel containing noise, tragedy, and secrets. Each and every one.

A long time ago, Sunny Sunnyland was a chaparral. That was before they paved it over. It was a big job to cover all that arid soil with concrete, but the Sunnylanders were determined. There had also been lots of orange groves, but eventually they managed to cut them all down too, and pave over the stumps. Every once in a while, some pesky grass shoots managed to sprout stubbornly through the cracks in search of daylight, but Sunnylanders were vigilant. Anytime they discovered a green offender, out came the poison spray, followed by more concrete to smooth it over again.

A few holdouts had insisted on keeping their lawns, but thankfully, that practice was put to rest once and for all when Chosen Leader Delbert Thorne declared Sunny Sunnyland the Free Nation's first Paved National Monument. With its new status came responsibility. To maintain a Paved Monument, all trees must be cut down. All lawns must be dug up, poisoned, or burned. And everything that grew must be paved over. So Sunny Sunnyland gave itself a fresh coat of concrete paint!

Sunnylanders liked to say their city was a "melting pot," but the truth was, it was more like a jigsaw puzzle. One piece of the puzzle was the Mexitino section—Mexitino shops, Mexitino signs, Mexitino men and women speaking their native language (*Hablo Mexitino solamente*). Cross the street and you'd be in the Asianese section—same planet, different worlds. Butted up against the Asianese were the Descendants of Africa. Who needed to travel? You could visit any country in the world, right here in Sunny Sunnyland. Back in the days when the Free Nationers still voted, the ballots were written in sixty-seven different languages. No wonder all the forests were gone!

If you speak Mexitino, press one now . . . If you speak Asianese press two now . . . If you speak Yurkistanish, press three now . . . If you speak Free Nationish, press sixty-seven now . . . ."

Then there was the sex. It was everywhere! Huge signs advertising:

SIN CITY! HOT 'N' HORNY BABES!
WET 'N' WILD TEENS!
ONLY A DOLLAR A POUND!

Sex on billboards. Naked girls on taxi cab roofs, bare bodies on bus stop benches. Massage parlors, escort services, porn shops, strip clubs, XXX Movies! TV ads, movies ads—SEX BIGGER THAN LIFE! Sex in Sunny Sunnyland was like the struggling grass shoots that sprouted through the pavement. So much life was covered over—it just had to find its way out somehow.

Needless to say, Sunnylanders took great pride in their city and declared it "The Pavement Capital of the World." When they weren't going somewhere in their cars, they loved to stroll the flat, earth-free sidewalks in their white shoes and pants that never got dirty or showed any unsightly stain of grass.

The other mandatory accessories to the Sunny Sunnyland ensemble were the wrap-around, polarized, fiber optic designer sunglasses, which not only shielded the wearer from the sun, but insured that nobody could see in. It was curious that Sunnylanders found it necessary to block out the sun with their shades—they *worshipped* the sun. If the sky was blue, sunny, and cloudless, this was known as a "beautiful day." A drop of drizzle was an unsightly blemish to be avoided the way a fashion model avoids a pimple. Gray sky was depressing. Honest-to-god rain was more dreaded than a nuclear attack—it threw the town into total chaos. Fortunately, nature had not given Sunnylanders any pimples, depression, or chaos for a long time.

Bob and his entourage stopped for gas again and saw a billboard that read:

WELCOME TO SUNNY SUNNYLAND!
DAYS WITHOUT RAIN: 423 AND COUNTING!

Four hundred twenty three beautiful days in a row!

Nobody in Sunny Sunnyland quite knew where their water came from, except that when they turned on the tap—there it was! Now that there weren't so many lawns to water, consumption was down, but still—it had been hot for a long time and there were lots of thirsty people and lots of swimming pools to fill. What most Sunnylanders didn't know was their water was delivered from Northern Sunnyland, hundreds of miles away, through an elaborate system of dams and pipelines. The once lush farms to the north were drying up and starting to look like a desert, but—oh well. Nowadays, the Sunnylanders got most of their produce from down south in Mexitino anyway, so *no problema.*

Shortly after Bob and his Carrier Pigeons stopped for gas and saw the second welcoming billboard, they needed to stop for gas again. There they noticed a huge chartreuse neon sign which read:

WELCOME TO SUNNY SUNNYLAND!
ENTERTAINMENT CAPITAL OF THE WORLD!

Well, yes and no.

In its salad days, Sunny Sunnyland had truly been the show biz mecca, not only of the world, but of the universe. Every blockbuster movie, every TV show, radio show, and hit record was born right there in the studios and sets of Sunny Sunnyland. Anybody who was anybody in show biz lived there then—the place reeked of fantasy, glamour, and glitz. Everywhere you looked, flashing signs with blinding lights blasted you with announcements of whatever movie, record, or celebrity was **NUMBER ONE!** Tour busses cruised the Street of Stars day and night: farting cylinders full of fans who hoped to catch a glimpse of fame in the flesh, hoped to have their brush with greatness.

The celebrities gave Sunnylanders a high standard to aspire to. People thought, maybe if I'm lucky, I too can be beautiful and glamorous, charming and witty, rich beyond imagination, adulated, adored, and spoiled. Maybe I too can live like my matinee idols: Exempt from pain, failure, and old age. Exempt from bad breath and shit and menstrual cramps. Exempt from dirt. Exempt from doubt. Exempt from being tongue-tied, confused, and stupid. Always in control. Always winning. Always defining reality to my advantage.

The celebrity standard had good news and bad news. The good news was: The sky was the limit! "Keep your feet on the ground and reach for the stars," said a popular DJ. The bad news was: Most Sunnylanders had a tremendous inferiority complex because, try as they might, they couldn't become rich, famous, or wonderful.

But this was ancient history. Truth is, most of the entertainment industry had been outsourced along with everything else. Movies and records could be made anywhere now. The stars from the Golden Era proved not to be exempt from pain and shit and death after all. Most of the ones who were still alive had fled Sunny Sunnyland long ago, opting for their villas in the country where they could get some peace and quiet.

This left a few fading stars like Gloria Varrone, who made infamous news just a week before Bob's arrival. It seems she had gone on one of her notorious drinking binges and somewhere along the way, she disappeared. No one had a clue where she was and her friends began to worry. There were rumors of foul play. Police began to investigate, but turned up nothing. The only clue they had came from her friend, masseuse, and sometime lover, Sergio, who explained to the authorities that he had been expecting her the night she disappeared, but she never showed up. His interrogators nodded suspiciously and declared Sergio a "person of interest."

Sergio lived in a suburban part of Sunny Sunnyland—one of those neighborhoods with rows and rows of stylish adobe homes, painted in earth tones and covered by tile roofs. The streets had Mexitino names like Via del Loro, Via de la Paz, and Via de San Miguel. Most of the people who lived there didn't know *loro* meant "parrot." They didn't know *paz* meant "peace." They didn't know San Miguel was the archangel, Michael. Most of them didn't know *via* meant "street," either. They just liked the sound of the names that vaguely reminded them of the Mexitino people from whom their ancestors had stolen the land so Sunnylanders could live there and be free.

Gloria Varrone disappeared on a Sunday, and by Thursday most people expected the worst. The whole thing got cleared up at three in the morning when Sergio heard a steady, insistent pounding on his door. He rolled out of bed, threw on his white terrycloth robe, padded across the living room, and looked through the peephole. There was Gloria, banging on the door as if she wanted to break it down. When Sergio opened up, he found her naked as Eve, except for the Free Nation flag wrapped around her head. In her hand was a mostly empty bottle of scotch.

"Well, *there* you are!" she sputtered sloppily.

"Gloria, where have you been?" asked Sergio.

"I've been looking for you for *days!*" she exclaimed. "Every one of these goddamn houses looks exactly the same!"

In truth, Sunny Sunnyland was looking more and more like Gloria Varrone every day: A once-glamorous star who was now aging, unrecognizable, and lost. A drunken caricature of her former self.

Or maybe, if Sunny Sunnyland had once been a high priced call girl, she was now an old whore, slapping on more and more make-up to cover up her age, hoping to turn one last trick.

Whatever. Gloria Varrone was last week's news. Today, all the buzz was:

Bob is coming Bob is coming Bob is coming!

He was poised to take Sunny Sunnyland by storm.

* * * * * *

"Get Jimmy Lee Mathers on the phone. I'm gonna make him my next Secretary of Religion."

"Excellent choice, Mr. Chosen Leader," said Aide #3.

"Astute thinking, sir," said Aide #2.

"Brilliant," said Aide #1. "I'll look up the number of the penitentiary."

"Brilliant, what?" asked Chosen Leader Delbert Thorne.

"Brilliant, *sir*, Mr. Chosen Leader, sir," said Aide #1.

"That's better," replied Thorne. "How many times do I have to tell you to call me sir? Or Mr. Chosen Leader. Or both. Anyway, why are you guys telling me to make Jimmy Lee Mathers my Secretary of Religion when he's in jail?"

"Our mistake, sir," said Aide #3.

"How stupid of us, Mr. Chosen Leader," said Aide #2.

"Please forgive us, Mr. Chosen Leader, sir," said Aide #1.

They were sitting on foldout chairs in the basement of the Executive Palace in Capital City, under leaky pipes, candles illuminating the dark. Chosen Leader Thorne had taken to making all important decisions in the bowels of the palace, having become convinced that every other room in the damn place was bugged. The only thing his Executive Office was good for anymore was watching baseball games and working out. He'd had his desk hauled away, and had turned the room into a world-class fitness center. There were eight different exercise stations: Exercise bike, treadmill, gut buster, "the whole shootin' match," as Delbert would say. Every day he worked out religiously for hours to an exercise routine tape that played music at the perfect rhythm for his heart rate. A woman's voice told him when to proceed to the next station. Delbert Thorne prided himself in being the most physically fit Chosen Leader in history.

Not that he didn't do any business in the Executive Office. He met lots of foreign dignitaries there. It was a common experience for a head of state to be led into Chosen Leader Thorne's office and see Delbert on the treadmill, tee-shirt drenched with sweat, giant erection straining at his red shorts, and to hear the familiar greeting of, "Hey Yuri, what's up?"

That's what he liked to call every foreign leader: "Yuri."

Athletes, girl scouts, religious leaders all made their daily parade through the Executive Office for their handshake and photo-op. But when serious business was to be done, notes were passed, meaningful looks were exchanged, and Chosen Leader Thorne would quietly slip into the dark and dank basement, discreetly followed by Aides #3, #2, and #1. Which was where they were at this moment, wrestling with the dilemma of whom to choose for the next Secretary of Religion.

"I kinda like that Arlen Husky fella," said Chosen Leader Delbert Thorne.

"Yes sir," said Aide #3. "I kinda like him too."

"Arlen Husky is a likable fella, Mr. Chosen Leader," said Aide #2.

"Everybody likes Arlen Husky, Mr. Chosen Leader, sir," said Aide #1. "Those boys in the pictures that are going around the Internet seemed to like him a lot, too."

"I don't think Arlen's right for the job," Chosen Leader Thorne decided.

"Sir, if I may . . . " began Aide #1.

"Number One, ask the question," said the Chosen Leader.

"Chosen Leader, may I?"

"Yes, you may."

"Mr. Chosen Leader, have you ever heard of Roland of Red Rock, sir?

"Yes I have," said the Chosen Leader. "Who is he?"

"Actually, sir, Roland of Red Rock is quite remarkable. He has established a ministry in the Southwest Region, and in a very short time he has developed a phenomenal following, sir."

"Yeah, Roland of Red Rock is amazing," said Thorne. "What's his religion?"

"His faith is right in line with yours, Mr. Chosen Leader. He preaches about Nebulon and Uncle Ominus, good versus evil, black versus white, sir."

"I've always thought Roland of Red Rock was a stand-up

guy," said the Chosen Leader.

"Roland of Red Rock is definitely a stand-up guy, Mr. Chosen Leader, sir," said Aide #1. "There's one potential problem, sir."

"Problem, Number One? You know I hate problems."

"Only a *potential* problem, Mr. Chosen Leader, sir. Roland of Red Rock preaches from a new doctrine called *The Book of Bob*, sir."

"*The Book of Bob*? What the hell is that?"

"I took the liberty of bringing you a copy, Mr. Chosen Leader, sir. It was written by a guy named Bob who claims God came to him one night and told him to take dictation. He says Bob is His son and told Bob to call Him 'Dad.' It seems to be consistent with the teachings of the One True Religion."

The Chosen Leader thumbed through *The Book of Bob*. He opened a page at random, held the book upside down, and looked puzzled. "Here," he said, handing Aide #1 the book. "I ain't got my readin' glasses on. What's that say?"

"Excellent choice of a passage, Mr. Chosen Leader, sir. It says:

> *Thou shalt not question thy Chosen Leader, for he surely knoweth best.*"

"Hey, that's pretty good. I like this book," Thorne declared.

"Yes, Mr. Chosen Leader, sir," said Aide #1. "It's a very good book. Would you like to hear more, sir?"

"Go ahead, Number One. Shoot."

"Well, Mr. Chosen Leader, sir, *The Book of Bob* also says:

> *All worldly problems will be solved when there shalt cometh upon this earth a great and wise man who doth beareth an unusual endowment.*"

"Hey, that's me," said the Chosen Leader. "He's talkin'

'bout me!"

"Yes, He is, Mr. Chosen Leader, sir," said Aide #1. "And if I may read just one more, sir?"

"Yeah, go for it," said Thorne. Now he was interested.

And there shalt cometh upon this earth a great and noble prophet whose name shalt beareth three R's; and he shalt join forces with the great and wise Chosen Leader of unusual endowment; and together they shall lead their people to the Promised Land.

"Three R's?" asked the Chosen Leader. "What's he talkin' about?"

"Could it be Roland of Red Rock, sir?" wondered Aide #1.

"I think the three R's must stand for Roland of Red Rock," declared Thorne. "What do you think?"

"Astute observation, Mr. Chosen Leader, sir," said Aide #1. "Do you think Dad is telling you to choose Roland of Red Rock as your next Secretary of Religion, sir?"

"As a matter of fact, I was just talkin' to Dad last night, and you know what He said? He said, 'Delbert,' that's what He calls me—Delbert, heh, heh . . . 'Delbert,' He says, 'Call up that Roland of Red Rock and make him your next Secretary of Religion.'"

"Excellent choice, sir!" exclaimed Aide #3.

"Roland of Red Rock! How do you do it, Mr. Chosen Leader?" asked Aide #2, incredulously.

"You have outdone yourself this time, Mr. Chosen Leader, sir," said Aide #1. "Roland of Red Rock will make a perfect Secretary of Religion, sir."

"Number One, get me Roland of Red Rock on the phone," said Chosen Leader Thorne, decisively.

XII. ROLANDWORLD

THERE ONCE WAS A FOOL WHO WALKED HOME DOWN A DARK ALLEY one night and fell into a deep manhole. To his good fortune, he managed to climb to safety with no more than a few bumps and bruises. He praised Dad for letting him live another day.

"I've learned my lesson," pronounced the fool. The next night, he walked down the very same alley, taking greater care. Although he walked gingerly, it was too dark to see, and he tripped over the very same hole. Fortunately, he fell to the side of the hole and landed unceremoniously on the ground with nothing injured other than his pride. Brushing himself off, he thanked Dad for sparing him from falling into the manhole.

"This time I have certainly learned my lesson," said the fool, and to prove his point, the next night he carried a flashlight down the very same alley. But when he approached the manhole, his toe caught on the rim, he tripped and nearly lost his balance. "Praise Dad," he declared, "for helping me keep my feet."

The next night, to prove he had learned his lesson once and for all, the fool chose to walk home down a different alley altogether. There, he was mugged by a gang of thieves who beat him up, stole his wallet and shoes, and threw him down a manhole.

Fables 12:13

* * * * * *

Traveling with their new friends toward the outskirts of Red Rock, Sophia Wise and Lakshmi Jackson gazed out the car window, awe-struck and starry-eyed, at the giant golden gates which parted and opened wide, revealing the enchanted path to:

ROLANDWORLD!
LAST STOP TILL NEBULON!

Rolandworld! *The Magic Empire of the Universe!*
Rolandworld! *A Paradise Where Dreams Come True!*
Rolandworld! *Take the wife and kids and buy your one-way ticket to Nebulon! Get on board and don't be late! Dad's a-comin' and you don't want to be left behind!*

What a place! Pictures didn't do it justice! You just had to see it in person to believe it!

It was amazing what Roland Brand had done. Starting at the south end of Red Rock, he had bulldozed a stretch of rust-colored canyons for miles around. Only a handful of people had ever made it to the top of one of those things before, but Roland of Red Rock just leveled 'em.

Then, after laying a twenty square mile base of finely ground sandstone and limestone, Roland created a combination Theme Park—Amusement Park—Worship Retreat—Golf Course—Casino—Residential Mansion in his image. This time he really outdid himself.

"I feel like I've died and gone to Nebulon!" exclaimed Sophia.

"I feel like I've died," Lakshmi replied.

Professor Matters eased the car through the gates and

stopped to admire the bigger-than-life bronze statue of Roland Brand that greeted him. The representation had Roland wearing his famous sequined jump suit, leering dramatically in his patented pose. Normal Bea Freee leaned out the window to snap a picture. Looking directly beyond Roland's statue, the Carrier Pigeons were amazed to see a sparkling castle with pillars and spires of real silver and gold. A church bell tolled in the eaves high above, greeting their arrival. Twelve white doves flew gracefully above the bell, circling the three magnificent bejeweled letters that shimmered at the top:

RRR

"Roland of Red Rock," whispered Donald LaFarge reverently. He sat in the back seat between Sophia and Lakshmi, clutching his white suitcase tightly to his chest.

"Or could it be Reactive Regression Response?" speculated Thaddeus Well.

As they approached the hulking oak doors, bolted with heavy timber beams to bar penetration into the castle, a deep voice boomed from nobody-knew-where, ordering: "Stop your engine and put your car in neutral."

"Maybe we should turn around," said Lakshmi.

"Are you kidding? This is fun," Sophia replied.

Professor Matters followed orders, and as he did so, the bolts magically lifted and the doors swung free. The passengers found themselves gliding as if in a car wash, passing through the entry into the magic land of **Rolandworld!**

And what a world it was! The most stupendous Ferris wheel anyone had ever seen, called The Nebulonic Circle. The death-defying Tower of Descension, in which passengers were shuttled five hundred feet straight up, then dropped free falling into Planet Ug. And, of course, the famous roller coaster that attracted thrill seekers from around the world—climb aboard Uncle Ominus' Last Ride—if you dare. And on the side of every car at every attraction, the familiar **RRR** logo, signifying supreme devotion to Dad.

The rolling road to Rolandworld transported the Carrier Pigeons' car to an expansive, overflowing parking lot, slipped them into a space and stopped.

"We're here!" bubbled Normal Bea Freee as they all piled out. Thaddeus and Professor Matters wasted no time heading straight for Uncle Ominus' Last Ride. Normal Bea proceeded directly to Witch's Doom Virtual Reality Center. Sophia and Lakshmi waited while Donald LaFarge faced south to say his prayers. Then the three went looking for Roland Brand.

Wading through a jostling sea of humanity, the trio stared in all directions with wide-eyed amazement: Over here was an outdoor stage on which actors portrayed The Birth of Bob, re-enacting the historic night when Dad came down and told Bob to write a book. Over there was a rap group barking something about having your "mug squashed like a bug on Planet Ug." Fortune telling booths, a Dunk Uncle Ominus booth, a sharpshooting booth where the targets were real-life non-believers—three shots for a dollar. Gift shops selling **RRR** cups and **RRR** caps and **RRR** pennants and "Genuine Rocks from Nebulon."

Finding Roland Brand was complicated by the fact that everywhere Sophia, Lakshmi, and Donald LaFarge went, they saw Roland of Red Rock impersonators. Most wore the trademark jump suit but there were some who disguised themselves as the early Roland. Many were a spittin' image of the real thing, which made Sophia and Lakshmi as confused as if they were in a house of mirrors.

They passed the Virtual Reality Center where they saw Normal Bea Freee being burned at the stake. The most popular attraction after Uncle Ominus' Last Ride was the Rocket Ship to Nebulon, where true believers could take a simulated trip and when they reached their destination, sit at the feet of Roland, Dad, and Bob. It was so realistic, you thought you were actually there!

But the capper was the ***RRR*** Casino. Fronted by gushing geysers, tropical waterfalls, and a lava-spewing volcano, the ***RRR*** Casino spread over the equivalent of three city blocks, the consummate icon of luxury, comfort, and restraint. Courteous red-coated footmen in white gloves waited at attention by the door to escort customers into the gaming room where they would be greeted by smiling, scantily clad women carrying trays of complementary pink champagne. The flashing neon signs above the chandeliers announced:

Play the RRR Slots and Win a Ticket to Nebulon!
Odds of winning: 1111 in 6 billion!

"Where can I find Roland Brand?" Sophia asked. Most people continued to walk by, heads down. A few shook their heads and muttered as they ducked anonymously back into the crowd.

"Something strange is going on," said Lakshmi. "Have you noticed that the women . . ."

"You mean what they're wearing?"

"Yes—those shawls around their heads," said Lakshmi. Are we the only ones who don't have them?"

"No—the women in the casino weren't wearing them. But they're kinda cool, aren't they? Let's go to the gift shop and pick some up. I want to get one with the ***RRR*** logo on it."

"Sophia, something's not right."

"I know, Lakshmi. I feel naked without a shawl when everybody else has one. Also, have you seen those tattoos on the women's foreheads? When we find Roland, I've got to get him to give me one of those. Look—there's a gift shop. Let's see what they've got. I wonder what the 'T' stands for?"

"Trouble," said Lakshmi.

Donald LaFarge waited outside while the girls went shopping. It was time for him to face west and pray.

As Sophia and Lakshmi approached the gift shop, they were

blocked by two non-descript white men with black hats and shades, black suits, black ties on white shirts, and shiny black shoes. They each had walkie-talkies attached to their black belts, and Sophia noticed a gun in a shoulder holster, peaking from inside the mid-sized man's coat.

"Are you looking for First Messenger Roland?" asked the other mid-sized man. His gun was showing too.

"Yes, we are," said Sophia. "I'm Bob's Minister of Wisdom, Sophia Wise. This is my friend, Carrier Pigeon Lakshmi Jackson. We're here to help Roland spread Dad's word to every man, woman, beast, and sprout."

"He's been expecting you. Come this way." The mid-sized man squeezed Lakshmi's arm roughly and the other mid-sized man gripped Sophia in the same manner. They led the girls briskly and purposefully through the teeming throng of *RRR* worshippers; past the long line waiting to enter the *RRR* Prayer Retreat; then the long walk around the immaculate *RRR* Golf Course where players were challenged by the 9th hole quicksand trap, the ring of fire around the 11th hole, and the atom-neutralizing lasers on holes 5, 7, and 18. Then they saw it: The *RRR* Mansion.

This wasn't your average run-of-the-mill six thousand square foot Colonial. This was something special. Sophia wished she could get a better look, but the non-descript white men in black suits whisked her and Lakshmi up the slate stairway so quickly that she could only catch fleeting glimpses of the ivy-covered brick walls, the magnificent stone towers and gables, the Roland statues, and the White Bengal tigers roaming free along the manicured grounds.

Into the elevator—the girls' eyes turned upward, watching the digital numbers as they climbed past 30 (funny, they hadn't seen so many stories from the outside), while their escorts stared straight ahead, behind black sunglasses.

At floor 42, the elevator stopped and the doors opened. Sophia and Lakshmi were led down a carpeted hall that could have been in a bank building or a corporate office. They stopped at a door with the familiar **RRR** insignia on it. The guards didn't knock. They stared ahead again, waiting, hand-over-hand in front of their belts.

"Bring them in," said Roland from the other side.

The mid-sized man opened the door, and the other mid-sized man motioned Sophia and Lakshmi to enter. When they had passed the threshold, the door closed behind them. They looked back and the non-descript white men in black suits were gone.

"Hello, Sophia. Hello, Lakshmi. So good of you to come."

Roland sat squarely in his luxurious black leather chair, behind a large mahogany desk. Roland looked dashing in his smart three-piece suit, the **RRR** cufflinks matching the pin in his silk tie. His skin was smooth and pampered, his black hair freshly clipped. He folded his hands on the buffed and bare desktop; his manicured fingernails shone. Behind him was a picture window with a view of Rolandworld, far below.

"So Lakshmi," said Roland Brand. "How's your mother?"

* * * * * *

"Mash my potatoes! This is the life!"

Indeed it was. Who would have thought just a few short months ago that Ivan Bunt would find himself living in the penthouse suite of the posh Silver Star Hotel, getting his hands massaged by Natasha and Bunny ("One for each hankerin' hand!"), sipping tropical drinks with umbrellas in them, catching rays, snoozin', Jacuzzin', and living the good life?

"Bake my beans!" he declared. "I *love* Sunny Sunnyland!"

Natasha and Bunny laughed. They thought Ivan was so funny. He was always cracking them up with things he said.

"Hey girls," Ivan said. "Would you mind moldin' the dough on my shoulders some more? They're tighter 'n a rassler's headlock."

"Sure, Ivan," Natasha giggled. "How about if I do your shoulders and Bunny does your head?"

"Oh me, and it's crumble my cornflakes! This is better than a yodelers' convention! A little to the left, please. Ooh—that's good. Bless your belly-button, Bunny."

Eldon and Larry were down at the pool, but Ivan knew they'd be up soon. In fifteen minutes it would be time for Bob's guest appearance on the *Allan Famous Show*. Of course, by now Bob had his own show, a daily sermon called *Helluva Deal!* It was wildly popular, but a spot on the *Allan Famous Show* would be a step up to a whole new level. Still, everyone was a little bit nervous because Allan Famous was notorious for ripping his guests to shreds. It remained to be seen if Bob could match wits with him.

Today was day number four hundred fifty-one without rain. Another beautiful day! Larry loved admiring how Eldon's tan was progressing. Also, this was day number forty-four for Eldon and Larry without a fight. There had been a slight argument over when to pick up Bud from Pierre's Pet Grooming Parlor. Larry wanted to get him before Bob's appearance on the *Allan Famous Show*, but Eldon needed seven and a half more minutes of sun on his back, which wouldn't leave them enough time. Larry said he was "feeling frustrated" that Eldon would be so selfish to think his tan was more important than Bud getting to see Bob on TV. Eldon made the point that if Larry hadn't procrastinated so much this morning, they could have gotten to the pool when they'd planned and had plenty of time to pick up Bud before the show.

"Procrastinated?" asked Larry, incredulously. "Just because some of us have the decency to cleanse our toxins in the sauna before we enter a public pool . . . ."

"I think the reason you procrastinate so much is you're passive-aggressive," declared Eldon.

They were in danger of breaking their forty-four-day winning streak, but then they remembered Dad's loving words, and besides, who could stay mad when it was such a beautiful day? They resolved the conflict by agreeing to call Pierre and ask him to let Bud watch the show from the Parlor.

When Larry and Eldon got to Ivan Bunt's room, they found him splayed out in his plush recliner, peering out from between Natasha and Bunny. Ivan was looking quite pampered and happy.

"Bless my pancakes! It's Eldon and Larry! Turn on the twitterin' TV, boys—it's time for the big show!"

Larry pressed the remote, and they all gathered 'round in delicious anticipation.

"Ladies and gentlemen, put your hands together for the *amazing* . . . the incredible . . . the one and only . . . A-a-al-lan Fa-a-a-mous!"

"Leapin' Lordy!" exclaimed Ivan, clapping his hands. "This is better than a room full of tubas!"

Excitement began to wane as they waited through Allan Famous' monologue followed by seventeen commercials. But at last the time had come.

"My first guest," said Allan Famous, sitting behind his desk and holding up *The Book* for the camera, "is a fellow who simply calls himself 'Bob.' He claims God speaks to him and tells him to call Him 'Dad.' Dad dictated a book to Bob, which I have right here—it's called *The Book of Bob*. His new TV show, *Helluva Deal* is on this network, and it's the Number Two show in the country. And whose show is Number One?"

"Yours is, Allan!" the audience shouted, reading from the cue card.

"That's right. And don't forget it for a minute. And how long has the *Allan Famous Show* been Number One?"

"Twelve years!" they read again.

"Twelve years and three months—but who's counting?"

Boisterous laughter.

"But Bob's got a nice little show and it's doing really well at the moment. So please, give a big welcome to . . . Bob!"

Bob ambled on stage and smiled slightly toward the camera.

Then he sat down in the "hot seat" beside his host's desk. The studio audience went crazy, as almost everyone did in Bob's presence. Everyone except Allan Famous.

"So, Bob," Allan began sweetly, "I hear you're pretty popular these days."

"I'm but a simple messenger, Allan. Dad is popular."

"Dad?" Allan Famous raised an eyebrow toward the audience, conspiratorially. They tittered. "Who is this . . . Dad?"

"He's just Dad. He's the one who made all of us."

"All of us?" said Famous incredulously. "Sounds like Dad needs to take some family planning classes."

Bull's-eye! The audience roared.

"Dude! With six billion of us, Dad must be getting some serious action!"

More laughter.

"By the way, where's Mom?"

"Mom? I don't know. I've never talked to Mom. Only Dad."

"Six billion kids! No wonder Mom never talks to you. She's too tired. Whew!" Allan fanned himself and winked at the audience.

What a pro Allan Famous was! He'd been playing this keyboard for a long time and he knew every button to push. He could carve up any guest without breaking a sweat.

"So what does Dad say to you, Bob?" He was closing in for the kill.

"Oh, he tells me lots of things. Mainly he says to be kind to every man, woman, beast, and sprout."

"Every man, woman, beast, and sprout," Allan pondered. "*Every* one?"

"Yes, every one."

"*Every* one?" he repeated in mock amazement.

"Yes, Allan. That's what Dad asks us to do." He smiled sweetly.

"Ok, ok, ok . . . Let me see if I've got this right? Suppose our Chosen Leader decides to take out the evil Abdul Kashmir in Yurkistan? Would Dad tell you that our Chosen Leader is wrong, that he should be *kind* to the evil Abdul Kashmir?"

The studio audience booed.

"Dad has some very specific things to say about war and conflict resolution."

"He does, does he? Sounds to me like your Dad isn't the Dad *I* know. *My* Dad is on the side of right! *My* Dad is on the side of the Free Nation! *My* Dad is on the side of our Chosen Leader! *My* Dad won't crumble like a gutless little wienie when it's time to take out the evil Abdul Kashmir!"

Wild applause! Allan Famous nodded his head with righteous indignation as the studio audience hooted, whistled, and stomped their feet in a zealous, patriotic display.

"So, Bob," Allan held up both hands, signaling his fans to calm down, "is Dad talking to you right now?"

"Dad always talks to me, Allan," said Bob.

"But I mean right now? Right this minute? Is He here right now? Is He here in the studio audience? Wait! I think I see him!"

The camera panned to a paunchy, laughing man in a baseball cap.

"Is that him?" cried Allan Famous. "Wait! Over there! I think I see Dad!"

The camera caught an elderly man picking his nose. The audience was in an uproar.

"So Dad is talking to you right this minute?" Allan continued.

"Yes, He is, Allan," replied Bob.

Then Allan Famous made a mistake that any first year law student knows not to make. He asked a question he didn't know the answer to.

"What is Dad saying to you, Bob?" he asked.

"Dad's saying it's much easier to tear something down than it is to build it back up," Bob answered. He listened for a moment and continued.

"He says it takes months to build a house, but all it takes is one match and a few minutes to burn it down.

"Now He's saying that cruelty, violence, and destruction are the easy way out; they're the paths of fools and cowards.

"He says to declare war is to declare failure; find another way.

"He says when you ravage the land to meet your own greedy desires, you're like a horse shitting in his own stall; find another way.

"He says when you get rich by climbing on the backs of the poor, you bankrupt yourself as well; find another way.

"Oh, and . . . wait . . . He wants to tell you something . . . Hold on a minute . . . Ok, I got it. Dad says, 'Allan Famous, you are a little man. Your heart is so shriveled up, even *I* can hardly see it. You are clever but you are cruel. You are small and you are wrong. Find the love in your heart, Allan Famous. Find the compassion. Only when you are able to treat every man, woman, beast, and sprout with loving kindness, will you find peace with yourself and the world. Allan Famous, find another way.'"

The audience stood as one. They had heard Bob, and they responded as all receivers of The Message did—weeping and wailing and rolling in the aisles. As for Allan Famous, he was reduced to a blubbering puddle of tears, for he had heard Dad's words and he knew them to be true.

"Beat my bagpipes!" Ivan Bunt shouted. "Bob did it again!"

"To declare war is to declare failure! Praise Dad!" cried Larry Smith.

"Yes, oh yes!" declared Eldon Smith. "We're horses shitting in our own stall! Praise Dad!"

"I think Bob's kinda cute," said Natasha. Bunny agreed.

"Oh, I've learned something today!" proclaimed Ivan, on a roll. "Oh yes, I've learned my livin' lesson today-ya! Better to be kind than cruel-a! Better to love than to hate-a! Better to build a happenin' house than to burn it down-a! Oh, I've got the spirit! I'm shriekin' with the spirit now-a! Oh, it's grease my gizzards and butter my bread! I feel better than a kangaroo at Christmas! Oh, it's holler hallelujah and *Helluva* deal!

"Natasha, will you mix me another one of them drinks with the strawberries, please?"

Helluva a deal is right. After that day, Bob's ratings soared straight to the top. He was the undisputed King of the Airwaves. The entire Free Nation was watching him now. As for Allan Famous, his show never quite had the same zip again. Although he was still liked by some, his ratings slipped noticeably. He just couldn't find it within himself to beat up his guests anymore. He became known for insightful discussions with eminent experts on the day's most pressing issues. After a while, he was given the axe by the network and was relegated to hosting a little show on public TV. He considered this the greatest success in his life and was finally a happy man.

* * * * * *

"My, how things have changed since we last saw each other," said Roland Brand.

Sophia and Lakshmi stood before him, separated by his opulent desk, speechless as two schoolgirls summoned by the principal.

"How's that friend of yours? What was his name? Oh yes— Bob—that's right—Bob. How is he?"

"Bob is awesome," said Sophia. "He's got his own TV show now, and . . . ."

"Enough!" said Roland, holding up a manicured hand. Sophia didn't know she had hit a sore spot.

"You know, don't you," said Roland, recovering, "that the television world is all politics. It's all about who you schmooze with. If I was in Sunny Sunnyland instead of this little podunk town of Red Rock, *I'd* be the guy with a number one show. I'd blow Bob out of the water."

"Speaking of Bob," said Sophia, "remember that Bob tattoo

you promised me? You wouldn't believe how ungrounded I've been feeling ever since . . . ."

Roland silenced her with a hand again. "As I said, circumstances have changed. Now I have all this." He gestured grandly toward the picture window behind him, displaying his domain below. "Do you have any idea how time-consuming it is to run an empire? There're bills to pay and board meetings to run and employees to hire and fire. There's security and lawyers and lawsuits—why, just last week Uncle Ominus' Last Ride broke down, and several people fell to their death. You wouldn't believe how much it cost to pay off the families and the press to shut them up.

"This thing has turned into one big headache. You think I have time to be piddling around with childish games like tattoos?"

"But . . . ."

Both Roland's hands went up. "Don't worry. I've farmed out my tattoo business to my able assistant. I have trained him personally in the mystic arts and have taught him all my secrets. Have you seen the T's on the women's heads? He did every one of those. Orvil does good work, don't you think?"

Sophia and Lakshmi exchanged puzzled looks.

"Roland," Sophia tried to start. "About Bob . . . ."

"Bob, Bob, Bob! All I hear is Bob!" Roland mockingly covered his ears. "Bob this, Bob that! Sophia, don't you know Bob is yesterday's news? How long do you think Bob will be hot? A month? Six months? A year? Where's your vision? Look around you. I have built an *empire*! And this is just the beginning. When Bob is back in his little house talking to his dog, I will be ruling the world!"

"Sophia, I think we'd better go," said Lakshmi.

"NO!" Roland shouted. The girls jumped. Roland stood up and leaned over his desk. "You will *not* go because I need your help. Didn't you hear me? I've got a dynasty to run, and it keeps getting bigger. Do you know how hard it is to find good help these days?

"No, you have to stay and help me manage Rolandworld. Sophia, I want you to be my Director of Operations. You're the only one I can trust. I know you will help because I'm asking you to. And Lakshmi," he leaned over his desk and penetrated her with his stare, "*you* will help because I'm *telling* you to."

"Sophia," Lakshmi tried again. "This isn't what Bob had in mind. We've really got to . . . ."

"Jules! James!" Roland pressed the intercom with one hand and silenced Lakshmi with the other. The door opened immediately and the two non-descript white men in black suits entered. "Jules and James, I would like to have a word alone with Lakshmi, please."

Jules and James took Sophia by the arms and led her out the side door.

"So, Lakshmi, you never did tell me—how's your mother?"

"My mother is not well. In fact, thanks to you, her life might be ruined."

"Me?" he said in mock surprise. "Why, I thought I was cleansing her. People never show gratitude anymore."

"Look, Roland, all I want . . ."

He held up his hand. "Lakshmi, I think there's something you should see. Jules! James! Bring in Donald LaFarge!"

Jules and James burst through the entry door, dragging with them a disheveled, cut and bruised Donald LaFarge.

"Donald LaFarge, I believe you know Lakshmi Jackson?"

"Roland of Red Rock!" LaFarge exclaimed. "Thank Dad I've found you! There's been a terrible mistake. I was praying facing west when these two thugs accosted me. They said I was a spy for Uncle Ominus and they beat me up. Tell them who I am. Tell them I'm the famous author of the *Are You Ready?* series and I have a seat reserved on the rocket ship to Nebulon. Tell them . . . ."

Roland raised his hand. "I have told Jules and James they are doing a splendid job. I have told them there are spies among us, and everyone is suspect. At the top of the list are overzealous authors who parade their religion as a front to infiltrate my organization."

"But Roland, I'm a True Believer. I was so looking forward to comparing notes with a colleague of equal stature."

"Equal?" Roland raised an eyebrow.

"Ok, not equal. There's no one equal to you, Mr. First Messenger, sir. But I thought maybe you'd like to collaborate on my next book?"

"Take him away," said Roland, whisking his hand impatiently.

"Now, Lakshmi, I urge you to reconsider," he continued, as Jules and James dragged a kicking and screaming Donald LaFarge out of his office. "It is imperative that Sophia assist me in my operations. As Bob's Minister of Wisdom, she can help me gain the credibility I need to corner the Bob market. But you are an obstacle. You don't want to be an obstacle to your friend Sophia, now do you?"

Lakshmi fidgeted.

"You've seen what happens to obstacles like Mr. LaFarge. I'm quite convinced you don't want suffer a similar fate. By the way, speaking of obstacles, have you seen your other friends lately?"

"Do you mean Normal Bea? Thaddeus and the professor?"

"Yes, that's exactly to whom I'm referring. Last I heard, Normal Bea Freee was being burned at the stake at Witch's Doom Virtual Reality Center. It's amazing how realistic they can make virtual reality these days."

Roland paused. "And your friends Thaddeus Well and Professor Matters are still on Uncle Ominus' Last Ride. I'm sure they'd like to get off sometime."

"What do you want?" asked Lakshmi.

"Haven't I told you? I want your help. Your friend, Minister of Wisdom Sophia Wise, is my liaison to Bob. I want you to do everything you can to insure her success."

"I don't think I have a choice."

"One always has a choice, Lakshmi. I'm sure you'll make the right one. Jules! James! Bring Sophia back in."

Jules and James hustled Sophia through the side door. They deposited her next to Lakshmi and made their exit.

"Now, Sophia," Roland began. A woman's voice on the intercom interrupted him. "Mr. Brand, you have a call from a man who says he's Chosen Leader Delbert Thorne."

"I'll take it, Patricia," said Roland, picking up the phone.

"Hello, Mr. Chosen Leader . . . Yes, yes . . . Yes sir, I do. You mean now? Yes, right away . . . Yes sir, of course sir . . . Why, yes sir, I'd be honored . . . Yes sir, I'll leave for Capital City first thing in the morning . . . All right . . . Thank you sir, thank you. I'll see you tomorrow . . . Very good, Mr. Chosen Leader . . . Thank you and goodbye, sir."

Roland spoke into the intercom and called, "Patricia, pack my bags. I'm heading for Capital City tomorrow."

Then he turned to the girls and smiled. "Sophia, Lakshmi, you are looking at the Free Nation's next Secretary of Religion."

XIII. THE GOLDEN AGE

Give a man a fish and he will have a meal;
Teach a man to fish and he will deplete the ocean.

Ironies 24:7

* * * * * *

THE FREE NATION WAS ENTERING WHAT WOULD LATER BE remembered as The Golden Age of the One True Religion. Faith flourished as it never had before. After millennia of speculation, people had finally figured out the secret to life and the mystery of the universe—they'd cracked the code. They had an intimate and personal relationship with Dad. They knew exactly who He was, what He looked like, and what He wanted from them. Since the beginning of history, people had been looking for answers. Now the Free Nation had them. It was about time!

One of the many things the Free Nationers knew for sure was, they couldn't afford slackers. "One germ can infect an entire city," Secretary of Religion Roland Brand warned his countrymen. One transgressor would make *everybody* look bad in Dad's eyes, and spoil their chances of getting to Nebulon. With the exception of a few isolated "troublespots," Free

Nationers breathed easy knowing that their neighbors who didn't worship sufficiently would be locked up and "re-educated." If they still didn't get it, they would be issued a cyanide pill and asked to "submit their resignation." If they refused, they'd be "fired."

Church bells tolled throughout the Free Nation every fifteen minutes, twenty-four hours a day, reminding people to face north, east, south, or west, and get on their knees and pray. This practice helped Free Nationers devote their lives to Dad and gave them an outside chance of making it to Nebulon. Also, with the entire sleep-deprived populace stumbling around like zombies, the quarter hour prayers were an effective device for Secretary of Religion Roland Brand to achieve his ends of spreading the One True Religion throughout the land.

Finally men could live free from the temptation of women. With twenty-twenty hindsight, it was amazing it had taken so long for people to figure out the problem. It was so obvious—it had been right under their noses the whole time. The problem could be summed up in one word: Women. It was women who caused men to do all kinds of stupid things like fight and rape and kill. Women caused them to whistle and yell "hubba hubba" and scratch their armpits like chimps. Men were always rear-ending people's cars because they were distracted by *women's* rear ends.

It was all women's fault, and finally the citizens were doing something to correct it. The first step was to remove temptation. Of course, women were required to wear the **RRR** shawl at all times, but that was just the basics. Now they were expected to don the black and formless "vaulted cloak" whenever they peeked into public. This served the dual purpose of completely concealing the delights that had previously reduced rational men to genuflecting buffoons. And, if men were still tempted, they would have about as much chance of unwrapping the prize as they would of robbing a bank.

Even with these precautions, letting women out in public

was risky business. You might be able to control what men saw and what they were able to do, but just the presence of a woman could cause a man's imagination to go wild. It was amazing what a woman could make a man dream up. But the problem was, women had to be let out sometimes—there was shopping to do. Therefore, Secretary of Religion Roland Brand thought it prudent to institute a compromise policy of "day pass rationing." There would be a finite number of passes issued per day so there wouldn't be too many women out on the street at one time. The passes worked on the odd-even system: Women whose husband's names started with "A" were given passes on even days; "Bs" were allowed out on odd days.

The only part of a woman's body that was allowed to show was the forehead, on which it was decreed that a "T" for "Temptress" would be tattooed. There were a lot of women in the Free Nation, so there was a lot of catching up to do. Roland Brand, having trained Deputy Secretary of Religion Orvil Swain in the mystic arts of tattooing, put Swain in charge of the project. They predicted within six months to a year, every woman over the age of twelve would be "T-ed up."

Women weren't allowed to vote anymore—you never knew *what* they might do—but the truth was, it was a moot point. After Delbert Thorne was elected Chosen Leader for the second time, he decided the Free Nation didn't need elections for the time being. They were expensive and time-consuming, and besides, everybody knew he'd win anyway.

The sacred covenant of marriage underwent a transformation. After much consultation with Deputy Secretary of Religion Orvil Swain, Roland Brand initiated the far-reaching "Marriage Reform Act," which finally restored the institution to Dad's original intentions. Among the most significant advancements was the following clause:

A man may marry as many women as he deems necessary to facilitate his worship of Dad; with the following restrictions:

1) A man may not take more than three brides per year without special consent from the Deputy Secretary of Religion.

2) A man may not take a bride under twelve years old without the consent of her father and the Deputy Secretary of Religion.

3) Divorce is strictly forbidden. If a man is no longer happy with his wife, he may:

> *a) Give her a cyanide pill and ask for her resignation; however, he may only employ the 3a clause if said wife is suspected of being in violation of Dad's laws.*

> *b) If said wife is not suspect, but husband is tired, bored, or ascertains she is 'not his type,' said husband may institute a 'Sacred Swap' with another husband for a wife of equal value. The Sacred Swap is subject to the approval of the Deputy Secretary of Religion who will be granted first right of refusal."*

Roland Brand also instituted long overdue "Abomination Reforms." Although most violators of Dad's laws were given the option to "submit their resignation" before they were "fired," there was one abomination that Roland deemed so *abominable*, that this act would bring upon the perpetrator(s) instant "termination of contract" by the state. That one abominable act was:

Any sexual activity that is not performed within a covenant marriage for the express and sole purpose of procreation.

That pretty much summed it up. Adulterers were rounded up and fired; gays were rounded up and fired; married couples over fifty years old who still had the spark were rounded up and fired.

As in much of life, there were gray areas. For example, self-touching was strictly prohibited, however, Free Nationers prided themselves in being clean. This created a dilemma—there was a concern that, in the course of normal hygienic care, the washer might cause him or herself to feel good. This and other problems were discussed frankly in the pamphlet, *How to Keep Uncle Ominus Out of Your Bedroom and Bath.* In it, practical tips and guidelines were offered on keeping "Cleanliness next to Godliness." For example, the following specific method was offered for washing:

If it is found necessary to wash the genitalia, the first question to ask is: What have you done to make them dirty in the first place? If your genitalia are dirty because of an abomination you have committed, proceed directly to your nearest Office of Religion and report the incident. However, if you can look yourself in the mirror and honestly say you've done nothing wrong (no cheating—dreams count, too), take the following hygienic steps.

1) Fill up your bath with warm water.

2) With the tap still running, pour in two caps of Mr. Binky's Bath & Body Bubbles.

3) Get in.

4) With arms tightly gripping the sides of the tub, swish torso to and fro, until genitalia are thoroughly clean. DO NOT put genitalia under a running faucet.

5) Upon exiting the tub, allow genitalia to air dry. DO NOT wipe, rub, tamp with a towel, or blow-dry.

(Note: The above is the State-approved cleansing method and is deemed sufficient for proper hygiene. DO NOT, under any circumstances, touch genitalia with hands, deliberately or "accidentally." If you do, you will have committed a severe violation of the Abomination Laws and you must proceed immediately to the nearest Office of Religion and report your transgression.)

Television was an important tool for educating the public. Along with his daily hour-long sermon, Secretary of Religion

Roland Brand also filmed short spots called "Roland's Reminders," which were broadcast every fifteen minutes at prayer time. Roland encouraged the networks to program many hours of cartoons, which he believed would "soften the brains" of the viewers for the more demanding messages he would deliver later. Secretly, he also urged programmers to step up the violence and gratuitous sex. This too, was part of his "softening up" campaign, and it had the added advantage of giving him something to rally the public against in his daily sermons.

Bob's *Helluva Deal!* show was a sore spot—it still held its number one position in the ratings. Roland realized that for the present, he was prudent to publicly embrace Bob and piggy-back his popularity onto Bobism. However, pretty soon it would be time to educate the public and "define their differences."

Secretary of Religion Roland Brand was on a mission to cut down all the forests as fast as possible. His point was: We should use up all our resources before Dad beamed one thousand, one hundred and eleven of us up to Nebulon, because we didn't want to leave anything for the undeserving slackers left on earth. Besides, when Uncle Ominus came to get them, Roland didn't want to leave any trees for people to hide behind.

The Golden Age of the One True Religion wasn't a phenomenon exclusive to the Free Nation—it was spreading like wildfire around the world. Secretary of Religion Roland Brand had decreed that it was the Dad-given right and responsibility of every man, woman, beast, and sprout to practice the One True Religion. It was amazing, when the Free Nation's soldiers invaded a country to help them out, how most foreigners agreed. Of course, there were some pesky "troublespots" around the globe, just as there were in the Free Nation itself, but it was only a matter of time before they came around. Yurkistan was still a problem, but when Roland was named Secretary of Religion, he promised Chosen Leader Delbert Thorne he would make it his top priority.

There were two main troublespots in the Free Nation—one

surprising and one not so. The not-so-surprising troublespot was Sunny Sunnyland. The natives there had always been out of step with the rest of the country. Maybe it was all the beautiful days—they'd had well over five hundred in a row now. All that sun seemed to make people lazy. Sunnylanders subscribed to a more self-indulgent form of Bobism rather than the stringent, spartan discipline that Roland Brand advocated. Sunnylanders figured if they were simply kind to their neighbors and friends most of the time, that was probably good enough. Besides, it was too hot for women to be going around in vaulted cloaks all day long. Women preferred to be tan and mostly bare, and in truth, most men *and* women liked it better that way. Bobism's permissive influence could be felt all the way up to the Northwest Region. It was a problem.

More surprising was what was happening in Rolandworld. If Roland had known when he left that in a short time he would be passing reforms that would return women to their Dad-given station, he never would have put Sophia Wise and Lakshmi Jackson in charge. But being Secretary of Religion made him see things from a broader perspective than when he had been a mere ruler of a modest empire. It all happened so fast—he had asked Sophia to be Director of Operations, then came the phone call from Chosen Leader Delbert Thorne, then Roland left in a flurry of activity and never was able to give proper instructions. Then came his reforms. Now, something had to be done because the way Sophia and Lakshmi were giving Rolandworld a make-over was not at all what he had in mind.

The first thing Sophia and Lakshmi did was open the gates to the poor, homeless, and afflicted. Sophia slipped naturally into her experience at The Shelter to organize a soup kitchen, medical unit, counseling center, and housing development. Lakshmi went to work on the golf course, transforming it into a world-class wildlife preserve.

They rescued Normal Bea Freee from the stake at Witch's Doom ("What a relief," Normal Bea exclaimed. "I had a premonition if I stayed much longer, I'd be burned up!"), where she did wonders transforming the Virtual Reality Center into The Virtual Reality Theology Library. With the miracles of new technology, visitors were able to experience any sacred event throughout history and see for themselves how it *really* went.

One of the best-attended exhibits was "Adam's Rib." Scholars, biologists, and engineers came to study how God made Eve out of Adam's rib, how He was able to extract the rib without an anesthesiologist, and whether or not He left a scar. But the most popular exhibit by far was "The Immaculate Conception." *Everybody* wanted to see how *that* was done. Boy, were they surprised!

Thaddeus Well and Professor Tyrone T. Matters took a few days to get over their dizziness after Sophia and Lakshmi helped them off Uncle Ominus' Last Ride. Then they went straight to work. Thaddeus Well took charge of the Counseling Center where he specialized in helping women who poured in daily from every corner of the Free Nation—they seemed to be having difficulty adjusting to Secretary of Religion Roland Brand's new reforms.

Professor Matters took on what would come to be known as the greatest engineering feat of his time: Rebuilding the red rock canyons that Roland Brand had torn down, and restoring them to their original state.

"Won't Roland be thrilled when he sees our improvements?" exclaimed Sophia.

"Sophia," replied Lakshmi, "we really have to have a talk."

The girls were nothing if not resourceful. They transformed the casino into an enormous greenhouse in which delicious organic foods were grown to feed the hungry multitudes. Flowers and gardens abounded everywhere. The rides were torn down, and materials from them were used for Professor Matters' other pet project: A system of panels and windmills that would soon enable all of Rolandworld to run on solar and thermal energy.

"We're really carrying out Dad's word, aren't we, Lakshmi?" exclaimed Sophia. We're practicing loving kindness with every man, woman, beast, and sprout."

"I don't think Roland will see it quite that way."

Sophia had even stopped worrying about getting her Bob tattoo lately. She was so busy transforming Rolandworld into a happy oasis on the desert, she'd forgotten about how ungrounded she was. Actually, her bare feet felt pretty firmly planted in the warm red sandstone as she welcomed newcomers who streamed into the thriving community. They all seemed so anxious to contribute, and it was fun to figure out how each person could help.

Lakshmi Jackson was worried. On one hand, she had never lived in such a paradise as Rolandworld. She felt more at home on the wildlife preserve she had created than anywhere she'd ever been in her life. She loved the creatures that roamed the territory who were finally free to live according to their true nature. Most nights she slept out in a tent, right where the 11th hole "Ring of Fire" used to be. The White Bengal tigers didn't bother her, except when they crawled in her tent to sleep and hogged the whole sleeping bag.

On the other hand, she didn't think Sophia was being very realistic about Roland Brand. Every time Lakshmi tried to explain her concerns, Sophia would dismiss her and say, "You're so negative!" Well, she'd just have to keep trying. As Lakshmi's dad would say, "Sometimes negative is realistic." Speaking of her dad, that was another thing Lakshmi was worried about. Ever since she'd gotten that letter from him she'd been on edge.

The one thing Sophia *did* worry about once in a while was Donald LaFarge. He was nowhere to be found. However, she was able to rest easy because Normal Bea Freee predicted he would turn up eventually.

* * * * * *

The letter Lakshmi received from her father said:

> *Dear Lakshmi,*
> *I know where Roland Brand is. Worry not. Vengeance will*
> *be mine.*
>
> > *Your loving father,*
> > *Ben*

Ben Jackson still hadn't gotten over what Roland Brand had done to his wife, Aruna. The truth was, she wasn't getting any better. She still spent many hours a day locked in the bathroom, washing furiously in the tub while clucking like a chicken and baa-ing like a goat. When she wasn't clucking and baa-ing in the bathtub, she could usually be found at City Hall's Office of Religion, where she volunteered her time assisting in the local T-ing up effort. The single file lines stretched down the hall and out the door; unT-ed women standing quietly, heads down and covered by **RRR** shawls, bodies hidden by black vaulted cloaks, dark glasses covering their eyes, trembling hands clutching the orange slips they had received in the mail informing them that this was the date they were to report to the Office of Religion for their tattoo.

In Ben Jackson's opinion, Aruna was taking things too far. She insisted on wearing her vaulted cloak and shawl at all times, even when she was in the house—even to bed, which was now in Lakshmi's old room. She certainly wouldn't be sleeping with her husband anymore, now that their procreating days were over.

Some nights, a worried Ben would sneak into Aruna's new bedroom and check to make sure she was ok. There he would find her, still in her sunglasses, the "T" tattoo peeking out from her layers of protective covering, snoring like a buzz saw beneath a life-size poster of Roland Brand in his pre-Secretary of Religion days, posing and leering in his gold-sequined white jumpsuit.

"I'm gonna kill him," he whispered.

Aruna became a leading exponent of Secretary of Religion Roland Brand's doctrines. If anything, she told Ben, she thought Roland was "too moderate." If it were up to her, she would take things a lot further. For one thing, why did the government waste so much time and money re-educating troublemakers and non-believers? They weren't going to make it to Nebulon anyway, so why not just fire them? She did have to concede that, given the permissive atmosphere in today's society, her solution wasn't practical. Realistically, you would probably have to give slackers the option of turning in their resignation before they were fired. She was willing to be flexible on that point, but she just couldn't see why Roland Brand wanted to give everybody so many chances. That's what happens when people become politicians, she explained to Ben. They come in with big ideas and high ideals, then they're forced to compromise and compromise until pretty soon, they forget who they are and where they came from.

"I'm gonna kill him," Ben muttered under his breath.

Ben was spending a lot of time at the shooting range these days. He had always been a crack shot with a pistol, only slightly above average with a hunting rifle, and admittedly sub-par with semi-automatic assault weapons. This would change. It was amazing what hours and hours of daily practice could accomplish. He got to a point where he could pick off a bee at four hundred yards with his double barreled, 16-gauge Sportsman's Special. While ripping off rounds with his army issue MX-247 Dematerializer featuring the telescoping stock, bayonet mount, and grenade launcher, Ben would laugh above the roar and shout, "No man, woman, beast, or sprout is safe with *this* baby!"

One night, while Aruna was sleeping in Lakshmi's old room she heard a blast downstairs. She looked in the mirror to make sure she was completely covered, then ran down to see what was the matter. There was Ben, sitting on the couch in the living room, pointing his still-smoking pistol at the TV, which he had blown to smithereens.

"Ben!" Aruna exclaimed. "What in Dad's name are you doing?"

"I saw your friend, Roland Brand," was his reply. "I was practicing."

Aruna took it upon herself to head up the Women's Vigilance Committee, wherein the members dedicated themselves to keeping an eye out for transgressors and reporting them. The committee members built up an impressive track record. They were three-time winners of the "Community Contribution Award" for turning in the highest number of suspected drinkers, fornicators, and dreamers. (A "dreamer" was someone who wasn't actually *accused* of committing a transgression, but was alleged to be *thinking* about a transgression.) The committee was going along fine until the members started turning each other in. Finally, Aruna was the only one left standing.

Ben had had enough. He hatched a two-pronged plan. The first prong was to give Aruna a change of scenery. The second prong was to kill Roland Brand. One night, he sneaked into Aruna's room. He expected to find her sleeping, but instead he found her on her knees by the bed, praying toward Roland's picture. Being a strong cop, trained in the art of combat, it was easy as buttering bread for Ben to overpower her and stick a needle into her arm. He tenderly kissed her unconscious cheek—the first kiss in he-couldn't-remember-when—then wrapped her in a large Free Nation flag, carried her in a bundle to the garage, opened the back door to the car, and gently laid her on the seat.

One more thing to do before he left—he ran back upstairs, taking two steps at a time, returned to Aruna's room where he violently ripped the poster of Roland Brand off the wall. He dashed back down the stairs, taped the picture to the fireplace, removed his MX-247 Dematerializer from the gun rack, and let 'er rip until all that was left of the picture and fireplace was dust.

Ben grabbed his pistol, his 16-gauge Sportsmen's Special, and the MX-247 Dematerializer and, not bothering to close the front door, dashed to the car. He jumped in, turned on the engine, and backed out of the driveway, burning rubber as he sped away. First stop: Rolandworld!

* * * * * *

Back in Sunny Sunnyland, Eldon Smith and Larry Smith were getting ready to turn in. They said their prayers and thanked Dad for helping them get through another day without a fight. It had been close. Eldon had complained that their suite was a pigpen because "some people" were such slobs. Larry countered by observing that Eldon was "so anal." There was a danger of escalation, but it was another beautiful day. How could anybody stay mad?

Bud was hiding under the dining room table where no one could see him. Everybody thought he looked so cute with his new haircut and the pink ribbon around his neck. Bud wasn't convinced. He wondered if, after everybody went to sleep, he'd be able to chew off the knit sweater they'd put on him. It made him hot and itchy.

Ivan Bunt was immersed in a boisterous game of "Indoor Wheelchair Rugby" with Natalie and Bunny. "Scuttle my scrum!" he shouted. "If I was dead, I'd be rolling in my grave!"

Bob was in his suite, engrossed in conversation with Dad. Dad was giving Bob a tutorial on the finer points of the 1031 Property Exchange clause and the benefits of offshore tax shelters.

In Capital City, Secretary of Religion Roland Brand sat in the same office at the same desk that his predecessors Gennisaw Tubbs, Conrad Shanks, and Rod Barkley had occupied before him. To his back was a map of the world. Roland opened the top drawer of his desk and removed three red pushpins. He stood up, turned to the map, and pushed the pins in three strategic locations: One in Yurkistan, one in Sunny Sunnyland, and one in Rolandworld.

Deputy Secretary of Religion Orvil Swain sat back, pulled the cork out of his corn liquor jug, and poured the hot juice down his throat. He was tired after a long day of T-ing up. He'd had a lotta purty gals today. The purty gals always took longer an' slowed things down.

Chosen Leader Delbert Thorne stood in front of the full-length mirror, trying on his new fighter pilot's jumpsuit. He pondered on the new Secretary of Religion. *So far, so good*, he thought. But he wondered if maybe this Roland of Red Rock guy was getting a little too big for his britches.

Back in Rolandworld, Lakshmi Jackson climbed out of her tent and padded over to the main house. Dexter and Sheeba, her two favorite tigers, were being particularly playful tonight. She decided to move to Sophia's bed so she could get a decent night's sleep.

Thaddeus Well poured himself a drink. He had just finished an intense group therapy session in which one of his clients had had a breakthrough and torn off her vaulted cloak. In a moving ritual, the group had lit a fire and she had tearfully threw the cloak in. She kept the shawl, however. Thaddeus guessed it would be years before she'd be ready to give *that* up.

Professor Tyrone T. Matters was at his drafting desk drawing up plans for the state-of-the-art recycling center he planned to begin building next week.

Normal Bea Freee was looking into her crystal ball for Donald LaFarge. She knew he was around somewhere.

Lounging in the living room, idly picking her mandolin, Sophia Wise heard a knock on the door. She laid her instrument on the couch and proceeded to the entry. A look of surprise came over her face as she opened the door to find her smiling parents on the porch.

"Natalie! Phil! What are *you* doing here?"

XIV. PARENTS' NIGHT

I LOVE PEOPLE. I'VE MADE THEM IN MY OWN IMAGE. I GUESS YOU could say I'm a "people person." Because I love them so much, I wanted to give them a good sturdy home. So far, Earth has held up really well. It's about four and a half billion years old. Four and a half billion looks like this:

4,500,000,000

Before I created Earth, I wanted to be sure it was in a good neighborhood. So twelve billion years ago, I made the Universe. Here's what twelve billion looks like:

12,000,000,000

Humans are my favorite creation so I built them to last. I keep tinkering with the design, and now they're able to live for about seventy years. Seventy looks like this:

I wanted my people to have a spacious home. So I made Earth seventy-nine hundred miles in diameter. That comes out to forty-one million, eighty thousand feet. Forty-one million, eighty thousand feet looks like this:

41,080,000'

My people needed light, so I worked out a way for their planet to travel around a star. I couldn't put them too close, though, or they'd burn up. So I put them ninety-three million miles from the sun. That's four-hundred seventy three billion, six hundred million feet. Four-hundred seventy three billion, six hundred million feet looks like this:

473,600,000,000'

I wanted my beloved people to be big and strong. They've grown over the years. They used to only be around five feet tall. Now, on average, they're almost a whopping five feet, six inches. Five feet, six inches looks like this:

5'6"

Light travels one hundred eighty-six thousand, two hundred miles per second:

186,200

In a year, a beam of light will travel approximately six trillion miles, which looks like this:

6,000,000,000,000

I wanted my humans to be athletic—almost God-like. There are a few who can even run a mile in less than four minutes. Imagine that! Four looks like this:

4

A long time ago, I decided to put planet Earth in a high-end neighborhood called "The Milky Way." If you were in a rocket ship traveling at the speed of light from one end of the Milky Way to the other, it would take you about six quintillion years to get there:

6,000,000,000,000,000,000

I didn't want my beloved earthlings to be bothered by aliens, so I put the next closest galaxy far, far away. It's called "The Andromeda Galaxy." A rocket ship from the Milky Way to Andromeda traveling at the speed of light would get you there in twenty-one quintillion years:

21,000,000,000,000,000,000

Here's how many hours it would take:

183,960,000,000,000,000,000,000

If you flew on a commercial flight, it would take a lot longer than that. You'd have to do a lot of planning to pack for THAT trip. Anyway, I love my little humans. They're just like me! It just goes to show: Size isn't everything.

Calculations:
3:141592653589793238462643383279502884197169399375

* * * * * *

"You see, Phil?" exclaimed Natalie on the porch. "I was right! Her hair *is* green this time. Do I know my daughter or *what*?"

Natalie's hair was bright orange, and unlike her daughter, she never changed it—just touched it up. Natalie stood a good six-foot-two-inches in her sandals, and was skinny and bouncy like a pogo stick. Phil stood in front of her, staring at Sophia. His head full of hippy hair barely reached Natalie's chin.

"Sunshine! We've missed you so much," he said.

"Natalie . . . Phil . . . What brings you here?" asked a puzzled Sophia.

"Actually, I can't stay long," Natalie looked at her watch. "I'm on my way to a see my new teacher, Baba Yogananda Brahmahudi. He's leading a consciousness-raising retreat right near here, in Canyon City. Wanna come? This is going to be a really good one. Have you heard of Baba Yogananda Brahmahudi? He used to be called Seymour Ross, but that was before he attained what he calls 'The Fifth Level of Enlightenment.' He's going to show us how to get there. I think you'd love it, Sophia—a whole week of movement, aromatherapy, spirit dancing, psychodrama, rebirthing, rolfing, meditation, face painting, and massage. Sophia, I've been doing a lot of work lately to get in touch with my inner child; Baba Yogananda Brahmahudi has been helping me heal my Anahata chakra and I think this time I'm finally ready to give up all my attachments and reach a new level of awareness. Wanna come?"

"Well, Natalie, I'm awfully busy . . . ."

"There'll be lots of yummy veggies." Natalie opened her eyes wide, making slurping sounds and licking her lips to show Sophia how yummy the veggies would be. "And it's all in a supportive, playful, non-competitive atmosphere."

"Natalie, I really can't . . . ."

"Say no more," she said, looking at her watch again. "Phil can stay here with you. He doesn't go in for that kind of thing anyway. I've been helping him work on himself, but he's shy about sharing his personal growth with others. Maybe someday he'll be advanced enough to go to retreats, but right now we just have to accept him for where he is. We all have our karma to work through and he's doing the best he can, just as we all are. I'm very proud of the progress Phil has been making, and who knows? Maybe one day he'll become enlightened just like that," she snapped her fingers, "and we'll all be sitting at his feet. Anyway, I'm late. Gotta run. Toodles."

Natalie dashed off. Phil stayed on the porch, hat in hand, hound dog eyes glued to Sophia as they listened to Natalie slam the car door, start the engine, lay a patch, and race away.

"Sunshine," said Phil, "I can't tell you how much Natalie and I have missed you."

"Come on in, Phil," said Sophia.

Phil walked through the door and stopped on the other side. He stood there, watching Sophia and waiting for her to tell him what to do.

"Do you want to take off your coat, Phil? Can I take your hat?"

"Oh yeah, of course. What was I thinking?" he said, fumbling with his coat and hat. He handed them to Sophia who went to the hall closet and hung them up. When she returned, Phil was still standing at the very spot she had left him.

"Um . . . Phil, can I get you something to drink?"

"No, that's ok," Phil said. "Well . . . maybe some water. Would water be ok? No, wait a minute—I think it's time for juice. Natalie says I have to get my blood sugar under control. But come to think of it, I just had some juice an hour ago, well, forty-six minutes—so I probably shouldn't have any more for a while. Do you have any tea? Not the caffeinated kind—I'll be up all night. If you have herbal tea, that would be nice—except not peppermint. I don't like peppermint. Well . . . unless peppermint's all you've got. Then I guess it would be ok. Maybe I should just have some water. Where does your water come from? Have you had it tested lately?"

"I'll get you some water, Phil. Come sit down."

"You sure it's ok? I don't want to be a bother. I could go find a motel."

"Sit down, Phil. I'll be right back." Sophia ran upstairs, opened the bedroom door, and shook Lakshmi Jackson who was curled up in a warm, peaceful lump on the bed.

"Lakshmi!" Her volume was a whisper, but her tone was a roar. "Wake up and come downstairs. I need your help!"

She returned to Phil with his water.

"This place is incredible," he said. "You've done wonders with it."

"Thanks, Phil. I can't wait till Roland sees it."

Phil opened his mouth to say something, then closed it. The night was quiet. Father and daughter staring at each other; no words could express . . . .

Phil opened his mouth to try again. He didn't know what would come out, but he couldn't stand the silence.

"Sunshine, remember when we used to watch the Three Stooges together? Remember how we used to laugh and laugh? Whoop whoop!" he cried in a high falsetto. "Those were the good ol' days, weren't they? Didn't we have fun? I remember one time you laughed so hard, you peed. Where's your TV? Maybe we could watch the Three Stooges just like we used to."

"We don't have a TV, Phil."

"Oh, of course not. I didn't mean . . . I mean why would you have a TV? You've got so many important things to do now. How would you have time to watch TV? That was so stupid of me to ask. Do you still play that mandolin over there? Remember when we used to play together? If there's a guitar around, maybe we could jam just like the old days. Or maybe that's not such a good idea . . . ."

"Lakshmi!" Sophia called. "Are you coming?"

"Is Lakshmi here? I remember her. She was such a nice girl. Natalie always said . . . ."

"Hi, Phil," said Lakshmi, yawning as she padded down the stairs in her pajamas and slippers.

"Lakshmi," exclaimed Phil. "You've grown! Last time I saw you, you were this high." He lowered his hand to show her how high she used to be.

"I'm all grown up now," Lakshmi smiled. "How's Natalie?"

"Natalie's great," he answered. "Well . . . she's great and

she's not. I mean, she's done some incredible growth lately, but to tell you the truth, Natalie's having a little bit of a problem with all the new rules your friend Roland is making. Not that I have any complaints—and she's not complaining either—it's just that Natalie's a free soul and she's been feeling a little cramped lately, with the vaulted cloak and the day pass rationing, and the Marriage Reform Act. Last week, she got her orange slip telling her to come in and get her T. That's why she came down here for Baba Yogananda Brahmahudi's workshop. I mean, she would have anyway because she's grown so much since he's been her teacher—she's really getting in touch with her inner child. You should see her—she's really amazing. But I guess you could say she's on the lam."

"You see, Sophia?" Lakshmi said. "This is what I've been trying to tell you."

"Are you saying she *has* to get a T?" Sophia asked. "I guess I thought it was sort of voluntary."

"Oh, it's voluntary all right," said Lakshmi. "You can volunteer to get a T, or you can volunteer to get 're-educated,' or you can volunteer to take a cyanide pill."

Sophia thought she heard a hint of bitterness in Lakshmi's voice. "But," she countered, "Natalie wasn't wearing the vaulted cloak tonight."

"She wore it all the way over here," said Phil. "She changed into her regular clothes when we got to Rolandworld. Sunshine, I don't think you know how bad it is out there."

"Bad?"

"Yes, it is. Another thing about all these rules Roland is making up is, it's really messing up our sex life . . . ."

"Phil, let's not go there, ok?"

"I mean, these days it's hard for Natalie to . . . ."

"NO, PHIL!" Sophia shouted over him. "I DON'T WANT TO HEAR . . . ."

"And it's affecting me, too. Half the time, I can't even get it . . . ."

"RADDA RADDA RADDA RADDA!" Sophia held her ears and shouted as loud as she could, drowning Phil out.

"Phil," Lakshmi said, sweetly steering him away, "I'm glad you're here. How long do you think you'll stay?"

"That's a good question. Natalie is doing her inner child work at Baba Yogananda Brahmahudi's retreat, but after that she said she might go to the Red Rock Spa for mineral water therapy and colon cleansing. Then she's off to Sunny Sunnyland to see her other teacher, Gemini Moonbeam, who is going to read her chart. I thought I could stay here and help out."

"Help out?" Sophia cried. "Phil . . . ."

"I think that would be wonderful," said Lakshmi. "You can help me tend the gardens. There's always work to be done at the wildlife preserve. There are so many invasive species—it's a constant job."

"That would be great," said Phil. "I mean, I don't want to be a bother or anything—I just thought if I could help in some way . . . Anyway, it's been so long since I've seen Little Miss Sunshine here—I've missed her so much! This'll be great. It'll be just like old times—well, not *exactly* like old times—I mean, it's different now, but it's sort of the same, too."

"Lakshmi . . . ." Sophia flashed her a desperate look.

"Another way you can help, Phil," Lakshmi turned back to him, "is explain to your daughter what Rolandism is doing to the Free Nation."

There was a knock on the door.

"I'll get it," said Sophia, bugging her eyes at Lakshmi.

Sophia escaped into the hall and took a deep breath. She opened the front door.

"Mr. Jackson, what a surprise! Is that Mrs. Jackson you're carrying? Is she all right?"

"Yes, she's all right now," said Ben. "But she's getting heavy. May we come in?"

"Lakshmi!" Sophia called. "You'll never guess who's here!" Her spirits had just picked up.

* * * * * *

"I need a plan to take out the Evil Klezmer in Franistan," said Chosen Leader Delbert Thorne.

"Yes sir, the Evil Abdul Kashmir is certainly a problem in Yurkistan," said Aide #3.

"We've got to get rid of Kashmir, Mr. Chosen Leader," said Aide #2.

"In Yurkistan, Mr. Chosen Leader, sir, and if I may . . ." said Aide #1.

"Delbert," Secretary of Religion Roland Brand interrupted, "I think before you go . . . ."

"That's 'Mr. Chosen Leader.' Or 'sir'—take your pick."

"Right, Mr. Chosen Leader. As I was saying, Delbert, I think you've got some fires to put out right here at home before you go running halfway around the world to Yurkistan."

"That's the trouble with people these days," said the Chosen Leader. "You don't think large. You don't have a vision. See, I got a vision. And my vision is to go halfway around the world and take out the Evil Krapster in Frankenstein. What fires you talkin' about, Roland?"

"Well, Delbert . . . ."

"That's Mr. Chosen Leader to you."

"Right. Sorry. Anyway Delbert, we're having a difficult time getting Sunny Sunnyland on board with our new reforms. Bobism is a plague of permissiveness that's spreading across the entire west coast. Millions of people across the country are watching Bob's *Helluva Deal!* show on TV every day. If we don't stop Bob in his tracks, he could take over the entire Free Nation."

"Yeah, we gotta stop Bob. He's gettin' too big for his bloomers," agreed the Chosen Leader.

"Take him down," said Aide #3.

"Gettin' too big for his bloomers," said Aide #2.

"Gotta stop Bob," said Aide #1.

"And the other problem, Delbert," Roland continued, "is one that's close to my heart. There are a couple of silly little girls who have taken over my own Rolandworld and made a mockery of it. They've removed everything that was sacred, and turned all of Red Rock into a pagan playground. As long as this kind of evil exists, the Free Nation will never be free."

"I see your point," said the Chosen Leader. "We gotta wipe out evil wherever it shows its ugly head. Speaking of evil, how come you guys haven't given me a plan to take out the Evil Klaptrap of Burkistan?"

"The problem Mr. Chosen Leader, sir, is our troops are already stretched too thin," said Aide #1. "All our military forces are tied up bringing freedom to neighboring Borak and Boran. If we send them into Yurkistan, we'll lose Borak and Boran to the evil foreigners who live there."

"There *is* a solution, Delbert, if you're willing to think large," said Roland.

"I'm all ears, Mr. Secretary," said the Chosen Leader. "Well, not *all* ears, heh-heh." He chuckled as he patted his protrusion. Aides #3, #2, and #1 laughed heartily.

"Nuke him," said Roland.

"Nuke who?" asked the Chosen Leader.

"Nuke the Evil Abdul Kashmir."

"Nuke the Evil Kringle of Burkenstock?"

"Think large, Delbert. Your aides are right. We don't have any troops to spare. Abdul Kashmir is a slippery target. The beauty of nuking him is it won't require any troops *and . . . ,*" he paused dramatically, "you won't even have to make a direct hit."

"I think I see where you're going, Mr. Secretary," said Delbert.

"Remember when you wanted to attack Boran but you hit Borak by accident?"

Delbert scowled. Aides #3, #2, and #1 fidgeted. They knew their Chosen Leader didn't like to be reminded of this.

"Well, Delbert," continued Roland, undaunted, "if you nuke

Yurkistan, you could miss by the same amount and *still* take out the Evil Abdul Kashmir. You'll be amazed at the margin of error nukes will give you."

"I think I'm on to something," said the Chosen Leader.

"Good idea, sir," said Aide #3.

"Nuke Yurkistan," said Aide #2.

"Excellent thinking, Mr. Chosen Leader, sir. What about collateral damage, sir?" asked Aide #1.

"What about collateral damage, Mr. Secretary of Religion?" asked Thorne.

"Level Yurkistan and we will be rid of the most evil menace the world has ever known," said Roland, putting his arm around the Chosen Leader's shoulders. "Every war has collateral damage. Small price to pay for freedom, don't you think, Delbert?"

"Small price to pay to be rid, once and for all, of the evil Krishna from the Yukon."

"And the beauty of your plan," continued Roland, "is after you've nuked Yurkistan, no one in Red Rock or Sunny Sunnyland will dare stand up to you. You'll be able to march right in and have your way."

"First Yogastand, then Red Rock and Sunny Sunnyland," said Delbert.

"Then the world, Mr. Chosen Leader," said Roland.

Later, alone on his exercise bike, Chosen Leader Delbert Thorne pondered the conversation he'd had with his aides. He was pleased with the visionary new ideas he'd come up with, and with the largeness of his thinking.

That new Secretary of Religion was working out pretty well, too.

But, thought Delbert, *I'd better keep an eye on him. He's gettin' pretty tall for his trousers.*

* * * * * *

After laying a groggy Aruna upright on the couch, Ben Jackson unburdened the Sportsman's Special and his MX-247 Dematerializer from his shoulder and laid them on the floor. Dressed in full camouflage uniform, he paced the room as he told Sophia, Lakshmi, and Phil the full story of events leading to the formulation of his two-pronged plan to bring Aruna to Rolandworld for a change of scenery and to kill Roland Brand.

As Ben talked, Sophia sat with a comforting arm around the dazed Aruna Jackson.

"I had no idea," Sophia said when Ben finished his story. "I thought Roland Brand was such a cool guy."

"Dad, you're not serious about killing Roland, are you?" Lakshmi asked.

"I've never been so serious about anything in my life," said Ben.

"Lakshmi," Aruna said in a weak and shaky voice.

"Yes, mother?"

"Where is your vaulted cloak? Where is your shawl? Hurry girl. Put them on and get down on your knees and pray for Dad's forgiveness before Uncle Ominus comes to get you. Don't you know he's on his way?"

"Mother, I don't think Dad . . . ."

"May I say something about that?" Phil interrupted. "My wife, Natalie—I think you've met her, Aruna—she has a really good teacher named Baba Yogananda Brahmahudi, and he says when you reach a higher state of consciousness, you give up all your attachments. You even give up attachment to Dad and Nebulon. I know this is true, because Natalie is almost there. The only attachment she's still clinging to is the attachment to letting go of attachments. Natalie says . . . ."

"As I was saying, Mother," interrupted Lakshmi, "I don't think Dad is as cruel as you think."

"Oh, you'd be surprised," said Aruna. "Your dad can be very cruel. He wants to kill Roland, and he wants him to die slowly."

"I meant *Dad*, not Dad," said Lakshmi.

"Oh, *Dad*," said Aruna.

"You're right, Lakshmi." Ben sounded sarcastic. "Dad is kind. Dad is good. He would never kill anyone. He just smites them."

"Bob says Dad learned from His mistakes, Dad," said Lakshmi. "He doesn't go around smiting people like He did in His youth."

"That's why I have to smite Roland," said Ben. "I can't wait around for Dad to do it for me."

"Maybe you're wrong, Mr. Jackson," said Sophia. "Maybe if you're patient, Dad *will* smite Roland."

"I'm not going to smite Roland," said Phil.

"You're not *Dad*, Dad," said Sophia. "You're Phil."

"And Dad, I don't think you should be playing Dad," said Lakshmi.

"Lakshmi!" Aruna exploded. "Don't talk to your dad that way! Haven't you been taught that Dad knows best?"

"Yes, I'm very sorry Mother," said Lakshmi. "Of course, Dad knows best. He teaches us to be kind to every man, woman, beast, and sprout."

"I never told you such a thing," said Ben.

"No, Dad, *Dad* told me."

"Dad told you he was going to kill Roland Brand," Aruna reminded Lakshmi. "That doesn't sound very kind to me."

"Funny you should mention that," said Phil. "Natalie was just saying the other day . . . ."

"Phil," Sophia interrupted.

"Don't call me 'Phil' anymore, Sunshine. I'd like you to start calling me 'Dad,'" said Phil.

"Why?" asked Sophia.

"Because I *am* your dad," he replied. "Natalie always wanted you to call us by our first names because she didn't want you to think of us as authoritarian. But all this talk about 'Dad' makes me realize that I miss being called 'Dad' by my Little

Miss Sunshine." His eyes started to tear up.

"Ok ok," Sophia relented. "Dad it is, Dad. So Dad, what do *you* think Dad would want Lakshmi's dad to do?"

"Well . . . I don't know for sure. On one hand, Dad is a loving Dad. Dad even loves Roland. But Dad also loves Lakshmi's dad who wants to kill Roland. Maybe Dad loves Lakshmi's dad so much, he doesn't want him to feel frustrated, but then if Lakshmi's dad kills Roland, he'd be killing one of Dad's creations . . . I don't know. It's like my dad used to say . . . ."

"Dad!" Sophia was exasperated.

"Praise Dad," whispered Aruna.

"Dad?" said Lakshmi.

No answer.

"Dad?" she tried again.

"Oh," said Ben. "Are you talking to me?"

"Yes, Dad," said Lakshmi. "Dad, I'd like to tell you about the Dad I know. He's kind and compassionate. He's a wonderful, loving Dad."

Ben broke down and began blubbering. "Oh thank you, Lakshmi. That's the nicest thing you've ever said to me."

"Oh," Lakshmi backtracked, "I wasn't talking about *you*, Dad, I was talking about *Dad*."

"Oh," said Ben, drying his eyes.

The phone rang.

"I'LL GET IT!" cried Sophia and Lakshmi together. They almost knocked each other down as they raced to the kitchen to get the phone.

Sophia won.

"Hello . . . Oh, really? . . . She is? . . . Ok . . . Yeah, ok . . . We'll be right there."

She hurried to the living room and announced: "Natalie's in jail. "

XV. THE ELECTRONIC BABYSITTER

The **RRR** Pledge:

> *I Pledge Allegiance*
> *To the Flag*
> *Of the United Regions of the Free Nation;*
> *And to the Regressive Party*
> *For which it Stands,*
> *One Country,*
> *Under Dad,*
> *Invincible,*
> *With Liberty and Justice for All White Men*
> *Over the Age of Twenty-One*
> *With the Following Exceptions:*

Members of the Progressive Party, Suspected Slackers, Draftees, Gays, and Other Enemies of the State.

* * * * * *

ALONG WITH RELIGION, ANOTHER FORCE THAT WAS EXPERIENCING its Golden Era in the Free Nation was television. Free Nationers watched an average of six hours per day, which took up one quarter of their lifetime. If they were lucky enough to get eight hours of sleep, they would spend three quarters as much time watching television as they did sleeping. Or another way to look at it was, Free Nationers spent fourteen hours a day in the combined activities of sleeping and watching. Almost sixty per cent of their lives! Add in work hours and commuting time, and there went the day. They called television the "Electronic Babysitter" (EB).

One of the amazing features of EB was, it moved really fast. In a fifteen-second commercial, an EB viewer might see thirty visual images or more. This caused Free Nationers who grew up on a steady diet of fleeting images to think quickly. Their nimble minds flitted from one thought to the next, without ever landing on an idea. On the down side, they found it hard to look at a tree.

EB taught Free Nationers the value of "sound bytes." A sound byte was created when a concept was boiled down to an idea, then filtered into a statement. The statement was then boiled some more and strained until all that was left was a memorable image. The broth at the surface of the memorable image was known as a "sound byte." Sound bytes insured that viewers wouldn't have to waste their valuable time sifting through a tangle of mind-boggling information. They were a shorthand—a code based on the assumption that everyone was starting from the same premise, enabling the sound-byter to get right to the point. For example, an unskilled politician might say:

"In order to most effectively address the problems that Abdul Kashmir presents to the Free Nation, we must put the situation in historical and cultural context and unravel the multi-leveled complexities that are inherent in our current conundrum."

The hapless fool would proceed to put everyone to sleep with a dissertation on the history of the region, the geopolitical intricacies, options and their ramifications, realistic goals and the sacrifices required to achieve them. Whereas, the wise politician would say:

"We have to kill the Evil Abdul Kashmir."

In the world of electronic babysitters, the most skilled sound-byter won every time.

Another way EB improved the citizens' lives was it helped them know not only *what* to think, but *how* to think it. Watching EB, people saw a world in which everybody had lots of things, and all those things seemed to make them so *happy*. It made watchers think if they had lots of things, they'd be happy too. They did their best to buy all the things EB told them to buy, but there was always something new—it was hard to keep up.

EB taught people that the world was actually a pretty simple place if you stopped to think about it. There were good guys and bad guys; right and wrong. Most problems took no longer than an hour to resolve. Political programs taught people that every issue had two equal but opposite sides, and if you yelled louder, longer, faster, and more cleverly than the other guy, you'd prove you were right.

EB helped people figure out what was important in life. For example, the Golden Era's most famous movie star, Beau Swanson, got into big trouble when he kidnapped his mistress and held her at gunpoint in a church for thirty days. His goal was to prevent her from telling his wife his deep, dark secret, which was that he was head of a sex slave ring. He had to stop his mistress from spilling the beans because he was afraid it would ruin his marriage. The press held 'round the clock vigils, camping outside the church and reporting every breaking development. Then there was the trial that dragged on for a year. The case of Beau Swanson had everything: Fame, fortune, sex, and violence. The media impressed upon the public the extreme urgency of the matter. Most people who could not locate the Free Nation on a map could tell you the names of Beau Swanson's wife, mistress, and each of his sex slaves. It was a matter of priorities.

In the end, Beau Swanson was found not guilty. He was just too famous, handsome, and charming for the star-struck jury to put away. Coincidentally, the day he was acquitted was the same day Delbert Thorne accidentally bombed Borak instead of Boran. The press explained people should be outraged that Beau Swanson was let off the hook. And they were.

Some EB shows played recordings of people laughing so viewers could learn what was funny. It taught people what kind of food they wanted to eat, what kind of afflictions they shouldn't have to put up with, and what was attractive in a partner. It taught people that being stupid and ignorant wasn't all that bad, really. In fact, it could be downright charming. EB watchers learned that "street smarts" were good, but beware of the intelligent and informed. They were not like you, and not to be trusted.

The Electronic Babysitter gave people so much power! If they didn't like what one show was telling them, all they had to do was point and click, and presto! There would be another show they might like better. It was magic! A person could sit in front of his EB and "channel surf" for six hours a day, and have total control of his or her life.

Most Free Nationers hoped one day they would be beamed up to Nebulon where they would be asked what they did with their lives. They were prepared to say proudly, "I watched a hundred and fifty-five thousand hours of EB."

* * * * * *

"Ladies and gentlemen, what time is it?"

"It's time for *Helluva Deal!*"

"Yes, it's time for *Helluva Deal!* Starring . . . Your favorite filibustering', flibbertyfibbin' fountain of faith . . . I-i-i-va-a-an Bunt!"

"YAY! YAY, IVAN!"

"Also starring . . . those two wacky Smith brothers, E-e-eldon and La-a-ar-ry!"

"YAY! ELDON AND LARRY!"

"And co-starring: The smashing and beautiful Natasha and Bunny!"

"YA-A-A-AY!"

"And NOW! . . . Who's the man who talks to Dad?"

"BOB!"

"Who's the man who wrote Dad's book?"

"BOB!"

"And who's the man who spreads Dad's word to you and me and every man, woman, beast, and sprout?"

"IT'S BOB!"

"Yes, it's time for Bob, ladies and gentlemen! And if it's time for Bob, it's TI-I-IME . . . FO-O-OR . . ."

"*HELLUVA DEAL!*"

"Yes, it's time for Helluva Deal. And now . . . . The star of the show . . . Mr. *Helluva* Deal himself . . . Please welco-o-o-me . . . BOB!"

"BOB! BOB! *HELLUVA* DEAL! IT'S BOB!"

"Thank you, thank you." Bob moseyed onto the stage, holding up his hands to show he didn't deserve such a fuss. Then he launched into his familiar theme song. When the studio audience heard the opening line, everyone jumped in eagerly and sang along.

Free Nationers were funny that way.

They acted so excited and surprised when told to do something they knew was coming all along. For example, the Free Nation had a dance called the "square dance." Participants would form a roomful of squares consisting of four couples each, while a "caller" stood above them on a stage, giving them orders so they would know what to do. Following the caller's instructions gave the dancers great joy. A square dance was considered successful when everybody followed instructions happily and well.

At the end of a series of maneuvers, the caller would order, "Now allemande left and dosey-doe," and the dancers would erupt with glee that they were being told to do this. Maybe they were relieved that they had done everything the caller had told them to do without messing up. Maybe they liked doing something easy and familiar. Hard to tell.

But when Bob started singing the *Helluva Deal!* theme song, the audience jumped on it like a bunch of square dancers being told to allemande left:

> *Dad is great!*
> *Dad is good!*
> *Come and love Him*
> *Like you should!*
> *The Book of Bob*
> *Is understood!*
> *Re-e-eal . . .*
> *Re-e-eal . . .*
> *HELLUVA-deal!*

"Thank you, brothers and sisters. Thank you. And Dad thanks you too."

"Thank *you*, Bob!" they shouted.

"We have a great show for you tonight, brothers and sisters. Dad has some very important things he wants me to tell you. But first, we have some special people in the audience tonight. Ethyl Widebody is here all the way from the Eastern Region, and guess what? Today is her birthday. She's ninety-two today! Ethyl, stand up."

Gracious Ethyl stood, and everybody cheered.

"Brandon and Jennifer are here from the Midwest Region. They're on their honeymoon. Brandon? Jennifer?"

The newlyweds stood up while the audience hooted and hollered.

"Brandon, Jennifer, it's your *honeymoon!* What are you doing *here?*"

Uproarious laughter.

"Little Brenda Miller is here tonight. She's five years old. She wrote me a note in her own handwriting. It says, '*Deer Bob. Plees ask Dad to find my cat. Not Tiger. He's ded. The othr wun. Blackie. Love, Brenda*'

"Well, Brenda," continued Bob, "I'll talk to Dad and see what He can do to help you find Blackie. Isn't she cute, ladies and gentlemen?"

Everyone clapped for cute little Brenda Miller.

"Ok, everybody. We've sung our song and said our hellos, so you know what it's time for now?

"It's time for 'Dad's Turn,' Bob!"

"That's right, ladies and gentlemen. It's time for 'Dad's Turn.' This is the portion of the show when we get real quiet and wait for Dad to talk to me. When he does, I will tell you what He said.

"Are you ready for 'Dad's Turn?'"

"We're ready, Bob!"

"O—K—then here we go."

Bob got real quiet. The audience got quiet with him. They waited with reverence, knowing soon Dad would be right there in the room with them and Bob.

"Yes, Dad, yes," said Bob looking toward the ceiling. He nodded to the audience. Contact had been made.

"Yes, Dad, I'll tell them . . . Are you sure? . . . Sorry—of course you're sure. You're Dad . . . Really? No joke? Cross your heart and hope to . . . I know, I know—I'm sorry. It's just that I'm up here in front of millions of EB viewers, and I just want to make sure you're not playing one of your jokes . . . Ok . . . . Thanks, Dad. Yeah, yeah, I'll tell them . . . Did you win that bet with Uncle Ominus last week? . . . You did but he won't pay up? Isn't that just like him . . . Yeah, right . . . Oh, by the way, do you think you could find Brenda Miller's cat? . . . No, no, not

Tiger . . . Yeah, I know he's dead. She wants you to find Blackie
. . . Ok, well, keep looking, will you? . . . Thanks, Dad . . . Ok,
I'll tell them. Boy, are they going to be surprised! . . . Yeah, I
know yesterday's show sucked. But you've gotta admit, the
guests were awful . . . I know, I know, I was off, too . . . . I'll try
to do better today. I'll talk to you after the show . . . Ok, Dad . . .
Love you, too. Bye."

Bob turned back to his studio audience, which was hushed
and awed after witnessing his talk with Dad.

"There He is, ladies and gentlemen. Put your hands together
for the Big Guy!"

"YA-A-A-AY!"

"I have good news today, brothers and sisters."

"What is it, Bob? Tell us the good news."

"The good news is: You're free! Dad says my First
Messenger Roland Brand has gotten a little carried away, and the
message he's spreading isn't quite what Dad had in mind."

A confused murmur washed through the room.

"Dad has a special message for the women in this room and
around the Free Nation. He says, 'Remove your shawls! I can't
see your faces!'

"Dad says, 'Remove your vaulted cloaks. I want to see your
lovely bodies that I created. Besides, those cloaks are too damn
hot!'

"Dad says, 'If you haven't gotten T-ed up yet, don't waste
your time. If you have, not to worry—you can always get your T
removed. It'll hurt worse than the tattoo itself, but small price to
pay for saving face.'"

As Bob spoke, the joyous women in the audience cheered,
ripping off their wrappings and tossing them into the air. Soon,
the stage was littered with cloaks and shawls. Bob was covered,
too.

This scene was repeated all across the Free Nation. Ecstatic
women tossing away their constraints in living rooms,
workplaces, and out the windows. In some cities, it seemed to be

raining shawls and cloaks.

"But this is just the beginning," continued Bob. "Dad says He's repealing all of First Messenger Roland's Marriage and Abomination Reforms. He says Roland really went overboard with that stuff. Dad says the reason He made sex so much fun is so you can enjoy it. Wait a minute . . . He's talking to me again . . . Ok, got it, Dad. Dad says:

'Go ahead! Knock yourselves out!'

"Wait, wait . . . He's saying something else. Now He's saying,

'Not here. Wait till you get home.'

"Another thing he wants me to tell you is to use birth control. Have you noticed how crowded it's getting? 'Stop making so many babies!' Dad says.

"He's also telling you to stop giving gay people such a bad time. He says, 'Gays are my children, too, and if you keep making babies, I'm just going to keep making more gay people, so get used to it.'

"Dad says stop worrying about Nebulon and Uncle Ominus and rocket ships and Planet Ug and praying in every direction. Stop chewing your leg off! He wants you to know that you visit Nebulon and Planet Ug every day of your life—which one you visit depends on your mood. Where are you right now?"

"Nebulon, Bob!"

"Dad also wants me to let you in on a little secret: He says Uncle Ominus really isn't as bad as everybody says. He and Dad have a regular poker night on Fridays. They keep a running tab, and so far, Uncle Ominus owes Dad over eight billion dollars. Dad says He'd hate for anything to happen to Uncle Ominus before he pays up."

The studio audience was never so happy as that night. This

was Bob's best show by far. It was as if, with each of Dad's new proclamations, he'd opened another gate at the animal shelter. The people were like dogs and cats breaking out of their cages, running down the corridors of the humane society shouting, "*Helluva* deal!"

"Now Dad's telling me He wants me to make a phone call," said Bob. "Natasha? Bunny? Can you bring me the phone, please?"

Natasha and Bunny entered stage left, wearing skimpy bikinis and carrying a small end table with a phone sitting on it. The crowd applauded, congratulating Natasha and Bunny on a job well done.

"Dad's telling me to call Roland Brand," Bob confided as he dialed. The audience heard the phone ringing on the other end, and then:

"You have reached the office of Secretary of Religion, The Honorable Roland Brand. If you are a True Believer, press one now. If you are a slacker, press two now. If you don't know, stay on the line and the next available operator will collect your pertinent data so you may be re-educated."

Bob winked at his audience and pressed one.

"You have reached the True Believer's line to the office of the Secretary of Religion, The Honorable Roland Brand. If you are Chosen Leader Delbert Thorne, press one now. If you are Dad, press two now. If you have reached this line in error, press three now, and the next available operator will collect your pertinent data so you may be re-educated. If you are not Chosen Leader Thorne or Dad, but still think you are important enough to be worthy of an audience with The Honorable Roland Brand, please stay on the line. And Dad help you if you're wrong."

Bob nodded, smiling at his audience, and stayed on the line. "He'll be so surprised to hear from me," he whispered with his hand over the phone.

"Hello, this is the office of the Secretary of Religion, The Honorable Roland Brand. This call may be monitored in order to track down enemies of the state. Please state your name."

"Bob."

"Occupation?"

"Dad's Messenger."

"Date of birth?"

"The day Dad came to me and told me to write His book."

"Purpose of this call?"

"To tell my First Messenger Roland that Dad says, 'Lighten up.'" Bob held a forefinger up to his lips, signaling his tittering flock to stay quiet.

"I will see if Secretary Brand is available."

Bob waited a moment. Then:

"Bob! So good of you to call! I'm watching your show. You know I'm a big fan."

"Hi, Roland, long time no see."

"What's that you say? Wrong time to flee?"

"Roland, is your EB still on?"

"Yes . . . ."

"Turn the sound down on your EB, Roland."

"Oh—ok—hold on a second . . . Is that better?"

"Much better."

"Bob, as I said, I've been watching your show, and I have to admit I'm a bit taken aback."

"Me too, Roland. But then, I'm always taken aback when I talk with Dad. After all this time, He still gives me chills."

"Bob, how do you know it's really Dad you're talking to?"

"Gee, Roland, I know His voice pretty well by now. He can imitate anybody, but nobody can imitate Him."

"Let me try another way . . . You come on EB every day, telling the Free Nation that you have the inside track to Dad. You've got everybody believing Dad wants them to do all kinds of radical things like throw away the shawl and cloak and have sex just for the fun of it. You see where I'm going, Bob?"

"Well, I'm not sure. But Dad also wants you to . . . ."

"I guess what I'm saying," Roland interrupted, "is how are

we in the Free Nation to know that you're not some sort of crack-pot who's hearing voices in his head?"

"Because Dad says . . . ."

"How do we know you're not making all this up because you have a hidden agenda to take over the world?"

"Roland, remember when . . . ."

"As a matter of fact, Bob, I've been talking with Dad myself, lately. And the conversations *I've* had with Him are quite different from the ones you claim to be having."

"Oh?" said Bob. "That's nice that Dad is talking to you now, too. Funny He never mentioned it to me. Oh, well . . . Don't you love talking with Dad? Has He told you the one about the preacher and the rabbi yet?"

"No, He hasn't. But my point is . . . ."

"Oh, that's a really good one. It seems there was this preacher and a rabbi, and they were . . . ."

"Bob!"

Roland took a deep breath and started over, more calmly this time. "Bob, here is what I want you and all Free Nationers to know: The reforms I have instituted are for the good of the country. Only when they are followed strictly and to the letter by every citizen will we be free to practice the One True Religion. Anyone who disputes my decrees is an agent of Uncle Ominus and an enemy of the state. *Anyone!* Do you get my point, Bob?"

"Roland, are you sure you turned off your EB?" asked Bob. "You still . . . ."

"My fellow Free Nationers, hear me now! I speak not to you as your Secretary of Religion. I come to you as Dad's spokesman. *I* am the one He speaks to now. The *only* one."

Roland paused, and a dark dread blanketed the Free Nation.

"Dad wants you to know his ways are harsh, but that's only because He loves you so much. Tough love. He has to weed out the slackers in your midst and make it possible for *you* to go to Nebulon. You do want to go to Nebulon, don't you?"

"Yes, Roland," said the studio audience. "Yes, Roland,"

said the citizenry in living rooms throughout the country.

"I thought so," said Roland. "I will be speaking more on this in the coming weeks. Dad's rules are going to get stricter. He's asked me to step up the program, because He's coming for one thousand, one hundred and eleven of us very soon. He wants to make sure He picks the right ones.

"So look for my new book, the **RRR Manifesto**, coming to your nearest bookseller soon. In it, you will read about my new, harsher regime, which all True Believers will recognize as the only road to Nebulon. You will read about how *YOU* can help Dad weed out the slackers so that *YOU* will have a chance.

"In the meantime, beware of false prophets who claim they speak to Dad. Especially pathetic, middle-aged men in shabby suits. They're fakes and not long for this world. Woe to him who listens to prophets other than me! *I'm* the only one to whom Dad speaks! *I AM THE ONE!*

"Nice talking to you, Bob." And with that, Roland hung up.

"Gee," said Bob, "I didn't even get to tell him about the preacher and the rabbi."

The studio audience filed out. They avoided looking at Bob, who stood alone on the stage, still holding the phone. They turned away before they could see Ivan, Eldon and Larry, Natasha and Bunny, forming a teary-eyed circle around him.

Across the Free Nation, women picked up their discarded shawls and vaulted cloaks, and donned them once again. The country heaved a collective sigh as the citizens hunkered down to await their next instructions for the best way to get to Nebulon.

* * * * * *

High in a stone tower overlooking the capital of the Free Nation, a haggard Donald LaFarge hunched over his small splintered desk beneath the one barred window his cold cell had to offer, scribbling by candle light, deep through the night and into morning. The desk was piled over his head with papers, and the floor littered with the overflow.

He heard the clinking of keys, followed by the creaking of the iron handle on the thick oak door. It groaned open.

"Ya done yet?" asked Deputy Secretary of Religion Orvil Swain, illuminated by the lantern he carried in front of him.

LaFarge didn't look up. "I'm getting there."

"Roland wants ta know how soon ya gonna be done."

"Tell Roland I'm writing as fast as I can."

"Roland says things'll go a lot better for ya if ya finish sooner rather than later. Hell, he still might even hold a seat for ya on the rocket ship." Orvil laughed.

"Tell Roland you can't rush art. It'll be ready when it's ready.

"Art? . . . Shee-oot!" said Orvil Swain. "Since when did you become an '*ar-tiste*'? Anyhow, can'tchoo read yer own writin'? Says right there in the first chapter there ain't gonna be no more art."

"Right," said LaFarge. "Well, Roland won't have to worry about art in this book."

"Well, tha's good. So when ya gonna be done?"

"I'm almost there."

"Roland wants to go on EB tonight an' address the nation. He wants to be able to show 'em that-there *RRR Manifesto* when he goes on. He's gonna be real disappointed if'n he don't have no *RRR Manifesto* to show folks. You don't want Roland to be disappointed, do ya?"

"No, I sure don't."

"Cause Roland don't like to be disappointed," continued the Deputy Secretary of Religion. "He might want me to come in an' do a little more re-educatin'. You don't want no more re-educatin', do ya?"

LaFarge shivered. "No, Orvil, I sure don't. Tell Roland he'll have his *RRR Manifesto* by tonight."

"Tha's good," said Orvil Swain. "Tha's real good. An'

don't be wastin' no time facin' every which direction an' sayin' them prayers every fifteen minutes. We ain't got time for that now."

"Don't worry, Orvil. Now go away, will you? I've got work to do."

"All right-ee. I best be on my way. Oh, I almost forgot, Roland said he wants more o' them '*thees*' and '*thou shalts*' an' stuff like that."

"You already told me. I spiced it up."

"Also, '*smites*.' Roland wants lots o' them '*smites*' in there."

'Got 'em."

"Good," said the Deputy Secretary of Religion. "Now you finish up in time, hear? Praise Roland. Praise Dad."

"Praise Roland. Praise Dad," said Donald LaFarge.

XVI. SHE'S IN THE JAILHOUSE NOW

EXCERPT FROM THE **RRR MANIFESTO**, CHAPTER 1:

Persons suspected of committing the following crimes will be deemed unsuitable for re-education or voluntary resignation; they will proceed directly to the Office of Religion where they will be fired:

1) Failure to recognize the One True Religion. This failure includes, but is not limited to the following infractions:
    a) Facing wrong direction while saying quarter-hour prayers.
    b) Failure by a woman to wear her shawl and vaulted cloak.
    c) Failure by a man to enforce the shawl and cloak strictures upon his wives.
    d) Failure to invoke Roland's name when speaking to Dad.
    e) Any mention of Bobism.

2) Sexual activity for any purpose other than procreation.

> *a) Female perpetrators will be fired; male perpetrators may be considered for re-education.*
> *b) Gay perpetrators of either gender will be fired.*
> *c) Use of birth control by either gender will be grounds for firing on the spot.*

3) Failure by any male adult to regularly ingest erectile dysfunction drugs. With the extra workload inherent in the mandatory polygamy laws, it is deemed necessary for even the highest functioning males to employ supplemental erectile enhancement.

4) Consumption of alcohol or any drugs not deemed necessary for erectile enhancement. This shall include but not be limited to: Hard liquor, beer, wine, marijuana, cocaine, coffee, tea, tobacco, cough syrup.

5) Teaching of any school subject that does not incorporate the One True Religion as the basis for curriculum. Example:
> *Wrong Method: 2+2=4*
> *Correct Method: Roland says 2+2=4*

6) Failure to meet quota of oil, water, and paper use as stipulated in the Mandatory Resource Consumption Act. Reminder: Each Free Nationer must do his or her part to assure there be no resources left for the slackers when the one thousand, one hundred and eleven of Dad's Children are beamed to Nebulon.

7) Failure to earn enough money to live above the poverty line. Poverty is an abomination and a reflection of Dad's displeasure with you.

8) Failure to respond to Tattoo Summons from the Office of Religion. All women must receive and display "T" tattoo on *forehead; all men must receive and display "**RRR**" on forehead.*

*9) Failure to properly exhibit Dual Loyalty Flags on premises and in vehicles. Dual Loyalty Flags must be displayed with **RRR** banner above; Free Nation banner below. Free Nation flag may be of smaller or equal size to **RRR** banner, however, may not exceed the **RRR** flag in size.*

*10) Production, distribution, display, participation in, or viewing of any film, EB (Electronic Babysitter) program, play, music, or art which is not approved by the **RRR** Freedom of Religion Board.*

*11) Reading, writing, or distribution of any book or written publication other than the **RRR Manifesto**. (Memo to Bob: This means you!)*

12) Failure by any citizen to fire a fellow citizen whom he or she suspects of committing a fireable offense; failure by any citizen to fire a fellow citizen whom he or she suspects of not firing a citizen whom he or she suspects of committing a fireable offense.

Reminder: Roland loves you. So does Dad. That's why they want to make sure those around you do the right thing.

* * * * * *

"Everybody reach for the sky!"

Standing in a circle, they reached for the sky.

"Stretch your arms high!"

They groaned in pain as their bodies were torturously stretched.

"I want you to scream!"

"YA-A-A-A-AH!" they screamed.

"I want you to jump!"

They jumped.

"Now jump and scream!"

They jumped and screamed.

"Now, close your eyes and feel Mother Earth's sacred energy as it surges through your feet, up your legs, through your straight spine, into your neck, and out the top of your head," said Natalie.

Her prison guards, barefoot and in a circle, closed their eyes and felt the energy.

"You're all so beautiful," she said. "I think you've really progressed today. Remember—when you stretch your body, you are stretching your soul. Are all our little souls stretched?"

"Yes, Natalie."

"Now—who would like to share his inner work with us today?"

"I would, Natalie."

"Sergeant Drillmaster. What did you get in touch with?

"Well, Natalie," Sergeant Drillmaster tried to begin. "This is hard to talk about."

"That's why we're here," said Natalie. "This is a loving group of men who will support you in your hard-to-talk-about feelings. Isn't that right, everybody?"

"That's right, Natalie."

"Well," Sergeant Drillmaster continued, "whenever I'm on the firing squad and we're shooting a slacker, I . . . ."

"Yes," said Natalie. "You can tell us. It's safe."

"I always miss on purpose." Sergeant Drillmaster broke down crying.

Natalie's eyes got moist too. "And why do you miss?"

"I do-o-on't kn-o-o-ow!" he wailed. "Ever since I was young, I've hated to kill things—even when I knew it was Dad's will."

"Has anybody else here ever had those feelings?" Natalie wondered.

A few men nodded and muttered yes.

"You see?" said Natalie. "Sometimes, when you're on a

firing squad, it takes more courage to miss the slacker than it does to shoot him."

"But what about Dad?" he asked.

"You must trust the Dad in your heart. If your inner Dad tells you to miss, you go right ahead and miss."

"But Roland says . . . ."

"Roland thinks all slackers should be shot. I support him in that. He has his karma to work out, and that's the path he's on. You don't want to shoot slackers—that's your path and I support you in that too. What do you think, everybody? Do you support Sergeant Drillmaster in his path to not shoot slackers?"

"We support you, Sergeant Drillmaster!"

"Thank you, everybody," he sobbed. "This means so much to me."

"I admire your courage, Sergeant Drillmaster," said Natalie. "Thank you so much for sharing with us. We've all grown from hearing your story."

"Thank you, Natalie," he whimpered. "I feel much better."

"Does anybody else want to share with us?"

"I will," said Sergeant Gonzalez.

"Good, Sergeant Gonzalez. What did you get in touch with today?"

"Well," Sergeant Gonzalez hesitated and gulped, "today I got in touch with little Andy. That's my name, you know— Andy. My mommy used to call me Andito." He began to cry.

"Andito," said Natalie in a soothing voice. "What does little Andito want to tell us now?"

"Andito didn't want to be a prison guard!" Sergeant Gonzalez bawled. "Andito wanted to be a figure skater! But when my father found out, he went into a rage and told me to never mention skating again."

"Poor Andito," said Natalie. "It's never too late, you know. You can skate anytime you want, Andito. You can skate right now. Come on, everybody! Let's show little Andito how he can skate."

And the next thing you knew, all the prison guards were skating barefoot, up and down the cellblock—twirling and pirouetting, and pretty soon, Sergeant Gonzalez was skating and blubbering. He was right in the middle of a triple axel when: "Natalie!" Sophia entered the prison with Phil trailing behind her.

"Natalie!" cried Phil. "Are you ok?"

"Of course, I'm ok," grinned Natalie. "We're skating. Come join us."

Sergeant Gonzalez executed a triple Lutz, followed by a double Salchow.

"What's my score?" he called to Natalie.

"A ten!" she called back. "No deductions here! Everybody gets a ten!"

"Um, Natalie," said Sophia as her mother skated by. "We heard you were in jail."

"Jail's a state of mind," Natalie called over her shoulder. "Your body might be locked in a cell, but if your heart and mind are open, you're free!"

"Sophia! Phil! Are you going to skate with us or not?"

The guards stopped skating and froze like statues.

"Did you say 'Sophia?'" asked Sergeant Drillmaster.

They all turned in her direction.

"Green hair . . . tattoos . . . her mother is Natalie Wise," said Sergeant Gonzalez.

"Men, I think we have Sophia Wise here," said Sergeant Drillmaster.

"Are you Sophia Wise?" asked Sergeant Gonzalez.

"Yes, I am," said Sophia, looking puzzled.

The guards closed in. "Sophia Wise," said Sergeant Drillmaster, "I have a warrant for your arrest. Secretary of Religion Roland Brand has declared you an enemy of the state and a Slacker-in-the-First-Degree. Men . . . ."

The guards grabbed Sophia and whisked her away.

"Sophia!" cried Phil.

"Tell Lakshmi!" she called as she was hustled out of sight.

"This could give Sophia an amazing opportunity for growth," said Natalie, following fast behind Phil as he ran to the car. "She can use this experience to really get in touch with herself."

Phil started the engine, and they sped off.

"I wish you could have seen the changes those men went through. The way they opened up was so inspiring. It's so hard for men to express their feelings—they need a wise woman to help them get in touch with their female side. I'm so happy to be able to facilitate them—it's an honor really, to witness their process. I bet I grew from their work as much as they did . . . ."

And on and on, all the way to Rolandworld.

* * * * * *

Actually, Chosen Leader Delbert Thorne was pretty easy to steer, Roland thought. Not at all like a finely tuned sports car with pinpoint precision. No, he was more like a pick-up truck. You had to muscle him and you couldn't take corners too tight. But you could blast your way out of any jam with Delbert— bounce over potholes, fly through the air, land hard, bounce again, and away you go. Stuck in the mud? No problem. Just ram the thing into four-wheel and bust on outta there. The main thing was keep a firm grip on the wheel, put your foot to the floor, and power on through.

Or maybe steering Delbert was like dancing with a clumsy fat girl, Roland reconsidered. If you didn't take charge, things could get really ugly. However, if you just grabbed a handful of midriff bulge and put some shoulder into it, she'd be happy to stumble in any direction you pushed.

Roland preferred finesse. He'd rather drive a Maserati than a pick-up truck. He'd rather tango with a lithe beauty who could match his grace. *But you have to play the cards you're dealt*, thought Roland. Someday soon, the world will be my Maserati, but for now, I have to play the Delbert card. I have to drive the Delbert truck. I have to dance the Delbert dance. Pick your metaphor.

The direction Roland was steering the Delbert truck was toward a world religion called "Rolandism." He was making progress. His creation of the **RRR** Freedom of Religion Board had been a big step forward. Through it, he was able to control the information that was disseminated into and ingested by the populace. The publishing of the **RRR Manifesto**, which Donald LaFarge had been so gracious to ghostwrite, had been a huge success. The simultaneous release of the book along with his prime-time address to the Free Nation, followed by the firing of two dozen slackers, convinced the Free Nation that Roland was the One True Spokesman for the One True Religion.

Bob was a nagging problem. Roland had no trouble steering Delbert into cutting Bob off the air, but he was having trouble negotiating the curve that would convince Delbert Thorne that Bob needed to be put in jail and fired. Always the politician, Delbert was testing the waters. He wanted to wait until Bob had been off the air awhile and his popularity had waned, thus avoiding a backlash. Roland didn't care about a backlash—he could ride it out. In fact, if the backlash whipped back in Delbert's direction, so much the better. Delbert could take the fall and Roland would rise to the top.

Another bumpy road Roland was driving Delbert on was the Yurkistan issue. He had gotten as far as convincing Delbert that nukes would be the best option. However, Roland was of the opinion that world domination started in your own backyard. What good would nuking Yurkistan do if there were bastions of permissiveness in Sunny Sunnyland and Rolandworld? Talk about backlash! If he took out Yurkistan before taking care of business at home, the slackers would be protesting in the streets and there's no telling where it would go. No—if he was serious about spreading the One True Religion throughout the world, he had to lay a foundation.

But, as Roland Brand knew, you could only ask so much of a pick-up truck. That was why he was hatching a third option, which was brilliant if he did say so himself. *Why not,* he thought, *nuke Yurkistan, Sunny Sunnyland, and Rolandworld simultaneously?* This would be a show of force the world had never seen. Any person or country that had any thoughts of resistance would freeze in their tracks.

Another advantage to "Operation Triple-Nuke" was Roland could use it as a wedge to force Chosen Leader Delbert Thorne out. Roland's friends in the military brass knew who was driving this truck and after the blitz, he'd go on the air and the Free Nation would know, too.

And then Roland would never have to drive a truck again; he'd have his Maserati.

* * * * * *

That Roland fella's gettin' too much size for his slacks, thought Chosen Leader Delbert Thorne. Every time they had a meeting, everything went along fine, but after Roland left, Delbert would get this twitchy little feeling in his gut that said he'd been snookered. Delbert didn't like being snookered.

He had that twitchy snookered feeling in his gut at this very moment. He didn't know why Roland Brand couldn't get it in his head that his top priority was to nuke the Evil Abner Krabner in Yuccasand. What part of that didn't he get? Just when he thought he had Roland on the same page, Roland would start in on Sunny Sunnyland or Rolandworld, and they were off on another dance. *Roland's right,* Delbert thought. *We gotta nuke those places, too.* It's just that a leader's gotta set goals and stick to 'em. And Delbert's goal was to nuke the Evil Abe Kohen in Yiddistein.

Another problem was this Bob fella. Roland was right— they had to do something about Bob. The guy was dangerous. Bob even had Delbert snookered for a little while—had him thinking that he and his book were speaking for the One True

Religion. Delbert never actually read *The Book of Bob*, but he watched his EB show every day and liked it a lot. Even yelled out *Helluva* Deal every once in a while. But then, when Roland came along with his book, well—Delbert knew the truth when he saw it, and the **RRR Manifesto** was closer to Delbert's truth than anything he'd ever seen. Still, there was a right way and a wrong way to go about things. Roland was still pretty new at this game—he hadn't learned when it was better to "starve the beast" and when it was better to take 'im out. He just had to keep explaining till Roland understood: With a guy like Bob, you starve the beast; with a guy like the Evil Knieval of Yellowstone, ya had to take 'im out.

Delbert liked the **RRR Manifesto** real well. But something was gnawing at him. For one thing, he wondered if Dad liked Roland better. Dad told Roland he was the "One True Spokesman for the One True Religion." Dad never said anything like that to Delbert. In fact, in their last conversation, Dad had said, "Delbert, you're a hopeless moron." Delbert didn't take it personally—*we're all hopeless morons in Dad's eyes*, he thought. But then, he didn't see anything in the **RRR Manifesto** that said Roland was a hopeless moron.

Also, he'd been keeping score.

In the last two weeks, Roland had gotten fifty-six hours of Electronic Babysitter time to Delbert's four. Roland had ordered two hundred eighty firings; Delbert had only ordered fifteen. Roland had been on eight magazine covers; Delbert on two. *Apples and oranges,* Delbert thought. I'm busy runnin' the world, Roland's just the Secretary of Religion. He's got more time to be muggin' for the camera. Still—every time Delbert thought about the score, he got that twitchy feeling in his stomach that made him wonder if he was being snookered. He didn't like being snookered.

Maybe he should write a book. He could get that LaFarge guy to ghost write one like he did for Roland. It worked for Roland; it could work for him, too. Delbert wondered what he could write a book about. Maybe LaFarge would have some ideas.

Anyway, thought Chosen Leader Delbert Thorne, *I gotta do something 'bout that Roland fella 'cause he's gettin' too large for his long johns.*

* * * * * *

"Well, that's that," said Bob.

He and his Carrier Pigeons had moved out of the penthouse suite of the Silver Star Hotel. Since the show had been canceled, the bills had piled up and they'd had to downsize their lifestyle. Bob and his Carrier Pigeons were situated in the Last Daze Hotel, a low rent dive in a dead end part of town. Natasha and Bunny were long gone. That was fine with Ivan.

"Flutter away, you fickle fly-by-nights!" he called to them as they clattered down the stairwell. "Rude riddance to rancid rubbish, I say!"

Eldon and Larry Smith had decided to cool it for awhile. They took separate rooms on different floors at the Last Daze, although they sneaked visits whenever it seemed safe. But with Roland's new decrees, they thought they'd better keep their heads down. The **RRR Manifesto** was very specific about the consequences of homosexuality, and now the truth must be told: Eldon and Larry were at risk because they were . . . well . . . gay.

Bob didn't seem troubled by the new developments. As far as he was concerned, nothing much had changed, really—same message different venue. He was still out every day, standing on his soapbox on the corner, holding up *The Book of Bob* and preaching the word of Dad. Some days he drew huge crowds. When the crowds got too big, the True Religion Squad would wade in, beat people with their clubs, round 'em up, shove 'em into paddy wagons, and with sirens wailing, haul 'em away while Bob continued to preach, undaunted. For the next few days after the police raids, people would shudder as they hurried by, avoiding Bob's corner and averting their eyes. But pretty soon, the crowds would swell again for the steadfast Bob whose message and delivery were the same—rain or shine, peace or riot, four listeners or four thousand.

There was always a guaranteed audience of four. First Carrier Pigeon Ivan Bunt sat loyally to Bob's left, echoing Bob's sentiments.

"Beat my brow and brew my beer!" he would exclaim to emphasize one of Bob's points. "Bob's rollin' the logs and rattlin' the house!"

When things got hot and heavy with the True Religion Squad, First Carrier Pigeon Ivan could be counted on to give his account of the proceedings.

"You gripin' goons are bunglin' my bum! Get yer bumblin' bees outta my buttermilk!"

Eldon and Larry never missed a sermon either. However, they hovered in the shadows at opposite ends of the block, and they made themselves scarce at the first sign of trouble.

And of course, Bud was a regular, stretched out by Bob's right foot, head resting on crossed forepaws. The truth was, he was tired, and he wished everybody would be quiet so he could get some sleep. Bud missed the attention he used to get from Eldon, Larry, and Pierre the pet groomer. He was troubled by all the new smells in the air—especially the one that smelled like blood, smoke, and danger. Most upsetting were the riots. At those times, he would sneak between Bob's legs and whimper. Bob just kept right on talking like he always did and didn't smell scared at all. This reassured Bud, but still . . . something wasn't right. On the other hand, Bud was glad to finally be rid of that knit sweater and the ribbon around his neck. Being an old dog, he'd learned by now that you take the good with the bad. But mostly he was tired and achy and wanted to sleep.

Unlike Bud, Dad didn't seem at all troubled by the course of events. "My messengers have always had problems," he informed Bob frequently. "This is nothing new. You just keep plugging away, Bob. Maybe if we're lucky, they'll kill you in a hideous public spectacle. I could get a couple thousand years of mileage out of *that*."

"Whatever you say, Dad," Bob replied. "You're the Boss."

* * * * * *

The only time Lakshmi Jackson had ever come close to being in charge of anything was when she was working by herself at the In 'n' Out market. But now Sophia Wise was in jail and in grave danger. When Natalie bustled in, chattering away about the news, all the clutter in Lakshmi's mind assimilated into sharp focus. She straightened her spine and interrupted Natalie politely.

"We must assemble in the meeting room at once," she said. "Phil, please fetch Thaddeus and the professor. Natalie, will you please go find Normal Bea? Mother, where is Father?"

"I don't know," said Aruna Jackson. "Baa-aa."

"I think I know," said Lakshmi. "Well, there's nothing we can do about that now. Mother, please stay here with me."

When Phil and Natalie had left the room, Lakshmi sat down next to Aruna, put her arm around her and whispered gently, "Mother, I know you've suffered greatly. You've taken care of me all my life, now I will take care of you. I'll be strong and won't let anyone hurt you. I promise you'll be safe with me. But you must trust me and let go of the past. No more scrubbing till you bleed. No more clucking and baa-ing. Let it go, Mother. Your life is at stake. So is Ben's. So are Sophia's and my own. The entire planet is in danger. I don't know what to do yet, but I will learn. First, I need you to be strong enough to give up the past and trust me. Can you do that, Mother?"

Aruna began to blubber, then thought better of it and stopped herself. She looked Lakshmi directly in the eye and said, "I will."

Phil rushed in with Thaddeus Well and the professor. Then

noisy Natalie burst in with Normal Bea Freee, and the five of them began bouncing off each other like so many ping-pong balls. Lakshmi stood to greet them and became very calm.

"Please sit, my friends," said Lakshmi. She continued to stand while they settled down.

"We all know by now that Sophia's in jail. There are certain truths I see very clearly. Don't ask me how, because I don't understand. But these things I know: Sophia's life is in danger. She will soon be transported to Capital City, where she will be taken before Roland Brand. Roland has a plan for her, which is still fuzzy to me, but it's coming into focus. It is up to us to go immediately to Capital City and rescue Sophia. Our lives and the very life of the planet depend on our delivering Sophia to safety. I don't know yet how we will do this, but I do know if are wise, all answers will present themselves in due time."

Lakshmi's friends were struck speechless by her graceful presence, by her sense of purpose. Something warm and glowing had entered this shy girl and filled her to the brim. They were mesmerized by her voice.

"If we are to succeed," she continued, "we must each find within ourselves our deep reservoir of courage, wisdom, and love. We must eliminate pretense, we must embrace our true selves. Let us travel with joy, mindful of every step. For if each step is sure, we will prevail.

"And our steps will be sure. We'll not hide our faces. We will show them openly before the world. We'll not be bound by oppression. We will walk in the freedom that is our true nature. We will arm ourselves with love and truth and the knowledge that those are the only arms we need."

What could they say? Thankfully, not much. They basked in Lakshmi's glow. They reveled in the rightness of her thought. They would walk with her and when they did, they'd find that, like Lakshmi, their feet would touch ever so gently on the ground.

XVII. LIFE IS BUT A DREAM

PEOPLE ALWAYS ASK ME:

Dad, what will happen to me when I die? Will I:

a) See a white light with my loved ones waiting for me on the other side
b) Choose my next incarnation to work out my karma
c) Go to Nebulon
d) Go to Planet Ug
e) Have the lights go out and fade into nothingness

I don't know why you don't get it. I tell you a million times a day, and my answer is always the same. Ok—let's try again. I'll lob it in real slow this time. Ready? Here's your answer:

Ok—NOW do you get it?

From *The Book of Bob*
Q & A 0:0

* * * * * *

Sleeping handcuffed on the hard, cold floor of her holding cell, flying high above the Free Nation in an unmarked plane heading for Capital City, Sophia Wise had a dream:

She dreamed *she was very old. Her hair was no longer spiked and multi-colored, it was long and flowing and multi-gray. She was able to look at herself, as we sometimes can in our dreams, and she thought she had never seen so many shades of gray as she saw in her hair. It was a rainbow of shades from black to white.*

She was very beautiful, this old Sophia. It was not a peaceful beauty; there was still too much life and mischief for that. This Sophia knew too much of the world to be at peace. She had lived life and fought many battles against its cruel, dark destruction (or was it simply erosion?). This Sophia had been fooled time and again by liars; she'd been disappointed by those who were lazy or stupid or asleep.

All the old foolishness and disappointment showed on her face. But what showed most was how awake she was. After all this time. Who would have thought this old woman would be more alive and more mischievous than that nineteen-year-old girl of so long ago? Who would have thought this old Sophia Wise would still be laughing belly laughs, still be starting food fights, still taking in strays? Who would have thought she could have lost so many battles and still have so much hope?

Old Sophia Wise was in the sky, spread out over the entire Free Nation, playing her mandolin. It was a beautiful song she was playing, rich and full—much warmer than the tinkly sounds she used to make. She played to all the nation, and every man, woman, beast, and sprout seemed to rise toward the music like a field of sunflowers following the sun.

All her old friends were there. They were much older now. There was Bob, hoeing a garden. There was Bud, hardly able to walk, stretched out on the cool earth, happily smelling the grass. There was Ivan Bunt—he was walking now. Ivan had a lurch in his gait, but there he was—wearing long pants and sputtering along. There were Eldon and Larry Smith holding hands—Eldon was gray; Larry's head was shaved and a ring dangled from his ear like Mr. Kleen. There were Normal Bea, Thaddeus Well, the professor, Natalie and Phil. They were bobbing up and down on merry-go-round horses—up and down, around and around and around. There was Lakshmi Jackson between her mother and father, her arms around their waists. She seemed to be holding them up.

My, but Lakshmi was beautiful. In fact, it didn't even look like her, but Sophia knew it was—the way we know these things in dreams. Lakshmi left no footprints when she walked. She seemed to know a secret she'd be glad to tell, but only if you knew the right question. And if you knew the question, you wouldn't need to ask. Lakshmi's beauty was as peaceful as Sophia's was wild.

And there was Roland Brand. He came in the form of a giant thundercloud, rolling into her space in the sky. He was no longer a mystery; she recognized him now. She was not infatuated or afraid.

"Oh, hello there, Roland," she said. Then she flew directly into the Roland cloud. She gave her mandolin a strum and when she did, the cloud dissipated, and a misty rain descended lightly over the Free Nation.

* * * * * *

Prong One completed, thought Ben Jackson. *Aruna is safe with Lakshmi. Now it's on to Prong Two.*

Ben stealthily guided his car heading east in the dead of night, staying in the middle lane, never exceeding the speed limit, never falling below. Eyes glancing frequently in the rearview; mindful to do nothing to attract attention.

"I'm a marked man," Ben said to himself. "But so is Roland Brand, and I'll get him before they get me."

Maybe Ben thought he was marked because he had blown Roland's picture and his fireplace to powder and left the front door wide open. Maybe he thought he was marked because Roland had gotten his wife and Natalie, and it was just a matter of time before Roland Brand got them all. Maybe he thought he was marked because of what he had let slip at the gun store when he bought the MX-247 Dematerializer. If he remembered correctly, his exact words were: "I won't miss Roland Brand with *this* baby."

Hard to tell. All he knew was, dressed in full camouflage with his weapons piled up on the front seat, Ben thought he'd better stay in full readiness mode. With the first rays of sunlight, he would pull off the highway and find a back road where he could slip out of sight and catch a few winks. If there was nowhere to hide safely, only then would he check into some fleabag hotel where he hoped the yahoo at the desk wouldn't ask any questions. He would register under an assumed name: Bill Marshall, Tom Wilson, Mike Johnson—good generic Free Nationer names that wouldn't attract attention. One old-timer did raise his eyebrows at the sight of this feller-name-o' Don Olson who was wearin' army fatigues an' packin' some serious heat, but Ben ("Don") explained to him that he was on his way to a secret spy mission in Yurkistan, and he'd better not blow his cover or he'd be getting a visit from the True Religion Squad. The old-timer lifted an eyebrow and said he wouldn't breathe a word. But still, Ben worried about leaving a trail.

That was why he decided not to stay with one car for long. Being a trained policeman, changing cars was as easy as changing channels. After he'd used one car for a night, he'd simply find himself a KonsumerWorld SuperStore, leave last night's car in the crowded parking lot, find another one he liked, jimmy the lock, hotwire the engine, and away he'd go.

Ben really started feeling like a marked man after he killed his first cop. The guy didn't leave him much choice. He was driving along at three a.m. in the black Land Pillager SUV he'd borrowed for the night—he was minding his own business in the middle lane, the needle hovering right at fifty-five, when he saw the flashing lights behind him.

Ben muttered a curse as he pulled over, checking his pistol to make sure it was loaded and ready. He had no intention of using it of course, but as a trained policeman, it was his natural reflex to be prepared.

Everything started out fine: "May I see your driver's license, sir? May I see your registration?"

But then the guy started getting nosy and asking Ben questions like, "Why are you carrying all those firearms in the front seat?" and: "Will you please step out of the car with your hands up?"

At that point, Ben didn't have any choice but to blow him away. It wasn't that Ben was trying to save his own skin. He wasn't a selfish man. It wasn't even his own need for revenge—if it had been that simple, Ben probably would have tossed in his cards.

No—it was bigger than that. At the very point the cop asked Ben to step out of his borrowed Land Pillager, Dad spoke to him. This is what Dad said:

"Blow this little sucker away, Ben. You've got bigger fish to fry."

What else could he do? If Dad tells you to blow someone away, the only question to ask is, "Which gun do you want me to use, Dad?"

Ben didn't even bother to ask. He knew from his police training that trying to point a hunting rifle or a semi-automatic out the car window at a target two feet away would be impractical. His pistol worked just fine.

"Good shot," said Dad. "Now take the cop car and beat it out of here."

From that point, Ben was in Dad's hands. Dad told Ben when to ditch the car, which new one to borrow, and when to blow the next cop away. Talk about leaving a trail! Sometimes

Ben would express remorse at all the dead cops he'd left behind, but Dad would remind him:

"We all have to go sometime, Ben. Look at the big picture—what's a couple dozen dead cops when the world is at stake? You're the only one who can save humankind. It's a heavy burden to bear, but you are the one I have chosen. Keep your eye on the ball, Ben. Your mission is to kill Roland Brand. Do whatever it takes."

"I will, Dad. I will," said a determined Ben. With the highway swimming before his glazed eyes, Ben careened into one lane and out the other, minding the speed limit no more, pushing his borrowed car past ninety-five miles per hour as he raced with impunity toward Capital City on his Mission From Dad.

* * * * * *

The fever was broken. After a year of delirious suffering, Aruna Jackson came back to herself. She was weak and shaky, but as she sat next to her daughter Lakshmi in the back seat of the car, she took inventory of her body and found all of it to be there. She listened to her thoughts and they were clear. As if she'd had a bad cold and blown her nose, suddenly she could breathe again.

She wanted to cry for all the time lost. She wanted to cry for all the suffering she had caused her family. She wanted to feel sorry for herself. But she had cried enough. Lakshmi was right—it was time to be strong and determined. So Aruna watched her beautiful daughter and tried to copy her.

She saw how straight Lakshmi sat, and Aruna straightened herself, too. She saw the mysterious radiance in Lakshmi's face and tried to imagine what the girl was thinking to have such an expression, and Aruna tried to think like that too. She remembered how her daughter behaved most of her life—what a shy girl she had been. Look how she was transforming before her very eyes! It seemed every time Aruna glanced at Lakshmi, the girl appeared stronger than the last. *Maybe I can be strong like that too*, Aruna thought. *At least a little.*

In the front seat, Natalie and Phil seemed to sense it also. Sometimes, Natalie would go on for too long, and Lakshmi would interrupt her. Aruna thought she'd heard Lakshmi interrupt people more in the last twenty-four hours than she had in her entire life. But she did it in such a pleasant way—it seemed to calm people down. Natalie would say:

"This will be such a life-expanding event for Sophia. I think we all should send out a whole bunch of positive energy in her direction right now. My teacher, Baba Yogananda Brahmahudi taught me this chant—I think we should . . . ."

"Thank you, Natalie, for the energy you are sending in your beloved daughter's direction. She will certainly gather strength from our calm resolve."

Once Phil had difficulty with a decision. He thought he'd stop for gas but he wondered if the next station fifty miles up the road might be cheaper but the tank was running low and he didn't want to get stuck out in the middle of nowhere but he'd rather stop at a station with an In 'n' Out market and he didn't think . . . ."

Lakshmi simply said, "Phil, I have to pee. Could you please stop at the next station?"

At these moments, it was as if Lakshmi opened the windows and let out the smoke. The air was clear and felt good to inhale.

Funny, thought Aruna, *Lakshmi never seems to mention Dad anymore.* Aruna had gotten so much in the habit of saying, "Praise Dad, thanks be to Dad," after every sentence, and lately it had been, "Praise Roland." It took some getting used to, being around people who didn't say this all the time. Aruna herself didn't say it much, either. She remembered how much power it used to give her to invoke Dad's name, then she realized, somewhere along the way, it started to drain her, so that every time she said, "Praise Dad," a few more drops of power dribbled away. The old Aruna would have chastised her daughter for not calling on Dad more, but the new Aruna noticed that Lakshmi seemed to be getting along just fine.

Lakshmi had asked Normal Bea Freee, Thaddeus Well, and Professor Tyrone T. Matters to stay at Rolandworld and keep things running. Hordes of refugees were piling in every day, and it was a big job to get them settled, put them to work, and heal the physical and psychic wounds they had suffered from Rolandism. The trio was happy to oblige, and they all seemed to inflate with pride when Lakshmi put so much faith in them.

With that arranged, Lakshmi had asked Natalie and Phil to drive her and her mother to Capital City as quickly as possible so they could rescue Sophia. Lakshmi repeated that she had no plan at present, but she was confident that when the critical moments came, she would know what to do.

The journey was surprisingly hushed. Lakshmi's fellow travelers noticed her quiet resolve, and they followed her lead. When there was talk, the discussion often revolved around Ben Jackson. Lakshmi warned her mother to expect the worst. Ben had become a warrior. Once a man becomes a warrior, she explained, it's very difficult to get him back, even if he lives. Each time a man kills, he kills a part of himself until nothing is left but that which he has destroyed.

Aruna wanted to blame herself. If she hadn't let Roland Brand drive her crazy, Ben would still be Ben and with her today. Lakshmi told her there was no one to blame. This was the oldest story in the world. A man is wronged by a warrior. Rather than right the wrong, he becomes a warrior himself and perpetuates the cycle. The saddest story in the world too, she added.

Just then, Lakshmi looked out the window and saw some medics lifting a policeman's body into an ambulance. She knew.

Phil drove with both hands on the wheel, hoping he wasn't driving too fast or too slow. He couldn't wait to see his Sunshine again.

Natalie breathed deeply. She wondered if Lakshmi was more enlightened than Baba Yogananda Brahmahudi. She observed her busy mind and took another breath.

Aruna had a sudden urge to wash her hands. Then she remembered they were clean.

* * * * * *

On this day, Bud felt better than any time he could remember since he was a puppy. He didn't know what was coming over him, but he liked it. The air was warm and smelled like spring. For a long time now, his body had been heavy and his legs had been creaky. But today he was so light, he thought he could fly. He wished there were some squirrels to chase. He could probably catch one today, just like he used to.

Bud remembered his mother. She was warm just like the air was now. He remembered crowding in with his brothers and sisters, latching on to a tit and sucking sweet milk, jostling with the puppies while they fought for a tit to suck. He remembered the gurgling and the nudging, pretty soon they'd all be asleep and dreaming and warm. Maybe his mother was asleep too . . . He didn't know . . . But she was calm and still and she let him sleep with a tit still in his mouth . . . The other puppies too . . . Mostly he remembered how warm she was.

Bud remembered the day Bob took him home. He had been rolling and growling and gnawing with his brothers and sisters and all of a sudden this man picked him up and took him away and his mother was gone and the puppies were gone and he thought he was falling in space.

That was the first time Bud ever rode in a car. The man kept right on talking to him while everything was whizzing by so fast he couldn't even see straight and Bud remembered how he wished the bouncing would stop. He threw up.

Bud remembered Helen. She patted him on the head once in

a while as she was walking by, but most of the time she didn't notice him much. When she talked, she mainly yelled at the back of Bob's head. Bob didn't talk much to her. He talked a lot to Bud, though, and Bud liked the sound.

Bud liked his happy life. He liked it when he got to be with Bob. He liked smelling all the things in the world. He liked to run. He remembered how he used to run and run and run because he liked how fast he could go and how his feet would kick up dirt and the grass was cool and he could feel the air better on his face when he ran.

Bud liked to smile and bark and chase things and pee on trees. He remembered how proud he was when he learned to lift his leg. One time, there was a female dog who smelled ready and told him she was ready—for him! And he got on top of her and it just felt too good to stop.

Bud felt like a puppy again. He was lying right there in the sun and he liked it so much. He liked lying on the warm earth, on the cool grass. He could feel the earth's heart beating. Life was good. He didn't understand why Eldon and Larry were crying. Ivan was too. Stop crying Eldon and Larry and Ivan. Be happy. Bob was sitting next to him, petting his head and talking to him. He liked when Bob did that. He hoped he would for awhile.

Bud was tired. He thought he'd sleep. That would be nice.

There was his mother. What a surprise. "Come with me, Bud," she said. Oh, how good it was to see her again.

XVIII. Looks Like Rain

There once was a pack of old mules,
Who built them a boat with their tools;
They put out to sea,
And before you'd count three,
They sunk like a big ship of fools.

Limericks 13:6

* * * * * *

"Bob?"

"Yes, Dad?"

"Bob, I want you to go out and buy a boat."

"What kind of boat, Dad?"

"Well, I've been doing some research. I think I found a good deal for you, but you'll have to move fast before somebody snatches it up. It's a forty-six foot cruiser, fourteen foot beam, bridge clearance five feet—fiberglass hull, 175-gallon fuel capacity, 220-gallon water capacity, loaded with extras. It's three years old and it's only got a couple hundred miles on it. I think it's a steal."

"Um, Dad?"

"Yes, Bob?"

"Why do you want me to buy a boat?"

"There's gonna be a flood."

"A flood?"

"Yes, Bob. A really big flood. It's going to annihilate the entire west coast. I want you to get your friends and head for dry ground. You're going to need a ship-shape boat that can weather the storm and take you all the way to Red Rock."

"But, there's not a cloud in the sky. We've had over five-hundred-fifty beautiful days in a row now."

"That's going to change."

"Wait a minute," said Bob. "You're not going to do what you did way back in the beginning, are you?"

"You mean the Forty Days and Nights Flood?"

"Yeah, that one."

"I didn't exactly *do* that, you know. I get so tired of being blamed for everything."

"What do you mean?"

"That flood happened way before people understood about weather systems. They didn't know about 'depressions' that whirl around and create 'air masses.' They didn't know about the heat energy that gets released as 'water vapor,' becoming condensed, then freezing inside a cloud. They didn't know that this heat energy creates powerful rising 'air currents' that swirl upwards to the tropopause. They didn't know about cool descending air currents that produce strong downdraughts below the storm. So they blamed me."

"You mean, you didn't cause it?"

"Use your head, Bob. Even if I could, why would I?"

"Well," said Bob, "I heard you got mad because humans were so wicked, so you said:

'I will destroy man who I have created from the face of the earth; both man, beast, and the creeping thing, and the fowls of the air; for it repenteth me that I have made them.'"

"*I* said that?" Dad asked.

"That's what I heard," said Bob.

"That was a long time ago—it's hard to remember. But I don't know why I would want to destroy all the beasts and fowls and creeping things. *They* didn't do anything to piss me off."

"Well, you *did* tell me you used to have a temper . . . ."

"Yes, but this seems extreme—even for *me*. It reminds me of a five-year-old destroying his train set because one car went off the tracks."

"You said it, Dad—not me."

"Anyway, that's not how it went. I wasn't *that* bad. And as I said, even if I wanted to, I'm not sure I could have pulled it off. That was a really extreme weather system they had back then."

"So why are you going to make a big flood now?"

"Aren't you listening to me? I just told you, it's not my fault!"

"I'm not following you, Dad."

"*Oy vey!* Will somebody help me out here? Bob—have you heard about the polar ice caps?"

"Yes. As a matter of fact, I got one just yesterday at the In 'n' Out market. It was really good—and so refreshing."

Dad decided to ignore his dense son and press ahead. "The polar ice caps are melting, Bob."

"I know, Dad. Yesterday I had to eat mine really fast—it was making quite a mess."

"Listen carefully, Bob. Huge glaciers that have existed for thousands of years are falling into the sea. The ocean is rising. The earth is warming up. Do you know why this is happening?"

"Because you told it to?" Bob guessed.

"It's happening because you people have been spewing so many greenhouse gases into the air."

"Then I guess we'd better stop building greenhouses," Bob ventured.

"Bob, your coal plants and electric plants are spewing carbon into the air. Your forests were supposed to trap that stuff, but you're cutting all of *them* down. Do you know what you're doing every time you drive your car, watch EB, turn on your air conditioner, or turn on a light?"

"Living the Free Nationers' Dream!" Bob was *sure* he got *that* one right.

"You're sending greenhouse gases in the air, Bob. When the sun's heat reaches the earth, the greenhouse gases trap it in the atmosphere. That's why you've had over five hundred and fifty beautiful days in a row in Sunny Sunnyland."

"So it's a *good* thing." Bob thought he was starting to get it.

"No, it's not a good thing, Bob. Your planet is in chaos. The Eskimos are skinny-dipping. The Mexitinos are buying snow plows. Everything is . . . ."

"I hate to interrupt, Dad, but if it's snowing in Mexitino, how could the planet be warming?"

"That's because the *average* temperature is rising. But the effect of that is chaos. Some places are warmer, some are colder—you've got hurricanes and tornadoes and drought and floods—that's why you've got to buy a boat."

"Because you're mad and you're going to make it flood?" Bob tried.

"NO, BOB! BECAUSE *YOU'RE* GOING TO MAKE IT FLOOD!"

"Me?"

"Never mind. Will you promise me you'll get that boat?"

"Ok. Do you want me to collect two of every species to put in it?"

"Why would I want you to do that?"

"Because that's what you did last time?"

"Oh, that. Now, that one I *know* I didn't do."

"Are you sure? I heard . . ."

"Bob, do you know what you call a species when there are only two of them left?"

"A couple?"

"Extinct."

"Oh. But the two can breed, can't they?"

"Probably not. But let's say for the sake of argument that they did. Do you know what you would call it if they had babies who bred?"

"Incest?"

"Bob, sometimes I underestimate you. Right—incest. And then, if the incestuous siblings manage to have babies—and that's a big if—then you get mutant forms, weakened genetics—it just doesn't work. Right now, there are about six hundred mountain gorillas left in the world. Do you know what they are?"

"Um . . . you just said they were mountain gorillas." Bob thought Dad was acting so weird, he'd better humor him.

"The six hundred mountain gorillas are almost extinct."

"So I'd better take two with me when I go?"

"FORGET THE MOUNTAIN GORILLAS, BOB! FORGET THE GREENHOUSE GASES! JUST TRUST ME!" Dad took a deep breath. "Just get yourself a boat, get your friends together, and get ready to take a trip."

"Whatever you say, Dad. One more question?"

"What now, Bob?"

"After I take my friends on my boat to Red Rock, will you let me live to be nine-hundred-sixty years old?"

Dad wanted to give up. "Why nine hundred-sixty, Bob?" He sighed.

"That's how old you let the last guy live after he took *his* boat through the Forty-Days-and-Nights Flood."

"I don't know, Bob. Maybe if you get lots of exercise and eat right . . . ."

"You think so? I haven't been paying much attention to that, lately."

"Well, you'll never get to nine-hundred-sixty at this rate. They say it's the upper body strength that's most important."

"I'll work on it."

"Also, you should lose that spare tire around your middle. They say that's a big cause of heart disease."

"Ok, Dad, I'll do my best. Dad?"

"What, Bob?" Dad wished this conversation would end.

"I heard the guy who took the boat through the Forty-Days-and-Nights Flood was six-hundred years old when he did it."

"That's what you heard?"

"That's right. Do you think this flood will be in five hundred and fifty years? That's about when I'll be six hundred."

"No, Bob. It's coming a lot sooner."

"Then I guess I'd better get that boat."

"Go get that boat, Bob."

"Ok. Um . . . Dad?"

"What, Bob?"

"Shouldn't you have said: '*I will destroy any man WHOM I have created*,' not '*who*'?"

"Go get that boat, Bob."

* * * * * *

Venecia Bosco had a headache. She had been sitting behind her desk at the Veteran's Resource Center for eight hours straight, and she wanted to go home to her cat. All day long, one client after the next, pulling on her for one thing or another. *It's not their fallutin' fault*, she thought with a sigh. *The grubbin' government sends 'em off to some wankin' war somewhere, and then they come home missing half their sombreros.*

There's just so many of 'em, she sighed again. *And there's so little I can doodley do. Blast my bloomers!* she said to herself. Oh well, she was glad she only had one client left, and then she could go home to her cuddlin' cat. She rubbed the temples beneath her shocking red hair.

She pressed the intercom. "Is Mr. Bunt in?" she asked.

"He's here," came the reply. "Shall I send him in?"

"Yes," said Venecia. "Send him in."

Ivan Bunt wheeled into Venecia Bosco's office in a dither. "Whomp my waffles! Plaster my pajamas! This ain't no way to run a ventilatin' veterans' center!"

"Hello, Mr. Bunt," she smiled. She was used to irritated clients. "I'm Venecia Bosco." She held out her hand to shake his.

"And I'm Bo Diddley! Buffaloes! How come you're a Veterans' Resource Center and you ain't got no wallowin' wheelchair access? Oil my onions! Don't you know some of us vets ain't got no leapin' legs?"

"Believe me, Mr. Bunt, I understand. As a matter of fact, just yesterday I was testifying before the resource committee. Do you know what I said? I tattled 'em that it makes me madder 'n a shark in a swimming pool that they treat our heroes so bubblin' bad. A shabby shame, I said!"

"A shabby shambles of a shame," said Ivan. "You snarled that?"

"I did," Venecia replied. Then she muttered under her breath, "A shabby shambles of a snorkin' shame."

"Well, goose my griddle!" said Ivan. "What else did you say?"

"Then I told 'em," said Venecia, warming to the subject, "if'n you want our boys to go out and fight for yer fiddlin' country, ya better start payin' 'em more than the price of a mousetrap, I said! I said if'n ya got one cigar box of decency left in ya, you could at least give 'em a whoppin' wheelchair access so they can grind their gonads through the door!"

"You said that?" asked Ivan.

"I diddley did," Venecia said.

"Well, chug my chittlins an' chisel my cheese," said Ivan. "I'm as speechless as a spatula!"

"Mr. Bunt, what can I help you with today?"

"Call me Ivan, Ms. Bosco."

"Ok, Ivan. Call me Venecia."

"Venecia," Ivan savored the name. "Venecia Bosco . . . That's prettier 'n a basket of bullfrogs."

"Oh, Ivan," she replied. "You flatter my flames. What can I do for you?"

"Well, Venecia," Ivan continued, "ya see, I was pretty down 'n' out, an' then I took up with Bob. He changed my lovin' life, he did. He taught me about Dad an he taught me to say, 'Hallelujah! Hootin' hollerin' *Helluva* deal!' Then Bob got an EB show—betcha didn't know you was talkin' to a straight-up an' struttin' EB star. Anyways, we was into the blue chips fer awhile, but then old Roland Brand rocked along 'n' pulled the plug and now, here I sit before you, a vagrant vet with no legs an' not enough money to buy a pistachio."

Venecia pulled out a tissue and wiped her eyes. "Oh, Ivan," she said. "I'm so sobbin' sorry."

Seeing Venecia tear up made Ivan tear up too. She handed him a tissue.

"A shabby snarlin' shambles of a shoddy snorkin' shame," she reiterated.

"Well, I ain't here on no mercy mission, Venecia. All I'm askin' for is some jelly on my just desserts."

"I understand, Ivan. Believe me, it's clear as toothpaste. I'll tell you what I'm gonna do—I'm gonna set it up so's you can get all the benefits 'n' beer nuts you deserve, and not only that, but you'll get back pay for every day they diddled their dally."

Ivan was overcome. "Oh, Venecia, I ain't been treated so good since the day Bob gave me them wieners in a jar!"

"But I'm not finished," she continued. "Ivan, have you ever thought you could walk again?"

"No, Venecia. Bob tried to help me walk once, but it didn't work."

"Oh, maybe you misunderstand me. Have you ever thought about prosthetic legs?"

"Prosthetic legs? What kind of kinky clowns do you think are creepin' in my closet?"

"Oh, no no, Ivan. Don't numb your nostrils. Prosthetic legs are artificial limbs you can attach to your knobs. I think you'd be a good candidate for 'em. Ivan, I think you can walk again!"

"Well, flog my football and spank my spam! You're not

ditherin' my dome, are ya?"

"Ivan, I'd never meddle your mind about something so staggeringly serious."

"You think I can walk again?"

"I think there's a big chunk of a chance you can, Ivan."

"Oh, popsicles in paradise! I feel better 'n' a bear in July!"

"Well, pound my penguins, Ivan! This makes me happier 'n' a houseful of blue-haired orphans! I'll call first thing tomorrow and set up an appointment for you."

"Oh, Venecia, how can I ever thank you?"

"No need to thank me, Ivan. I'm just doing my job. Ivan?"

"Yes, Venecia?"

"Do you like stroganoff?"

"Stroganoff? Why, stroganoff's my favorite flavor."

"Well," she continued shyly, "I just happen to be making stroganoff tonight. Would you like to come to my house tonight and swallow some stroganoff?"

"Would I?" exclaimed Ivan. "Well, take my violin off the wall and fiddle me a saw! That sound's better 'n' a monkey in a grapefruit tree!"

"It does?"

"Oh yes, it doodley-does."

"It doodley-does?" Venecia laughed.

"Oh my, yes! It diddley-doodley does!" Ivan laughed too.

"Well, diddle my doodle!" she exclaimed.

They both became silent and shy. Then:

"Ivan?"

"Yes, Venecia?"

"Do you like cats?"

"Do I like cats? Why I like cats better 'n' a belly dancer on Tuesday. You got a cat?"

"I do. A brand new kitten. And you'll never guess her name."

"Umm . . ." said Ivan, thinking. "Let me guess. Zuzzana?"

"Nope."

"Octivania?"

"Nope."

"Ok, give me one more try. Let's see . . . Florinicity?"

"I named my kitty Helluvadeal."

"Helluvadeal? You mean? . . . ."

"That's right, Ivan. I'm a Bobist."

"Well, bless my bees! Did you ever see me on our EB show?"

"No, I never did. I'm afraid I don't have an EB. But I read *The Book of Bob* every night."

"Well, Hattie hide the doorknobs! Turn on the lights! The rooster's comin' home!"

"Oh, Ivan, I feel better 'n' a witch on Halloween!"

"Oh, Venecia, you're the prize in my Crackerjacks!"

"Oh, Ivan, you're the gravy on my cake!"

"Oh, Venecia!"

"Oh, Ivan!"

"*HELLUVA* DEAL!"

XIX. PRAISE DAD

If you want an educated populace, you must start your children young. If the basic **RRR** *values are not ingrained in them by ages six to twelve, chances are they'll be lost. Lay the* **RRR** *foundation early and your children will build on it for life. Neglect the early seeds of growth, and civilization will flounder. Give your children a chance in life! Teach them* **RRR**: *Readin', Ritin', & Rithmatic!*

Letters 18:3

* * * * * *

THE TROUBLE WITH PEOPLE, SOPHIA WISE THOUGHT, *IS THEY talk too much.* She was amazed it had taken her this long to figure it out.

It was also surprising that her thoughts became so clear on an empty stomach. She couldn't remember when she'd been given something to eat, but she knew it had been quite a while. The first day was the hardest. All she could think of was food. Now, with twenty-twenty hindsight, maybe it was a blessing. The hunger pains had taken her mind off the cold dark cell and the hard floor she was forced to sit on because her hands were chained to the bars. She had been too hungry to be afraid that first day.

Now she was beyond all that, although—what she wouldn't give for a drink of water! Being thirsty was much worse than being hungry. She didn't think about food much anymore, but she thought a lot about water.

Sophia thought about all kinds of things—she had lots of spare time. She was happy she had come to the realization that people talk too much. Most of the world's problems could be solved, she concluded, if people would just shut up! Talking was like technology—it seemed like a good idea at the time, but most often, not much good came of it. Early humans learned to use stones for all kinds of useful tools, but pretty soon they were beating each other over the head with them. Later they made cars, which turned travel into a miracle, but pretty soon everybody was stuck in traffic jams and choking on their own smoke. Atomic energy was supposed to be a *good* thing and maybe it was, but you'd have a hard time convincing the residents of any nuked city that it was such a brilliant idea.

People used language the way they used stones, cars, and nuclear power, Sophia reasoned. Great tool, bad application. For every enlightened thinker, there were ten charlatans. For every charlatan, there were thousands of parrots who would blab forever about what the charlatan had said. For every parrot, there were a thousand more who talked and talked without saying anything, simply because there was some space to fill and they thought it was their job to fill it.

Sophia decided not to be one of them. She took a vow of silence. She would not speak until she was sure she had something worthwhile to say. It was amazing what you noticed when you shut up and paid attention. Even in her cell, she could hear little shifts in the breeze outside. In the dim light of day, she would stare at the cracks in her cage for hours until the wall was no longer a wall; the cracks were no longer cracks. She saw clearly that she was sitting in a living, breathing mass of cells that melded, swirled, transformed, and flowed in and out like the tides. Cool!

She thought she was learning to smell as a dog smells. She transcended the gross surface odors of shit and piss and sweat; she was able to "read the news" just like a dog—she knew the smell of fear, the smell of anger. Right now, she smelled thirsty. When Orvil Swain made his visits, she didn't listen much to his words. Like a dog, she listened to the tone of his voice, and she smelled his smell—that told her everything she needed to know. She even knew the smell of boredom now, although it didn't come up much anymore, because with all the new things she was learning, she was hardly ever bored.

She could amuse herself for a long time with something as simple as an itch on the end of her nose. Being unable to scratch, she had the opportunity to really zero in on it. She could bat it around in her mind the way a cat plays with a catnip toy. She'd visualize the itch as a singular, silver pinpoint of light. From its center, she'd see golden rays emanating in all directions. About then, she would realize she had a star sitting right on the tip of her nose. The star vibrated hot and cold, light and dark, birth, death, and rebirth. This star was the source of some divine energy. *Very* cool!

The pain didn't bother her all that much.

She wasn't sure if she could move her left arm—hard to tell when it was chained to a bar. She thought the right side of her head must be pretty swollen by now. It wasn't that she liked pain—it was just that she had a lot of time to look at it. When she peered directly into the pain, it looked like an angry red volcano, spewing hot molten lava straight up in the air and flowing down its sides. When she descended right to the core, the volcano looked very similar to the breathing cells in her prison walls, the smells she could read, and the silver itch on the tip of her nose. It was pure energy!

Mainly, Sophia was thirsty and she thought people talked too much. With all the bad things Orvil Swain did when he came to "re-educate" her, what she disliked most was how much he talked. Oh, how she wished he'd shut up! By the tone of his voice, she knew he was often asking questions, but it seemed like such a waste of time because she had taken a vow of silence, so what was the point?

When Orvil Swain talked or asked questions or slapped her around or invaded her body, she studied him. She came to know him well. The disorder in his brain smelled so strong, she could see it. His mind looked like a dark, dilapidated house that had been ransacked and abandoned; all the furniture was shattered and strewn; the current residents were spiders and rats.

She saw that Orvil had been beaten the way he beat her. Actually, much worse and more often—so far. He had never been touched by love. Never. Occasionally, Sophia would hear him say the words, "Dad's love," and she would tune in for a little bit, but then she'd realize he still wasn't saying anything worth listening to, so she'd tune out again. She knew when Orvil talked about "Dad's love," he was confused—he knew as much about love as a fish knows about badminton. Poor Orvil. Sometimes after he'd left, she cried for him.

She could see that his body had been invaded. Actually, when Orvil came in to "re-educate" her, she hoped he would invade her quickly. That way, he'd stop talking. Also, it didn't take long and after that, he'd go away.

Sophia thought a lot about Lakshmi Jackson. My, she was different now! Sophia could tell by the way Lakshmi walked, by the tone in her voice. When Sophia conjured her up, Lakshmi smelled of tigers; her scent was sure and whole and full of earth. Lakshmi interrupted her sometimes, and argued with her now. Sophia didn't like it at first, but now she was glad Lakshmi did. Lakshmi was usually right, and she only talked when she had something worthwhile to say. Sophia thought, *If Lakshmi were here right now, I'd break my vow of silence.*

Poor Natalie, Sophia thought. She says so many words, and most of them are right—how come she's so mixed up? She remembered Natalie saying, "Give up your attachments to material things, Sophia." She was right about that. Natalie would say, "Love and compassion are the true paths to wisdom." Right again. Natalie even told Sophia that going to jail could be an opportunity for growth. It was true. So how is it, Sophia wondered, that Natalie is right so much of the time, but still doesn't have a clue? It just goes to show, she concluded—words will only get you so far.

It made Sophia happy to think about her friends—Ivan Bunt, Eldon and Larry Smith, Bud, Normal Bea Freee, Thaddeus Well and the professor, Natalie and Phil, Aruna and Ben Jackson, and of course, Lakshmi . . . When she thought about how she loved them, she would travel as deeply into the love as she traveled into her prison walls, the volcano and the itch on her nose. When she arrived at the center of love, she discovered the same pure energy. She expanded with love energy until her jail cell and every other barrier dissolved and her love blanketed the earth. She didn't pray—that would just be more words. She simply radiated light toward her friends, and she knew it filled them up.

Funny, Sophia thought, the one person she couldn't picture was Bob. Try as she might, she couldn't remember what he looked like. It was as if he didn't exist. She knew the words of him—he was middle-aged, balding, paunchy—but he was invisible. *There you go again*, she thought: Words aren't everything. She couldn't smell him or see him at all.

The cell was dark now. No more studying the cracks till morning. Oh well—there were plenty of things to do. There was good news and bad news: Orvil Swain said he wouldn't be coming tomorrow. Good news. The bad news was Orvil had told her that Roland Brand would be paying her a visit to give her a special tattoo. She hoped he wouldn't take too long. She especially hoped he wouldn't talk too much.

She jumped a little when she heard the door grind open. Squinting toward the light, she saw two figures. The large figure in back pushed the smaller one in front into the cell and slammed the door behind him. She heard Orvil's voice calling from the other side:

"Hey, Sophia! I got a present for ya! Donald LaFarge! Roland told me ta send 'im over ta soften you up!'"

"Sophia! Are you ok?"

"Hey, Donald, how're you doing?" Whoops—she forgot her vow of silence. Ok—she wouldn't say another word. *Anyway*, she thought, *I'm sure Donald LaFarge will do enough talking for both of us.*

* * * * * *

Dad is a hard taskmaster, thought Ben Jackson. *It's a good thing he chose me. Not too many people would be equal to this job.*

Dawn's light had broken, so Ben was trying to catch a few winks in a ditch, some seventy-five miles east of Capital City. He had quit borrowing cars—Dad had told him it was getting too risky. "You're going to have to go on foot from here on out, Ben," Dad had said. "The roads are swarming with cops."

Dad has a way of stating the truth, plain and simple, thought Ben. The roads *were* swarming with cops. There were roadblocks at almost every mile.

"The reality is," Dad told Ben, "at this point, you can get to Capital City faster by foot then you'd be able to by car." Right again. With all the roadblocks and checkpoints, the highway was a parking lot.

Ben still traveled by night, jogging double-time down dark and desolate side roads. However, he never felt alone anymore— Dad was a constant presence.

"Keep your eye on the prize," He would tell Ben. "You're the only one I can depend on to rid the world of the evil Roland Brand." Or:

"This kid coming toward you on his bicycle—you'd better shoot him, Ben. He might know who you are." Or:

"Don't worry about that last family, Ben. If they had lived, they might have prevented you from carrying out your mission."

The family Dad was referring to had lived in the last house Ben had borrowed. After he stopped borrowing cars, he started borrowing houses. He would find a house to borrow just when daylight threatened to break—Dad preferred that it be isolated—an old farmhouse out in the boonies was perfect. Ben would use his police training to approach the house holding his rifle shoulder high, gliding along the walls sideways like a cat. Then in one swift motion, he'd kick down the door, slide in behind it, point his gun directly at the nearest head, and shout, "DON'T ANYBODY MOVE OR I'LL SPLATTER THIS ASSHOLE ALL OVER THE WALLS!"

"Good job, Ben," Dad would say. "Now tie them up."

Once the people in the house were bound and gagged and the phones ripped out of the walls, Ben could spend the rest of the day sleeping on their beds, eating their food, taking a shower, watching himself on the EB news, and getting ready for next night's double-time jog.

But there had been a problem with the last family.

"I have a funny feeling about these people, Ben," Dad had told him. "I think they're going to snitch."

"What makes you think that, Dad?" asked Ben. He remembered the wide-eyed stares the mother, father, and their three children had given him.

"I don't know, Ben. Sometimes I just get an intuition about things."

"What should I do, Dad?"

"I think you'd better blow 'em away."

"You want me to blow 'em away? Shoot them in cold blood?" Ben could hear their screams muffled by their gags; he remembered their looks of terror.

"You have to, Ben. I have chosen you to kill the evil Roland Brand. Consider these people collateral damage."

So it was with great sadness that Ben did what Dad called on him to do. He blew 'em away.

After that, Dad told Ben he would have to curtail his

practice of borrowing houses, too. Now, when morning broke, he would have to sleep in the woods or a ditch or a dumpster. His trials grew more burdensome and his body grew weary. Ben was just glad it was *he* who was called to carry out this mission and not someone of weaker constitution who would not be up to the task.

The media were in heaven. This was the biggest story since Beau Swanson kidnapped his mistress. The airwaves were besieged with stories about Ben Jackson's shooting rampage, the latest killings, and psychological profiles of Ben, Aruna, and every one of Ben's victims. Maps were displayed tracing Ben's headlong charge from Rolandworld toward his destination, which it was now generally acknowledged, was almost certainly Capital City. The maps were lit up at each point at which a murder had been committed.

The journalist who was most on top of this story was, not surprisingly, Logan Berry, star reporter for the Free Nation Network (FNN). Logan Berry, with the perfectly chiseled face, cleft chin, and blow-dried hair; Logan Berry with the basso profundo voice. Logan Berry: *"Setting the Standard for Journalistic Excellence and Integrity for Twenty-five Years!"*

Logan Berry earned his stripes back when Delbert Thorne had aimed his missiles at Boran but hit Borak instead. It was none other than Logan Berry who informed an anxious Free Nation that their Chosen Leader's "miscalculation" had turned into a stunning victory because it thwarted the Evil Abdul Kashmir's sinister plans.

When things got dicey at one of Chosen Leader Thorne's infrequent press conferences, Logan Berry could always be counted on to relieve the tension by asking questions such as, "Mr. Chosen Leader, is it true you spoke with Dad last night and it was *His* idea to cut school lunches?"

Logan Berry won the coveted Golden Shovel Award for the dirt he dug up on the Beau Swanson fiasco, which at the time was **The Story of the Century!** Of course, the Roadside

Slaughterer blew Beau Swanson out of the water and was the new **Story of the Century!**

Incidentally, that was what the new Story of the Century was called: **The Roadside Slaughterer!** It was none other than Logan Berry who coined the phrase, and it stuck.

Roadside Slaughterer Strikes Seven! screamed the headlines.

Race to Rein in Roadside Slaughterer Still Stymied! said another.

Can Anyone Stop the Roadside Slaughterer's Stranglehold on the Streets? was the question of the day.

It was a good thing the Roadside Slaughterer came along when he did. The Free Nation was going through a "slow news cycle." The only things that were going on were Chosen Leader Delbert Thorne's plan to nuke Yurkistan, the astonishing rise in poverty, several of Chosen Leader Thorne's corporate friends getting caught with their fingers in the till, and Roland Brand's meteoric rise as Secretary of Religion. All in all, people were getting bored.

Incidentally, when Logan Berry asked Chosen Leader Thorne the question: "Mr. Chosen Leader, is it true you spoke with Dad last night and it was *His* idea to cut school lunches?" Delbert Thorne's answer was:

"Yes."

For all of Logan Berry's journalistic triumphs, this was the capper to his career. He couldn't believe his luck when he got a phone call from none other than Ben Jackson, The Roadside Slaughterer, inviting him to come give an exclusive interview. Ben wanted to tell his side of the story.

Upon promise of confidentiality, Ben told Logan Berry where to find him. His instructions were specific, demanding that Logan come alone in a rented SUV, carrying his own camera, sound equipment, lights, generator, network feeds, and a large white backdrop. "Make sure your vehicle is a four-wheel," the Roadside Slaughterer had recommended. "The terrain is pretty tough."

When he arrived, Logan was surprised to find Ben Jackson in high and jovial spirits. He did appear a bit emaciated and unkempt, but no more than you would expect of someone who had been sleeping in ditches and was on a nationwide shooting spree.

As Logan Berry set up his equipment, Ben repeated the ground rules: One camera would be trained on the two participants standing before the white backdrop, revealing them only from the chest up. There would be no visuals that would leave clues as to Ben's whereabouts. Logan was not allowed to drop any hints either. Ben assured Logan that Dad would alert him if he tried to speak in code. Logan was to protect Ben's confidentiality with the same commitment he would give to any anonymous source. Finally, the tape would be aired live to insure no creative editing would be done.

The Free Nation was gripped with suspense. Schools and businesses closed early. The only people who didn't come home were the ones who had Electronic Babysitters in their workplace. The entire country was on the edge of its collective seat, waiting to see what The Roadside Slaughterer was really like, and how the media giant, Logan Berry would deal with him.

"Good afternoon," Logan Berry began, his deep voice matching the gravity of the situation. "I come to you from somewhere in the Free Nation."

"Careful, Berry," Ben Jackson's voice was heard in the background.

"As every Free Nationer is aware, two weeks ago, the Roadside Slaughterer began the most murderous massacre in memory, plundering the population and pillaging every person in his path."

My, Logan Berry looked great! Evenly tanned and physically fit—he had a two-day stubble that showed he wasn't

XIX. Praise Dad   287

just sitting on his butt in the studio—no, he was out in the trenches; just a working reporter digging up a story. He was decked out in a flannel shirt and waterproof vest and a camouflage hat—clean and creaseless and fresh off the rack from EnviroWorld, the most stylish outdoor store in the Free Nation.

"Today, you're going to hear his story. I warn you: There are elements of his tale you may find disturbing. If blood and guts and mayhem are distasteful to you, you may want to turn your EB set off now."

Nobody turned it off.

"So now, let's talk one-on-one with Ben Jackson, The Roadside Slaughterer."

Ben joined Logan Berry in front of the white backdrop and grimly faced the camera. His Sportsman's Special was strapped over one shoulder, the MX-247 over the other. As agreed upon, the camera only showed the men from chest up. If it had ventured downward, the viewing audience would have seen Ben petting his pistol, as if to calm it down.

"Mr. Jackson," Berry began, totally professional with just the right balance of impartiality and passion, "I will ask you the question the entire Free Nation wants to hear: Why?"

"Well, sir," said Ben, looking directly into the camera, "I'll make a long story short: Dad told me to do it."

"Mr. Jackson," said Berry, "some people would say that Dad doesn't tell them to travel across the country in camouflage uniform, stealing cars and killing people."

"I don't think Dad would tell most people to do that. But He told me," said Ben.

"But why would Dad tell you to do such a thing?"

"Collateral damage, sir."

"Excuse me? Collateral damage?"

"That's correct, sir. Dad has explained that it's too bad these poor people had to get in the way, but my mission is too important to let them stop me."

"And what would that mission be?"

"To kill Roland Brand."

"Let me get this straight--you're saying Dad is sending you on a mission to assassinate our Secretary of Religion?"

"That's correct, sir."

"And why is that?"

"Now we're getting to the message I want to deliver to every citizen of the Free Nation," said Ben Jackson, looking meaningfully into the camera. His voice cracked a little as he said, "Roland Brand is an evil man. He destroyed my wife and now he's set on destroying the country. He won't be satisfied until the entire world is under his thumb. Because of my training and my constitution, Dad has chosen me to stop him. He wants you to stay out of my way so I can do my job. If I have to kill you, I'm terribly sorry. Dad says He's sorry too. But sometimes you have to look at the bigger picture. If Dad says your life must be sacrificed for the greater good, who are you to argue with Him?"

"For the sake of argument, Mr. Jackson, I can hear some of my countrymen asking, 'Who is this guy, and how do I know he's really talking to Dad?' After all, most of us have never heard Dad talk like that."

"With all due respect, sir, most of you have not been chosen. I have."

"Chosen? To kill our esteemed Secretary of Religion? To kill anyone who crosses your path?"

"That's correct, sir."

"Aren't you concerned that in publicizing your plan, you will alert the Secretary of Religion and he will increase his security?

"No amount of security can protect him from Dad. Besides, Dad says scared people make mistakes, so I want him to be scared. You hear that, Roland? I'm coming after you!"

This was going better than Logan Berry had ever dreamed. Up until now.

"Tell me, Mr. Jackson, how often do you speak with Dad?"

"I speak with Him all the time. Mostly, He speaks to me. When Dad talks, I listen."

"Is He speaking to you right now?"

"Yes, sir, he is."

"Mr. Jackson, would you care to tell the Free Nation what Dad is telling you at this moment?"

"He's telling me, 'Blow this sucker away.'"

"What?"

"That's right, sir. Dad wants me to blow you away."

"But why?"

"I don't know. Dad says there's just something about you that pisses Him off."

And with that, before a shocked and riveted Free Nation, Ben Jackson blew Logan Berry away.

Free Nationers had always been prone to Rubber Neck Syndrome. This was a disorder that originated on the freeways. A massive traffic jam would occur—people would be stuck in their cars for hours, and when they finally got to the source of the problem, they would discover an accident had occurred on the other side of the highway, and everybody, including themselves, would have to stop and stretch their "rubber necks" to see the carnage as they crept by.

On this historic day, every Free Nationer was gripped by Rubber Neck Syndrome. The entire country shut down so people could stay home and watch the ghastly moment over and over and over on their Electronic Babysitters. It was amazing how much there was to say about the subject. Although there was only one camera angle, the networks managed to spice it up with slow motion, fast motion, in and out zooms, and computerized simulations of the bullet's entrance and exits through Logan Berry's head.

"Stop the film here," a reporter would say. Then, with the victim's half-blown away head in a freeze frame, the reporter would point a laser light to identify a particle of Berry's brain.

People had never had so much fun being appalled and

disgusted. FNN registered the highest single-day ratings in its history.

Back in the trenches, Ben Jackson continued his lonely mission to rid the world of Roland Brand.

"Good job," said Dad. "I think we've got his attention now."

* * * * * *

"Good morning, Mr. Secretary."

"Good morning, Delbert."

"Mr. Secretary, before the large decision we're about to make, I think we should pray. I always like to say a prayer before I make large decisions."

"Good idea, Delbert."

"Being the Secretary of Religion, I think you oughtta say it. You got one?"

"Yes, Delbert. I've got one. Let us bow our heads:

> *Our Dad who art in Nebulon,*
> *Hollow be thy name,*
> *Thy will be done*
> *With great big guns,*
> *We'll blow the Evil Kashmir,*
> *To Kingdom Come."*

"Praise Dad."

"Praise Dad."

"Mighty pretty, Mr. Secretary. Praise Dad."

"Thanks, Delbert. Praise Dad. Listen, I was talking to Dad last night and . . . ."

"That's funny. I was talkin' to Him too," said Delbert. "What time were you talkin' to Him?"

"I'm not sure . . . Maybe around eight?"

"I musta talked to Him right after you. I talked to Him

around nine."

"Did He tell you what we talked about?"

"I'm not sure. Which part?"

"Operation Triple Nuke," Roland answered.

"Yeah, yeah," said Delbert. "I think I remember talkin' to Dad about that."

"Dad told me He wants us to go ahead with Operation Triple Nuke. Praise Dad."

"Yeah, that's what Dad told me, too. He said, 'Delbert'—that's what He calls me, Delbert—heh, heh. 'Delbert,' He says, 'you tell that Secretary of Religion of yours to go ahead with that Operation Triple Nuke.'"

"It could be risky," warned Roland.

"That's the trouble with you, Mr. Secretary. You don't think large! Dad told me, 'Think large, Delbert!' He calls me Delbert."

"You have a point. Ok, Delbert. If the Chosen Leader *and* Dad put their vote in for Operation Triple Nuke, I have no choice but to go along. Praise Dad."

"Praise Dad," said Delbert. "So, Mr. Secretary, what did Dad tell you about Operation Triple Nuke?"

"Dad thinks we should nuke Yurkistan, Sunny Sunnyland, and Rolandworld simultaneously. What did He tell you?"

"Why, He told me the same thing."

"Dad works in mysterious ways," said Roland. "Praise Dad. I guess it's a go, then?"

"Of course, it's a go! It's Dad's will! Operation Triple Nuke! Praise Dad.

Um . . . Why did Dad tell you to nuke Sunny Sunnyland and Rolandworld?" asked the Chosen Leader. "Aren't they part of the Free Nation?"

"Well, they are and they're not. Dad's very angry with the way they're disregarding my *RRR Manifesto*. He's afraid if we don't stop them now, they might lead a revolt against the Free Nation and the One True Religion."

"Yeah, that's what He told me, too. They're dangerous,"

Delbert agreed.

"They're very dangerous, Delbert. They're as dangerous as the Evil Abdul Kashmir."

"We better nuke 'em. Praise Dad."

"All three at once. Praise Dad."

"Show everybody what happens when ya cross Dad."

"Dad also told me He thinks we should nuke 'em next week," offered Roland.

"That's what Dad told me, too. He says, 'Delbert, I wantcha to nuke 'em into next week," said the Chosen Leader."

"Nuke 'em *next week*, Delbert. Dad wants us to nuke 'em into next week *next week*. Praise Dad."

"Praise Dad. Speaking of dangerous, did you watch the news yesterday?" asked Delbert.

"How could I miss it?"

"Ya gotta hand it to that Roadside Slaughterer. He's thinkin' large."

"I know. The problem is, the large thinking he's doing is about blowing me away."

"Did ya see that Logan Berry feller's brains?"

"Yes, Delbert. I did."

"Splattered all over the damn place."

"What are we going to do about the Roadside Slaughterer?"

"Too bad about that Logan Berry feller. I always liked ta call on him at my press conferences."

"Do you think we could increase my security detail?"

"One time I was in a little pickle, so I call on that Logan Berry feller and he says, 'Mr. Chosen Leader, are the members of the Progressive party traitors, or are they in cahoots with Uncle Ominus?'"

"I'm thinking we should at least double my security."

"So I says, 'Ya know, Logan,' I says, 'it's been so long since I talked to one of 'em, I don't believe I know yer answer. Maybe they're both.'" The Chosen Leader got a good laugh out of his joke.

"Around the clock."

"Yeah—too bad about that Logan Berry feller. For a reporter, he was ok."

"Delbert?"

"Yes, Mr. Secretary?"

"Are there plenty of security guards around this basement?"

"Why, my security's so tight I can't even flush the toilet without them tryin' it out first. Why?"

"Just checking," said Roland, looking around. "The reason I ask is, last night, Dad told me he wanted my security doubled."

"Yeah, seems to me I remember Him mentioning something like that to me, too," said Delbert. "We'll get you all the security you need. I'd hate to see you end up like that Logan Berry feller. Didja see that close-up of the side of his head?"

"I did," said Roland squirming. "You'll get me that security Dad asked for?"

"No problem," said Delbert. "I just remembered another thing Dad told me."

"What's that?"

"He says, 'Delbert, I want you to push the button.'"

"The button?"

"The nuke button. Dad wants *me* to push it. Praise Dad."

"Dad wants *you* to push the button that sends the nukes to Yurkistan, Sunny Sunnyland, and Rolandworld?"

"That's what He said."

"Well, Delbert, if Dad wants you push the button, who are we to say no?"

"I've never pushed a nuke button before."

"There's a first time for everything. Praise Dad."

"Praise Dad."

"Delbert?"

"Yes, Mr. Secretary?"

"You'll get right on it with that extra security Dad wants me to have?"

"I'll get right on it.

"Praise Dad."
"Praise Dad."

XX. FAITH-BASED FACTS

I LIKE FACTS. I GUESS YOU COULD SAY I'M A FACTS MAN. DID YOU know:

Fact: I once made a guy who begat two sons after he was five-hundred years old. And that was way before erectile enhancement drugs.

Fact: I once made a guy who disobeyed me, so for punishment, I had a fish swallow him. I made him think it over inside the fish's belly for three days and three nights, after which time he got the message. So I saved him by making the fish vomit him onto dry land. To this day, we in Nebulon have to keep our distance from him—he never was able to get rid of the smell.

Fact: I once made a guy who said the earth revolved around the sun. You can imagine the trouble he got into. His persecutors' point was he was contradicting Me when I said I "hangeth the earth above nothing." He was forced to renounce his position and state the obvious: "The earth does not move under our feet." It doesn't take a rocket scientist to figure that out.

There are two kinds of facts: Proven facts and faith-based facts. I like faith-based facts the best. They're the most reliable. Consider the Source.

Factoids 3:65

* * * * * *

"Sophia!" Donald LaFarge exclaimed. "What have they done to you?"

This is different, thought Sophia Wise. *They've never turned on the overhead light before.*

She guessed they wanted her to be able to see Donald while he talked. If she hadn't taken a vow of silence and if there had been somebody to tell—two big ifs—she would have said she didn't need the light. She could smell Donald LaFarge's fear and his bruises. She didn't need to see his confusion—she could hear it in his voice. *Maybe,* she thought, *they wanted* him *to see* her.

"Sophia, this is terrible!" he continued. "Being all chained up like that, how are you able to face in the right direction for your quarter-hour prayers? You'll never get to Nebulon this way!"

"Donald, would you mind scratching my nose?" she asked. Whoops—she broke her vow of silence again. Oh well, technically her vow was that she wouldn't talk unless she had something worthwhile to say.

"That's good. A little to the left, please?" That was worthwhile, she guessed.

Donald was all in a stew about Nebulon and Uncle Ominus and something about how the guards had taken away his suitcase, and if the rocket ship came for him right now, he didn't know if he could survive the trip. Sophia thought she heard him ask if, when they were on the rocket ship, would she mind letting him borrow her toothbrush?

She smiled as she watched him talk. Oh, how she loved poor, mixed-up Donald LaFarge. He talked too much, but then, so did most people. She sighed. She wanted to say, 'Donald, you take things way too seriously.'

But she knew if she said that, he'd just take that seriously, too. And then he'd be off talking too much and too seriously about why it was important to take things seriously. *No*, she thought, *better to just let him run out his string.*

There was a lot of string to run out. The first string was about Roland Brand. Sophia tuned in long enough to hear that Donald LaFarge couldn't understand why Roland thought he was the enemy.

"How can I convince him we're on the same page?" he implored. He unraveled a string about how supportive he was of the **RRR Manifesto** and the more rigorous regime, and how you *had* to have strict rules so people could be free to practice the One True Religion.

"We *agree* on that!" he exclaimed.

He continued his string about the one narrow road to Nebulon, and how few people were on that road; that he and Roland Brand were brothers, walking that path side-by-side.

"If only brother Roland could see," he lamented.

From there the string wound back to the familiar territory of Dad's greatness and how we wait for the rocket ship to Nebulon—but *it* won't wait for *us*, so we'd better be ready to climb on board; and the wrath of Uncle Ominus and the terrible things that happen on Planet Ug and the one thousand, one hundred and eleven who will escape that dreadful fate . . . .

Sophia was glad the light was on after all. It turned out, there *were* things you could see that were hard to hear and smell. She watched Donald's eyes and saw they were very far away. They reminded her of marbles or the eyes on a deer's head she had once seen mounted on a hunting lodge wall. If the cell had been dark, she might not have known how much Donald LaFarge worried about flies. She watched his hands as he spoke, and they kept waving in all directions, as if he were chasing away a swarm of flies.

Sight or not, Sophia probably would have known Donald

LaFarge didn't like living very much. He couldn't wait to go to Nebulon so he could get away from all of this. He paced frantically as he talked, but Sophia knew he wasn't moving nearly fast enough to dodge whatever it was he was trying to escape. She knew *he* knew it too.

Time to pray. She watched him get down on his knees, head to the ground, butt in the air, hands clasped in front of him, rocking back and forth, tearfully asking Dad why Roland Brand didn't trust him, and exhorting Him to explain to Roland that Donald LaFarge was a friend, not a foe. Then he got up, dusted himself off, and said, "You missed your quarter-hour prayer, Sophia. You'll never get to Nebulon at this rate."

Then he was back to being tangled up in the string that questioned why Roland didn't trust him.

"I know I've sold a lot of books, and for many years I was the leading exponent of the *Are You Ready?* school of thought," LaFarge reasoned, "but Roland has nothing to defend against me. He's the *Secretary of Religion*! I'm *happy* that he's climbed on my shoulders and outgrown me. I *defer* to him. He has my total respect and devotion. I'm the teacher learning from the pupil.

"Sophia," she heard him say, "maybe *you* could talk to him. He listens to *you*."

She wondered what he was like as a child. Little Donald LaFarge. She imagined he liked school—especially when the teachers were strict. He'd like the ones who punished him in front of the class if he broke a rule. Little Donald LaFarge probably didn't like recess. He would have been lost and confused and scared because there was no one on the playground to tell him what to do. Except the bullies. He probably hung close to the bullies. He'd be relieved when he got back into the classroom again, with the strict teacher who gave him clear instructions and demanded they be followed.

And still, LaFarge hadn't run out his string. Sophia figured it might take a while before he noticed she hadn't said anything.

Well—she *did* ask him to scratch her nose. For Donald LaFarge, that amounted to an entire conversation. He wouldn't notice it was Sophia's turn again for quite some time.

She guessed this was how Roland meant to "soften her up." She had to admit, Donald LaFarge's talking got pretty tedious, but there were plenty of ways she could amuse herself. She could look deeply into his face until it wasn't a face anymore but swirling liquid, just like her prison cell. She could make his face melt or change colors. Who is that? Donald LaFarge's face turned into somebody she didn't know, but then she figured out it must be his father. No wonder Donald's like that, she thought. His father is one scary dude.

She wanted to say, 'Oh Donald, I'm so sorry your father scared you and made you think you had to have all the answers in order to make sense of this crazy world. I'm sorry you had to hang with the bullies at recess. Just quiet down and listen to the birds. Go to the ocean and smell the salt. Feel your heart thumping, Donald.'

But she knew if she said those things, it would just give him more to talk about. She smiled a sad smile.

"Time's up," said Orvil Swain, lumbering in.

"Already?" asked Donald.

"Yup," answered Swain. "Roland's gonna be here in just a few minutes, an' if I was you, LaFarge, I wouldn't wanna be around when he comes."

"Orvil, tell Roland I'm on *his* side. Will you do that? Will you tell him I'm his brother?"

"Sure, LaFarge. I'll tell 'im. Roland'll be so relieved!"

"Oh, thank you, Orvil. You're my brother, too. Bye, Sophia. Nice talking with you."

Poor Donald LaFarge.

Orvil turned to Sophia. "Roland'll be payin' you a visit real soon with that special tattoo. He says ta tell you that if you'll talk, things'll go a lot easier for ya."

He started to shove LaFarge out the door. "Don't go

anywhere," he called to her over his back and chuckled.

"Hey, Orvil!" called Sophia.

"You say somethin'?" he asked, surprised.

"Tell Roland to bring me a drink of water."

She knew she was breaking her vow of silence, but she thought it was a worthwhile thing to say.

* * * * * *

Chosen Leader Delbert Thorne straightened his tie as he settled down behind his desk, facing the camera. Tonight was the momentous night he would address the Free Nation in prime time to announce his plan for Operation Triple Nuke. He was guaranteed a good audience. Ever since the citizens had witnessed the Roadside Slaughterer blowing away Logan Berry right before their eyes, every citizen had been glued to the EB to find out what would happen next in the soap opera known as the Free Nation.

Behind Delbert Thorne was a wall-sized Free Nation flag. The design was simple yet elegant: The top half was black, the bottom half white. In the top left-hand corner was a golden "D" for "Dad." The "D" had a crown on top of it. Chosen Leader Thorne often liked to point out that the "D" could stand for "Delbert," too.

After Delbert's problematic speech before the League of Steadfast Devotionists, he wasn't taking any chances. In the event of another teleprompter malfunction, there was a back-up teleprompter on hand, ready to take over seamlessly. And, to cover all his bases, Delbert kept a paper copy of the speech on the desk in front of him. The "hard copy" served the dual purpose of providing a security blanket in case of teleprompter malfunction, but equally important, in making a show of reading it, Delbert aimed to dispel the rumors that he couldn't read. Those rumors were nothing but vicious lies spread by his enemies in the Progressive party. Of course, Delbert could read!

With a small dose of Visactra, Delbert could read anything!

Visactra was the new miracle drug that helped people who suffered from Reading Dysfunction. One little yellow pill would have a first-grader reading Shakespeare, Homer, and Chaucer for up to thirty-six hours. Side effects might include: Headaches, dizziness, nausea, stroke, seizure, and death. "If you find yourself speaking in verse for more than four hours, call your physician immediately," the ads said.

Unfortunately, reading-enhancement drugs hadn't caught on the way the pharmaceutical companies had hoped. The problem was most Free Nationers didn't know they *had* a Reading Dysfunction because it had been so long since they'd tried. That narrowed the market down to a few college students who were cramming for finals, and specialty cases like Delbert Thorne, a world leader with a speech to read.

Delbert straightened his tie one last time, adjusted his erection vertically so it pushed his pants above the desktop, took a sip of water and a deep breath. He was ready to give the biggest speech of his life.

"Ladies and gentlemen: The Chosen Leader of the Free Nation."

"Good evening, my fellow citizens. I wish to speak to you tonight on a matter of grave importance . . . ."

"Don't say 'grave.'"

"What?" Delbert looked around.

"It's Dad, Delbert. Don't say 'grave.' When you're about to start a nuclear war, 'grave' has all kinds of bad connotations."

"Heh, heh, Dad's such a joker," said Delbert, forcing a smile."

"They can't hear me," Dad told him. 'Only you."

"Lemme start over, Delbert tried again. "Good evening, my fellow citizens. I wish to speak to you on a matter of . . . large . . . importance."

"Large?" asked Dad. "Oh well, your choice."

"As you know," Delbert continued to read, "we have

enemies in our mitts."

"Midst, Delbert. That's 'midst.' How long ago did you take that Visactra?"

"I just took it this morning, Dad. It oughta be . . ." Delbert caught himself and refocused. "Anyway, we got enemies in our midst. The Evil Abdul Kashmar . . . ."

"Kashmir," Dad corrected.

" . . . is threatening to take over the world. We can't let that happen, because Dad wants *me* to take over the world."

"I can hardly wait. Who wrote this speech?" Dad asked.

"I wrote that line myself. Pretty good, huh?"

"You ought to fire your speechwriter."

Delbert's eyes flitted around as if trying to locate the unseen voice. Back to the camera.

"But now, we have new enemies looming on the horizon."

"Ok—sounds a bit paranoid, but keep going."

"Um . . . Where was I? Oh yeah—enemies on the horizon. My Secretary of Religion Roland Brand, has informed me that in Sunny Sunnyland and in his own Rolandworld over there in Red Rock, pockets of rebellion have arisen."

"Pockets have arisen? Wait—don't tell me—you wrote that line, too?"

"What's wrong with 'pockets have arisen,' Dad?"

Delbert Thorne always prided himself in his ability to stay on message, but Dad had a compelling voice and could be pretty distracting.

"Never mind, Delbert. Just do your best."

Out in the Free Nation, people were starting to get a sense that something strange was going on. They were used to their Chosen Leader's speeches being somewhat of an adventure, but tonight he seemed even more confused than usual. He kept stopping to look around, and he seemed to be talking to somebody who was off-camera. Oh well, they thought, this is a really big speech for him. Maybe he'll settle down.

Delbert Thorne appeared to be hanging in there for a while,

but then out of nowhere, the entire Free Nation heard their Chosen Leader shout: "DAD! YOU'RE DRIVING ME CRAZY! CAN'T YOU SEE I'M TRYING TO GIVE A SPEECH? EVERY TIME YOU TALK TO ME, I GET DISTRACTED AND LOSE MY PLACE! CAN'T WE TALK ABOUT THIS AFTERWARDS?"

They saw his face turn red and perspiration appear above his lip. His hair stuck out in the places he had pulled while he was yelling at Dad. Many citizens got down on their knees and prayed that their Chosen Leader wouldn't melt down. Others didn't bother to pray because they knew the line was tied up—Dad was busy talking to Chosen Leader Thorne.

"Just trying to help," said Dad.

"Anyway, as I was SAY-ying," Chosen Leader Delbert Thorne started again, "we've got three big enemies: The Evil Krisco in Yokelstan . . . ."

"Aargh . . . ."

" . . . the creeping permissiveness of Bobism in Sunny Sunnyland, and the blasphemous rebellion in Red Rock, led by the Godless Gorilla Girls."

"Um . . . I hate to interrupt, Delbert. Nice alliteration, but that's 'guerilla.'"

"That's what I said, Dad—gorilla! Anyway, I have a message for the Evil Ab . . . dul Kash . . . mir . . . ."

"Good . . . ."

" . . . and for Bob in Sunny Sunnyland, and to the Godless Gorilla Girls in Red Rock, and that message is: The world isn't big enough for both of us!"

"Oh, Lordy, Lordy! Delbert, I'm sorry, but I've got to stop you. You can't say, 'The world isn't big enough for BOTH of us!' Don't you know? That would mean it's not big enough for you and one other person, like maybe you and Abdul Kashmir. I understand—you were trying for a rhetorical flourish. But it doesn't work. If you're talking about more than two, you can't say 'both.'"

Delbert stood up and shook his fist in the air. "WHY DON'T YOU WRITE THE GODDAMN SPEECH, THEN?! WHY DIDN'T YOU SAY SOMETHING BEFORE, INSTEAD OF WAITING TILL NOW TO TELL ME?!"

"Sit down, Delbert. The Free Nation is watching."

Dad was right. The Free Nation was watching and holding its collective breath.

Delbert sat back down, wiped the sweat off his brow with his sleeve, took a deep breath, readjusted his erection, and collected himself.

"My fellow citizens, I'm going to level with you," Delbert Thorne said, dramatically throwing away his script. "Turn off the teleprompter, boys."

"Uh-oh, don't you remember what happened last time?"

"Truth is, my fellow citizens," he continued, "I been havin' some long conversations with Dad, deep into the night. He's with me all the time in this dark hour. Fact is, He's with me right now."

Free Nationers across the land nodded their heads. Now they were beginning to understand.

"Dad's got a plan—it's called Operation Triple Nuke."

"Don't bring ME into Operation Triple Nuke—that was Roland's idea."

"Like I say, Dad come to me one night an' He says, 'Delbert . . .' That's what he calls me, 'Delbert.' Heh, heh. 'Delbert,' He says, 'I want you to take out Yurkistan, Sunny Sunnyland, and Red Rock all in one shot. I call my plan Operation Triple Nuke. It's gonna be hard,' Dad says. 'Lots of innocent people gonna die.' You know what Dad calls that? He says it's 'commandable damage.'"

"Delbert, you're on your own. I'm outta here."

"Dad says a few million lives is a small price to pay when you're rootin' out evil."

"I said that? Why are you guys always misquoting me? I said TALL price to pay."

"Dad says once we're done with Operation Triple Nuke, the world'll be free and we can all finally live in peace. Praise Dad."

Praise Dad, said the Free Nation.

"Delbert . . . ."

"Dad wants you to know, even if you're one of the ones that ends up bein' collapsible damage . . . ."

"Delbert . . . ."

" . . . He wants you to know collisional damage is a commendable thing if . . . ."

"DELBERT!"

"Hold on a second. Dad's pagin' me," Delbert told the Free Nation. Then to Dad, "What is it, Dad? Can't you wait till I'm done with my speech?"

"Delbert, I want to speak to the Free Nation. Will you pass on a message for me?"

"Oh . . . sure, Dad." Delbert was always happy to be Dad's messenger.

"Tell them I said they're all my children."

"Ok, heads up everybody. Dad's talkin' to me an' He wants me to tell you something. He wants you to know you're all His children. Ok, Dad, what's next?"

"Tell them I love each and every one of them. Tell them I would never think of any idea like Operation Triple Nuke. Tell them using nukes makes you wrong."

"Ok," said Delbert dutifully. "Let's see if I got it. Dad says He loves each and every one of you. He thinks He was clever to come up with the idea of Operation Triple Nuke. And He says using nukes will make me strong."

"Delbert, you're myopic."

"Dad says, 'Delbert, you're my pick.' That's what He calls me—'Delbert.' Heh, heh."

"Goodbye, Delbert. Good luck. Send my love to the Free Nation."

"Bye, Dad. Good luck to you, too. Hey everybody, Dad sends His love. Let's hear it for Dad."

Delbert led the applause, and in living rooms throughout the land, people put their hands together for Dad.

"Ok, like I was sayin'," Delbert continued his speech, "Dad come to me with this idea for Operation Triple Nuke, an' He says, 'Delbert, I want you to be the one to push the button.'"

The citizens of the Free Nation went to bed happy that night, knowing their Chosen Leader and Dad had a plan to finally rid the world of evil. However, many residents of Sunny Sunnyland and Red Rock began packing their bags and loading up the car. As much as they supported Operation Triple Nuke, they decided it was in their best interest to not be collateral damage.

* * * * * *

"I brought you some water, Sophia."

It was Roland Brand.

"Here," he said. "Let me undo one of your hands. It'll be easier to drink that way."

She had a reflex to say thank you, but she decided it wouldn't be worthwhile. Thank you for what? He was the reason she was sitting here hungry and thirsty, beat up and chained to the prison bars. She took the cup and drank very slowly. She savored the cool water and felt her body revive like a dry fern in the rain.

Of course, Roland was talking too much. Something about how she had let him down. They could have been partners in this grand adventure. The world was his and it could have been hers, too. But no—instead, she and her silly little friend had to go and undo everything he had worked so hard to build and set a bad example for the rest of the nation that understood the importance of his decrees and he was so disappointed in her and blah, blah, blah . . . This was the best tasting water she had ever had in her life. It's a good thing she took a vow of silence. It was much better to drink water than it was to talk.

Oh, how she wished Roland would go away and leave her to her water. But he kept talking, as she knew he would. *I guess he'll go on for quite a while,* she thought, as she took another slow luxurious drink. Now he was on a riff about how it wasn't too late. She could still join him. He could do this alone, but it would be so much easier if she came on board—"a woman's touch"—did he actually say that? *My, it felt good to wet her throat.*

"Aren't you going to say anything, Sophia?"

She studied Roland. Interesting—she'd never seen him before. She used to think he was quite handsome. She realized the way she used to see Roland Brand was the way you look at something out of the corner of your eye. With peripheral vision, you could mistake a road sign for a tree. *You have to look at things straight on to really see them,* she thought. *You have to look at them with your whole body, not just your eyes.*

"Sophia, you're not making things easy for yourself."

She was glad she had finally learned to look at things straight on with her whole body. When she did, she realized Roland wasn't handsome at all! That gleam in his eye was a black light that tied a knot in her stomach. Those white teeth she used to so admire now were fangs that made her flesh crawl. She tried an experiment. She squinted to make him blurry.

"Sophia!"

When he was a blur, he appeared symmetrical. His face, hands, body, all in perfect balance. Then she opened her eyes as widely as she possibly could and looked again. What a change! Beneath the symmetry was a grotesque and frightening tangle of snakes and worms and bad intentions, illuminated by black light.

"Sophia! Are you going to talk to me or are you just going to sit there and . . . ."

Better to not look too hard. She could feel Roland's innards creeping into her own. Better to take another drink of water.

" . . . leave me no choice."

Delicious.

" . . . make an example of you."

Amazing how a simple drink of water can wash Roland right out of your body. All you have to do is look at the water straight on as it travels down.

" . . . a 'T' tattoo on your forehead. But not the generic 'T' we've been issuing to the female masses. Their tattoos have been small and plain, no bigger than a nickel, really. The purpose has not been to cause them unnecessary discomfort, merely enough to remind everybody who's boss and to assure they're all on the same page.

"No, for you I have in mind something much more elaborate. I will apply it myself. The base of the 'T' will start at the bridge of your nose and branch out like a tree across your entire forehead. The design I have in mind will be multi-colored, ornate, and time-consuming. But, you're an old hand at the tattoo game. I'm sure you won't mind."

Sophia had been nursing her water. It was about half gone now. She wondered if he would give her some more when she ran out.

"But that's just the preliminary," Roland continued. "As I said, I must make an example of you. If my manifesto is to be successful, it is of critical importance that the citizenry witness the consequences of defying my decrees. Therefore, in three days you will be paraded through the town square with your new, custom-designed tattoo on your forehead, and there, before the entire Free Nation, you will be declared a witch, an enemy of the state, a Slacker of the First Degree, and you will be burned at the stake."

Sophia took another drink, a little too fast.

"It's a pity, really," said Roland. "My tattoo masterpiece will be so new and we'll have to burn it up. Oh well—do you know there are cultures that create a piece of art and destroy it immediately upon completion? Something about the transience of life."

Sophia felt her heart thumping in her chest and heard it in

her ears. *My, it's working hard*, she thought. She looked directly at it and saw her heart pumping, saw the rich blood rushing fast through her veins; saw the fear that sent a shot of adrenaline to her beloved heart, thrusting it into action. She was glad she had learned how to look at things. She was sure she would learn to see more clearly still, as she went through the last days of her life, followed by a burning death. Better start now, she thought. With hands slightly shaking, she took another sip of water.

"I will now call in Orvil Swain. He will assist me in your ordeal of the tattoo. This might be your last chance to speak, Sophia. Are you sure you have nothing to say?"

Sophia thought for a moment, weighing the worth of her words.

"Could you ask him to bring me some more water?" she asked.

* * * * * *

Traffic into Capital City was impossible. Lakshmi Jackson came to the same conclusion that her father, the Roadside Slaughterer, had come to earlier: Better to get out and walk. She asked Phil to pull into the next rest stop, and with her mother's hand in hers, she led Natalie and Phil on their long march to Capital City.

Most people stuck in the traffic jam were content to sit in their cars, breathing fumes and cursing their luck. However, when they saw Lakshmi and her little band marching resolutely past them on the side of the highway, they concluded she might have a better idea.

"Where are you going?" some asked.

To which Lakshmi would reply, "We're marching to Capital City. Our friend, Sophia Wise has been wrongfully imprisoned and is in grave danger. It is our mission to free her and deliver her to safety."

There was something about Lakshmi's conviction that made people want to follow her. That, and the fact they were tired of sitting in their cars, breathing fumes and cursing their luck. That and the fact that Follow-the-Leader was the Official National Game of the Free Nation. They never got tired of it. So, when the motorists saw Lakshmi Jackson, a radiant young woman with an uncovered head, marching forward with strength and determination to right the wrong that was being inflicted upon her friend, many were compelled to follow. They got out of their cars and abandoned them.

By the time they reached the outskirts of town, the numbers of people who marched behind Lakshmi had grown to a thousand strong. The story of Sophia Wise's persecution had spread like an electric current through the crowd. As if they'd been shaken awake from a long sleep, the people came alive with resolve and purpose. They followed young Lakshmi Jackson through the gates of Capital City, bolstered by her strength and propelled by her cause.

* * * * * *

Slithering on his belly through the tall grass like a snake was Ben Jackson, the Roadside Slaughterer. Dad had informed him that for the duration of his journey, he would have to travel in this fashion.

"There are too many people looking for you, Ben," He had said. "You're going to have to keep your head down."

Oh, the trials Dad put him through. Once again, Ben thanked Dad for the strength He had given him to carry out his demanding task. Though his knees and elbows were rubbed raw, his clothes tattered, though he grimaced as he gasped for each breath, he never faltered and he never failed, for his spirit was strong and his loyalty to Dad was absolute.

"I'd give my life for you, Dad," he said.

"I know you would, Ben. And you will."

Ben had learned from the couple he had blown away that morning that there was to be a public execution in the town square the following day. Before they had the misfortune of seeing him, he had overheard them talking by the side of the road.

"Did you hear about the witch they're going to burn at the stake tomorrow?" asked the woman, hidden by her veil and vaulted cloak.

"Yes," her companion shuddered. "I hear she's guilty of the most horrible abominations."

"I was told she is so unspeakably evil," replied the woman, "that none other than our Secretary of Religion, Roland Brand, will preside over the ceremonies."

Ben jerked involuntarily and rustled the brush.

"What the . . ." The unfortunate pair looked in the direction of the noise and there, camouflaged in the weeds, lurked Ben Jackson. Faster than you could say "Roadside Slaughterer," he was on his feet, rifle trained at the man's head.

"Tell me quick," he said. "Where and what time?"

"N . . . n . . . noon in the center of town," the man stuttered. "Please sir, spare our lives. We've done nothing to you. We won't breathe a word."

"Dad? What do you think?" Ben put the question to the Higher Authority. "Dad says thanks for the tip. You've been a big help." And with that, the Roadside Slaughterer turned the poor couple into one more case of collateral damage.

"Noon in the center of town," Ben whispered to Dad as he panted and slithered along. "I've almost reached the end of my journey."

"Don't put the cart before the horse, Ben. The most important part of your task is yet to come."

"Don't worry, Dad. I won't fail you."

"I know you won't Ben. That's why I've chosen you."

By night, Ben had reached Capital City. He located the thirty-five story FreeCorps building at the center of town. He emptied his backpack, blackened his face with charcoal, and then, with only the use of ropes and suctions, he scaled the side of the building until he reached the top.

Lying flat on the roof, he scanned the scene below through his night-vision goggles. There in the center of town, he saw a platform. On the platform was a high pile of straw and logs with a tall stake protruding from the center.

At noon tomorrow, thought Ben, *Roland Brand will appear on that very platform with the evil witch.* He lined up the target in his gun site and prepared for the night's lonely vigil on the rooftop.

"Just a few more hours and I'll be home," he whispered.

XXI. MELTDOWN

People often ask me: "Dad, how do I know it's really you who's talking to me and I'm not just some wacko hearing voices?"
And I always answer the same way: "That's a good question."

Riddles 3:17

* * * * * *

THE FREE NATIONERS WERE UP EARLY. THE CAPITAL CITY residents began gathering in the town square before sun-up, and by mid-morning, the place was packed. Across the rest of the land, people stumbled out of bed and, while still in their robes, headed straight to the Electronic Babysitter and turned it on. Then, over breakfast and coffee, they watched the preliminaries and heard every angle covered in-depth about the evil witch who was to be burned at the stake that day. Live from the nation's capital!

With so much to talk about, the biggest suspense was whether the talking heads would get it all in before the execution. There was much historical background to be covered on the Evil Witch Sophia Wise; many questions to be answered about what had led her down the road to wickedness, and speculation about her motives in defying Rolandism. Legal experts and theological scholars were trotted out to parse the difference between a slacker and a Slacker-in-the-First-Degree.

Pyrotechnicians offered an array of techniques for witch-burning and discussed in detail the methods to be employed in today's spectacle. It turned out the combination of straw, oil, peat, and large logs that had been meticulously erected was designed for slow burning to maximize the amount of time the victim would suffer.

There were countless panel discussions pitting practical members of the Regressive Party who passionately defended their Secretary of Religion's uncompromising methods versus the Progressive Party permissives who argued that a less extreme form of capital punishment such as hanging would be more humane.

In keeping with his flair for dramatics, Secretary of Religion Roland Brand declared this day National Medieval Day. All cars were parked outside Capital City, and the town was given a makeover. The streets were turned to cobblestone; buildings were covered with facades of brick and crumbling rock. Vegetable stands were set up on corners; venders with wheelbarrows patrolled the crowd calling, "Pumpkin bread! Pumpkin bread!" Toothless beggars sat on the ground, arms outstretched, pleading for alms. The townspeople were ordered to dress in peasant garb and say things like "Yea, verily," and "Forsooth," and "Take up thy quarterstaff and defend thyself, scurrilous varlet," and "Hark! O hark, O lady fair; wilt thou beest mine own true love?" lending authenticity to the event.

All in all, it was an exciting day for Free Nationers who were treated to a first-hand civics lesson. "Freedom in Action!" was the rallying cry across the land. Most citizens thought they would be relieved when the world was finally free from the evil witchcraft of Sophia Wise. Many were also privately relieved that it was she who would be burned at the stake and not they. But why would they be burned at the stake? They would never do what she did.

As the time grew nigh, the Electronic Babysitter news stars made much of the route the Evil Witch Sophia Wise would take, leading to her fate. Photos of the square were brought out, and analysts traced the path she would travel—first down the cold stone steps from her cell, high in the prison tower; onto the street where she would be shackled standing in a donkey-drawn hay wagon, then paraded slowly in a clockwise circle around the square, detouring here and there up side streets, and finally arriving at her destination: The large wooden platform on which a stake was mounted in the center of an enormous kindling construction, which, when lit, would become a bonfire that would consume the evil witch along with the entire platform.

The tower bells struck twelve, and it seemed for a moment that no one in the entire Free Nation took a breath. The peasants of Capital City turned their eyes toward the prison tower, from where they knew the Evil Witch Sophia Wise would soon emerge.

And there she was! The first thing they saw was Sophia's shorn head. After all the news about her frequent changes from one wild color to the next, most people had expected to see a shock of bright green, purple, or orange. But no. Her captors had cut off her locks, leaving only a stubble on her bare skull. The nakedness of her head accentuated the "T" tattoo that began at the bridge of her nose and branched out across her forehead. It was magnificent indeed—a swirling and colorful ornamental design, complimented by the graceful lines that were Roland Brand's trademark.

Sophia was free of her filthy prison rags, and in their place she had been clothed in a ceremonial robe of purple velour that touched her bare feet. As the men-at-arms with swords and spears, clad in shining mail of linked chain, lifted the shackled

Sophia Wise into the donkey cart, a hush fell over the crowd. They were not prepared for this—she looked positively regal!

The peasants had collected their tomatoes and rotten fruit, and had counted the moments until the Evil Witch would appear so they could yell, "A pox upon thy breast, ye vixen!" and let 'er fly. But not an object or a curse was thrown.

How could they? She was the most beatific sight they had ever seen. Each person in the crowd thought Sophia looked directly into his or her eyes as she passed, and her expression penetrated every core. Her slight smile revealed a mysterious mix of joy, sadness, and acceptance. Her body stood straight; seemingly ready to embrace whatever fate might befall her. No one had ever been in the presence of such serenity, and they were rendered speechless. It was so quiet, they could hear the squeaking of the wagon wheels and clopping of the donkey's hooves as the glowing Sophia Wise passed them by.

The entire Free Nation was dumbstruck. In living rooms across the land, people laid down their pizza, popcorn, and beer, and silently witnessed. Even the EB talking heads were rendered speechless. Nothing but the sound of the six wooden steps creaking beneath Sophia's bare feet as the men-at-arms led her onto the stage. Nothing but the sound of clanking chains as they secured her to the stake. And still—that expression—if anything, stronger than before, reaching out to every man, woman, beast, and sprout with love.

A hatch on the floor of the platform opened, and from down below, Secretary of Religion Roland Brand rose upwards until he stood level with the floor. Like Sophia, he wore a long, flowing robe of velour, although his was gold in color and displayed the *RRR* insignia on the chest. He looked like a sorcerer with his tall triangular hat—some people had to admit to themselves it looked a bit like a dunce cap. Orvil Swain lumbered up the stairs behind the platform, his pale, hulking arms folded over an open, leather vest which came to rest upon his bare, bulging belly. From the back of the platform he withdrew a long, flaming torch, and brandishing it conspicuously, he took his place next to Roland. Up on the roof of the FreeCorps building, Ben Jackson cursed. For a brief moment, he'd had Roland in his sights, but now this big guy with a torch was blocking his view.

"Be patient, Ben," said Dad. "You'll get your chance."

"My fellow Free Nationers," began Roland Brand in the most dignified of tones, "we come together at this dark hour to carry out our solemn task."

It was so quiet, a dove could be heard cooing on some distant rooftop.

"There is no joy in the duty with which we are charged today," Roland almost whispered into the silence he mistook for a somber mood befitting the occasion.

"We, who love and value life," he continued, slightly raising his tone, "know that in order to preserve life, we must sometimes destroy it. And when we come face-to-face with godless wickedness in its purest form, as we do today in the form of the Evil Sophia Wise," his voice shook slightly as he built toward an emotional crescendo, "we are left with no choice but to get on with our thankless job and BURN THE WICKED WITCH UNTIL THERE IS NOTHING LEFT OF HER BUT ASHES!"

Roland was an old hand at working a crowd, and at this point he expected his listeners to be stirred to a fevered pitch. So, why were they staring at him like that? Why was everything so quiet? This scene felt strangely surreal. He decided he'd better backtrack and review Sophia Wise's transgressions. Maybe his timing was off and he'd moved too quickly. Maybe if he reminded everybody of atrocities she had committed that had brought her to this point . . . .

Ben Jackson wished Roland would hold still. For a second, he thought he had him in his sights, but then he moved too close to Sophia. Then he was behind the big guy with the torch again. All he needed was one clear shot . . . .

The people in the crowd were puzzled. They had come to

bask in the presence of their great Secretary of Religion, Roland Brand, and they had looked forward to getting worked into a frenzy by his fiery oratory. They had counted on him to infuse them with bloodlust so when the time came to destroy the evil witch in a terrible pyre, they would not shirk and they would not turn away. No, they would rally him on as he stoked the flames of their righteousness, as he stoked the flames of Sophia's terrible death.

So why was it the Evil Witch Sophia, shorn, tattooed and chained to the stake, awaiting her deserved doom, looked so angelic while their revered Secretary of Religion Roland Brand, outfitted in formal ceremonial garb, speaking with passion, justice, and Dad on his side, looked so . . . well . . . how could they put this . . . ? Lame?

As Roland continued his litany of Sophia's offenses, as the crowd pondered these questions in eerie silence, as Ben peered into his sights, looking for one clear shot, a faint chant could be heard near the entrance to the square. The chant grew louder as it approached.

"Free Sophia! Free Sophia!"

Everyone turned to see: A parade of a thousand men and women, entering the square and progressing steadily toward the platform. The crowd parted to make way.

"FREE SOPHIA! FREE SOPHIA!"

At the front of the parade marched Lakshmi Jackson, arms linked with her mother, Natalie, and Phil. Lakshmi did not chant. She walked in the lead with noble assurance. She seemed to be carrying the followers on her back. As she looked at Sophia their gazes locked, and for a moment they conversed with their eyes about love, transcendence, and strength of will.

Then, every person in the town square took up the cry: **"FREE SOPHIA! FREE SOPHIA!"**

Lakshmi mounted the six steps to the platform and stood in front of Sophia Wise. Roland Brand ordered his guards to seize her, but they were mesmerized along with everybody else.

"My name is Lakshmi Jackson," she announced. "I am a friend of this good woman before you, Sophia Wise. She has been wrongfully accused and her life is in our hands. And I say to you, as surely as morning follows night: There will be no killing today!"

The townspeople erupted in cheers.

"I will not speak to you about right and wrong; you already know.

"I will not remind you to 'Do unto others . . .' You know that, too.

"There is only one thing I can tell you that you don't already know, so this is what I will say:

"You have been in a long, deep sleep. **WAKE UP!**"

Another wild eruption as people did indeed wake up. And when they did, what did they find? A beautiful young woman bound before them, on the brink of being burned alive; a man in a robe and a dunce cap scaring them with fairy tales about witches and rocket ships and a guy named Uncle Ominus. They awoke to find Lakshmi Jackson shaking them from their long, dark slumber. And when they emerged, they found they had been sleepwalking through Capital City, drifting in a hazy dream in which thought and action were suspended, in which feelings and will were lost, in which reality was defined by decree.

Roland saw his empire slipping away. He realized, as the crowd advanced toward him, that the trance had been broken. He must act quickly, he thought. He raised his hands to silence the people and for a moment, they reflexively recoiled.

It was at that moment that Ben Jackson, the Roadside Slaughterer, stood on the rooftop and centered Roland Brand's heart directly in his cross hairs. His finger found the trigger but he heard Dad's voice say, "Now, Ben!" which distracted him and caused him to freeze for a split second. And in that frozen moment, Lakshmi leaped in front of Roland, crying above the crowd, "No, father, no! There will be no killing today!"

Unfortunately for Ben, Roland's bodyguards, who were

stationed at the top of two adjacent buildings, didn't agree. They shot him with startling efficiency and speed—CRACK!-CRACK!—sending bullets through each of his shoulders. The force of the impact blew Ben Jackson off his feet and sent him hurtling toward the ground, thirty-five stories below.

For the first twenty-five stories, Ben fell with terrifying acceleration. Then, time . . . began . . . to . . . cra-a-awl. Ben was amazed at how slowly he was falling and how clearly he could think. He no longer heard Dad's voice—it was the first time Dad hadn't been with him in a long time. Somehow, rather than miss Dad, he felt as though he had cleaned out his hopelessly cluttered desk.

He saw his beloved Aruna. She was whole again. She looked at him with deep love and sadness as she spoke to him.

"Ben, I love you," she said. "I'm sorry my craziness made you crazy. In the end, it was you who suffered most. I'm free now, and in a moment, you will be free, too."

Then Aruna was gone and his beloved daughter, Lakshmi, took her place. My, she was beautiful now. Lakshmi didn't say anything. She simply smiled at him, and he felt at peace. When he looked into her eyes, he knew his daughter had become strong and wise—much more than himself. He was glad for her. She reached out her hands to him, but his fall was accelerating and she couldn't catch him . . . .

The last thought that passed through Ben Jackson's mind before his body slammed into concrete and he returned to his source was:

"I think I fucked up."

Lakshmi watched her father fall to his death, and she knew she would grieve later. At this moment though, her mind was fixed on the task at hand: Free Sophia and get her out of Capital City. But the human tide was rushing in, and she had no more control over it than she had over the ocean. Neither did Orvil Swain, who, drowning in a sea of people, was stripped of the keys that would set Sophia free. Someone opened the locks, and

Sophia's shackles fell to the deck in a rusty heap. Then, the human tide rolled back out again, carrying Sophia on its shoulders, away from Capital City and toward safety.

Lakshmi gathered her mother, Natalie, and Phil, and hurriedly picked through the crowd, straining her neck to keep Sophia in her sights. As Lakshmi reached the edge of the square she heard pandemonium behind her, and she turned to look. Standing on the platform, far in the distance, was Roland Brand, shouting and waving his arms frantically as he tried to stop the next human wave from crashing the stage. Orvil Swain stood by his side, confronting the angry sea, swinging his torch in all directions, trying to fight back the tide. But he lost his footing as the huge mass broke over him and down he went. The torch flew from Orvil's hand, and the straw began to burn. Then the entire platform collapsed under the weight of people, and Roland too, disappeared beneath the crush.

The pyrotechnicians who had meticulously engineered the kindling to produce a slow burning fire, should have lost their jobs. For within moments, the stage on which Sophia Wise was to have been burned alive, was engulfed in flames, a hellish bonfire raging at the heavens. Lakshmi shuddered as she thought, *That is the last I will ever see of Roland Brand.*

* * * * * *

This isn't going the way I planned, thought Chosen Leader Delbert Thorne.

In fact, nothing was breaking his way. First, his address to the Free Nation, in which he unveiled Operation Triple Nuke, didn't seem to be having the desired effect. True, the citizens were generally supportive of the idea. Free Nationers could always be counted on to rally around their leader in times of war. But Delbert hadn't anticipated the mass exodus from Sunny Sunnyland and Red Rock.

What's the point of nuking 'em if there's no one there to

nuke? he wondered.

He thought the Sunnylanders and Red Rockers were shortsighted and selfish to be fleeing their homes to get out of harm's way. *That's the trouble with people these days,* he thought. *They're always putting their own interests ahead of the common good. They just can't see the big picture.*

Not only were ordinary citizens picking up and getting out, but there were reports of *slackers* leaving, too. *Don't they know, if they set up camp in another city, I'll just have to nuke 'em there?* he wondered. *At this rate, I'm gonna have to nuke the whole damn country!*

Maybe he'd shown too many of his cards. *I shouldn't have warned them about collaborative damage,* Delbert thought. *I guess I scared 'em away.*

It turned out, lots of people were trying to get out of Yurkistan, too. But one person who stayed put was the Evil Abdul Kashmir. He immediately issued a statement challenging Chosen Leader Delbert Thorne to a no-holds-barred, one-on-one Battle to the Death at any location of Delbert's choosing. Then, he stood on the steps of his palace, dressed in combat fatigues, stogie clenched in his teeth, shooting his gun into the air, shouting defiantly, "I'm right here, Delbert! Come and get me, you moron!"

That was the Evil Abdul Kashmir's big mistake. Not that Delbert came and got him. But a whole lot of Kashmir's countrymen did. They figured, with Kashmir in jail, maybe that lunatic running the Free Nation would lose interest and leave them alone.

They figured wrong. In fact, they played right into Delbert's hands. Delbert Thorne knew it was only a matter of time before the Evil Kashmir escaped and retook Yurkistan, at which time he would be more dangerous than ever. With Kashmir locked in jail, Delbert had a sitting target.

Hittin' the Evil Crushmeyer in prison with a nuke will be like stealin' candy from the broadside of a barn, thought the

Chosen Leader.

Then there was the Roland Brand fiasco. *I knew I couldn't trust that guy*, he thought. *I'm gonna have to tell Aides #2 and #3 to remind me to fire Aide #1. I don't know what he was thinkin' when he talked me into signin' up that Roland feller.* Brand had totally botched the witch burning, and now the natives were restless.

Another Secretary of Religion, been and gone. *That makes four*, Delbert thought. He knew he had to stop the losing streak and he had to stop it quick. So, he made a bold move that contained the two ingredients that were the staples of every Delbert Thorne decision:

Ingredient 1: Decide fast while the thought is still fresh in your gut, before it has time to reach your brain.

Ingredient 2: Do it yourself.

The two-ingredient decision Delbert made was to appoint himself Secretary of Religion. *I wish I had done this a long time ago*, he thought. *It's so hard to find good help these days*, he continued his line of thinking. *Sometimes if you want a job done right, you just gotta take matters into your own hands.*

If the thought that stayed in Delbert's gut had made it to his brain, he might have remembered there was a jinx on the Secretary of Religion. He was zero for four. If he had given his idea a chance to complete its cycle, it might have occurred to Delbert that when he appointed himself Secretary of Religion, he ran the risk of becoming zero for five. But to Delbert's thinking, he needed a Secretary of Religion, and he was the only one he could count on to do the job right.

In his dual role as Chosen Leader and Secretary of Religion, Delbert Thorne realized events were spiraling out of control and he would have to reassert himself. He couldn't wait until next week to nuke his enemies into next week. He had to do nuke 'em into next week *now*.

Chosen Leader and Secretary of Religion Delbert Thorne summoned his aides. They'd all be fired after this was over, but for now, he needed them. Once they assembled, he led them to the bowels of the Executive Palace and into the underground tunnel, through which they walked the two hundred yards to the top secret Nuclear War Room.

There was a bit of a mix-up getting in. Only a handful of people on the entire planet had the top security clearance necessary to enter the Nuclear War Room. Of course, Chosen Leader Thorne had such a clearance. Aides #3, #2, and #1 also had it. Unfortunately, Secretary of Religion Delbert Thorne did not. The non-descript guards explained that the rules were very clear on this point: Absolutely no one was allowed in without the proper pass—no exceptions. It looked as though they had reached an impasse, when Delbert came up with a brilliant idea: He fired himself as Secretary of Religion. That was good enough for the non-descript guards, who punched in the combination, waited for the light to blink green, and turned the heavy wheel that opened the massive, impenetrable door. It looked to Delbert as though they were stepping into a bank vault.

Once inside, Delbert chuckled as he whispered to Aide #1, "I had my fingers crossed."

"Brilliant idea, Mr. Chosen Leader and Secretary of Religion, sir," whispered Aide #1.

Delbert had only been in this dark underground room once before, and that was when he first became Chosen Leader, so many years ago. He had been given a tutorial on how to operate the console with the boggling array of switches, knobs, and buttons; the complex grid of computers, monitors, and programs. He had been shown how to pinpoint any location on the wall-size map, and how to program the robot-driven missiles to hit a cockroach halfway around the world.

Of course, he didn't remember any of that. That's what aides are for, he had thought. Neither did he remember the Nuclear Consequences lecture he had been given covering such topics as:

—Annihilating Hundreds of Thousands of People in One Fell
   Swoop: Pros and Cons
—Nuclear Fallout: When Is It Safe to Breathe?
—Environmental Degradation: Where Did All the Birds and
   Rabbits Go?
—Post-Nuke Diplomacy: What To Do When Your Enemy
   Holds a Grudge for More than a Hundred Years

Nor had he paid much attention to the Nuclear Ethics
lecture he had received, with the twenty-point checklist it was
recommended he tick off before nuclear weapons (NW) were
employed. If he had remembered the checklist, he might have
stalled on such items as:

**#3: NW should be used only if the Free Nation is under NW
   attack itself.**
**#4: In such event, NW should only be used upon the country
   that is nuking the Free Nation.**
**#7: Every attempt should be made to warn and evacuate
   innocent citizens before launching NW.**
#12: NW should never be used in anger or to get even.
#20: Get a second opinion.

Whatever, Delbert had thought at the time. And that was
what he was thinking now: *Whatever.* He only remembered one
thing from that introductory session, and for twelve years as
Chosen Leader he had bided his time, waiting for the day when
he could throw off all constraints and man the controls to the one
panel in the Nuclear War Room that he understood: The one
panel that, in his hands, would be the key to ultimate power; the
panel that had captured the new Chosen Leader's imagination
the first time he laid eyes on it twelve long years ago and had
occupied his fantasies and dreams ever since; the panel he now
gazed upon with the same combination of love, tenderness, and
lust with which a groom gazes upon his bride on their wedding

night. Delbert Thorne was not given to great fits of sentimentality, however, he was nearly overcome with emotion as he admired the understated beauty of the panel displaying nothing but three buttons: A red button on the left saying, **READY**, an orange button in the middle saying, **AIM**, and a green one on the right that said, **FIRE**.

The three-button panel rested in a vault behind the bulletproof glass door that required three keys to open it. Tradition had it that no one person would be the custodian to all three keys, and on this day, Aides #3, #2, and #1 each had one. Delbert ordered them to open up. When they did, Delbert lovingly lifted the panel out of the vault and stood it on the console so it faced him. His eyes lingered with longing over each of the three buttons, spaced a foot apart so there would be no possibility of pushing the wrong one in error.

"Before we do the deed, boys," said Delbert, "we need to pray."

Aides #3, #2, and #1 followed Delbert's lead and bowed their heads.

"Dear Dad," Delbert began, "I want to thank you for giving me the idea for Operation Triple Nuke. Thank you for helping me to think large. If it weren't for you, I might have only nuked Yurkistan. It's only your largeness of thinking that helped me understand I needed to nuke Sunny Sunnyland and Red Rock too. That's the difference between me, you, and everybody else. Me and you think large. That's why I'm the Chosen Leader and you're Dad. That's why everybody else is . . . well . . . everybody else.

"Thanks again, Dad, and may your large hand guide me in this large task I'm about to undertake. Love, Delbert." Then:

"Are we ready, boys?" he asked, hitching up his pants.

"Ready, Mr. Chosen Leader and Secretary of Religion," said Aide #3.

"All set, sir," said Aide #2.

"All three nukes are good to go, Mr. Chosen Leader and

Secretary of Religion, sir," said Aide #1. "Do you know how to work the controls, sir?"

"Of course I do," said Delbert. "What could be simpler than **READY, AIM**, and **FIRE**?"

"Nothing could be simpler, Mr. Chosen Leader and Secretary of Religion, sir," said Aide #1. "But the one most important thing you have to remember is: When you press the **AIM** button, keep holding it down while we train the targets on Yurkistan, Sunny Sunnyland, and Red Rock. Otherwise . . . ."

"Roger, Aide #1. I copy that. Now, I got an itch that's been waitin' twelve years to get scratched and I'm gonna scratch it right now."

As Delbert told Aide #1 about the itch he wanted to scratch, he pressed the **READY** button. However, there was one problem he hadn't counted on. When Delbert Thorne pressed the **READY** button, he made the fatal mistake of leaning in too far, inadvertently pressing the **FIRE** button simultaneously with his enormous erection.

"Sir! No, sir! Back up!" his aides cried frantically.

But it was too late. Delbert Thorne's enormous erection had fired three nuclear bombs before he could press the **AIM** button, causing the nukes to explode right where they sat—in Capital City.

The last thing Chosen Leader and Secretary of Religion Delbert Thorne said before he was vaporized along with the entire capital was: "Ya just gotta think large!"

XXII. THE WATER'S WIDE

I ONCE MADE A GUY WHO BECAME A GREAT JAZZ SAXOPHONE player. His name was Charlie Parker, but his nickname was "Bird." One day, Charlie Parker was asked the secret to improvising music, and this is what he said:

"First you master the instrument, then you master the repertory, then you forget all that shit and just play."

That's the lesson of life I would like to leave you with when you read my Book of Bob. *Study it! Learn it! Then forget all that shit and just play!*

While we're on the subject, I once made a great jazz pianist named Thelonious Monk. He used to walk in circles--around and around—for reasons no one knew. I made him a wife who helped him get dressed in the morning, pointed him toward the door, and sent him on his way. I made him a mistress with whom he spent part-time. His wife knew about her and didn't seem to mind—she was probably relieved to get a break. Once, at a recording session, two of his musicians were puzzling over an unreadable musical score he had written. One of them got up the nerve to ask, "Monk, is this note a C or a C-sharp?" To which

Monk replied:

"It don't matter."

Incidentally, most people say Charlie Parker got his nickname because he lived and played as "free as a bird." However, there are some who hold the belief that he acquired his nickname one day when he was riding in a car with his group, and they accidentally hit a chicken. He made the driver stop and pick up the chicken so he could ask his landlady to cook it for dinner.

Free as a bird or chicken for dinner. You choose. It don't matter.

Life Lessons 9:16

* * * * * *

Sunny Sunnyland's streak of consecutive beautiful days ended at 599. On day six hundred, people grew irritable when the sky became overcast and there were isolated reports of a few pesky drops. On day 601, it began to drizzle, and Sunnylanders got downright depressed. On day 602, they were plagued by genuine rain, and on day 603, it poured.

On day 602, the "First Rainy Day," most Sunnylanders who had not already fled because of the nuclear threat or because of the drizzle, had had enough. They headed for their nearest In 'n' Out market, where they stocked up on the provisions they thought they would need to see them through the crummy weather. Then they drove straight home where they intended to hole up until the next beautiful day.

Of course, many never made it home. Sunnylanders were out of practice driving in the rain—you might as well have laid a sheet of ice on the road. Cars were slipping and sliding, colliding into each other, and crashing through storefronts. The streets were littered with overturned cars, shattered glass, and broken bodies. Ambulances didn't have much better luck—the streets were littered with them, too. Driving in Sunny Sunnyland on a rainy day required the skill of a demolition derby driver and the nerves of a trapeze artist. It was dangerous business.

An interesting phenomenon took place on day 599, the "Last Beautiful Day." Sunnylanders looked up to see a black cloud moving eastward in the sky. It took them a moment to adjust their eyes before they realized they were not looking at a cloud at all, but a massive migration of birds. The Sunnylanders who happened to look down noticed swarms of ants and cockroaches heading in the same easterly direction. Bees and wasps, grasshoppers, frogs—every critter that could walk, crawl, or fly seemed to be packing up and heading east with single-minded purpose.

On day 600, the "Gloomy Gray Day," animal shelters throughout Sunny Sunnyland were inundated with phone calls. People were losing their pets in record numbers. Those who were brave enough to step outside saw a parade of poodles, labs, and cats running east. Those who managed to contain their pets were kept up at night by their frantic scratching at the door and the animals' desperate attempts to tunnel out.

The Electronic Babysitter news stations picked up the odd development, and for several nights they ran "human interest" stories on the "Peculiar Pet Pilgrimage." The local anchors joked that maybe the cause for the sudden exodus was that the pets were slackers who wanted to escape Chosen Leader Thorne's nuclear wrath. The more serious journalists speculated that someone in the Eastern Region was calling the pets with a whistle of a frequency undetectable to human ears. The theory took hold and pretty soon all of Sunny Sunnyland was buzzing about the "Pet Pied Piper." Whatever the reason, by Day 602, "The First Rainy Day," there was not a sign of wildlife anywhere, and Sunny Sunnyland was suffering from a plague of missing pets.

Eldon and Larry Smith shared the funk that had taken over the city. Eldon was depressed because he couldn't work on his tan outside. To complicate matters, Larry was back to his old ways. He had just taken out a loan to buy a new sports car, which he immediately totaled on Sunny Sunnyland's treacherous streets. This meant Eldon had no transportation to the tanning booth. He had already lost a precious layer, and he was watching all his hard work slip away. Needless to say, Eldon and Larry were both in ill humor, and things were getting tense.

Ivan Bunt and Venecia Bosco, on the other hand, were happy to see the rain. It gave them a good excuse to do what they were mostly doing these days anyway—staying inside.

"Turkeys a-gobblin', Venecia," Ivan would cry. "You're the cheese in my macaroni!"

"Oh, Ivan," Venecia would reply. "You're the raisins in my bran!"

Bob was taking Bud's death as well as could be expected.

"Well, that's that," he had said when Bud was gone.

On Day 599, "The Last Beautiful Day," Bob was deep in conversation with Dad. Dad seemed preoccupied with the boat Bob had just acquired and was grilling him on every minute detail.

"Did you fix that crack in the hull, Bob?" Dad asked.

"Dad, you know I did. You were hovering over me the whole time."

"Just checking," said Dad. "What about the generator? Did you buy that generator I told you to get?"

"Yes, Dad. Remember?"

"Bob, it's always better to be safe than sorry. Your power is bound to go out in the storm. Have you checked the generator?"

"I did."

"When?"

"Yesterday."

"Check it again."

"Dad," Bob said, "why are you so edgy? Can't you see it's a beautiful day? There's not a cloud in sight. I don't know why you're so convinced there's going to be a storm."

"I don't like the way the toilet's working," was Dad's reply. "It seems a little sluggish. You'd better put in some drain cleaner. It's going to be a long trip."

At any given hour of the day, Bob could be seen conversing with Dad as he toiled over His little craft to make it shipshape. By day 602, the rain had soaked through Bob's clothes as he continued his preparations. By day 603, the Boat of Bob was rocking wildly under a torrent of horizontal rain pellets. The sea thrashed and swelled so violently that many of the boats in the marina crashed and shattered where they were docked. By noon, the sky turned ominously black, making the world look as though it had been hurled into a howling, starless night. If the rain didn't knock you down, the wind would. If the wind didn't knock you down, the careening of the boat under the chaos of waves would certainly sweep you off your feet.

Then came the hail. Bob had to scramble for cover to avoid being stoned to death. Huddled in the rocking cabin, he heard Dad's voice penetrate the deafening clatter on the roof:

"Gang, gang, the hail's all here." Then:

"Speaking of gang, Bob, don't you think it's time to go get your friends?"

"You want me to go out in *this*? How about if I wait till the weather lets up a little?"

"No time for that, Bob. You'd better go now."

"Do you think you could ratchet down the hail for a little while, Dad?"

"Bob, how many times do I have to tell you? It's out of my hands. Remember what I explained to you about weather systems and jet streams?"

"Oh, yeah."

"Time's a-wastin', Bob," said Dad. "You'd better tell your friends to get on the boat."

"Ok, Dad," said Bob. "Just let me find something to cover myself with."

Holding *The Book of Bob* like a hat on his hunched-over head, Bob climbed off the Boat of Bob into the hailstorm in search of Eldon and Larry Smith. The Sunny Sunnyland streets were empty, but for the hail bouncing like ping-pong balls and for the lonely figure of Bob staggering head down in the dark against nature's violent elements, taking step after purposeful step into the onslaught, determined to deliver his flock to safety.

Finally, he arrived at the Last Daze Hotel, where he hoped to find his friends. He knocked on Eldon's door.

"Who is it?" called Larry.

"It's Bob," he replied.

"Can you wait just a minute, Bob?" Larry asked.

"You'd better hurry, Larry. Dad says we don't have a moment to lose. Is Eldon in there?"

"Keep your socks on, Bob! I'll be right there."

"Actually, my socks are pretty wet. I'd rather take them off. Larry, Dad's getting impatient."

"Ok, ok! Tell Dad to pour Himself a good stiff drink and sip it slowly. Gracious, He gets so pushy!"

Bob knocked again. "Larry, we really . . . ."

"I'm coming! I'm coming!"

Larry swung the door open. Peering into the dark, Bob could see Larry holding an ice pack over his temple. In the candlelit room behind Larry, Bob saw an upended table and a broken chair; the floor was a riot of broken dishes. Crumbled plaster and splintered wood dangled out of a fist-sized hole in the wall, which gaped like an exclamation mark beneath a shattered mirror.

"Things have been a little tense, lately." Larry was sheepish.

Sitting in a corner on the floor was Eldon. He, too, held an ice pack over one eye. In the other hand was a sun lamp.

"The power went out," Eldon mourned.

"Eldon's suffered some severe setbacks with his tan," Larry explained. "I bought him that sun lamp, but when the power went out, that was the final blow."

"All that hard work snuffed out like a candle in the wind," Eldon waxed poetically. The candles flickered in the dark room.

"Eldon, Larry," said Bob, "remember I told you Dad said we'd have to leave on a boat pretty soon? Well, now is the time."

"Ok, Bob," Larry answered. "Just give us a . . . ."

"I can't go *now*," Eldon wailed. "I refuse to be seen until I get my tan back to *at least* a Level 3!"

"Larry, Dad says we've got to get out of here," Bob insisted. "I have to go find Ivan Bunt and Venecia Bosco. Promise you'll meet me at the boat."

"I promise, Bob," said Larry Smith. "You go ahead to Venecia's house. I'm sure that's where you'll find them. Don't worry about Eldon. I'll get him to the boat."

As Bob headed down the hall, he heard Larry's coaxing voice.

Then Eldon's pitiful cry: "I have my standards!"

"Good job," Dad told Bob as he gnashed his teeth in the storm. "That was the easy part."

Upon arriving at Venecia Bosco's house, Bob overheard familiar voices on the other side of the door.

Knock knock.

"Oh, Venecia, my galivantin' grapefruit," he heard Ivan say. "How did I yearn all these years without you?"

Knock knock knock.

"Oh, Ivan, my magnificent mastodon," he heard Venecia reply. "This is the tastiest time of my loopy life!"

KNOCK KNOCK KNOCK KNOCK!

"Ivan! Venecia! I have to talk to you!" called Bob.

"Meddlin' monks! Mutterin' mimes! Who's the rapscallion who's rappin' on the ragin' door and poopin' my party?"

"It's Bob," said Bob. "Ivan, Venecia, open up. Dad says it's time to get on the boat. He says there's not a moment to lose."

"Get on the blunderin' boat, my bones!" exclaimed Ivan. "I'd no sooner leave Venecia's house than I'd chop down a gumball tree! I'm not . . . ."

"Ivan, my manly minstrel," came Venecia's soothing voice. "If Dad says it's time to go, then we'd better gobble up and go."

"But Venecia, my nutritious nacho," Ivan countered, "we were having a totally tootin' time till Bob came along and rained poodles on our parade. Baste my baloney, Venecia! I don't . . . ."

"Ivan," Bob heard Venecia behind the door. "We can have more fun than a fistful of fish on the Boat of Bob. Didn't I ever tell you I like a sexy sailor?"

"You do?"

"I doodley-do. I think a sailor is sexier than a six-pack of snails."

"You doodley-do?

"I diddley doodley-do.

"Well, shave my shish and clone my kebobs! Why're we sittin' here waggin' our weasels? Let's bump aboard the Boat of Bob and bon the voyage!"

Bob called through the door again. "I've got to get back to the boat and make final preparations. Can I count on you to meet me there?"

"We'll be there before you can count your calories," called Venecia.

"Ok, then. Goodbye," called Bob.

"Buy your goods and fairly well," called Ivan and Venecia in unison. Bob heard them giggling as he headed into the storm.

* * * * *

All hands on deck, and not a moment too soon. By the time Ivan, Venecia, Eldon, and Larry joined Bob on the Boat of Bob, the hail had subsided, but in its place came torrents of rain propelled by monstrous winds. While Bob manned the wheelhouse, Eldon and Larry scampered around the deck, pulling up anchor, releasing the ropes from their moorings, and bailing water. Meanwhile, Ivan and Venecia lashed themselves firmly to a pillar on the bow. With hair and clothes drenched and plastered

against their skin, they squinted into the storm, passed the bottle
of grog, raised defiant fists in the air, and shouted things like:

"Avast ye hollerin' hearties!" And:

"Shiver me blowhole, timber me down!"

And they sang merry sailor songs like:

"Sixteen men in a dead man's dress; yo ho ho and it's bottle
my bum!"

The day was dark as midnight. The only time the crew was
able to see beyond the faint light that shone from the Boat of
Bob was when lightning cracked and lit up the sky. At those
times the entire sea shook, the boat rattled, and the crew felt very
small indeed. Bob tried to steer the craft into open water, but was
constantly rebuffed by the relentless onslaught of violent waves.
It was only through masterful seamanship that he was able to
avoid being smashed to splinters on the dock.

"Don't be in such a hurry," Dad told Bob. "Just put the boat
in neutral and let the ocean do the work."

Sure enough, like a terrible giant taking a deep breath, the
ocean suddenly receded, sucking everything in its path—
including the Boat of Bob—with astonishing speed. The great,
impersonal mass accumulating tons by the second and rising to
skyscraper heights; withdrawing into itself, ripping away rock
and sand at the bottom; leaving miles of land exposed that had
not breathed air in eons.

Farther out to sea the Boat of Bob hurtled, lifting higher . . .
higher . . . riding the crest of an enormous saltwater volcano . . .
and rising higher still, looking down on bare land that used to be
the middle of the ocean.

"Tell Eldon and Larry to put on their seat belts, Bob," said
Dad. "Are Ivan and Venecia tied up securely?"

Bob scrambled around the careening boat, checking on his
passengers.

"All secure, Dad," he reported.

"Ok, get to the wheelhouse and put the boat in first gear.
Now, strap yourself in and get ready for the ride of your life."

Dad wasn't kidding. For one pregnant moment after Bob fastened his seat belt, the receding ocean froze, and the Boat of Bob hovered precariously at the top of the motionless crest while time . . . stopped . . . .

Then the terrible giant who had been inhaling the Boat of Bob out to sea, exhaled. And when it did, the entire sea exploded back the other way.

"A little to the left!" Dad shouted above the roar as the boat flew down the face of the wave like a barrel down Niagara Falls. "No! No! You're overcorrecting! Make smaller adjustments! There, that's better. Easy on the gas, Bob! What're you trying to do—flip the boat? Ok—see that mass of whitewater to your right? You're gonna have to shoot right through the curl! There you go—stay in the tunnel . . . WATCH OUT FOR THAT LOG!"

With Dad directing traffic, Bob maneuvered the tiny vessel like a NASCAR driver. Time seemed to slow down as Bob negotiated each hairpin turn and harrowing drop. As terrifying walls of water crashed the boat and tried to devour it, Eldon and Larry shivered with cold and tried to spit out the taste of salt. At times the boat went airborne, but Bob kept his hands steady on the wheel and never missed a beat as he bounced like a skipping stone on the compact water.

Meanwhile, Ivan and Venecia were having the best roller coaster ride of their lives.

"Hands up!" Ivan would cry as they went flying down the face of a hundred foot wave. They stretched their arms high in the air, screaming and shrieking all the way down. After a particularly wild ride, Ivan would shout things like:

"Oh, it's flibber my gib and batten my hatches!"

To which Venecia would respond, "Eye for an eye, cap'n! What shall we doodle with the drinkin' sailor?"

To which Ivan would sing, "Ear-li moles in morning!"

Bob hung on as the monstrous ocean rampaged toward Sunny Sunnyland, showing no intention of mercy or sign of fatigue. Bob faced a new challenge as houses and high-rises crumbled like toys, and he was forced to finesse his way around the rushing turmoil of debris. To the horror of the crew, Sunny Sunnyland was underwater in a matter of minutes—a modern day Atlantis—and still, the watery wall raged further eastward, uprooting and leveling everything in its path.

"How long is this going to go on?" Bob asked Dad. "I hope we're not going to have to go through forty days and forty nights of this."

"Bob, how many times do I have to tell you? People in those days had no sense of time. They exaggerated everything."

"Can you give me some kind of estimate? My arms are getting tired."

"I might be Dad, but I'm not a psychic."

"But you saw this coming. You told me to get a boat and get ready."

"Bob," said Dad, "I once made a guy who wrote a whole bunch of great songs. His name was Bob, too. Do you know what he said in one of his songs? He said: 'You don't need a weatherman to know which way the wind blows.'"

"So, what's your point?"

"Just keep your eyes on the road, Bob. WATCH OUT FOR THAT BILLBOARD!"

* * * * * *

"Look back," Sophia whispered to Lakshmi.

Five hundred miles west of Capital City, Lakshmi Jackson turned around to see the brown mushroom cloud. Then Aruna Jackson, Natalie, and Phil looked back and saw it too. Phil turned on the radio and they heard the news.

"Capital City's gone," declared Lakshmi.

"Poor Donald LaFarge," Sophia said.

"Poor *everybody*," Lakshmi said.

"At least we won't have to worry about Roland Brand

anymore," said Aruna, sitting in the back seat between her daughter and Sophia Wise.

"At such a price," Lakshmi shuddered.

They drove toward Red Rock in sober silence, each absorbed in grief. Sophia thought if only she had died, maybe somehow Capital City might have been spared. Lakshmi prayed that all the people who had paraded Sophia out of the city had kept going and escaped the disaster.

Aruna thought about her husband Ben up on that roof and began to cry. Lakshmi knew why her mother was crying. She also grieved for her father—not only for his fate, but for what he had become. She started to cry, too.

Sophia thought about what Roland Brand had done to her. She could hardly imagine what kind of hate, pain, and darkness someone would be burdened with to make him do what Roland did. She cried for the torment Roland Brand must have suffered.

Natalie held her husband Phil's hand while he drove. They were overwhelmed after witnessing the spectacle in which their daughter had been the central player. They had never experienced so much anguish and terror. Now they were overcome with relief that their little girl was safe, and they were in awe of the strength she had shown. They exchanged knowing looks, and both burst into tears.

Thus, the little car containing Sophia, Lakshmi, Aruna, Natalie, and Phil sped along the highway toward Red Rock, bouncing with the sobs of its passengers who cried for the devastation behind them; cried for loved ones lost; cried for a world gone crazy.

* * * * * *

Two days later, as they neared the Red Rock city limits, Sophia and Lakshmi sensed something strange.

"Look," said Sophia. "Seagulls."

At first they only saw a few, but soon, whole flocks swooped overhead.

Lakshmi opened her window and sniffed the air. "Smells like salt," she said. A cool, damp breeze blew in, refreshing her and making her think of home in the Northwest Region.

Sophia heard a low, churning rumble in the distance. She wondered if her ears were ringing, but the constant noise became louder and more defined as they approached Red Rock. She heard what sounded like the dull thud of waves crashing, followed by a higher pitch like water spreading out, then the broken clatter of rocks inhaled by the sea.

"Sophia," said Lakshmi, "what do you do when you smell the ocean, hear the ocean, feel the ocean, but you can't see the ocean?"

"Maybe we should close our eyes so we can smell, listen, and feel some more," was Sophia's reply.

Sophia and Lakshmi closed their eyes as the car wound its way through Red Rock toward the south end of town. Red Rock had never smelled, sounded, or felt like this before. When they finally opened their eyes, they looked in the distance and their suspicions were confirmed: Rolandworld had become beachfront property!

Phil guided the car past the new sand dunes that covered the wildlife preserve. Lakshmi wept again when she saw her two favorite tigers, Dexter and Sheeba.

"Stop the car!" she yelled. Lakshmi jumped out to roll in the sand with the tigers and give them treats. When she returned, Phil put the car in gear and drove his passengers toward the ocean. They passed Normal Bea Freee, Thaddeus Well, and Professor Tyrone T. Matters standing in front of the Virtual Reality Library, waving happily.

"I *knew* they were coming back," cried Normal Bea Freee, jumping up and down.

Sophia shouted out the open window, "You've done wonders with the canyons, Professor Matters!"

"Good as new," he called back.

Phil stopped the car in the parking lot next to the west

entrance to Rolandworld, which was now a sandy beach. The passengers piled out of the car and gazed in awe at the green surf pounding the new shoreline. All that remained of the castle was a broken brick wall the ocean had yet to fully claim. Sophia and Lakshmi wasted no time in throwing off their clothes, wiggling their toes in the warm sand, and plunging naked into the sea, surrendering to Mother Ocean and asking her to wash them clean.

As Sophia joyfully gave herself to the cold salty ocean, allowing it to pummel her however it would, she felt free, pure, and nurtured like a baby in her mother's rough and loving arms. She wanted to swim farther and farther until she couldn't come back. Mother Ocean spoke to her:

"Sophia," she said, "I will take you for this little while, then you must return to shore. Be careful what you give and whom you give it to; be careful *how* you give. Even I, who love you, cannot stop Father Sea from devouring you if you give me too much. Give yourself to me, take me in, then carry me back with you to dry land."

"I will, Mother," Sophia said as she plunged under the next wave.

Then Father Sea spoke to her. "Sophia," he said, "I love you, too. But my love comes in the form of a test. You must fight with me. I will always win, but I'll make you strong. You may carry my strength on your shoulders and your mother's love in your heart."

"Yes, Father," said Sophia, as a wave spun her in somersaults.

"And Sophia," Mother Ocean continued, "now that you've celebrated and you've suffered, you know there is nothing to fear. Both joy and pain will make you wise."

"I know, Mother," said Sophia as she dove to the sandy bottom, pushed off with her feet, and shot through the surface into the air.

"And one more thing, Sophia," said Mother Ocean.

"Yes, Mother," said Sophia, cavorting like a seal.

"Visit us often."

"I promise I will," she said.

And with that, Sophia looked toward the horizon and saw what seemed to be a boat, far away but heading toward shore.

"Lakshmi, look," she started to say, but Lakshmi had already trained her eyes on the incoming shape. As it grew from a speck to a dot to a boat, details emerged into focus.

Two red points on the bow eventually became heads attached to people. A little closer, and the two red-headed people seemed to be sitting and waving. Closer still, and two more people, a black man and a white, climbed out of the cabin—they appeared to be jumping up and down and waving, too.

Sophia and Lakshmi heard voices, first faint, then stronger. They heard boisterous shouting and lusty singing, but the boat was too far away to make it out. Then:

"Man the mizzenmast, maties! This ship is shipshape and shootin' for shore!"

"Aye fer an aye, Captain Bligh!"

Sophia and Lakshmi looked at each other and grinned.

"Well, bleach my bloomers and bungle my bunt!" exclaimed Sophia. "It's Ivan!"

"But who's that with him?" wondered Lakshmi.

Then they heard singing from all hands on deck:

Oh, it's heave your ho and ahoy we will go,
The life of a sailor is bully for me,
So scuttle me sails and starboard we blow,
With a bottle of rum on my knee-o,
A bottle of rum on my knee.

By the time the sailors had finished their joyous song, a welcoming party of Aruna, Natalie and Phil, Normal Bea, Thaddeus, and the Professor had formed on the shore. They waved happily as the battered boat sputtered and staggered toward land. But Sophia and Lakshmi couldn't wait. Like a couple of Tahitian native women, they dived in the water and swam to the Boat of Bob, then clambered aboard to greet the crew.

XXIII. Sacred Covenant

And they all lived happily ever after.

Epilogue 99:99

* * * * * *

THE ENTIRE TOWN OF RED ROCK SHORES WAS ABUZZ WITH anticipation of the big event. Invitations had been mailed, announcements placed in papers, and a gift registry placed at KonsumerWorld SuperStore. Gourmet caterers were busy making preparations, florists were put to work creating elaborate bouquets, and a fleet of the best interior designers had swarmed into Red Rock Shores (formerly known as Rolandworld), where they proceeded to transform the Meeting Hall into a venue of festivity tempered by holiness; celebration balanced by sobriety. In sum, all the elements befitting this most blessed ceremony on this most blessed of days: The marriage of Venecia Bosco to Ivan Bunt.

More than five hundred of their closest friends packed the Meeting Hall in good cheer. Today, the nuclear holocaust in Capital City, nature's destruction of Sunny Sunnyland, and the demise of the Free Nation would all be set aside as people came to witness the sacred union.

As the well-wishers entered, they were greeted by the sublime sounds of Lakshmi and Sophia, perched in front, stage right, playing piano and mandolin. Their goal was to break the world record for the longest Pachelbel Canon ever played. However, at one hour and twenty-three minutes, they came up far short.

As the music stopped, the audience turned to see Bob walking slowly and solemnly up the aisle toward the stage. Taking his place front and center, opening his *Book of Bob* and facing the congregation, he looked serene as ever. He still wore his crumpled suit and hat, along with his trademark tropical tie. People were reassured to see that some things never change.

Next came Ivan's best men Eldon and Larry Smith, looking elegant in their white tuxes and black bow ties. They took their places to Bob's right, and waited for the groom to arrive. Then the maids of honor: Sophia, Lakshmi, Natalie, and Normal Bea Freee, who lined up to Bob's left, spreading petals as they entered. Aruna Jackson took Lakshmi's seat at the piano and the stage was set.

All eyes turned toward the back of the hall, and when they did, no one could believe the miracle they witnessed. For there was Ivan Bunt, cutting a dashing figure with his long red hair slicked straight back, beard trim, sporting a powder blue tux and standing on his own two feet! And before the congregation had time to question *this* miracle, they were further amazed to see Ivan, cane in hand, making his tottering, bowlegged way down the aisle on his new prosthetic legs.

"Well, fiddle my sticks and rumple my stilts," Ivan Bunt muttered to himself as he lurched determinedly toward the front. Memories of the first time Bob tried to make him walk flooded his mind.

"Bob promised I'd wobblin' walk someday," he muttered some more. "And looky look and looky here—here I am, just like he said—waddlin' down the aisle on my weddin' day."

When Ivan reached the front, he turned to see the entire congregation standing and cheering him on. There was not a dry eye in the place, including Ivan's.

"Clobber yer clocks! Bamboozle yer bumpkins!" he shouted, waving his cane. *"Now* look at the muddlin' mess you've made o' me," he said as he pulled out his handkerchief and blew.

Everyone remained standing while the familiar strains of "Here Comes the Bride" rang from Aruna's piano. All eyes turned once again toward the back of the hall, and they saw a radiant Venecia Bosco, arm-in-arm with Phil. As Venecia and Phil progressed down the aisle in their slow two-step procession, people marveled at how ravishing the bride looked in her streaming white dress and lacy veil. Her cheeks blushed red as her hair. Her smile was an endearing mix of shyness and joy. She fixed her eyes on the groom who, flanked by his best men Eldon and Larry, stood waiting for his bride.

Phil released Venecia and found his seat. Ivan and Venecia took each other's hands and giggled.

The well-wishers sat down and waited for Bob to begin.

He looked over the flock and said, "Let us pray:

"Dear Dad," he began, "we ask that you be with us today and give your blessing to the sacred union of Ivan Bunt and Venecia Bosco. We thank you for bringing them together and pray you give them many years of love, health, and happiness. Please help them practice good birth control so they don't crank out lots of babies—the world's too crowded. Impress upon them that one or two little baby Bunts will be more than enough. Also, please give them the strength, love, and wisdom to beat the odds and make their marriage one of the fifty per cent that doesn't crash and burn. Sincerely, Bob

"Dearly beloved," he addressed the congregation, "we are gathered here today to bear witness as Ivan Bunt and Venecia Bosco begin their life journey together in holy matrimony. It is our duty as friends to stand by them through good times and bad, and support them in their commitment to each other. When things get tough, it is our job to remind Brother Ivan and Sister Venecia that life isn't always long walks on the beach and lingering kisses by the fireplace. It's not always ecstatic nights of wild abandon in the bedroom or the living room, or on the kitchen table or on the Ferris wheel, or on the fifty-yard line at the football stadium.

"No, sometimes life gets rough and the marriage gets put to the test. Believe me, I know. My wife Helen used to get so mad when I'd go out and have a few drinks after work and forget to call her—and I'd get mad too, because she didn't keep my dinner warm. Plus, we had different styles of getting angry. *My* way was to lock myself in my woodshop and turn on the power saw so I couldn't hear her when she was getting mad in *her* way, which was to yell and scream and pound on the door and try to break it down . . . .

"My point is, these two are going to need all the help they can get. So, if there is anyone here who, for any reason, objects to this marriage, I would like you to leave right now before you screw this whole thing up.

"Ivan, Venecia, marriage is the voluntary commitment of a man to a woman and a woman to a man; or a man to a man, or a woman to a woman; or in some areas they allow polygamy, and that's usually one man to several women. In bee colonies, they practice one woman to lots and lots of men.

"Ok, here we go. Ivan and Venecia have decided to say their own vows. Ivan, you're up."

Ivan faced Venecia, took both her hands in his, looked her in the eyes, and gave her the following vow:

"Venecia, I take thee to be my wedded waddlin' wife, to handle and to hold, every daily day, for better or bitter. I'll love you if'n I win the liberatin' lottery. I'll love you if'n I hit the scufflin' skids. I'll love you if'n yer sicker than a stork. I'll love you if'n yer healthy as a hog. Peck my parasites, Venecia! I promise to love 'n' honor 'n' cherish yer chunky chassis as long as we both shall lewdly live!"

"Oh, Ivan," said Venecia, wiping away a tear. "You have such a whirly way with words."

"Venecia," said Bob. "It is time to say your vows."

Venecia gave her nose a good honk and began:

"Ivan, as I invite you to share my lovin' life, I promise to respect your needlin' needs—except for that thorny thing you told me about last night—you can forget about *that*. I promise to be kind, and kind of kinky. I promise to jingle with generosity and trample you with trust. I take thee Ivan Bunt, to be my hankerin' husband, to handle an' to hold, for better or burst, break the bank or brokedown broke, fit as a fiddle or sick as a swamp as long as we both shall loudly live.

"But, Ivan," continued Venecia, "one thing . . . ."

"What's that, my scintillatin' soul mate?"

"Usually, the bride is supposed to say she'll obey the groom. But I won't say that."

"You won't?"

"Wiggle my windows, I won't obey anyone or anything except my own convolutin' conscience."

"Venecia, I'm relieved as ravioli to hear you say that. It's hard enough to chase *my own* chariot without havin' ta steer yours straight, too."

"Thank you, Ivan," said Venecia. "And, just one more thing."

"Yes, my mystic morsel?"

"If I'm going to take your natural name, then I think you should take a tumble with mine, too."

"You mean? . . ."

"That's right: Ivan Bosco-Bunt. And I'll be Venecia Bosco-Bunt. What do you think?"

"Well, crash my crutches!" replied Ivan. "That sounds prettier 'n a chisel on a chalk board!"

"Well then, Ivan, put a fork in the fryer 'cause this deal is done!"

"I thought *I* was supposed to say that," said Bob.

"Time's a-tickin', Bob," said Ivan. "The train's a-tootin' down the tracks. If'n ya don't wanna be late, ya better bump on board."

"The rings please?" Bob hurried.

Phil and Larry handed Bob the rings. He handed one to Ivan and said, "Ivan, repeat after me: With this ring, I thee wed."

"With this romancin' ring, I thee weepin' wed," said Ivan as he placed the ring on Venecia's finger.

Then Bob said, "Venecia, repeat after me: With this ring, I thee wed."

"With this ravishin' ring, I thee worthily wed." She placed it on Ivan's finger.

Bob clapped his hands, snapped his fingers, shook a fist above his head and exclaimed, "*Helluva* deal!"

And before he could say, "You may kiss the bride," they were at it. He guessed he'd skip that part since they were way ahead of him, so he went straight to: "Ladies and gentlemen, I present to you Mr. and Mrs. Ivan and Venecia Bosco-Bunt."

The crowd stood and cheered as Ivan and Venecia Bosco-Bunt continued to seal their marriage with a kiss.

The sealing of the Bosco-Bunt marriage continued for quite some time. After a while, people weren't sure what to do so they shrugged their shoulders and filed into the reception hall where they were greeted by the most magnificent spread they had ever laid eyes on: A large plate of mangled mangoes, piles of petrified porridge, great gobs of greasy gizzards, and the main course—the rare and delectable delicacy of marinated mole meat.

Corks flew from cherry champagne and warm watermelon wine flowed as the guests dug into the sumptuous feast. It wasn't until bellies were full and heads were spinning with spirits that the new Ivan and Venecia Bosco-Bunt made their entrance, hand-in-hand. Ivan's face was smeared with lipstick. His bow tie was askew, as was Venecia's hair. No one had ever seen a happier couple, and everyone crowded around to give them hugs and best wishes. Toasts were proposed, testimonials given, and the groom made the first cut in the wedding cake, which of course, was a banana-berry bundt cake.

Sophia and Lakshmi struck up the music, and all looked on with happy tears as the newlyweds took the floor to perform a titillatin' tango. When Ivan and Venecia dashed to their awaiting car under a rain of rice, they found bouncing boots tied to their bumper, and written in shaving cream on the rear window was, "Munch my Mug! Married 'n' Merry!"

The history of the human species before and after the fall of the Free Nation has been one of unimaginable suffering, mindless destruction, appalling stupidity, and astonishing short-sightedness. If people survive another hundred years, they're probably in for more of the same. And yet, we humans are a stubborn lot. We cling to hope. And as we look for rays of hope, we need look no further than the sight of Ivan Bosco-Bunt, walking upright on his own two feet, carrying his bride in his arms, across the threshold, into their honeymoon suite.

* * * * * *

The Bosco-Bunt wedding was the last time Dad ever talked to Bob. At first, Bob tried to contact Dad and ask Him questions as he always had before. However, Bob's attempts at conversation were greeted with silence. After a few weeks, Bob saw the writing on the wall and knew Dad would not be back.

"Well, that's that," he said, as he hoed another row of radishes.

In truth, Dad had become somewhat of a burden. He was very demanding, and it had gotten pretty tiring trying to keep up with Him. It always seemed to Bob that just when he'd finished one task, Dad would get a new idea and put Bob to work again before he could catch his breath. Also, Bob thought, having Dad around all the time was like having your house bugged. It was difficult to live your life while you were being watched all the time.

Bob wondered if he'd have time to put up that window frame before dinner.

Not that he was complaining. Being Dad's Messenger had been interesting, but it just happened that other work was coming his way now. It happened that Sophia had put him to work doing odd jobs, framing houses, and tending the garden. It happened that the caretaker's shed was vacant and he was invited to move in. All the new things that happened were fine with him. Things hadn't changed that much, really—somebody gave him a task and he did it. But Sophia was easier on him than Dad, and that was fine with Bob.

It happened that Bob's memories of Dad were fading fast. Before long, when somebody happened to mention Dad, Bob would ask, "Who?"

People would explain to Bob that he had been Dad's messenger. They'd tell him about all the great things he had done and adventures he'd had. But to Bob, it all sounded like some big fairy tale. He wondered if they were making the whole thing up.

He was happy doing odd jobs, framing houses, hoeing the garden. He couldn't remember a time when he'd done anything else. The dinner bell happened to be ringing. Guess he wouldn't have time for that window frame after all. Bob shuffled to the tool shed and hung the hoe on a nail.

"Well, that's that," he said, as he went in to wash up for dinner.

When Bob arrived at the long table in the Dining Hall, most of the Red Rock Family happened to be seated already. Natalie was eating dinner with her usual gusto, smacking her lips loudly as she recounted her day's work to Thaddeus Well. She and Phil had been doing intake and orientation for the fugitives who continued to flock into Red Rock Shores from east and west. Many would be directed to the Thaddeus Well Counseling Center, where they would get help coming to grips with the horrors they had encountered. Some needed food, clothes, shelter, and rest. Others were ready to go right to work—there was plenty to do.

Professor Matters was explaining to Normal Bea Freee about the solar energy system he had designed. He hoped by next week, it would be up and running and servicing all of Red Rock. Then the whole town would have power again.

"I *knew* my library would be solar powered," exclaimed Normal Bea.

Eldon and Larry Smith were engrossed in their wedding plans. They had been so inspired by Ivan and Venecia's wedding that they had decided to renew their own vows. Since they had washed up on Red Rock Shores, they hadn't had a single fight. They were probably too busy. They were working harder than they ever had in their lives, and at the end of a long grueling day, who had the energy to fight?

As the new artistic director of Red Rock Shores, Eldon had his hands full. He couldn't believe how tastelessly the last person had "designed" the interiors.

"This will never do!" he exclaimed. "There oughtta be a law!"

Larry Smith and Venecia Bosco-Bunt were doing wonders at the Health and Services Center, but the most amazing of all was Ivan. When Thaddeus, Larry, or Venecia had a hard case that made them want to throw up their hands, they'd send that person to Ivan. He'd set 'em straight. In no time, that same hard case who had been given up for hopeless would be seen marching in the Bunt Brigade. With Ivan in the lead, the rag-tag lot would walk, limp, or roll with much noise and fanfare to put out any fire, right any wrong, help wherever help was needed. In this way, many lost souls were healed.

Ivan and Venecia Bosco-Bunt would not be joining the Red Rock Family for dinner on this night. They had decided to spend a nice, quiet evening at their home near the north end of town. They were gearing up for a big day. Another boat had been spotted, making its way toward shore from the direction of Sunny Sunnyland. They'd be getting up early.

In the Dining Hall, Aruna Jackson was serving dessert. As they did every night, the Red Rock Family gave her a big round of applause. Since Aruna had started cooking delicious meals over the outdoor fire pit, no one besides Ivan and Venecia ever wanted to eat anywhere else again. Once, when Aruna took a couple days off, Eldon and Larry took over the cooking chores. The Red Rock Family did so much grumbling, you would have thought they were being served Spam. Actually, they *were* being served Spam, but Eldon and Larry's feelings were hurt because they thought they'd spruced it up pretty well. Everyone breathed a big sigh of relief when Aruna came back on the job.

Aruna took her bows as the Red Rock Family gave her their nightly standing ovation. She even smiled and managed a funny little curtsy. *My, she felt strong now*, she thought. She still cried every night for Ben; still felt the wound in her heart where craziness and despair had punctured it. But every day, the tissue grew more firm. She knew she would always have a scar, but the injury would heal.

Or maybe, she continued her thought, *it would be like an old war wound*. Maybe she was like Ivan Bunt. She too, had had her legs shot out from under her, but like Ivan, now she too, could walk.

She had become so strong that when Lakshmi told her she was leaving, Aruna didn't panic. Sad, yes, but she was surprised to find that she felt no fear. In truth, Aruna was happy for Lakshmi. Her daughter was following her path, and it was right.

Aruna was the second person Lakshmi told. The first was Sophia.

"I've been dreaming every night," Lakshmi said. "I keep dreaming about a river somewhere in the Northwest Highlands. This guy with half his head shaved says, 'Find the river, Lakshmi Jackson. The river tells no lies.'"

"What do you think it means?" asked Sophia.

"I don't know," Lakshmi replied. "But I have to find out."

If someone were to draw a map of the Free Nation, it would

look quite different now. Capital City was leveled, and vast areas around it became uninhabitable wasteland due to nuclear fallout. In the west, the area from Sunny Sunnyland to the Northwest Region, was underwater. The peaks of the great Northwest Highlands, the mountain range that used to loom high over the Northwest, were now a new group of islands, isolated in the midst of a desolate sea.

"Bob's got a boat," Sophia offered.

"Do you think he'd let me use it?" Lakshmi wondered.

"I'll ask him," Sophia replied. "I'm sure it'll be ok."

Then Sophia thought a minute and asked, "Who will you take with you?"

"No one," said Lakshmi. "I have to do this myself. Somewhere in the Northwest Highlands, a river is calling me. I don't know what it wants to tell me, but I have to find out."

"How can you trust you'll find this river?" asked Sophia.

"When I came to get you out of Capital City, I didn't know what I'd find or what I would do—I only knew I had to go, and the answers would come to me as I needed them. I was right then, and I think I'm right now."

"Good luck, Lakshmi Jackson," said Sophia, as they hugged.

* * * * * *

Sophia Wise lit a candle in her dark room as she got ready for bed. She was tired after a long day. So many people—so much suffering. She was glad she had survived so she could help make Red Rock Shores a refuge for people to come and start over.

Today had been a good day. Two more stragglers from Sunny Sunnyland had rowed in on a lifeboat. A middle-aged man had walked in all the way from Capital City and had tested free of radiation. A pair of wolves had been sighted on a far ridge. Normal Bea Freee swore she saw an eagle. Signs of life.

Sophia looked at her candlelit reflection in the mirror. Her hair had grown out and was its natural color of brown. It wasn't that she didn't like the green, orange, and purple shades of old—it was just that with so many needs to be met, she didn't think about her hair much these days.

She scrutinized the "T" that extended from her nose and crossed her forehead. You had to hand it to Roland—he did beautiful work. It didn't look like a "T" at all. To Sophia, it was a "Tree of Life." She would keep it. However, she had decided it would be her last tattoo. She had other things to do now.

She wondered about Roland Brand. Most people said he had been burned up in the fire that day. If not, he was probably nuked along with the rest of Capital City. Still, there were rumors that he had been tarred and feathered and ridden out on a rail, far enough to escape the blast. One person even reported seeing someone who looked like Roland Brand running a little tattoo shop in the Far North Region. Sophia guessed it didn't matter much if Roland had lived or not. If he didn't, there would be others.

Sophia remembered her last conversation with Lakshmi before she climbed into the Boat of Bob and began her solo voyage to the Northwest Highlands. Lakshmi had asked her, "Do you think people are doing their best?"

"What do you mean?" Sophia had asked.

"Your mother always says everybody's doing the best they can," Lakshmi had said. "She thinks if we mess up, it's not out of laziness or bad intentions—it's only our level of consciousness that's holding us back. She thinks even if you're lazy or have bad intentions, it's only because of your level of consciousness."

"That's Natalie," said Sophia. "She calls it 'unskillful behavior.'"

"I hope she's wrong," was Lakshmi's response.

"Why do you say that?" Sophia asked.

"Look around," Lakshmi said. "If this is the best we can do, we're doomed. Our only hope is that we're lazy or have bad intentions. Then, at least, maybe we can change."

"We could become more 'skilled,'" Sophia ventured.

"I guess," Lakshmi replied. "But we've been at this for a long time. What's it going to take?"

"Maybe we need a book of instructions," said Sophia.

Lakshmi laughed. "There are lots of those."

"Isn't *that* the truth," said Sophia. "And then we get into fights over what the instructions mean."

"And who's got the right book," Lakshmi added.

"Maybe we'll just have to figure things out for ourselves," said Sophia.

"Do you think we will?" Lakshmi had asked.

* * * * * *

Sophia cupped the flickering candle as she set it on her nightstand and climbed into bed, still thinking about that last conversation with Lakshmi. She had never answered Lakshmi's questions. Are we doing the best we can? Is it worse if we are or if we're not? Will we ever get it right?

Sophia buried herself under the warm quilt and thought about the next day: Lots of people would need her tomorrow. She was grateful to all her friends who gave so much of themselves to make Red Rock Shores a welcoming home for every man, woman, beast, and sprout; an oasis where people could live in harmony with each other and the earth; a safe haven where the broken and the suffering could heal.

She was glad she had the strength to support so many people who needed to lean on her. They all did—Bob, Natalie, Phil—everybody. That was ok—she was up to it. Funny—the only person who didn't lean on her was Lakshmi, and now that she was gone, the person who leaned on her the least, was Aruna who was getting stronger every day—developing a strength that only comes from trial by fire. Aruna Jackson seemed old and wise now.

"I think I'll spend more time with her," Sophia decided. They had a lot in common.

Sophia sighed as she watched the candle waver in the dark. She would miss Lakshmi. She thought once more about Lakshmi's last question: "Are we doing the best we can?"

Sophia hoped not.

Oh well, tomorrow's another day. Another day to try again, thought Sophia Wise as she blew the candle out.

ABOUT THE AUTHOR

PAUL CHASMAN has been a professional guitarist, teacher, and composer his entire adult life. He recorded his first album in 1979, and now has a dozen full-length releases in his name.

In May 2003, following the United States' invasion of Iraq, Chasman wrote a letter to President George W. Bush telling him he liked the Dixie Chics and suggested he check them out. He signed the letter, "Carl Estrada."

The next day, Carl wrote another letter to President Bush giving him the heads-up that his American flag lapel pin was crooked. So began a year-and-a-half of daily letter writing under aliases of Carl Estrada, Brad Cahoon, and a cast of characters.

Chasman set up a web site: **www.thecarlletters.com** on which he posted his letters and subsequent replies. During the 2004 American presidential elections, Chasman put his guitars in the closet to devote his full time to the Carl Letters and other political activities.

The day after the elections, Paul Chasman began writing *The Book of Bob.*

To order additional copies of

The Book
of
Bob

As revealed to Paul Chasman

send $16.95 (plus $2.00 shipping/handling)
in check or money order to:

Bay View Arts
Post Office Box 1115
Yachats, Oregon 97498

Or use the order form at: **www.thecarlletters.com**